Don't Make Me Over

By: Jessica Terry

This is a work of fiction. Similarities to real people, places, or events are entirely coincidental.

DON'T MAKE ME OVER

First edition. March 14, 2026.

ISBN: 979-8999506986

Written by Jessica Terry.

To all my readers, supporters, author homies, coworkers, and especially my family and friends, I love and appreciate you SO freaking much. Thank you for having this swooning author's back. :)

Chapter 1

"Yes, Mollie," Myles Cornwall droned, his eyes on his computer screen as he scrolled through the spreadsheet his assistant had just sent him. "Your comedy set thing is tonight. I haven't forgotten."

"Oh I know that, because I won't *let* you forget," his sister chirped. "What I need to hear from you, though, is if I'll be seeing your face in the place."

"I've told you I'd be there."

"No you haven't. You just keep acknowledging the invitation, foolishly thinking I won't notice that you never actually accepted it. You think you're slick."

Sighing, Myles removed his glasses and rubbed the bridge of his nose. He should've figured he wouldn't get away with that. The truth was, while he loved his little sister, he wasn't the biggest supporter of her burgeoning comedy career and didn't exactly to rush to her shows. He wished she'd just accept his tepid support from afar.

"Fine," he finally acquiesced through gritted teeth. He knew she'd keep him on the phone until he gave a definitive confirmation. "I'll be there promptly at eight."

"Nice try. It starts at seven."

"Ugh. *Fine.*"

Mollie hung up and Myles resisted the urge to outwardly groan. He was tempted to slow down on the work he needed to do so he'd have an excuse to work late, but that would drive him crazier than having to go to the show at all.

Putting it out of his mind for the time being, he refocused on his work, frowning slightly as he perused the numbers in front of him. He grabbed a pen and started jotting down some notes, getting lost in his work.

After a while, his colleague and friend Ethan Fields knocked on the door to his office before poking his head in.

"Hey, buddy."

Myles pursed his lips, not loving that moniker but not wanting to be called a stick-in-the-mud yet again for saying so. "Hey, Ethan. What can I do for you?"

"About to head to an early lunch with a client." He fully entered the office, leaning his six-two frame just inside the door and folding his arms. "Got a full plate today?"

"Always."

"You'll be up in here late tonight, won't you?"

"I wish, but no. I have to go to my sister's comedy...*thing* tonight." He brightened, his eyes snapping to his friend. "You could come along. Maybe it'll be more bearable if I don't have to sit through it alone."

"I would, but I have to be home tonight. Brianna is coming over to get the rest of her things," Ethan replied, a slight frown forming between his sculpted brows. Myles still didn't totally believe his claim that he didn't get them shaped. "I don't really trust her there alone, since she's still salty about the breakup."

"I'm surprised you finally pulled the trigger on that," Myles muttered, pulling up his email and absently skimming over one that just popped in before immediately starting to type out a reply. "You've been dancing around it for months."

"I *was* in love with her, Myles." Ethan stepped forward and grabbed the back of the chair facing Myles's desk, leaning his weight on it. "It's not always the easiest to walk away from the one you love, even when you know it's the right thing to do."

"If you say so."

"Anyway, what you'll be doing sounds more fun than me playing watchdog to my ex to make sure she doesn't take any of my stuff out of spite."

"Or burn it."

"I thought it was your sister that told the jokes."

"I'd offer to trade places with you if I didn't know it would send Mollie into a whole hissy fit. And there's no telling what juvenile prank she'd try to pull on me in retaliation."

"Why are you talking like you're dreading this? I've been to a couple of Mollie's sets; she's a hoot."

"Yeah a *hoot* that tells crude jokes that makes me want to wash out my own mouth with soap. It's like all she knows how to talk about is sex. There *are* other topics, you know."

"You sound like an old man, buddy." Ethan chuckled, standing upright. "And a bit of a prude. When's the last time *you* had any-"

"We're at *work*," Myles hissed, his hazel eyes darting towards the open door. "Can we not?"

"You brought it up. And anyway, you act like it's some kind of monastery around here. This is nothing compared to some of the other things people talk about in this office, especially those juvenile boneheads Morton and Dennis."

"Well, we don't have to emulate that behavior in here. Let's save it for after-hours."

"Whatever, man." Ethan glanced at his watch and turned to leave. "I've gotta jet. Have fun tonight. Say hi to Mollie for me and don't be a grouse while you're at her set, please. At least *pretend* to laugh."

"I don't enjoy pretending but can when I need to," Myles stated, finishing the email he was working on and clicking 'Send' before reaching for a file on his desk. "Like when I pretended to like Brianna for the entirety of your relationship."

Ethan stopped. "What?"

"Don't you have a lunch to get to? Tardiness isn't becoming of a banking executive. I hope things go amicably tonight. Don't bother saying hi to Brianna for me."

Glaring at Myles for a moment, Ethan started to respond before just shaking his head and walking away.

Myles couldn't help being in something of a foul mood several hours later as he headed across town to Mollie's comedy set after first going home to quickly shower and change. As he always did before being roped into attending these things, he told himself it wouldn't be that bad and to hold out hope that maybe his sister would elevate her material this time and wouldn't spend the entire half hour of her set talking about penises and bodily fluids.

He frowned slightly when he realized his Cadillac was running differently. There was some funny noise that wasn't there that morning, and Myles didn't even bother trying to guess what it was. His knowledge of cars was elementary, at best.

"Great," he muttered, heaving a long sigh. "*Another* thing to worry about."

Making a mental note to call his mechanic later, Myles continued on to the venue where Mollie's comedy set was taking place. He hated going to this part of Brodence, the growing south Georgia city he'd grown up in. The streetlights seemed dimmer, the streets were narrower and full of potholes, and everything just seemed bunched on top of each other, from houses to businesses. And so many strip malls.

Once Myles pulled into The Laugh Vat (and scoffed at the name), he carefully maneuvered through the shotty parking lot, trying to find a space that was far enough from other cars while still not so far that he wouldn't feel comfortable walking back to it afterwards once it was dark. This wasn't exactly the part of town that was highlighted on the Chamber of Commerce's website.

His car parked, his hand stamped, and his order placed for a gin and tonic (Mollie neglected to mention there was a two-drink minimum), Myles glanced at his watch as he wondered how long he was going to have to stay there. He hoped Mollie was up first so he could leave right after her set was done. Comedy shows weren't his thing so he didn't have plans to just make a night of it and enjoy all the acts.

The small venue was about half full and Myles glanced around, taking in his surroundings. About eight small round tables, some with mismatched chairs, littered the floor that was covered in thin gray carpeting that looked older than

Myles. A small raised boxy stage with a microphone stand was waiting for its first occupant of the evening, flanked by heavy red curtains that were purely for show. Muted lighting fell on the audience while the brighter lights blared towards the stage. Myles wondered if the sparse décor was intentional or circumstance. Or if the owner just didn't give a damn enough to upgrade anything.

A fawn-colored woman poked her head around the left side of the curtains, her long goddess braids hanging. Her narrow brown eyes swept around the room and when they landed on Miles, she broke into a grin.

Myles waved at his sister, unable to resist returning her smile. He might not have been thrilled to be there but it made him feel good that it meant so much to her that he was. He told himself supporting his sister was worth a couple hours of misery.

Having verified that her big brother had actually shown up, Mollie disappeared back behind the curtain and Myles checked his watch again.

Finally, the show kicked off. Myles's hope that he'd be able to make a relatively quick exit was dashed when some comic other than Mollie was introduced first. Then another. It took every ounce of Myles's willpower not to pull out his phone and check some emails, or fold his arms on the table and take a nap like he did in kindergarten and wake up when he heard Mollie's name announced.

After about an hour, his sister finally graced the stage. She actually skipped to the microphone, already earning a few laughs. Myles just pursed his lips.

"How y'all doin' tonight?" Mollie practically yelled, causing Myles to wince. He hoped she wasn't going to bellow through her entire performance. "Have those drinks kicked in yet? This is one time when taking advantage of your liquored-up state is a *good* thing."

People around him chuckled while Myles sat stone-faced. He pushed his second half-finished gin and tonic away.

Mollie continued through her act, launching into a tale of a hookup from a sex site that Myles could only hope was made up. His ears burned as he listened to her describe how some guy fumbled through foreplay after having bragged on his skills for weeks.

"He was actually rubbing my titty like this," Mollie screeched, moving her hand in a circular motion. "And *swore* he was doing something! Buddy was looking at me like he expected me to cum at any second. And I'm laying there thinking, what are you, a fucking DJ?? It's a titty, not a turntable!"

The crowd cracked up while Myles shifted in his seat, feeling increasingly uncomfortable.

"You're wastin' your time," Mollie continued recalling her response to the inept lover. She was gripping the microphone in both hands in a way that Myles told himself wasn't supposed to be indicative of anything. "It was so sad, y'all. I had to guide his hands where they needed to go like he was some kind of blind virgin. It was like trying to teach someone to walk for the first time. Except it was, you know...fucking."

Oh god, Myles thought, forcing the scowl from his face when Mollie's eyes flitted to him. *When is this gonna be over??*

After another twenty minutes or so, he was finally put out of his misery and Mollie wrapped up her set, thanking everyone for 'hitting the g-spot of her ego' with all their laughter before doing some kind of dance off the stage.

His duty fulfilled, Myles wanted to go ahead and leave. But he didn't want to endure the tantrum Mollie would have if he did so without at least speaking to her first.

There was only one more comic after her, and his set was graciously short since he got mere giggles for his jokes that seemed to be solely about his dog. Red-faced, he muttered something about needing to pee before scurrying off the stage barely halfway through his allotted time. Which of course the host clowned him for.

Mollie bounded from backstage and joined Myles at his table as soon as everything was over. She dropped into the slightly-rickety chair across from his, throwing one long leg over the other and grinning at her brother.

"So what'd ya think?"

Myles shot her a *you know better* glance. "We had an agreement, Mollie. If I had to come watch, you wouldn't ask me for any feedback."

"I just wanted to see what you'd say. It's not like I didn't notice you barely cracked a smile while I was up there, let alone laughed at anything. It's a good thing my self-esteem is rock solid."

"It would have to be."

"You can be such a fuddy-duddy. I don't know how the hell we're related."

"You're my sister in every way that counts and I love you dearly but we're *not* related by blood, Mollie. You're adopted, remember?"

"Our parents must have sensed that you'd need someone to bring some joy into your life."

"My life is fine as is."

"Oh please. All you do is work, play racquetball, and watch those disturbing-ass crime shows. You *so* need to loosen up. When's the last time you had any pus-"

"I am *not* discussing that with you."

"That long, huh?" Mollie flashed a grin that was frustratingly triumphant. "Well, in case you wanted to know, *I* got some just last night. That's why my skin has such a glow."

Myles winced. "I *didn't* want to know. I'm already trying to purge the things I heard you say onstage from my memory. Those *were* just jokes, right?"

When her grin only widened, Myles held up a hand. "Never mind. Mollie, I get that this comedy stuff is fun for you but when are you going to get a real job?"

Her smile flattened and her eyes rolled. "Not this shit again."

"You need a career. A *real* career. You're barely able to pay your bills with this. Let me get you a job at the bank."

"I do fine. I'm more than capable of taking care of myself, Chubby, *and* Clap."

"While I know how much you love those cats of yours, I'm not worried about them. I'm worried about *you*," Myles insisted. "You've been trying to break into this comedy stuff for years now and are still only doing these tiny club shows with half-hour sets, and whatever that stuff is you do on the internet. How many auditions have you gone on that went nowhere? How many so-called promoters that made all these grand promises that ended up stiffing you? What are you even paying your manager for?"

"Are you finished?"

"You're thirty years old. You need to start making some better decisions. Get serious about your future."

"I'm paying my dues, Myles. Shit doesn't happen overnight. I do temp work to keep me afloat between gigs. Being a comedienne is what I love to do just like being a Corporate Banking exec is what *you* love to do. I think that's boring as hell but I don't bug you about it, do I?"

"You more than make up for it with the other stuff you bug me about."

"The point is, I respect that you make your own choices, whether I agree with them or not. And I usually *don't*, by the way." She stood as everyone else around them started slowly making their way towards the exit. "Do me the same courtesy, sir."

Dropping it, Myles stood and glanced at his watch. "You ready? I'll walk you to your car."

They headed out a few minutes later after Mollie got her things and chatted with a few people, taking pictures with a couple of them. Once they were outside, Mollie glanced at his starched gray button-down, black and white pinstripe slacks, and shiny black Johnston and Murphy shoes. "You must've come here straight from work. You were the only one in the crowd looking like a Sunday school teacher."

Myles rolled his eyes. "For your information, I went home and changed first."

"And that's what you chose to wear?"

"I'm perfectly comfortable."

"I swear, if I ever saw you in anything casual, I'd melt into a puddle of goo."

"This *is* casual. I'm not wearing a tie. Or a jacket."

"Oh god." They reached Mollie's Honda Accord and she turned to give him a tight hug. "Thank you for coming. I love you, you big dud."

"I love you, too. You need me to follow you home?"

"You can follow if you want, but you'll just be going with me to East Tony to meet up with my date."

Myles frowned. "You're going to East Tony this time of night? That's not exactly the safest area, Mollie."

"You forget; I grew up in the 'hood before our parents adopted me. They still know me out there. I can handle myself, big bro."

"Why doesn't your date come to you?"

"He doesn't need to know where I live yet. You remember what happened the last time; that woman started popping up, trying to move in on the sly. No thank you."

Myles sometimes forgot that his sister was bisexual; he tried to retain the least amount of detail about anything regarding her sex life as possible. "Text me when you arrive so I'll know you made it safely."

"Yes, dad." Mollie playfully rolled her eyes but her grin showed her appreciation for his concern. She leaned up to give him a parting kiss on the cheek, her sleepy eyes and slightly-pointy nose (that she hated) seeming extra pronounced under the flickering streetlight. The gloss on her pouty mouth shimmered. "Maybe *you* need to think about trying to get your own hookup for the night. You need it. You're thirty-six and stuffier than twenty aristocrats in a closet. With colds. Break out that little black book, bro." She winked. "See ya."

Myles watched as she got into her car and pulled off, sticking her tongue out at him as she passed. He just headed to his car, unable to resist a chuckle.

Once he was back on the road, he was reminded of something going on with his car when he heard that noise again. Giving no thought to the hour, he immediately voice-dialed his mechanic, Chet.

"What have I told you about calling me after-hours, man?" Chet's agitated voice greeted him through the Bluetooth.

Myles was unfazed. "You're supposed to be available to me twenty-four-seven, Chet."

"I'm not a damn doctor. What do you want?"

"Something's wrong with my car."

"Are you driving it right now?"

"Yes..."

"Then it can't be that bad, can it? This could have waited until tomorrow."

"When can you fix it?"

"What's wrong with it, Myles?"

"How am I supposed to know? *You're* the professional. It's making some kind of noise."

"Even if I could determine anything from that vague-ass response, there's nothing I can do about it tonight. It's almost ten o'clock and my wife is over here mean-mugging me 'cause the phone woke her up. She has to work the early shift tomorrow."

"My apologies to your wife, but-"

"You know the drill, Myles. Call the garage in the morning and make an appointment to bring it in. And let this be the last time you call me this time of night for this shit; I am not at your beck and call. I *do* have a life, you know. Get yourself one."

Myles was shocked when he heard the dial tone. His anger flared that Chet had actually left him hanging. He wouldn't even *have* a garage if it weren't for Myles's family loaning him the money to open it. Never mind that he'd already paid the money back; Myles still felt Chet should've acted a little more grateful and made exceptions for him, regardless.

Sighing, Myles just turned up the music from the jazz station he was listening to and concentrated on getting back to his side of town. He wondered how things had gone with Ethan and Brianna that evening, with her getting the rest of her things from his house. He wondered who it was that Mollie was going to meet. Her suggestion that he hook up with someone had gone unacknowledged but it certainly wasn't the first time someone said that to him. Everyone seemed to be under the misconception that Myles had no love life whatsoever and that was the reason for his perceived 'stuffiness.'

This was just the way Myles was, and he liked himself. His life might not have been perfect but he had way more to be grateful for than to complain about. And contrary to what people seemed to believe, he dated enough. The relationships usually didn't go very far, but Myles could attribute that to a number of reasons, many of which didn't have to do with him.

Truth be told, Myles was over the dating scene. From his experience, women just couldn't be trusted; they always seemed to want something from him, knowing the affluent and well-connected family he was a part of. It usually ended up being more about appearances than anything else, trying to tweak him to fit their image of an ideal mate. And on the rare times it wasn't, and he met a woman that actually had some substance, some conflict would inevitably arise that would drive too big of a wedge between them, and it was decided that the effort to fix it wasn't worth it. Myles had resigned himself to focusing on his career, his philanthropic efforts, and looking after his parents, even though they were more active than him and showed no signs of slowing down any time soon. They were in the number that constantly stressed for him to loosen up and have some fun, and there had been more than a few hints about wanting grandbabies at some point.

Myles figured he'd leave that duty to Mollie, who he knew wanted children someday once her career was off the ground. He had accepted that he'd probably never meet a woman that would accept him just the way he was.

Chapter 2

"*Take it off!*"

Jackie Malone danced in her seat as the women around her screamed for the man on stage to lose the cowboy getup he was sporting as they threw money at his feet. She grinned, enjoying the show and the atmosphere, but her dollar bills stayed tucked in her bra. She was waiting on her favorite dancer to make his appearance and then she had every intention of making it rain like a deluge.

When they finally announced Ringo and the opening chimes of Jodeci's "Freek'n You" began to play, Jackie eagerly scooted forward in her seat. The first cheer erupted from her throat when the bow-legged dancer with the oiled-up caramel skin did a teasing slow walk onto the stage, his long black locs hanging over his shoulders and his eyes scanning the screaming horny crowd as if looking for prey. When his gaze landed on Jackie, he smirked and eyed her up and down for several moments before going into his dance, which only made her scream louder.

Jackie bolted out of her seat and made a beeline to the front, boxing a couple of women out of the way and ignoring their glares. Her big brown eyes stayed locked on the man in front of her, grinning wildly as she fished the thick wad of money from her cleavage and began tossing it at his feet several bills at a time. When his attention landed on her again, she winked at him and bit her plump bottom lip, feeling her whole body wake up. Clearly, her pre-show pep talk she'd had in the car about controlling herself was a waste. Ringo was her favorite and always had that effect on her, despite her best efforts.

She'd just tossed her last bill when he slithered over to her side of the stage, his muscles popping and flexing as he did a couple of stage-humping push-ups before jumping to his feet, landing directly in front of her. His eyes were mischievous as he bit his bottom lip and held out his hand to her, and Jackie wasted no time grabbing it. She flashed a smug grin to the jealous ladies around her as Ringo helped her up on stage, immediately sliding his hands down her hips and behind her thighs before hoisting her up. Jackie grinned, more than willing to hold on for the ride.

Someone quickly brought a chair onstage and Ringo lowered her onto it before stepping back and resuming his show, this time just for her. Once his clothes started coming off and he was dancing for her in nothing but a black leather speedo, all composure went out the window. Jackie screamed until her throat hurt, writhing in her seat and trying to resist the urge to tackle this man right there on the stage. She was feeling extra heady thanks to being the one Ringo chose to come on stage and get all of his attention, and she was enjoying every second of it.

Later, once the show was over and Jackie was back in her car, she sat in the parking lot checking her appearance in the visor mirror. She raked her fingers through her super-short black hair and refreshed her lipstick, admiring her pecan brown skin in the dim light. Satisfied that she still looked delicious, she flipped the visor mirror closed and adjusted her low-cut v-neck top before digging into her purse for her lavender vanilla body mist, giving her cleavage a refresher spritz. Her body was still buzzing with energy and she wasn't ready to leave just yet.

Her phone rang with a call from her friend Cassidy, and Jackie glanced out the windows around her before answering.

"What's up, Cass?"

"Hey, girl. What you up to?"

"Nothing much; chillin'," Jackie replied, her eyes sweeping the parking lot again. "What's going on?"

"Waiting on Orion to get back with my heating pad. I wrenched my back last night."

"How'd you do that?"

"Girl, trying some new position he saw online somewhere. 'It'll be fun', he said. Now I'm laid up."

Jackie couldn't help but laugh. "I tried to tell you men like more than missionary sometimes."

"Whatever. And I don't know why you're laughing."

"Because it's funny."

"You're the one that likes to be all adventurous, not me. Missionary is a top-tier classic. Orion had me doing all kinds of shit last night. And I think he actually spit on me when he was getting it from the back. Can you believe that??"

Jackie wrinkled her nose, even though her giggles continued. "I can, actually. And I know we go way back but you don't really have to go *that* deep into detail of your nasty newlywed sex."

"Since when are you so skittish? I'm usually the one that has to cover *my* ears when you're talking about your raunchy exploits. And you're supposed to be the one I can complain to about my new husband so you're just gonna have to suck it up."

"Ugh."

"I tried to stay in the moment and everything but knowing he did that kinda took me out," Cassidy continued. "We started fussing about it while we were still sexing, and things got more and more intense, and then he tried to twist me into some kind of crazy position and I hurt my damn back. I thought sex injuries were supposed to happen during hoe phases, *not* once you finally settle down."

Resisting the urge to laugh louder, Jackie shook her head. "If you're having sex, you can get sex injuries, hoe phase or not. Which you never had, by the way. I *am* sorry you hurt yourself, though; you gonna be all right? You going to see a doctor?"

"Nah, I don't think it's that bad. I'm sure the heating pad and some extra strength Tylenol will get me right. Don't worry, I'll be at work on Monday."

"That's not why I was asking but good to know. You're pretty irreplaceable."

"Of course I am. Nobody else is gonna put up with you."

Just then, there was a knock on Jackie's window. She grinned when she looked over and saw Ringo standing there, his gold tooth gleaming as he smiled down at her.

"I've gotta go, Cass," Jackie announced hastily as Ringo leaned to where he was eye-level with her. "I'll check on you tomorrow."

"Why you rushing off all of a sudden? You're supposed to be keeping me company in my time of need-"

"And I did. Now I have to handle something. Bye." Jackie hung up and turned her attention back to Ringo, jerking her head towards the passenger's seat. She unlocked the door as she watched him round the front of the car and get in.

"I figured you'd still be here," Ringo greeted, his dark eyes snaking down her body and back up again. "Wasn't ready to call it a night, huh?"

"After that show you just gave me? Hell no."

"You know I'm not gonna see you and not give you special attention. I appreciate you coming out."

"Wouldn't have missed it. You hungry?"

"Starving."

"Let's go eat, then. I'll bring you back to your car later."

"Don't try to kidnap me."

"That was *one* time!"

They headed to a nearby diner, which was pretty full since apparently many others that had been at the male revue had the same idea. Jackie recognized several women's faces that had been in the audience, and they didn't look too happy when she strutted past them with Ringo.

"Don't start nothin' in here," Ringo playfully warned when Jackie blew a mocking kiss to a sneering woman. "We're just here to grub, that's it."

"They're the ones giving me the evil eye."

"And you're loving it."

Jackie didn't bother trying to deny that.

Once they were seated, Ringo immediately grabbed a menu. "So what's been up with you, Jacks?"

She smirked. "You know I never loved that nickname. I think you say it to mess with me."

"You never minded it before."

"You mean when we were still together? Yeah, I tolerated it. Mostly because I got to enjoy that body of yours whenever I wanted. But another woman has that privilege now."

"I'm just a piece of meat to you, huh?"

"Of course not. We're still friends, first and foremost...with occasional benefits."

He arched a brow at her. "That was before."

"You don't have to remind me."

They placed their orders and proceeded to get caught up, since they hadn't seen each other in a couple of months. Their romantic relationship had ended a few years earlier and Jackie didn't always hide her resentment of that well, since that decision hadn't been hers. She was grateful that they were still at least in each other's lives, even if it wasn't in the capacity she wished for.

"How's business?" Ringo asked, cutting into this medium-well steak. "Is the hottest mechanic in Brodence still busy as hell or have things slowed down some?"

"Some, but we're still booked more days than we aren't." Jackie took a sip of her orange juice. "We're hitting our two-year stride, finally."

"I'm still trippin' that you actually left that bougie-ass corporate job and opened your own car garage."

"Why? I've said I would for years."

"Plenty of folks talk about it but don't be about it. But you *did* that shit. No wonder you were always hogging my TV with your car shows and hanging out at AutoZone like most women hang at the mall."

"I love cars," Jackie shrugged. "Always have."

"Hey, you can fix a carburetor better than I ever could, so I'm not mad at it."

They continued with their meals and conversation, their easy rapport as buoyant as always. Once Jackie paid the check ("*I* invited *you,* remember?" she reminded when he protested), they headed back out to her car, Jackie's hand lightly clamped to the crook of Ringo's arm.

"You might as well come on back to my place," Jackie suggested as Ringo opened the driver's side door for her. "We both know you won't be going to bed any time soon, anyway."

Ringo didn't look at all surprised by her invitation. "As tempting as that is, I shouldn't."

"Why shouldn't you?"

"You know why, Jacks."

"I know you're not saying that girlfriend of yours that's *way* across the country is the reason we can't even hang out as friends."

"I'm not, 'cause that's what we just finished doing." He met her challenging gaze, standing pretty much eye-level with her five-seven height. "But we both know you're not inviting me over just to drink rum and play cards."

"We can do that, too."

He sighed and shook his head. "Jacks..."

"Look, Ringo, I'm not trying to be messy, here. But do you *really* think she's way over there not doing her own thing? You two only see each other a couple times a year. I don't even get why you're bothering."

"It's not for you to get."

"Don't get snippy. Just get in the car." She stepped closer, her ample bosom grazing his chest. "You know you want to."

"I want to do a lot of things I shouldn't."

"How 'bout if I offer to return the favor from earlier and put on a personal show for *you*?"

She could see his eyes brighten despite the rest of his expression not budging. He didn't speak for several moments, them facing off as people milled around them to and from their cars. Jackie prepared herself for anything, more than willing to wait him out.

"You still have those heels?" he finally asked in a low voice.

Biting her lip, Jackie nodded. "My one and only pair."

"Aight." He held the door open and stepped back, a lustful shadow now darkening his eyes. "Let's go."

Grinning, Jackie got in the car.

The following Monday morning, Jackie was at her garage, The Auto Loft, getting ready for the day. Cassidy, who worked as her receptionist and office manager, hadn't made it in yet, so Jackie went ahead and took a peek at the calendar. She beamed when she saw nearly every slot on the calendar full.

A lot of people thought she was nuts when she left her thriving executive career to open her own garage. And those who didn't figured it was just a sign she could no longer cut it in that environment. Jackie didn't care what anyone thought about it. She hated being buttoned-up Jacqueline Malone, whose days revolved around so much corporate minutiae and red tape and veiled smiles that it made her stomach turn, and she decided she didn't want to live like that anymore. She'd been putting away money for years, never having planned to answer to anyone forever. And with her lifelong love of cars, it wasn't a hard decision as to what she would do next. She enjoyed being under a car hood more than she did being in anyone's conference room. Now, she could just be Jackie.

She only employed two other mechanics and an assistant so far, and was looking forward to when she could expand and hire more. Cassidy often joked that she was running a 'boutique' garage, with the seafoam green-painted lobby/waiting room, comfy seating and R&B music that played throughout the day. Artificial green plants and colorful artwork added to the vibe. The other mechanics, both men, also teased her about that at times. Jackie took the ribbing, always reminding them that her loving cars didn't mean she didn't love pretty things, also.

Cassidy arrived, laden with coffee and breakfast sandwiches for the both of them. Her expression was pinched in annoyance as she stomped around the front desk.

"What's the matter with you?" Jackie asked her, frowning in concern.

"Ugh, those *ass*holes!" Cassidy placed the coffees on the desk and dumped her bags into the chair. "Did you know Lula's Cup might be closing?"

"Why??"

"Because some developers have been breathing down their necks about buying them out so they can have the land. Probably want to build some damn car wash or chain restaurant that we already have a million of. Nobody gives a damn about preserving the small businesses anymore."

"Oh..." Jackie blew out a measured breath as her frown melted. "And Ms. Lula doesn't want to sell, I assume." Ms. Lula was the owner of the beloved coffee shop.

"Of course not. But they're steadily trying to wear her down, borderline harassing her, knowing she's old and won't have the energy to fight them off forever." Cassidy brushed the bang of her shoulder-length brown wig from her eyes and pressed her hands to her round cheeks, taking a couple of deep breaths. "Oh, and good morning."

"Look, don't worry about Ms. Lula, Cass...she's stronger than she looks. Greedy land developers aren't anything new around here. Now please tell me you got my egg, bacon, and guacamole croissant. My stomach is going *off* right now."

"You know I did."

They quickly ate their breakfast as they chatted about the rest of their weekends, Jackie skipping over her night with Ringo. She didn't have the energy to go into the details that Cassidy would surely insist on. They'd had many discussions about Jackie and Ringo's friendship, and Cassidy veered from encouraging Jackie to go for hers to advising her to leave him alone altogether, depending on the day. Jackie didn't want to risk hearing what it might be on this particular morning.

Once Jimmy and Irv, the other mechanics, arrived, everyone got their days started. Jackie popped her first piece of gum for the day and dove in, immersing herself in oil changes, battery replacements, and other things, actually loving how progressively dirty her coveralls got over the course of the day. As it sometimes did, her mind drifted to wondering what she might be doing if she were still at her old job, knowing that she was going to come out on top regardless of what it was. The most hated job in her garage beat the easiest day in that office any day of the week.

Towards the later part of the afternoon, Cassidy let her know a customer wanted to speak to her. Rolling from underneath the Challenger she was under, Jackie wiped her hands on the towel she kept in her pocket and headed to the reception area. A frowning red-haired man stood there, his arms crossed over his chest.

"Mr. Blaithe has some concerns about the work we just did on his car," Cassidy informed Jackie with a pointed look.

Already sensing where this was going, Jackie reminded herself to keep her cool and stepped forward. "Yes, sir. Is there a problem?"

"There most certainly *is* a problem," he immediately snapped, his nasally voice biting. He waved the itemized printout of his charges in the air. "You charged me for a new alternator when I didn't need one."

"You *did* need one, Mr. Blaithe," Jackie patiently responded, still chewing on her gum. It helped keep her calm. Customers, especially male customers, questioning her decisions wasn't anything new. "And I let you know of that possibility up front."

"You could've done it without it."

"Sure. But I assumed you wanted your car to actually run. So if I'm correct on that, I in fact *couldn't* have done it without it."

His face reddened. Cassidy ducked her head as she pretended to look for something in her purse, trying not to laugh.

"The price is pretty high," Mr. Blaithe persisted, unwilling to let it go. "You can't tell me that you couldn't have gotten this part for cheaper. Most mechanics *I* know keep spare parts on hand so they don't have to gauge their customers-"

"Mr. Blaithe, you drive a '67 Pontiac LeMans. That's pretty rare and you don't just get parts for that right off the shelf. So while, yes, I do tend to have some parts on hand, the one you needed isn't one of them." Jackie leaned her hip against the desk, her eyes never wavering from the fuming customer's. "And since this was a rush job - at *your* insistence - it was extra to get it here as quickly as possible. None of this is new information; I told you all of this up front and you agreed to it. Did you not?"

His jaw clenched as his grip on the printout tightened. "Yes."

"Yes. So, remind me again what the problem is?"

Dropping his eyes to the ground, he muttered, "Nothing. Um, never mind."

He stepped over to the desk so he could pay his bill and Jackie stood, her own arms now folded, watching the transaction with an even expression. Mr. Blaithe barely looked at her as he quickly grabbed his receipt from Cassidy and scurried out, mumbling his thanks.

As soon as he was gone, Jackie and Cassidy shared a look before breaking into laughter.

"I should've known we wouldn't get through a Monday without *something* happening," Jackie commented.

"Yeah, well." Cassidy unlocked the bottom drawer of the desk and lifted a large glass jar half full of various denominations of dollar bills. "That's another deposit into the Disrespect Jar."

"Girl, at this rate, we'll be going on that vacation by the end of the year." They each stuffed a few dollars into the cut-out slit in the jar's lid.

"Jamaica, here we come."

Not an hour later, a call came in requesting a quote. Jackie happened to be manning the phone while Cassidy went to the restroom, and the customer had an all-too-familiar condescending tone, questioning Jackie as if *she* was the one that needed *his* help and actually asked if there was someone else he could talk to. Jackie wrapped up the call just as Cassidy came back to the desk, heaving a heavy sigh.

"Another one, huh?" Cassidy surmised.

"Unfortunately, yes. If shit keeps going like this, we're gonna be able to go to France."

Chapter 3

Myles wasn't in the best mood.

He still hadn't been able to get his car serviced because Chet claimed to be too booked, and refused to bump anyone to make room for him or take him outside of business hours. Myles even offered to bring his car in early, but Chet wasn't going for that, either.

"If I let you do that now, you'll expect it next time and the time after that," Chet had told him. "You'll try to deny it but you know it's true."

"And why *shouldn't* I get some special treatment? Have I not earned that?"

"I know you're not saying that because of the money your folks loaned me."

"Well, *actually-*"

"For one, *your folks* loaned me that, not you. Two, I paid them back, *with interest*, over a year ago. And three, even they didn't hold it over my head or expect me to treat them like the king and queen of the world despite them helping me out like they did."

"Even so, Chet-"

"But I'd gladly make concessions for them because they still treat me with respect and not like some kind of peon that's beneath them like you do. So you either wait for one of the next available spots on my calendar or take your damn car somewhere else."

Myles's jaw dropped, not believing his ears. He seethed at Chet's refusal to budge.

So Myles had to find another garage to take his car to, which annoyed him to no end. He called a couple of places to get quotes, but he knew he'd have to just choose a place and take it in since he wasn't exactly sure of the issue and wouldn't get a definitive answer until he was.

It didn't help his mood when he got a call from Cynthia, an ex that he still tolerated more than he should've. She had a tendency to randomly pop up, usually when she wanted something.

"Hello, Cynthia," he greeted, already pinching the bridge of his nose under his glasses.

"Myles, darling. It's so good to hear your voice."

"Why is that?"

"It always is."

Not in the mood for her buttering up, Myles sighed and bluntly asked, "Why are you calling me, Cynthia? What do you want?"

"Why do you assume-"

"I don't have time nor am I in the mood. What is it?"

"Fine," Cynthia huffed. "I wanted to ask you to accompany me to the charity gala my ladies' league is hosting this weekend. I'm on the planning committee and I'd rather not show up without an escort."

"I'm sure there's someone else you actually get along with that could escort you to this."

"You and I get along perfectly fine when we're not wasting time denying our feelings for each other. I miss you, Myles, and I know you miss me, too."

"You're mistaken."

"Myles. Darling. Must you be that way? You talk as if you hate me."

"No. But our relationship didn't work because you were so self-centered. And you ignored my concerns whenever I tried to broach them to you. You didn't even put up much of a fight when I ended it, so I took that to mean you were as aware of our incompatibility as I was."

"On the contrary. I figured you just needed some time to regroup. Sow any *oats* that you men need to sow before you can settle down. I had every expectation that we'd pick up where we left off when an appropriate amount of time had passed."

"Yeah, that was another issue. You made a lot of assumptions."

"Well I don't think the fact that Daddy would love to see you at the gala would be much of an *assumption*," Cynthia retorted. "He mentioned you just the other day, in fact."

Myles perked up. He'd temporarily forgotten that Cynthia's father was chairman of the Titan Executive board and the key to Myles getting the seat he'd been coveting for the past couple of years. That board was made up of some of the most powerful individuals in Brodence and surrounding cities and Myles itched to be a part of it, just like his father once was before giving up his seat to focus on his ailing wife.

"Is that so?" Myles asked, trying to sound unaffected. "That's surprising, since he's been rather unresponsive to my attempts to connect."

"Daddy is a very busy man, as I'm sure you know. But he'll be at the function. Prime opportunity for you to speak to him."

Myles wondered if getting another stab at making his case for that board seat was worth allowing Cynthia back into his life again. He'd tried going around her many times already and gotten nowhere. Maybe one night as her escort wouldn't be so bad if it led to him getting what he wanted.

"I'll think about it," he finally said. "I have to go right now but give me a call tomorrow and I can verify for sure if it works with my schedule or not."

"Absolutely, darling. I understand you're a busy man, also. Do you still do those little kits for the homeless? I always thought that was adorable."

Myles felt his face tighten. "I do, yes. Talk to you tomorrow, Cynthia."

"Yes you will."

Ending the call, Myles rubbed the bridge of his nose again. He was all but sure he'd be attending the function with Cynthia but he didn't want to agree too easily and appear eager. Nor did he need to let her know that his attendance would be more for his own benefit than hers.

Still, the prospect of spending an evening with Cynthia, for *any* reason, soured his mood even more. And he wasn't shy about venting about that and several other things when he was out to lunch with Ethan later.

"It's just been an awful past few days," he groused in conclusion, sitting back in his chair after tossing his napkin on top of his half-empty plate.

Ethan eyed him for a moment as he finished chewing his roasted duck. "You done?"

"Yeah, I'm not hungry anymore."

"No, I mean are you done complaining. Because you haven't stopped since you sat down."

Myles frowned. "Excuse me?"

"Come on, man. Ever since we got here, you've fussed about your sister's comedy set, your car, Cynthia, your meeting getting cancelled this morning, the weather. Do you not realize that?"

"All of those are valid grievances."

"You really need to lighten up. So you didn't like your sister's jokes and she doesn't want to work for the bank; get over it. She's doing what she loves to do. Cars mess up; it's not the end of the world. And your mechanic had a point about you expecting special treatment. It rains sometimes; big deal. And Cynthia...well, you're bringing that on yourself by even entertaining her at all."

"It's not about her. I'm still hoping her father will consider me for a seat on the Titan board."

"Myles, they've been dangling that board seat over your head for at least two years now and you haven't even gotten close to it. When are you going to accept that it isn't going to happen? If he wanted to appoint you, he would have done it by now."

Myles stilled. It had honestly never occurred to him that Cynthia and her father might be stringing him along. He thought, if anything, that he was being vetted or tested. But now he wondered if Ethan was right and he'd just been fooling himself this whole time.

"I'd hope that isn't the case," he muttered, drumming his fingers on the arm of his chair.

"I'd like to think it isn't, either, but all evidence points to the contrary."

"Yeah, well. My immediate concern is my car. I need to take it to get serviced in case whatever's wrong with it is something progressive."

"There are plenty of mechanics in Brodence, Myles. Just choose one."

"I'm not taking my car just anywhere."

"I don't mean to interrupt, but if you're looking for a good mechanic, I can make a recommendation," their server chimed in, having just stepped up to clear their plates.

"Yes, please," Ethan immediately replied.

"The Auto Loft, over on Lynn Boulevard. I've taken my car there several times and have never had any issues. The prices are fair, too. Jackie, the owner, is awesome and will take good care of you."

"Thank you for that." Ethan smiled at her as she scurried off with their dirty plates before turning his dark brown eyes to Myles with a triumphant single clap of his hands. "There you go; problem solved. You can go this afternoon. I'll go with you in case they're able to take your car immediately and you need a ride back."

"Fine. That might be one of the places I called already. They all started blending together after a while."

"It's not a life decision. Don't make it more difficult than necessary. Like you usually do."

Myles started to protest that but figured there was no point. Ethan certainly wasn't the first one to say that about him.

A couple of hours later, Myles headed over to The Auto Loft with Ethan following him. After pulling into the lot and killing the engine, Myles stepped out of the car, frowning slightly at the white brick exterior. It looked too 'clean' to him. If it weren't for the open bays where he could see people working, he wouldn't even believe it was a garage.

He pulled open the door to the reception area, his frown deepening when he heard the R&B music playing and saw the comfortable, clean seating and clearly carefully-chosen décor. There was a water fountain with disposable cups and a snack machine along the wall, as well as a coffee station. And the air smelled of...jasmine?

Is this a lounge or a garage?

"Good afternoon, gentlemen," the lady at the desk greeted them. She had a cute round honey brown face, heavy-lidded eyes, a nose ring, and brightly-painted pink lips. And Myles was almost certain that the straight black hair that hung to her belly was courtesy of a wig. "I'm Cassidy and welcome to The Auto Loft. How can I help you today?"

"My buddy's car is making some kind of noise and he needs someone to take a look at it so he can stop fussing," Ethan spoke up before Myles could say anything, patting his friend on the back. Myles cut his eyes at him.

Cassidy giggled. "We're more than happy to help, if we can. And as luck would have it, we have room for you today thanks to a cancellation."

"Great!"

"I drive a Cadillac CT4," Myles spoke up. "Do you all have any experience dealing with those?"

Her smile fading slightly, Cassidy leveled her gaze on Myles. "Our mechanics are more than capable of handling that and any other car, sir. That's what they're trained to do."

"It's just that it doesn't seem you've been in business all that long," Myles replied, glancing around him. "Everything looks so...*new* in here."

"Sometimes people need to wait in here and we want them to be comfortable. We try to leave the grease in the work area."

"Looks great to me," Ethan quickly spoke up before Myles could retort, clamping a firm hand to his shoulder while shooting him a pointed glare. "And we appreciate you fitting him in."

"No problem at all."

Cassidy proceeded to get the necessary information from Myles regarding his car, politely fielding his interjected questions or comments that seemed to multiply no matter what assurances she gave that his car would be in good hands. She was visibly relieved when a mechanic walked in from the bay area, chewing heavily on a piece of gum.

"Good afternoon," she greeted the men with a smile.

"Good afternoon," Ethan replied with a smile of his own. Myles barely nodded, his shock at seeing a woman emerge as one the mechanics as plain as day.

"Mr. Cornwall here is leaving his car with us to take a look at," Cassidy informed her, nodding her head in Myles's direction. "He said it's making a strange noise."

"Yeah? Well, I'm sure we can get to the bottom of it," she replied confidently.

"If you find it to be something too difficult, you can call Chet over at Ultimate Automotive," Myles spoke up. "He's my regular mechanic and knows what to do with my car."

Her eyes narrowed slightly, looking at Myles with renewed interest. "Your voice sounds familiar...did you call here for a quote the other day?"

Myles's own eyes narrowed. "I did, I think. Wait, are *you* the one I spoke to?"

"I surely am."

"You weren't very pleasant."

"I was following your lead."

Ethan coughed into his hand to keep from laughing and Myles glared at him.

"I was simply asking the questions that I felt were necessary," Myles defended, his tone clipped. "It wasn't anything personal."

"Sure."

"I'm not sure I love your tone *today*, either," Myles noted, folding his arms. His eyes traveled from her scarf-covered head to her dirty work boots. "If you didn't come recommended, I'd just take my business elsewhere. I was assured Jackie would take good care of us. Is he available? I'd like to speak with him, if I may."

The ladies shared an amused look as Ethan squeezed his eyes shut, shaking his head.

"*I'm* Jackie."

Myles's eyebrows shot up. "I beg your pardon?"

"I'm Jackie Malone." Jackie stood straighter, loving how utterly shocked Myles looked at the revelation. "Owner."

"You're the..." Myles looked at Ethan, who was actually grinning. "*You're* the owner??"

"Yes, sir. And we'd love to be of service to you but if you have some kind of problem with a little ol' woman touching your precious car, we can give you your keys back right now and wish you a good day and I can get back to work on the cars of customers whose mindsets *aren't* still stuck in the nineteen-fifties."

Ethan didn't try to hide his laugh this time and Cassidy was eyeing Myles with amusement, waiting to see what he'd come back with.

Myles didn't appreciate the intimation that he was chauvinistic but he couldn't help being shocked that it was a woman that would be servicing his car. He'd never met a woman mechanic before.

"I suppose it'll be fine to leave it here," he finally muttered. "I figure you could use the business and all."

Jackie's brow arched sharply. "What was that?"

"Is that not true? This young lady here mentioned there was a cancellation and I figure that has to be for a reason. Does that kind of thing happen here often?"

"You know *what-*"

"Please forgive him, Ms. Malone," Ethan quickly stepped in, fully recognizing that Jackie was about to go off. As much as Myles deserved it, Ethan didn't want to risk her sending Myles and his car packing because he'd ticked her off. Then he'd have to listen to even more of Myles's complaining. "Sometimes my friend here doesn't know when to shut up. Myles, *shut up*."

"Can't say I'm surprised to hear that, after these couple of dealings with him," Jackie replied pointedly. "Unfortunately, it's nothing we're not used to."

Several minutes later, Myles and Ethan were heading back to Ethan's car with assurance from Jackie that Cassidy would call them with a definitive quote as soon as she determined what the issue with Myles's car was.

"You were such an asshole in there," Ethan muttered as he started his engine.

Myles actually looked affronted. "Was that necessary? Just because I-"

"There's no way you can justify how you acted towards those women, Myles, so don't make yourself look worse by trying."

"They weren't exactly peachy towards me, either, Ethan. Where's the vitriol over that? They can't throw tantrums when they have challenging customers if they're going to be in the service industry."

"Oh, so you're an expert on that, too, huh? You know, it's times like this that I wonder why the hell I'm friends with you. You can be a condescending jerk, Myles, and it's *not* becoming. You need to check yourself, for real."

Myles couldn't help being a little hurt by his friend's words. Ethan wouldn't even look at him, his annoyed expression locked on the road ahead of them as they pulled away from the garage.

"It's not like I'm *trying* to be that way," Myles muttered after a few tense moments.

"I can't tell."

"Am I really that bad? I wasn't aware you thought that about me."

"Yes, Myles, you're that bad. But thankfully, it's something you can fix. And it needs to start with an apology to those ladies when you go back to get your car once they're done with it."

Myles pursed his lips, eyeing the buildings they were passing. He felt he'd been justified in the moment but now that he'd had some distance, he could acknowledge that he could've been more gentlemanly. His mother certainly wouldn't have been pleased if she'd heard how he behaved. Mollie would have probably cursed him out.

But he also couldn't help thinking he'd sue if that woman messed up his car.

"Fine," he groused, partially to appease Ethan. "I guess you have something of a point."

Silence prevailed for several minutes before Ethan finally spoke again.

"Did Jackie look familiar to you?" he asked, stopping at a red light. "It feels like I've seen her somewhere before."

Myles shrugged. "No."

"In any case, she sure is cute. Even with the grease on her face and the dirty clothes. Those coveralls couldn't hide that figure of hers."

"I didn't notice."

"I'm sure you didn't, since you were too busy acting like a pretentious snob. *I* surely noticed, though."

"In the midst of all of your ogling, did you also hear how she kept popping that gum she was chewing? It was horrendous. And *so* unladylike."

"So what? That's not a big deal. It's probably just something she does while she works but regardless, it doesn't diminish how attractive she is. I'm almost tempted to start taking *my* car there."

"And what would you tell Chet? That he's losing your business because he's not *cute* enough?"

"There are worse reasons. I checked out Jackie's garage after that waitress suggested it earlier and pretty much all the reviews were positive. Some even said they wouldn't trust their cars to anyone but Jackie."

Myles's head whipped around, his glare almost accusatory. "So you knew she was a woman before we went?"

"I did."

"Why didn't you tell me?"

"Why does it matter?"

"I..." Myles didn't have a response that didn't make him sound even more chauvinistic than he'd already come across as. "It just would've been nice to know, that's all."

Ethan glanced at him but didn't respond. They just rode the rest of the way back to the office in silence.

Chapter 4

Myles had been at the gala with Cynthia for less than an hour and he was already regretting agreeing to accompany her.

Cynthia was hanging onto his arm, barely letting him have a moment to himself, giving everyone the impression that they were back together. Myles bit his tongue, justifying to himself that correcting her wasn't necessary since she hadn't flat-out told anyone that they were a couple again; she just hinted at it. And Myles didn't want any friction before he had a chance to talk to her father, Donald, who he hadn't yet seen. He could only hope he would actually be there and Cynthia hadn't misled him about that like she was misleading the guests about the status of their relationship.

"Are you having a good time, darling?" Cynthia asked him, reaching up to straighten his bowtie. "You look so dapper."

"Thank you."

"It may be unladylike to say in public, but," Cynthia leaned up so her lips were at his ear, "You have me rather hot and bothered, Mr. Cornwall."

Myles felt his face flush at the unexpected comment. When he looked down at her, he could see the lust in her sepia brown eyes, and he took a step back. Cynthia was attractive enough, and her ice blue off-the-shoulder gown, jet black hair that hug in waves to her delicate brown shoulders, and expertly-applied makeup certainly enhanced things. But he had never been on fire for her, even when they were together, and that hadn't changed. He only hoped that she wasn't expecting sex at the end of the evening.

"Thank you," he repeated.

"'Thank you'? That's your response?"

"Cynthia, this really isn't the time or place for that kind of discussion. When is your father arriving?"

Taking a step back, Cynthia glanced around and shrugged halfheartedly. "I don't know. I'm sure he'll arrive shortly."

"He *is* going to be here, right?"

"Yes, Myles. Can you stop worrying about him and focus on us being here together? You've barely smiled all evening."

He resisted the urge to express how he didn't *want* to be there. "I apologize."

"Thank you. Come on, there's some people that just came in that I'd like to introduce you to."

Myles tried to smooth out his countenance and make the most of the evening. If nothing else, he was among a lot of influential people and could get some valuable contacts. And when he met someone who shared his concern for the homeless, he almost forgot Cynthia was even there.

"I hate that we don't have a shelter in Brodence," the woman who'd introduced herself as Veronica stated. "Many have talked about it for years but no one has actually made it happen."

"That's definitely one of my goals, to change that," Myles stated. "This is an issue rather close to my heart; my sister was homeless for a short time before my parents took her in, then ultimately adopted her. And I've seen so many that used to thrive but were just hit with a string of bad luck. So many think that homeless people are just lazy or unmotivated but that's often not the case at all."

"That is so true. Many of them just need a chance, but people treat them with such disdain. My husband and I are working on a foundation that will work towards getting them jobs, any needed medical attention, places to live, all that. We're just in the beginning stages but we're determined."

"That sounds amazing. Please let me know if you all need any help; I'd love to be a part of that. I make kits for them that I keep in my car with snacks, water, and a few toiletries, but it never feels like enough."

"That's wonderful! I know, it *never* feels like enough, does it? But you're helping; that's not to be dismissed. And I'll absolutely be reaching out to you about the foundation. We'll need all the help we can get, especially from someone with your passion."

"What about passion?" Cynthia appeared at Myles's side, taking hold of his arm.

"Myles and I were just discussing the ways we can alleviate the homelessness problem in Brodence and surrounding cities," Veronica informed her with a pleasant smile. Myles was sure she wasn't blind to the possessive way Cynthia was holding his arm and how she leaned into him. Either Cynthia wasn't aware that Veronica was married or she thought Myles was the kind of man that wouldn't care about the fact that she was.

"Oh yes, Myles has always had a soft spot for that," Cynthia commented, smiling up at him as she rubbed his arm. "It's so endearing."

Wanting to tell her to go away but refraining from doing so in front of Veronica, Myles just eyed her for a moment before resuming his conversation, tuning Cynthia out.

A few minutes later, Veronica went to find her husband and Cynthia linked her fingers through Myles's. "Are you ready to call it a night? We can head back to my place for a nightcap."

Myles just looked at her, extracting his hand from hers. "Your father isn't coming, is he?"

Her peanut brown skin flushed slightly as her eyes flitted off to the side. "I'm sure something came up."

"Cut the bull, Cynthia. He was never coming and you knew it."

She sighed, her eyes closing briefly. "I wasn't trying to deceive you, Myles. He *did* say that he might make an appearance but it wasn't set in stone."

"Of course you neglected to tell me that part."

"I assumed he would show."

"There you go with the assumptions again." He glanced at his watch. "I'm going home."

"Already?" Cynthia hesitated, her eyes dropping to her wrist even though she wasn't wearing a watch. "The night is still young."

"You weren't saying that a moment ago when you were suggesting we leave."

"Yes, *together*. It's bad enough I had to practically beg you to share a ride so we could make an entrance. Now you want to leave simply because my father didn't show?"

"The clueless act isn't endearing, Cynthia. You know the real reason."

"Well, I'm not ready to leave," Cynthia huffed, folding her arms and lifting her chin defiantly.

"Feel free to stay, then. I'll call my own car."

"Myles, darling, why are you behaving like this?" she hissed, dropping her arms and stepping closer to him. "We were having a nice evening-"

"You've just been stringing me along this whole time," he accused, not bothering to pose it as a question, because he already knew. Ethan had been right, as much as he hated to admit it. "All this time you've been acting like you were going to recommend me to your father; that he was seriously considering me and that I had any chance in hell of getting that Titan board seat. But it was all lies, wasn't it? I was never being considered, was I?"

Heaving a deep sigh, Cynthia's lip quivered momentarily before she couldn't bear to hold his challenging gaze anymore.

"No," she finally admitted, her voice barely audible over the dim music and conversation surrounding them. "I spoke to him about you, but...not for that purpose. The board seat was actually filled six months ago."

Myles felt his entire body heat with anger, at her but also at himself. He couldn't believe he'd let her dupe him all this time.

Without another word, he turned and headed for the exit. He needed to get away from Cynthia because he was having visions of causing a very unbecoming scene that he knew he would regret later, no matter how good it might feel in the moment.

And people wondered why he had no interest in dating.

"Myles!" Cynthia caught up to him outside, her heels clicking rapidly against the pavement thanks to her teeny tiny steps. The long chiffon skirt of her gown flowed behind her. Myles had just ordered his ride, which thankfully was only a few minutes away. She grabbed his arm, her French-tipped nails digging through his suit jacket. "I really cannot believe you're behaving like this. Look, I'm sorry if you think I deceived you-"

"You did." He didn't even look at her.

"I might not have been the most forthcoming but that doesn't mean we can't still have a nice evening together." She stepped in front of him, her hair blowing slightly in the evening breeze. Any beauty she had was muted by his frustration. "I only did what I did because I want us to reconcile, Myles."

"And you thought dishonesty was the route to take for that?"

"I tried the direct approach but that didn't work. I apologize. Can we just..." She stepped forward, hesitating briefly before placing a hand to his chest. Her pleading eyes roamed his face. "Can we just start over together? My feelings for you never went away. If you still feel anything for me, we can make this work. And let's not forget, we *both* made mistakes in our relationship. But I forgave *you*."

Myles's eyes dropped to hers.

"This can be our clean slate, darling." Her hand slid down and around to his back, under his suit jacket. Her chest was now pressed against his body. "Come back to my place tonight. We can have some drinks, get reacquainted, and just enjoy each other." Her other hand slid behind his neck and eased his head closer to hers. "However you'd like."

Myles hated that he was tempted. He'd lost track of how many months it'd been since he had sex. Images of Cynthia's lithe brown body underneath his began rolling through his mind, and his body started to react, much to his chagrin. And Cynthia's triumphant grin indicated that she noticed it, too.

That snapped him out of it. He couldn't let himself do something foolish for a couple hours of pleasure, and giving in to Cynthia would be foolish. Even if he told her up front that it would just be sex and nothing else, and even if she agreed to whatever terms he may lay out, she would internally take it to mean more. It wasn't like she had a good track record of keeping her word.

A black SUV pulled up and Myles stepped back, removing Cynthia's hands from his body.

"It's not happening, Cynthia," he told her, his voice unyielding. "Not tonight, not ever. Don't call me again."

Her jaw dropped, and he sidestepped her and verified that the SUV was for him before getting into the backseat. He didn't even glance Cynthia's way as they pulled off, his head falling against the headrest once they were down the street.

Myles was mildly surprised when he got the call from The Auto Loft that his car was ready. They had estimated that it might not be for another day, and Myles had figured it would be even longer. There had been a few times when Chet went beyond the estimated time getting his car back to him. Myles had automatically thought it would be the same or worse with Jackie.

He got a rideshare to the garage, since he knew Ethan was busy. When he noted that every bay in the street-facing garage was occupied and there were several other cars in the graveled lot, his eyebrows shot up in surprise. They certainly didn't seem to be lacking for business. He noted his car neatly parked in the small paved portion of the lot, which he figured was the section for the completed cars. If he didn't know better, it even looked cleaner than when he brought it in.

There were a couple of people ahead of him when he entered the reception area, and he just stood and waited after a brief glance at his watch. A woman and small child sat on the nearby loveseat, the child reading a children's book and the woman flipping through a magazine as she bopped her head to the R&B music. An older man was helping himself to the complimentary coffee, and Myles noticed there were even individually-wrapped muffins from a local bakery that apparently were free on a first-come-first-served basis. His fingers itched to take one of the last two but he resisted, feeling like it would be embarrassing even though he didn't know why.

When he was finally at the front of the line, Cassidy looked up at him with a smile. He was expecting attitude after his last visit, but if she recognized him, she showed no signs of it. His previous suspicions about her hair being a wig were confirmed, since today's 'do was short and pink and reminded him of something on one of Mollie's dolls from back in the day.

"Good afternoon Mr. Cornwall," Cassidy greeted him.

Myles blinked in mild surprise. "You...remember my name."

"Sure do. Hope you're having a good afternoon so far." She punched a few buttons on the computer in front of her. "We have your car all ready for you. The final price ended up being a little different than we anticipated; let me get you a printout of the charges and the breakdown."

"Different, huh?" Myles shook his head. He knew it. Of course something else 'popped up' once they got their hands on his car. Anything to justify squeezing a few more bucks out of him. Even Chet had tried that on him a few times, so he wasn't even surprised.

When Cassidy held out the breakdown to him, he practically snatched it, ready to dispute whatever the extra (and unapproved) charges were. But when he saw the final price, his eyebrows shot up in surprise yet again. It was actually a hundred dollars *lower* than quoted.

All the fiery words that had been at the ready were suddenly eviscerated into ashes that were now coating his throat, leaving him speechless. He looked at Cassidy, whose smirk and arched brow clearly screamed *busted*. And Myles knew he was.

"Um..." He cleared his throat.

"Do you have any questions, Mr. Cornwall?" Cassidy asked sweetly.

He swallowed, trying to gather himself. He could feel the flush of embarrassment in his cheeks and hated that Cassidy probably could see it, too. "Not at this time, no."

"One of our mechanics can accompany you to your car so you can let it run and verify that we've taken care of the issue for you, as well as answer any questions you may think of. We want to be absolutely sure that you're *totally* satisfied with us today."

She was enjoying this, and Myles couldn't even blame her. He was just glad that Ethan wasn't there because he knew he'd never let him live this down.

"Yes, if Jackie could do that, I'd appreciate it," he managed to say.

"Oh, it would be one of our other mechanics or our garage assistant. Jackie is swamped and can't step away. But Irv or Jimmy are more than capable of assisting you."

"Oh..." Myles felt a surprising wave of disappointment. "Never mind, then. I mean; I'm sure it's fine."

"All right, then," Cassidy shrugged. "Feel free to call or come back if you *do* think of any questions or concerns later. How would you like to pay today?"

Myles completed the transaction with Cassidy, feeling what he could only describe as weird. No one had to tell him that he owed Jackie an apology, and he hated that he wouldn't be able to give her that before he left.

"Thank you for using The Auto Loft and we do hope you come back to see us," Cassidy said, handing him his receipt and his car keys. "And here are a few of our cards, if you'd like to spread the word. We do offer service discounts for referrals."

"Sure, yeah." Myles plucked a few cards from the holder at the edge of the desk. There was someone waiting behind him and he knew he needed to go ahead and leave, but he couldn't resist a last-ditch effort. Leaning in slightly, he asked, "Would it be possible to leave a message for the owner? I mean, for Jackie?"

"One and the same," Cassidy winked at him, reaching for a small notepad. "Absolutely. What's the message?"

"Um, I'll just jot it down myself, if that's all right."

Cassidy handed him the notepad and a pen, and Myles scribbled out his name and number, along with a short request for her to call him at her earliest convenience. His eyes didn't quite meet Cassidy's as he handed the pad and pen back to her. He didn't know why he felt so silly but he hated it. "Thank you."

"My pleasure, sir. I'll be sure Jackie gets this as soon as possible. Have a great day!"

"You, too."

Myles turned and headed for the door, almost bumping into the woman behind him. He mumbled an apology before scurrying out.

He headed over to his car, the wind hitting his heated face. Once he got closer to his car he realized it had in fact been washed since he dropped it off, which was a pleasant surprise.

"They do that for everybody?" he wondered to himself, getting into the driver's seat.

Once he started the engine, it purred like it did the day he bought it. The noise was nowhere to be found, and when he pulled out of the lot and headed down the street, it even seemed to ride smoother than before. And when he glanced around, he realized that the floorboards had been vacuumed, too.

Now he really felt like an idiot.

Part of him wondered if this was their standard level of service for everyone or if Jackie had chosen to go above and beyond just to show him up. He couldn't even fault her for it, if that was the case. In truth, he could see himself doing the same thing.

He headed back to the office to get some more work done, already mentally working out what he'd say to Jackie when she called.

"You have a message, boss lady."

It was the end of the day and Jackie was tired and achy, barely having had a break all day. She couldn't wait to get home and take a long, steamy eucalyptus shower and have a glass of rum the size of her head. She glanced at Cassidy as she rubbed her aching lower back. "What have we said about you calling me that?"

Cassidy shrugged. "I'm not sure what the big deal is. That's what you are."

"Whatever. What message?"

"Myles Cornwall. He asked to speak to you earlier when he picked up his car but I told him you were busy, per your instructions." She tapped the note Myles had left. "He wants you to call him."

"I see. Hand me that?"

Cassidy handed her the note and Jackie immediately spit her gum into it, then balled it up and tossed it in the trash. Cassidy's jaw dropped.

"Was that really necessary? It seemed like he wanted to apologize to you."

"You don't know that."

"I saw the look on his face once he got the revised price. Straight shook. He probably thought we were going to pad the bill with some bullshit." Cassidy shut down her computer and stood, pulling her shimmery sweater down over her round belly. "And he specifically requested *you* when I offered for someone to do a final check on his car with him."

"That doesn't mean anything," Jackie dismissed, taking a fresh piece of gum from her pocket and popping it into her mouth. "He might've just wanted to get me alone so he could spout more of his condescending bullshit in private. No thanks. We fixed his car, he paid; we don't have anything else to talk about."

Cassidy turned, leveling her friend with a thoughtful gaze. "You really need to lighten up sometimes, sis."

Rearing slightly, Jackie's brows lifted. "What?"

"You act like men are supposed to be perfect. Like they're trash that don't deserve second chances if they mess up one time."

"I never said that. But you saw how he acted when he was in here the other day."

"And I'm not defending it. But is it not possible that he realizes what an asshole he was and wants to make amends?

I'm telling you, I really think he was humbled earlier. If he's sincerely sorry-"

"He could've just apologized to *you*, then, because it's not like it was just me he showed his ass to. But he didn't do that, did he? So it doesn't seem like he's all that sorry to me."

"You're the damn owner, not me." Cassidy sucked her teeth as she tossed the book she read during her breaks and a couple of other things into her bag, shaking her head. "I swear I hate when you get like this. All stubborn and shit and refusing to give folks the benefit of the doubt. As if you don't want people to do the same for you."

It was almost like she was talking to herself, but Jackie still felt pricked by the words. She knew she had a tendency to hold a grudge but she was surprised that Cassidy was so annoyed by it, since she usually advocated pettiness.

"So it's like that, huh?" she asked, her tone missing its earlier edge.

"It's like that." Cassidy put a hand on her hip, facing off with her. "How many times have you had to prove yourself since you opened this garage to men that didn't think you could handle the job, or that questioned your skills? You wanted them to give *you* a chance, right? What about when you messed up your relationship with Ringo and was crying to me that he wouldn't talk to you for weeks? What if he just gave you one big brush-off like you did to this Myles guy and never forgave *you*?"

Anger surged through Jackie, her nostrils flaring. She hated that Cassidy was throwing that in her face but also that she had a point. She met skepticism every day as a mechanic, just because she was a woman. Some men questioned her every move and every decision, just because it was her. But if Irv or Jimmy told them the exact same thing she had, they'd take it as gospel. One or two times, people had left altogether once they saw she was the owner. It was both sad and infuriating that people still had those kinds of attitudes in this day and age.

And Ringo...Jackie didn't like the reminder of how she ruined their relationship. She was the first to admit she'd been a bit too possessive, copping an automatic attitude any time a woman so much as smiled in his direction or left flirty comments on social media. She didn't like sharing him, and had even bugged him to give up being an exotic dancer and do something where he didn't have to show off his body and have women groping at him. He refused, insisting that it was something he loved to do for now, and asked if she'd give up working on cars just because he didn't like how a few men spoke to her. They had many an argument about it, but Ringo had enough after Jackie caused a scene at one of his shows, getting into a fight with a woman Jackie felt was being a little too handsy. He dumped her that same night.

Jackie had been miserable, and pleaded for another chance. She was actually embarrassed at how she'd behaved, not just at that show but any time she and Ringo were out in public and someone flirted with him, or when she cussed strangers out on social media for leaving him so much as a heart-eyed emoji. Ringo had never given her any reason not to trust him but she still showed her ass at every opportunity, and she couldn't even blame him for being upset, yet she still hoped he'd take her back. He eventually took one of her calls, and over time forgave her and opened himself back up to a tentative friendship and some occasional flirting and fooling around, but he shut her down whenever she mentioned them getting back together. Jackie had told herself she accepted that, but there was a part of her that still hoped he'd change his mind.

"I guess you have a point," she grudgingly admitted to Cassidy. "That's something I need to check myself on, I suppose."

"It is." Cassidy slung her bag over her shoulder. "You never know; you might end up actually liking the guy. He's not bad to look at, either."

"I didn't notice all that." And she didn't. All that had registered to Jackie after her encounter with Myles was that he was a bespectacled stick-up-the-ass Black man who thought she was beneath him. "Might not hurt to check him out." Cassidy winked at her as she rounded the desk. "His eyes are really sexy behind those glasses. He has a pretty nice set of lips on him, too."

"If you say so. If I speak to him again, it would be to hear him out so he can say whatever he needs to say and that's it. Then him, his sexy eyes and nice lips and whatever else you happened to notice can go on about their business."

A couple of hours later, Jackie was feeling worlds better after her shower and first glass of rum. She wandered into her kitchen and opened the refrigerator, chewing her lip as she pondered what to make for dinner. A quick one-pan pasta, some broiled fish, burgers...all of it sounded good but she decided she didn't have the energy for any of it. So she grabbed her phone and ordered a meat-filled pizza and some breadsticks, opting for something she didn't have to make herself. It thankfully didn't take all that long for it to arrive, and she hurried to the door as soon as the doorbell rang without thought. The delivery guy almost dropped her food as soon as he saw her.

"Damn!"

"Oh shit, my bad..." Jackie eased behind the door, hiding her naked body. It was the norm for her when she was at home alone and it had totally slipped her mind to cover up before her food arrived. "Sorry about that. Um, you can just put the food right there." She pointed to the small table just inside the door where she usually stashed her keys and mail.

The guy wordlessly did as asked, trying to keep his eyes averted yet steal another glimpse of her on the sly. She had already included his tip when she paid on the app so thankfully the awkward encounter didn't have to go on any longer, and he mumbled his thanks before easing back out the door. Jackie quickly closed and locked it behind him, moving over to the window to make sure he actually got in his car and left. She sighed in relief, knowing that could've gone way left. She'd have to be more careful.

She enjoyed her dinner in front of the television, watching her favorite car show, *Custom Salvage*. When she got a text from Cassidy telling her about yet another thing going on with her and her husband Orion, Jackie felt an unwanted pang of jealousy. As happy as she was for her friend, she sometimes hated how eager Cassidy was to regale her with all of the details of her newlywed life. It only reminded Jackie that she didn't have anyone of her own to dish about. She didn't want to be one of those women who lamented day in and day out about not having a man, and she usually managed to convince herself that she was fine on her own, but that particular declaration wasn't working as often as it used to. Jackie would've loved to have someone to spend her life with; to have something more than just hot showers and rum to rush home to after a long work day. Part of her still wanted Ringo in that role, but she knew better than to hold out hope for it; he had made it abundantly clear that he couldn't go there with her again, and all they'd ever be was friends. Plus, he was in a relationship, even if Jackie chose to believe it didn't really count since it was long distance.

Figuring there was no sense yearning for something she wasn't going to get that night, Jackie forced those thoughts from her mind. She put away her leftovers, double-checked all the locks and turned out the lights except the lamp by the couch, which was something her father always taught her to do so the house didn't look completely dark. She headed to her en suite bathroom and got ready to call it a night, brushing her teeth and wrapping her hair. The surrounding quiet felt pronounced for some reason, so she turned on one of her favorite entrepreneurship podcasts to fill the silence.

Before diving onto her queen-sized bed, Jackie eyed the affirmation whiteboard that she kept by her mirror. Every couple of days, she wrote an encouraging affirmation or note or mantra to herself, and it had been a great source of comfort for her during the time she was considering leaving her corporate job and when she opened her garage. Going to the board for a bolster of confidence or assurance had become almost automatic. She grabbed the dry erase marker and paused briefly before writing:

He's coming. Make sure you're ready.

Stepping back, she eyed the statement with a smile before capping the marker and returning it to the whiteboard's ledge. Grabbing her phone, she switched from the podcast to her slow jam playlist, then grabbed her never-fail dildo from her bedside drawer and climbed into bed, hoping the day would soon come where she wouldn't need it.

Chapter 5

It was Sunday morning and Jackie was glad that her garage was closed. It had been a long week and while she loved working, she was looking forward to having the day off.

She was out picking up a few groceries when she heard someone call her name.

"Jacqueline Malone."

Jackie turned to see Chanel James heading towards her with a big smile on her face. She immediately pulled Jackie into a tight hug, towering over her by several inches.

"Good to see you, Chanel," Jackie replied, a good-natured smile now on her own lips. "But you know I prefer to be called Jackie."

"My bad. I forgot you're not 'corporate' anymore." Chanel stood perusing her as if trying to figure out a riddle. Her highlighted brown hair hung in microlocs over her shoulders, and her dark brown skin gleamed as if she was fresh from the spa. She sported a red fitted pantsuit and nude heels, leaving Jackie feeling rather underdressed in her oversized off-the-shoulder sweater, leggings, and slides, even though they were just in a grocery store. "How's the garage doing? Every time I ride by there, you seem to have a full house."

"Yeah, business is great. Almost doubled our earnings from last year. I'll be able to hire another mechanic soon enough, if things keep going like they are."

"I love to see it. Black women doing the damn thing with their own businesses; it does my heart good." Chanel slung an arm around Jackie's shoulders, leaning in. "So is that why I haven't heard from you about my offer? I think I've left six messages, at last count."

Jackie knew she'd have to deal with Chanel sooner or later, and she'd been hoping it was later. Chanel worked for the land developers that were trying to oust several of the local businesses in the area, including Lula's Cup. She initially approached Jackie a couple of months earlier, and Jackie gave her the brush-off, refusing to entertain any offer or discussions.

But it wasn't for the reason it appeared to be. She might have given Chanel the impression she wasn't interested when the truth was, she wouldn't have minded selling. In her mind, she could just build a bigger and better garage somewhere else. She'd moved to Brodence about fifteen years earlier and while she loved living there, she didn't have the same attachment to it or the local businesses that others did. And she knew it wouldn't go over well if she expressed her opinion that bringing some new business to the area, even if they *were* chain businesses, wouldn't be the worst thing in the world. It didn't mean all small businesses had to go away. If handled correctly, a healthy mix was possible.

She knew she was in the minority on that, though, so she kept it to herself; she hadn't even told Cassidy. She had good relationships with most of the people in the community and she didn't want them thinking she was a sellout. Jackie had made the internal decision that she would basically go with the majority; if most of the other businesses stayed put, so would she. She'd still expand down the line either way.

"I believe I already gave you my response on that, Chanel," Jackie reminded her, easing from beneath Chanel's arm. "Don't be like these thirsty men out here that can't take a hint."

"Persistence is part of the job. I'm already getting pushback on damn near every turn, and now the mayor is waning even more thanks to all the complaints." Chanel shook her head as she mindlessly thumped at a box of croutons. "You'd think we were talking about burning everything down and starting over. We're trying to enhance, not destroy."

"That's not how folks see it. It's not like you're *not* trying to run them out so you can put some big-name business in their place. And some of these places have been in business longer than you've been alive."

"I get that. But sometimes change is necessary. At some point, folks have to get off the treadmill and onto the road so they can actually *go* somewhere." Chanel shook her head, as if catching herself falling into a familiar rant, and plastered on a smile. "But anyway. You know, I was over at Joswell recently, visiting some former associates. It still seems strange seeing someone else in your old office."

Jackie scoffed. "I hope they're enjoying it more than I did."

"Come on, Jackie. You were one of the top executives there. It couldn't have been *that* bad."

"It wasn't terrible but it wasn't what I wanted to do with my life. I started dreading being in that environment; the people, the stuffy corporate culture, the unspoken expectation that the job take precedence over everything else in my life. No ma'am; I couldn't keep living like that."

Chanel eyed her thoughtfully. "And you don't miss it at all?"

"Not even a little bit."

"Well, hey; good for you," Chanel concluded with a shrug. "As happy as I am for you, I hope you don't think this means I'm going to stop trying to change your mind about selling."

Jackie just shook her head before turning to walk off down the aisle. "I don't doubt it, Chanel."

Myles couldn't believe he hadn't heard back from Jackie yet.

He wondered what Cassidy had told her, or if she had discouraged Jackie from getting back to him. It hadn't occurred to Myles until after the fact that he owed Cassidy an apology, too, a fact that surely wasn't lost on her. It wouldn't have surprised him if Cassidy tossed his message the moment he walked out the door.

Telling himself to think positively, he decided to call the garage again. It was totally possible that Jackie had just been too busy to get back to him. Or maybe she forgot. He imagined she had a lot on her plate, running the business and all. Hopefully he could catch her between appointments or she'd be able to give him a minute to say what he needed to say.

But no such luck.

"She's not available right now, Mr. Cornwall," Cassidy informed him. "She's elbow-deep in somebody's engine right now."

Myles tried to tamp down his frustration. He couldn't fault Jackie for working, but all he wanted was to give her the apology he owed her. It would take two minutes, tops. It wasn't like he was trying to sit and talk all day.

"Do you know when she might have a break?" he asked. "You *did* give her my message, didn't you?"

"I did, yes. And she's got a full day today so there's no telling when she'll be done."

Sighing, Myles pinched the bridge of his nose under his glasses. Why was this so hard?

"Fine," he sighed. "Well, since I have you, I want to apologize to you for how I acted on my visits there. I was rude and out of line when you were just doing your job, and I'm sincerely sorry for that."

There was a brief pause. "Thank you for that, Mr. Cornwall. I appreciate it. It's not often that customers willingly admit that so it means a lot."

"I'd like to apologize to Jackie, as well, if she would just...if she would be so kind as to return my call."

"Yeah...maybe you should try coming here to talk to her in person? It might go further with her, you telling her that face-to-face. Just sayin'."

"Hmph," Myles couldn't help but scoff. He was willing to apologize but he wasn't about to jump through hoops. What difference did it make where he apologized as long as it was sincere? What if he went there to apologize to her face and it *still* wasn't good enough? She might try to make him sweat some other way just because she didn't like him, and he was sure she didn't.

He was a busy man, too. If him calling to humble himself with an apology wasn't enough for Queen Jackie, then that was just too bad. He didn't have time to be strung along.

"I'll keep that in mind," he made himself say, not wanting to be rude again. "In any case, I hope you let her know why I called. Thank you for your time, Cassie. *Cassidy*," he quickly corrected.

"No problem, Mr. Cornwall. You have a good day."

"You, too."

Myles ended the call, still simmering with frustration. He'd hoped to knock that task off his to-do list for the day and it annoyed him that it was still unfinished because Jackie wanted to be stubborn, because he had a feeling she could've gotten back to him by then if she wanted to.

"I tried," he muttered, shrugging before checking his watch and standing, grabbing his phone and a couple of files for the meeting he was headed to. As far as he was concerned, he did his part.

"Knock, knock."

"I'm at work, Mollie."

"Come on, don't be such a fuddy-duddy. Knock, knock."

Myles sighed, not in the mood but figuring it would be quicker to just comply and get it over with. "Who's there?"

"Etch."

"Etch who?"

"Bless you!"

Myles rolled his eyes while Mollie cracked up at her own joke. He forced patience as he waited for her to calm down.

"Why did you call me, Mollie?"

"I didn't call you 'Mollie'. Your name is Myles."

Mollie laughed even louder at herself again and Myles sighed, seriously considering hanging up on her and just apologizing later.

"Mollie."

"Okay, okay. Geez, I'll be glad when you get a sense of humor." Mollie took a moment to compose herself. "Mom asked me to call and let you know they want us to come over for dinner tonight."

"What? Since when?"

"Since today, I guess. She just called me. I had other plans but had to change them because you know there's no refusing her."

Myles held his tongue, only because he didn't put it past Mollie to 'accidentally' tattle on him if he went off. He usually wouldn't have minded having dinner with his parents; it was the relatively short notice that annoyed him.

But he loved his parents, and his mother wasn't in the best health, having Lupus along with some other ailments. So if she wanted them to come over for dinner out of the blue for seemingly no reason, he'd be there.

After verifying the time of the dinner, Myles ended the call with Mollie and went back to the research he'd been doing. He was working on a proposal for funding to buy several empty houses in downtown Brodence and have them converted into shelters for the homeless. It was something of a pet project, but he fully intended on approaching his superiors about possibly getting on board as investors, which was why he didn't have any qualms about working on it during business hours. He could've had his assistant pull the information for him but this was so important to him, he wanted to do it himself.

He was concentrating so hard he didn't notice Ethan standing in his doorway for a couple of minutes.

"You really should be more aware of your surroundings, buddy."

Myles glanced up, his frown of concentration now also about being interrupted. "I'm concentrating."

"Clearly. What are you working on? Something for that big Morlock account?"

"Just information-gathering for now," Myles replied evasively, not wanting to get into it right then. He sat back in his seat, momentarily removing his glasses to rub his eyes. "That Morlock account is keeping me plenty busy, though."

"I bet. That's a major one that our colleagues are still salty they didn't get. Some of them are pressed that a Black man got that over them. You're a shoo-in for a promotion if you nail that."

"I'm aware, of both facts. I'm feeling the pressure as well as seeing the glares. I've even heard whispers that my parents had something to do with me getting the account."

"That's ridiculous! You've earned everything you have here on your own by busting your ass for the past ten years. Your folks had nothing to do with it."

"Absolutely not. But truth doesn't soothe bruised egos as well as fabricated reasoning. Rumors aren't anything new or anything I can't handle. I don't let that nonsense concern me. What's going on?"

"You remember Chanel James?"

Frowning slightly in thought, Myles took a beat before replying, "The name sounds familiar. Who is she, again?"

"Works for the land developer. They've been all around town recently, poking at most of the small businesses. I happened to see her at the grocery store with that hot mechanic you pissed off."

Myles had been mindlessly eying something on his computer screen but hearing that got his attention. "You mean Jackie?'

"I surely do," Ethan confirmed, amused at how Myles perked up upon her being mentioned. "At first I was curious that they seemed so friendly but then I remembered where I knew Jackie from."

"Where?"

"She used to work for Joswell International. I recall dealing with her indirectly while working that merger few years back, and also seeing her name mentioned several times at conferences and in publications or whatnot. She was a pretty big deal. Jacqueline Malone; she was COO before she left to go into business for herself."

"Really?" Myles hadn't been expecting that at all. The same woman he'd seen with a doo-rag on her head and grease on her face and coveralls covered in dirt and annoyingly popping gum was a former executive? A *big-time* executive, at that?

"That's certainly a surprise," Myles admitted.

"I bet. I don't suppose you've spoken to her again and made amends for how you acted yet."

"I tried. She won't return my call."

"You *called*? Seriously?" Ethan's groomed brows bunched together.

"Yes," Myles shrugged, not seeing what the problem was. "I had every intention of apologizing to her but she refuses to call me back. And I don't think it's just because she's so *busy*, as her receptionist claims. She's just being stubborn."

"Maybe she'd appreciate the apology the same way she got the disrespect; to her face."

Cassidy had hinted the same thing. Myles still didn't see why it mattered. "In any case, I'm sure Cassie – ugh...*Cassidy* – will relay the reason for my call. So either way, Jackie will know I intended to apologize even if she didn't hear it directly from me."

Ethan shook his head, the displeasure clear on his chiseled features. He always got more than his share of attention whenever he and Myles were out together, women apparently appreciating the attractive result of his Black mother and Greek father's union. Women noticed Myles, too, but he wasn't usually as welcoming of the attention as Ethan was.

"What?" Myles asked, noting the glare his friend was giving him. "Like I said, I tried."

"You didn't try hard enough," Ethan quickly retorted. "And you couldn't have been very sincere if you're willing to give up so easily."

Sighing, Myles ran his hands over his conservative low haircut a couple of times before dropping them into his lap and resting his head against the back of his chair.

"You're not gonna leave me alone about this, are you?" he asked.

"What do you think?"

"All right, *fine*. I will take time out of my schedule and go way across town so I can deliver the almighty Jacqueline her apology on a silver platter."

"Great." Ethan turned to leave. "Before you do, though, get all this smart-ass stuff out of your system. Otherwise, you might as well not even bother. You'll just be even further in the doghouse with her than you probably already are."

Several hours later, Myles was trying not to think about the work he could be doing as he sat at his parents' dining room table. He was glad to see them, as always, but he just wasn't in a very sociable mood.

It didn't help that Mollie was regaling them with the details of some web show she was recently a part of. Of course, her recounting was chock full of her usual crude humor.

"We actually made a game out of how many genitalia colloquialisms we could come up with in thirty seconds," Mollie recalled. She flipped her braids from her shoulder with a smug smile. "I won, of course."

"What did you win? An associate's degree?" Myles couldn't help asking. "Or maybe a lifetime supply of...sex toys."

"I *wish*! Do you know how much money that would save me??"

Myles was surprised when his parents actually laughed. They'd always found Mollie hilarious, and Myles used to think it was because they were just trying to bolster her confidence. Or that they were taking pity on her. But after so many years, he no longer thought that was the case, if it ever was.

"And by the way, there's nothing wrong with an associate's degree, Mr. Elitist," Mollie continued, rolling her eyes at Myles. "And you always seem to want to forget that I have a bachelor's."

"That you're not using," he muttered, cutting into his lamb chop.

"She can always use it down the line if she needs or wants to, son," their father, Hampton, spoke up.

"Of course. Because French Literature degrees are in *such* high demand..."

"Myles," his mother Agatha spoke up, her rich voice booming from across the table. "*When* is the last time you got laid?"

Myles dropped his fork while Mollie burst out laughing. Hampton chuckled, his hand partially covering his mouth.

"Mom!" Myles felt his face flush. "Did you really just ask me that??"

"Well, I figure maybe that's at least part of the reason you're always so stodgy. You can't even loosen up enough to take a joke, honey. Do you realize you've barely smiled since you got here, let alone laughed?"

"He hardly laughs at anything," Mollie scoffed, waving a dismissive hand at Myles before grabbing her glass of Ramey. "He'll try to say it's because he doesn't like my dirty jokes but I doubt it would make any difference who was saying it or what they were talking about. It's like he's programmed on 'stiff.'"

"I would've said 'stoic', but either one applies," Hampton noted, reaching for another helping of seafood salad from the crystal bowl near the middle of the table. "You've been extra sour and pouty since you broke things off with Cynthia. Though you were never exactly the life of the party before that."

"Maybe she'd be agreeable to one last roll in the hay to try to knock a crack in that stone exterior of his," Mollie suggested. "Maybe he's just backed up and needs to release a few rounds of-"

"Can we not?" Myles interjected. "I do not need to be *released* and even if I did, I surely wouldn't choose Cynthia to assist me with that. She has cemented that she can't be trusted."

"So who can we call, then?" Mollie drained the rest of her wine before tapping her chin, her eyes rolling to the ceiling in thought. "Ooh, how 'bout-"

"We are *not* doing this. There's no need to even go through this pointless exercise because I do not need any of you to help me find a date."

"It doesn't have to be a *date*-date. You've heard of booty calls, right?"

"You've had one of those, right, son?" Hampton asked.

Momentarily stumped by his father asking him such a thing, Myles stammered slightly as he replied, "Isn't there something else we can talk about? You all are acting like I'm some kind of stodgy old coot and I'm far from it. I just have a more elevated sense of humor-"

"Mama, are you sure *I'm* the one that's adopted?" Mollie asked behind her hand even though she purposely asked the question loud enough for Myles to hear. "'Cause when it comes to this family, one of these things is not like the others and it's *not* me. Hint: he's sitting over there ramrod straight like he's in the military or something and carries wet wipes in his pocket."

The three of them laughed as Myles cut his eyes at his little sister. He didn't love that they were talking about him like he wasn't there, just like he didn't appreciate the implication that he was the outsider of the family. Just because he knew how to keep his composure and didn't laugh at silliness like they did.

If Myles was honest, though, he could (silently) admit that Mollie had a point. The truth was, Mollie was more like their parents than he was, despite him actually being their biological child. Agatha and Hampton didn't behave like the multimillionaires they were. Not to mention Agatha also being a descendant of one of the original founding families of Brodence, and her and Hampton known pillars of the community who practically ran the city with an iron fist covered in suede, as they never abused the immense power they had, only wielding it when necessary. They owned successful corporations, sat on the most coveted boards, donated millions to charity every year, but there they sat in their formal dining room each wearing jeans and t-shirts from their recent trip to Disneyland. Agatha even had Mickey Mouse ears perched on her head, her thin grey hair gathered in a ponytail. Mollie wore a cropped hoodie under a pair of fashionably-distressed overalls. Myles was the one that stuck out in his full suit as if this was a business dinner.

He actually felt a little silly, even though his sixty-seven-year-old mother was the one sitting there in Mickey Mouse ears. Being among the overdressed in any room wasn't anything new for him, but this was a rare time that he wished he'd opted for something a tad less crisp. It crossed his mind to at least remove his jacket, but he didn't want to let them (namely Mollie) know they'd gotten to him.

"Anyway, I'm so glad to spend this evening with my beautiful family because I had a pretty unpleasant experience this morning," Agatha stated with a sigh, pouring a little more thyme gravy over her mashed potatoes.

Her husband looked at her with concern. "What happened, baby? You didn't mention anything about that earlier."

"I didn't want to give it any more energy, really." Agatha paused to take a bite of her potatoes, lightly bobbing her head side to side in contemplation before adding a touch more gravy. "But it's been stuck in my head so I figured venting might help move on past it."

"Yeah, tell us about it, Mama, so we'll know whose ass is now on the line," Mollie requested. "You don't need to be stressing out over anything."

"I'm fine. But some people nowadays are just so *ugh*." Agatha took another bite of potatoes before putting down her fork and sitting back in her chair, adjusting her Mickey Mouse ears. "I was getting gas this morning and noticed one of the tires could use a little more air, so I went to the air pump station. I was minding my business when some man pulled up behind me and asked if I needed any help. I thanked him but said I was good. He asked me if I was sure; I said yes. Then he proceeded to stand there and watch me, like he was some kind of evaluator."

"Did you ask him to leave you alone?" Hampton inquired, frowning.

"I politely let him know I'd be done shortly, but he insisted that he was just trying to make sure I didn't put too much air in the tire. Because that's 'what all women tend to do,'" Agatha mocked, air quoting with her fingers. "Then I guess that's when he noticed what kind of car I had because he made a couple of comments about how a woman of my 'advanced age' probably doesn't know about new technology. I was like, dude, I'm putting air in a tire, not recalibrating the windshield sensors."

"You should've called me. This is why I don't like you going around town alone, baby."

"You can't watch me twenty-four seven, sweetheart." Agatha smiled at her husband, placing a brief hand to his cheek. "I love you for it but that'll just drive us both nuts. I know I'm not in the best health but I can handle running basic errands."

"And didn't this man know who he was dealing with?" Myles asked, incensed. The idea of anyone harassing his mother infuriated him. "As much as you've done for this city, nobody should *ever* dare mess with you."

"I'm not arrogant enough to think that every single person in Brodence knows me on sight," Agatha dismissed. She added even more gravy to her potatoes before mixing it all together and taking another bite. "Not everyone grew up here or keeps up with that kind of stuff. And even if they *do* know, it doesn't mean they'll care. I'm not royalty."

"You practically are."

"That's not even the point, Myles. I just didn't appreciate the assumption that I didn't know what I was doing just because I'm a woman," Agatha stated, her voice taking on a slight edge. "And the fact that I'm a grey-haired Black senior citizen probably only added to his assumptions of my ineptitude. Some men are just determined to hold on to that antiquated way of thinking."

Myles's eyes fell to his half-empty plate. His mind immediately went to Jackie and how he'd treated her, assuming she wouldn't know what to do with his car. He even suggested she call Chet, which almost made him wince with embarrassment. He could only imagine what his mother would say if she knew how he'd acted.

His earlier resolve that he'd done enough towards making amends to Jackie was forgotten and his desire to make it right was renewed, but now he felt a simple apology wasn't enough. He wanted to do something more for her, feeling the urge to show that he wasn't like the jerk that had bothered his mother that morning or anyone else who thought like him. Myles certainly believed women could do whatever they were determined to do, even if he hadn't exactly showcased that to Jackie.

His mind was on what he could do to make it up to her as his mother went on to describe how she handled her unwanted helper from earlier, and then Mollie launched into a story about a recent date that didn't go as well as she'd hoped.

Then it hit him. Myles smiled as inspiration started sprouting in his mind like Jack's beanstalk. He knew exactly how he could both make amends to Jackie and do a good deed. Already proud of himself, he picked up his fork and asked his mother to pass the gravy.

Chapter 6

There was an idling car in the parking lot when Jackie arrived to work, exhaust flowing from the tailpipe in the early morning cold. Jackie frowned curiously, knowing she'd seen the car before but unsure as to where.

Still, she kept her hand on her Glock 19 in her bag as she cautiously approached the car, ready for anything. But when the driver's door opened and Myles stepped out, she was caught totally off guard.

"What the hell are *you* doing here?" she spat, automatically on the defensive. She only marginally loosened her hold on her weapon.

Myles blinked, slightly taken aback by her aggressiveness. "I wanted to have a word with you before you got your day started."

"We have a phone."

"I'm aware. I tried using it but you never returned any of my messages. Or did your employee not give them to you?"

Jackie hesitated slightly, fleetingly tempted to just lie and let the blame fall on Cassidy. But she knew that wasn't right, especially since Cassidy had been the main one bugging her to call him back.

"She did." Jackie sighed, removing her hand from her bag and adjusting the strap over her shoulder. "I've been busy."

"I'm sure you have." His tone and expression indicated he didn't buy that excuse. "Because taking a moment to return a paying customer's call would just eat up your entire day, huh?"

Jackie's attitude immediately flared. "You know what? You *and* your call can-"

"Okay, okay," Myles interjected, holding his gloved hands up in surrender. "I didn't come here to argue with you, Ms. Malone. Look, the main reason I was trying to reach you was because I wanted to apologize for the way I behaved when I brought my car in."

She folded her arms over her chest. "Is that so?"

"Yes. It is. And you not returning my call turned out to be a good thing because it gave me reason to come here, since I realized it was something that needed to be done in person, anyway." He stepped closer, sure to still keep a healthy amount of distance since her wary frown was still locked in place. "I sincerely apologize, Ms. Malone. There is no excuse for my behavior. Neither you or your employee deserved the difficulty I gave you and I do hope you'll be willing to forgive me."

Jackie just stood there, eying him skeptically. He certainly *seemed* sincere. But she wasn't that quick to let her guard down.

"So now we're supposed to just hug it out and go about our business, right? And all is forgotten?"

Myles didn't appear fazed by her sarcasm. "I'm not surprised if you'd like to make me sweat a bit. I was a jerk to you, plain and simple. And for the record, you did an excellent job on my car and I appreciate it."

That made Jackie smile. She couldn't help it, and part of her hated that she'd revealed one of the main ways to get on her good side.

"I'm glad to hear it," she made herself say, figuring there was no reason to be a total bitch. He was trying to be nice, so she could put away the claws. "But if you *really* want to thank me, send me some customers."

"I've already mentioned your business to a couple of people in my office."

She hesitated, unsure whether to buy that or not. "For real?"

"Absolutely. And my friend Ethan, the guy that was with me that day, said he might start bringing his car here, as well. He's a fan of yours simply for how you humbled me. Finishing on time *and* below the estimate – not to mention the washing and detailing, which I hadn't expected – really had me feeling like a first-class idiot and he got a lot of enjoyment out of that."

Jackie was liking this Ethan already. "Well...thanks. I'll take just as good care of him, if he ever decides to come through."

"I'm sure he will."

They stood in awkward silence for a couple of moments. Jackie found herself finally taking note of Myles's details; he looked to be about six foot one. It was hard to tell much about his body through his suit and overcoat but he looked sturdy enough. He had a buttoned-up conservative air about him that wasn't as repulsive as Jackie usually found it on other men. And if she was honest, she could see Cassidy's point about his eyes and lips.

Catching herself, she shook her head and looked away. Who cared what he looked like? She still hadn't totally moved him from her 'dislike' file yet.

"Was that all?" Jackie finally spoke up. She pulled her phone from her coat pocket. "I need to get inside and start getting things going."

"Right," Myles quickly agreed, as if snapping out of his own momentary trance. "Sorry. Actually there *was* one more thing...given how badly I acted, I didn't think a simple apology was sufficient. So there's something else I'd like to do for you, Ms. Malone."

"You don't have to keep calling me that, you know."

"Okay, then. Jacqueline."

She paused, her eyes narrowing slightly. How did he know her first name was really Jacqueline? Sure, it was a likely assumption, but... "Jackie is fine. I actually prefer Jackie."

"Very well. I know this is going to seem *extremely* out of the blue but I'd like to fix you up with someone."

Rearing, Jackie actually backed up a couple of steps. "What??"

"I guess I should have asked first if you were otherwise attached. Are you?"

"I mean, no, but..." Jackie blinked and huffed a befuddled breath, which billowed and vanished into the air in seconds. "Is this a joke? Are you messing with me?"

Myles immediately shook his head. "Absolutely not. I get that this is a little unorthodox, seeing as how we hardly know each other-"

"You think?"

"But I know someone I think you'd really hit it off with and once the idea of introducing the two of you was in my head, there was no getting rid of it. I figured this was the perfect way to make amends to you."

"You really think I need help getting dates?"

"I'm sure you don't, Ms. Malone. I mean, Jackie," Myles amended, hoping he wasn't digging a deeper hole and ticking her off more. Or worse, insulting her again. "This isn't intended to be anything but a gift to you, for lack of a better way of putting it. The person I have in mind is great and I'm sure you'd think so too, if you gave them a chance. Just have a casual meet-up and go from there; that wouldn't be so bad, right?"

Jackie hated that she was at all intrigued by this but she was. She hadn't exactly been hitting it out of the park in the dating arena lately. Most of her recent affirmations had been relationship-centered, due to her increasing loneliness. And it wasn't looking like Ringo was going to change his mind and take her back, as much as she'd like him to.

Jackie chewed her lip, contemplating. Her eyes wandered back over to Myles and her growing interest began to skid to a halt.

"Look, don't take this the wrong way," she began, scratching her head through her blue beanie, "But I imagine you have to be pretty close to whoever this person is to recommend them, and if they're anything like you, I'm not sure we'd hit it off. No offense."

Myles's eyes narrowed slightly, a furrow appearing between his brows. "Hard not to take offense to that, Jackie. I acknowledge that I didn't make the best first impression but that doesn't make me a bad person."

"That's not really what I meant," Jackie replied, feeling surprisingly pricked for offending him. "I'm talking more in terms of compatibility. You're kinda...*buttoned up* and that's not really what I go for."

"You don't have to worry about that. That's one thing this person and I *don't* have in common. We're pretty much opposites, in that regard."

Only partially convinced, Jackie shifted in her stance. She glanced up the street, knowing Cassidy would be arriving shortly. Jackie could only imagine the conclusions Cassidy would jump to upon seeing the two of them out there talking. She needed to wrap this up and send him on his way.

"And this person...they've already agreed to this?" she asked, her eyes flitting up the street again.

"I wanted to see if you'd be open to it first. But I'm sure once I describe you to them, they'd be totally on board."

Jackie felt a tiny tingle somewhere in the deep recesses of her body at that statement. Did that mean Myles found her attractive? Or did he just think this potential date would? She was suddenly curious how Myles saw her, to her complete and total shock. What did it matter what he thought? It wasn't like he was asking her out himself; he was just initiating a hook-up. And Myles certainly wasn't her type so his opinion on her looks was irrelevant.

"What the hell," she finally acquiesced, throwing up a hand. "I guess it couldn't hurt. I'm down, if they are."

Myles grinned, almost looking like a different person. He hadn't shown so much as a smirk before then.

"Wonderful! I'll get everything set up and get back to you. May I have your personal number?"

Her eyes widened. "For what?"

"So I can inform you of the details when I get them."

"Oh." Jackie felt foolish. She should've known that.

"Don't worry; I won't pass it along to them without your permission," Myles assured her. He glanced at his watch before fishing one of his business cards and a pen from his inside coat pocket, taking a few steps closer to her. "Here, you can jot it down on this. I'm not trying to rush you but I need to get to work."

"Yeah...me, too." Jackie cleared her throat as she accepted the card and pen. Her fingers tingled as she scribbled her name and number on the back of it before handing it back to him. "There. We good?"

"I'd say so. I'll be contacting you soon. Thanks for being open to this." He glanced at the card before sliding it into his pocket. A small smile remained on his lips; he actually looked quite proud of himself. "I'm already looking forward to seeing how this all plays out."

Jackie didn't want to admit out loud that she was, too, so she just shrugged. "I guess we'll see. Thank you for coming by, Mr. Cornwall."

"Please, call me Myles."

"All right, then. Myles. Hope you have a good day."

"Same to you, Jackie."

She turned on her heel and went to unlock the door to her building, sensing that he was watching as she did so. As soon as she was inside, she turned to see him finally head to his idling car, get in, and carefully back out of the parking lot before riding off down the street.

"What the hell did I just agree to?" she muttered, snatching the beanie off her head. Part of her hated that she didn't get Myles's number as well, in case she changed her mind about this weird hook-up. But she remembered she had it on file in her computer system if she needed it.

Telling herself it wouldn't be that bad, she went about getting everything fired up and prepared for her work day. She wasn't going to obsess about it; it was a date, not an arranged marriage. And it wouldn't hurt for her to shake things up a little.

It wasn't until that afternoon that Jackie got a few minutes to dish to Cassidy about Myles's visit that morning. It was a somewhat light work day, and Jackie had just finished replacing someone's catalytic converter before sending them on their way. Irv and Jimmy had gone to lunch and the next appointment wasn't scheduled for another hour or so, so the ladies had the place to themselves for the time being.

"He was actually outside waiting for you when you got here?" Cassidy marveled.

"Yep."

"Wow. He must have really been eager to apologize. Is that why you didn't call him back? So he'd come up here again?"

"What? No! I wasn't scheming; I was fully prepared to never see him again."

"I wonder how long he was sitting out there before you showed up."

Jackie gave her strange look. "What does *that* matter?"

"Just saying. I told you he was probably sincere. So now not only did he come to apologize in person, but he asked you out on a date, to boot. I *so* love this turn of events!"

"Is that wig hair stuck in your ears? He didn't ask me out; he only offered to hook me up."

"And you bought that?" Cassidy sat forward in her seat, actually laughing. "Girl, you can't see that was just him being slick? This whole hookup thing is just a ruse."

"A ruse."

"Yes! He probably figured you'd shoot him down if he just asked you flat-out so he came up with this hookup go-around. Which doesn't surprise me because he's not exactly the smooth type, from what I could tell."

Jackie considered her friend's words, then shook her head. "Nah, I don't buy that. He said this person is nothing like him."

"Of course he did. Did he give you a name? Tell you anything about what this guy looks like? Where he works or what he does for a living? *Anything*?"

"No...come to think of it, I should've asked for more details. Between my shock at the suggestion and us standing out in the cold, I wasn't as quick on my feet as usual."

"He would've offered up all those details on his own if there was actually another man on the other end of that invitation. I'm telling you, Jackie...*Myles* is the one you're going to be meeting up with." Cassidy tapped Jackie's knee from where she was perched on the desk. "He just didn't want to get his face cracked. It's kind of cute, when you think about it."

"How is a man not having the confidence to be straight-up 'cute'? Not that it matters because I still think you're wrong about all this."

"Watch what I tell you. And I'm not mad at it 'cause I already told you how nice-looking I think he is. You two would make an attractive couple, I think."

Immediately scoffing, Jackie shook her head. "Please. We are *so* not compatible."

"How do you know? You've talked to him for all of maybe twenty minutes, total. Yeah, he seems kinda nerdy but those can be some of the sexiest ones. Look at Clark Kent."

"Really? That's the best example you could come up with?"

"Fine...Dwayne Wayne. Kyle Barker. Carlton Banks."

"Those are all sitcom characters, and old school ones, at that. I'm not saying Myles hurts my eyes or anything but he damn sure doesn't make me weak in the knees."

"Doesn't mean he wouldn't be a good match for you. You just have to open your mind to something new. Not everyone is going to be ripped tattooed bow-legged walking sexiness with dreads like Ringo. Sometimes it's more understated, more subtle. I'd bet Myles is an animal once you unleash that side of him."

"Ugh." Jackie shook her head. "Well, I'll never know. I'll admit he seems like he's an okay guy but that's not exactly a road to a love connection. Between you and me, I wouldn't mind if the hookup was with that friend of his that he had with him that day; Ethan, I think his name was. Now *that's* a sexy nerd I'd like to get to know."

Cassidy mulled that over. "Yeah, he was pretty hot. He doesn't strike me as 'nerd', though...just a fine man that gets suited up when he needs to. I can just as easily picture him tossing back some beers in a bar or getting his hands dirty fixing something. Myles doesn't seem like the type for either of those kinds of things."

"Even more of an indication that he and I aren't a match; I don't need a man that's more worried about breaking a nail than I am. I need someone that can get down and dirty with me."

Her brow arching, Cassidy verified, "Are we talking in or out of the bedroom?"

"Both."

They shared a laugh as the phone rang. Jackie slid off the desk as Cassidy answered it, going around to throw away some disposable cups that customers had left sitting around the waiting area earlier. The more she thought about the possibility of Ethan being her blind date, the more excited she got. He was cute, respectful, polite, *and* he had checked Myles that day when he was being a jerk. That won him big points right there.

Jackie still wished she'd pushed for more details with Myles earlier but it didn't douse her growing excitement. If it *was* Ethan on the other end of this hook-up, she hoped he agreed to it and that he was as anticipatory as she was. Especially since Myles was so sure they'd hit it off.

She bit her lip in anticipation, hoping Myles didn't take forever getting back to her. Now that the blind date was on the table and she was warming to the idea, she wanted to get on with it. Her mind was already scrolling through her closet, deciding what to wear. The date wasn't even set in stone yet and she was already getting a little giddy, which she would never admit out loud.

If things went as well as she hoped, she'd owe Myles big time.

"You all ready for your date?"

Myles was on the phone with Ethan a couple nights later as his friend prepared to go out for the evening. Having no plans of his own, Myles was going over some files for the Morlock account as he ate leftover Thai.

"Just about," Ethan muttered. Myles could tell he had him on speakerphone. "First dates are always a little nerve-wracking. I even bought a new shirt in a color I almost *never* wear for this."

"I'm sure you have no reason to be nervous. It's gonna go just fine."

"I hope so. I've been looking forward to this for the past couple of days...she's been on my mind ever since we met a little while back. I'm nervous only because I want it to go well but I'm mostly excited."

"It's been a while since I've felt like that," Myles noted. His hand that had just picked up a silver pen from the coffee table where his files and dinner were spread out stilled as he thought about it. "Wow, it's been a *long* while since I've felt like that. That first date anticipation and the excitement over new possibilities...it almost seems foreign."

"It doesn't have to be. You imposed a dating ban on yourself, for whatever reason. Put yourself back out there."

"Ehh."

"Not all women are like Cynthia or the ones before her." There was some rustling on Ethan's end, as if he was pulling a shirt over his head. "Maybe you should step out of your comfort zone and try a different kind of woman. Shake things up."

"I don't think that would make any difference."

"You don't know that. There seems to be a part of you that misses companionship. Look at how you helped me out, with my date for tonight. You should do that for yourself."

"It's easy to help with other people's issues. I'm in no hurry to expend energy on a woman only for it to crash and burn in the end."

"So you can see the future, huh?" Ethan chuckled. "Stop being so pessimistic, buddy. The past isn't always indicative of the future. Take those experiences and improve your discernment so you don't end up with another Cynthia."

Myles sipped from his water bottle, knowing there was merit to his friend's words. Still, he shook his head. "I'd rather not waste my time."

"The time is going to pass regardless. Might as well put forth the effort. Especially since I know you want to spend your life with someone, despite what you say. I'm telling you, Myles, expand your horizons a little. Try someone that *isn't* a former debutante or socialite that's worried more about how the two of you look together than she is actually getting to know you. Someone you can actually be friends with as well as lovers. Can you say you've *ever* been friends with someone you've dated?

Myles had never even considered such a notion but now that it was on his mind, the answer was pretty sobering. "No, actually."

"That's what I figured. Just think about it, that's all I'm saying. You can't get different results doing the same thing."

Ethan ended the call shortly after to leave for his date and Myles's thoughts strayed to Jackie. As crazy as it was to even consider, she certainly was different than any woman he'd been with, or even thought about being with. He didn't know her very well at all but she seemed *so* far out of the realm of what he was used to...he was sure Ethan wasn't thinking of someone like her when he suggested Myles step out of his comfort zone.

He made himself clear his mind of such thoughts. Even though Jackie had marginally cooled off towards him, he didn't imagine her ever being interested in him romantically, for many reasons. And truth be told, he couldn't see himself with her, either.

More importantly, though, he'd already set her up on a date with someone he felt she was compatible with. And he was already looking forward to hearing about how it went later.

"She's gonna thank me for this," he muttered to himself with a tiny smile, taking another swig of his water before setting the bottle down and sitting forward on the couch, diving back into his work.

Meanwhile, Jackie gave herself a final once-over in the mirror, excitement already skittering over her body. She felt a little silly for how much she was looking forward to a blind date but she couldn't help it. Something told her that this night was going to be one she wouldn't forget. She'd even noted it on her affirmation board:

This could change everything. Be open to it.

She'd decided on a green one-shoulder top and matching wide-leg pants set, which was admittedly one of the few dressy-ish outfits she owned. When she left corporate America, she donated all of her business clothes and most of her dresses to the Goodwill. She only kept a small contingency of 'hot' clothes, and one pair of heels that went with most of them, for the occasional times she might need them (which thankfully wasn't often, because she hated wearing heels). She dated often enough, but she rarely had reason to actually get dressed up. Most of the men she went out with were just fine with her in jeans and a cute top. Anyone she had to constantly get dressed up for wasn't someone she'd be interested in, anyway.

After making sure she hadn't messed up her short hair somehow and she spritzed some supposed 'pheromone' perfume (a gift from Cassidy) onto her neck and wrists, she grabbed her purse and keys and headed out. She had tried to get some more information out of Myles when he contacted her with details about the date but he wouldn't budge, saying he wanted her to be totally surprised. All he would tell her was that her date would be in yellow, and that the reservation was under his last name.

Jackie danced to the Gucci Mane song playing on the radio as she drove to the restaurant. She wasn't typically brimming with optimism but something in her gut told her that it was going to be a great night. Despite Cassidy's opinion that it was Myles that was really interested in her, Jackie had convinced herself that it'd be Ethan waiting for her at that restaurant wearing yellow. Though she couldn't imagine why in the world he'd choose that color.

"I guess he *is* a totally different person outside of that suit," she muttered.

She pulled into the parking lot of Spasagna, a pasta restaurant, which was only around half full. Once she was parked, she yanked down the visor mirror and needlessly applied another coat of lip gloss before telling herself to get a grip and get out of the car. It was one thing to be nervous and excited but another to go overboard with the primping. She was plenty cute as is.

"Hey, good evening," Jackie greeted the hostess once she was inside.

"Good evening. Are you dining alone tonight or are you expecting more people? And if I may say, I love that short hair on you."

"Thank you, girl!" Jackie grinned, smoothing a hand down the back of her hair. Her nervousness eased some. "I'm actually meeting someone; the reservation is under Cornwall."

"Oh yes, your party is waiting for you," the hostess confirmed, noting something on the tablet in front of her before turning towards the dining area. "Follow me."

Jackie's smile grew a tiny bit with every step they took. But it disappeared in an instant when the hostess stopped at a table where a woman was sitting. A pretty woman, but still...a woman.

"Umm..." Jackie looked back and forth between her and the hostess with a confused frown. She leaned a little closer to the hostess and hissed, "I'm sorry...I thought I said *Cornwall*. I'm not sure what you heard, but-"

"Yes, I heard you correctly; this is your table," the hostess assured, now sporting her own confused frown.

The woman at the table stood, pushing her yellow sweater dress down her hips before extending a hand to Jackie, who was still wondering what the hell was happening. Jackie couldn't help but note that whoever this was didn't seem as floored as she, so clearly Jackie was the only one who'd gotten their wires crossed somewhere.

"Hi," the woman greeted as the hostess scurried away. "Jackie, right?"

Jackie hesitantly took her hand. "Yeah..."

"Looks like I'm your date for tonight. I'm Mollie...and you look like you could use a drink."

Chapter 7

Jackie had never been more shocked – or confused – in her life. She literally could find no words, even as she made herself slowly ease into the chair across from Mollie, who looked almost amused by her state.

"Let me guess," Mollie began, sitting back in her seat and crossing an arm over her knee, looking like the definition of unbothered. "You're straight."

"Uhh...what?"

"You're not family, right? You like men and men only, don't you?"

"Yeah." Jackie cleared her throat, her hand resting on her neck. "So...Myles actually set me up with you? He...he thinks I'm a lesbian?"

"Apparently," Mollie shrugged. "Personally, I go both ways. And apparently me doing so much bitching about my dating life recently prompted him to set me up with his – and I quote – 'nice-looking mechanic lady.'"

Jackie's jaw dropped slightly as realization oozed over her like cold motor oil. Myles assumed she was into women just because she was a mechanic? She couldn't decide if she was more shocked by his ignorance or pissed at his assumption.

"I..." She shook her head, still floored. "Is this for real? Like, am I the brunt of some practical joke? Is this for social media? There's some hidden cameras around here somewhere, aren't there?"

Mollie laughed. "'Fraid not. That's something *I* would do. I'm a comedienne and a bit of a prankster when I'm in the mood to be. Can be quite the little stinker, actually. But my brother? Ehh, not so much."

"Brother?" Jackie's eyes snapped to Mollie. "Myles is your *brother*?"

"Not blood, but yeah. I was adopted when I was ten. Not that that matters; I just like telling people that."

Jackie plunked back in her seat, eyes on the floor. A potent mix of embarrassment, sadness, and fury coursed through her. She felt ridiculous for trusting Myles and letting herself get her hopes up about this date; she'd actually let herself believe he was hooking her up with Ethan, and that's where the sadness came in. Not just because it wasn't him specifically, but because it was someone that she could only be friends with, at best. She didn't date women. The fury was because she felt deceived; Myles had clearly told Mollie about her but he chose to keep *her* in the dark. If he was so sure she was a lesbian, why couldn't he have just told her up front that he intended to set her up with his sister?

"My head hurts," she groaned, placing a hand to her forehead. "I really cannot believe this is my life right now..."

"Look, girl, I get it; you've been blindsided." Mollie hunched a shoulder. "My brother is a good guy but he can be an idiot at times when it comes to women. I don't know why he chose to handle things the way he did. I'll leave him to explain all that to you. In the meantime, though, we might as well have dinner."

"Seriously?"

"We both know it's not a date. It's just two women plotting how to get back at a man whose heart might have been in the right place but who has the common sense of a cardboard box. He got both of us here under false pretenses – well, mostly *you* – and he must pay. And we might as well get full and drunk since neither of us will be getting any tonight."

Despite herself, Jackie couldn't help the smile that tugged at her lips. She realized she actually liked Mollie, and could appreciate her attitude about all this. Jackie was still trying to process everything and was nowhere near over it, but it didn't mean her evening had to be totally ruined.

So she and Mollie proceeded to get to know each other as they ate and drank to their heart's content, even more so once Mollie revealed that it was on Myles. He'd given her his credit card to pay for their evening.

"He probably only offered it to butter me up," Mollie surmised, slurring slightly. She downed the rest of her Hennessey. "Since he's always making cracks about me getting a 'real' job and shit. I'm sure he thought I wouldn't be able to afford taking anyone on a date on my own."

"Your brother seems like a snob," Jackie observed, forking the last of her shrimp scampi and twirling it in the air before sticking it in her mouth.

"He definitely has his 'snob' moments. Which is wild because our parents are some of the most down-to-earth people you'll ever meet, despite how much money they've got. Not sure how Myles came out as such a stiff dick."

Jackie hated to acknowledge that she'd been hoping to get some *stiff dick* of her own before the night was over with. The reminder that that wasn't in the cards only soured her mood even more. She chuckled wryly. "Just another reason not to like him."

"Oh, come on, now," Mollie groaned, belching softly behind her hand before pushing away the rest of her alcohol and reaching for her water glass. "This is where I feel I need to obligatorily defend my brother. He's a nice guy. Has been a great brother to me, despite how he gets on my nerves about the job stuff. But even with that, I know it's mainly out of concern."

"Hmph."

"He sees about our parents, especially our mother; she's been sick for a while. He's big on helping the homeless..."

"Because of you?"

"I'm sure that's a big part of it. I think he also just hates to see anyone in that situation. He always says no human being should have to sleep on the street or scrounge for food."

Jackie couldn't help but be touched by that, despite her annoyance towards Myles. "Well, I can't help but agree with the bastard on that."

"Yeah. So he definitely has his flaws but he's far from a bad guy." Mollie leaned her elbows on the table, a mischievous gleam in her eyes. "But that doesn't mean we can't get him back for this bullshit blunder he committed tonight."

Jackie grinned. Maybe the night wouldn't be a total bust. "Now you're talkin'."

Myles had run out to get some juice, but mostly it was just an excuse to get out of the house. The quiet, which he usually relished, was deafening on this particular evening.

He knew it was mostly curiosity. He couldn't help but wonder how things were going with Jackie and Mollie. It had been tempting to tell Jackie more details about his sister, but he figured he'd have a higher chance of her showing up if he kept things vague, hoping her curiosity would make her go through with it. He wished he could've seen the look on her face when she got to the restaurant, though he didn't know if Mollie was even her type.

"Hey, mister."

Myles looked over to see a homeless man standing near the stop sign he'd just pulled up to. He was holding a sign asking for food, shivering slightly in the cold night air. Myles felt the familiar tug in his chest that always appeared when he came across someone in such a situation.

Not caring about the cars behind him, Myles retrieved one of the care kits he kept in his backseat. Rolling his window part of the way down, he smiled at the scruffy man inching towards his window. "Good evening, sir; here you go." He eased the kit through the window opening. "This is for you."

The man quickly stepped forward and grabbed the canvas pouch, clutching it to his chest in gratitude without even having opened it. "Thank you *so* much, mister."

The driver behind him honked their horn but Myles ignored it. "Take care of yourself out here tonight; it's cold and the temperature is supposed to drop some more."

"Yeah, I heard. I'm about to head down the street to the mattress store; the owner lets us sleep on the back dock at night, on some old mattresses. Sometimes he leaves a heater out for us."

Myles was both glad the guy had somewhere to go and upset that he still had to be outside on a cold night. It only reminded him that he needed to focus even more on his efforts to get more shelters up and running.

"What's your name, sir?" Myles asked, ignoring the impatient honks from the cars behind him.

"Dirk."

"Dirk, I'm praying for you and your safety. Here," he grabbed the fuzzy blanket he had in the backseat that had been a secret Santa gift from someone at work, but it wasn't his taste so he'd never even taken it out of the car. He shoved it though the window opening. "Take this."

The man's scruffy face lit up, grabbing the blanket and immediately throwing it around his shoulders. It was as if someone had given him a diamond, he looked so appreciative.

"Thank you!"

Myles chatted with him for a few more moments before finally pulling off, wishing Dirk a good night. If he couldn't take him somewhere warm for the night, the least he could do was treat him like a human being and give him some attention along with the items that would hopefully help make his evening at least a little more bearable.

His mind was still on Dirk and others like him when his phone rang. He smiled upon seeing Mollie's name flash across his dashboard screen. Though he was a little surprised to hear from her; he figured she and Jackie would still be enjoying their evening. It wasn't even nine o'clock.

"Hey, Mollie," he greeted, answering the call. "Everything okay?"

"No," Mollie immediately replied, her voice wavering.

Myles's smile melted and he sat up straighter with concern. "What's wrong?"

"Um, can you come over? I did something...kinda bad. Well, *really* bad. And I've been freaking out and I need you to tell me how to handle it."

"Mollie...what did you do?"

"I don't wanna talk about it over the phone. Just hurry up and get over here!"

"Okay, okay." Myles didn't know what to think as he steered his car towards Mollie's apartment building. What in the world could have happened? Mollie was always getting into some kind of mischief but he thought they were past the days of him needing to bail her out of messes. And where was Jackie during all this? Did she have a hand in...whatever this was? Somehow, the idea of her getting into trouble didn't surprise him.

He figured he'd been right on the money with setting her up with Mollie.

He arrived at Mollie's in less than twenty minutes, locking his car and rushing up to her second floor apartment. Mollie must have been eying the peephole because she swung the door open before he even had a chance to knock.

"Ugh, thank *god*! Get in here!" Mollie shrieked, pulling him inside by the arm.

"What in the world is going on?" Myles asked, looking around for anything amiss. Her place was just as cluttered and disheveled as ever. Her cats, Chubby and Clap, were lounging on their respective beds like they didn't have a care in the world. "What's wrong?"

"Back here, in the bathroom."

Myles followed his sister to the hall bathroom, noting her yellow sweater dress and bare feet. It was in the back of his mind to ask what happened to her date but he figured it wasn't the time.

When Mollie flicked on the bathroom light and squealed, pointing to the floor, Myles's brow furrowed at the smattering of what looked like ashes on the dingy gray tile.

"What's this?"

Mollie was now hopping up and down on her toes, flapping her hands in front of her face. "It's...it's Grandma!"

"What?!" He jumped back, bumping into the wall thanks to the cramped space.

"I was playing with the urn and accidentally dropped it!"

"You were..." Blinking as if trying to catch his bearings, Myles touched his fingertips to his forehead. "You were *playing* with the *urn*??"

"Yes, Myles!"

"Why would you-"

"Can we focus?? That's not really the point right now, is it?? You've gotta help me get this up!"

"Why *me*??"

"I can't touch it! Even *looking* at it is freaking me out! All I can think about is Grandma baking cookies in the kitchen and the time I tried to do it by myself and got to talking on the phone and forgot about them and burned them and how they were practically black by the time I got them out and now these ashes are like-"

"Do *not* finish that sentence, Mollie!"

"You can*not* tell Mama and Daddy about this, either; they'll kill me!" Mollie patted her hands rapidly against her cheeks before plastering them to her face and hopping around in a circle just outside the bathroom door, her eyes red and frantic. "Myles, please? Pretty please??"

"Okay, okay!" Myles tried to calm himself, despite being a little freaked out himself. Looking around, he asked "Where's the urn?"

"I kicked it into my room."

"I cannot believe this..."

"Myles!"

"Ugh!" Myles released a long breath, tucking his keys in his pocket and flexing his fingers, as if hyping himself up. "You *so* owe me for this! Okay, bring me a broom and dustpan, a couple of wet rags and some-"

"BOOM!"

"*Aaugh!*" Myles screamed louder than he ever had, banging hard into the wall again when Jackie jumped from behind the closed shower curtain, scaring him half to death. His heart was beating a mile a minute and he pressed a hand to his chest, breathing rapidly as he tried to figure out what the hell was happening. He looked over at Mollie, who was now literally on the hallway floor laughing. Jackie stood there, looking almost like a different person outside of the dirty coveralls he was used to seeing her in, breathing fire as she scowled at him with her arms folded over her chest.

"What in the world is going on??" Myles demanded, looking back and forth between Jackie and his sister.

"You asshole!" Jackie spat, her arms shooting down her sides, fists clenched.

"Wh-what?"

"Did it ever occur to you, you genius, to ask if I dated women before setting me up on a blind date with your sister??"

"You..." Myles froze, his eyes widening slightly. "You don't?"

"No. I *don't*."

"I..."

"I've gotta say, big bro, I'm a little disappointed in you," Mollie stated, having calmed down and appearing in the doorway with a small broom and dustpan. "And you always fussed about your ex making assumptions."

"You thought I was a lesbian just because I'm a mechanic!" Jackie accused, her eyes shooting daggers at Myles. "Without asking or trying to get to know me, you just jumped to an uninformed conclusion based just on what I do for damn living. For your information, you plugged-ass imbecile, I like men. *Men*. What if I went around making ignorant assumptions about you? Would you like that shit? *Would you*??"

Jackie proceeded to curse him out while Mollie calmly swept up the fake ashes she and Jackie had bought (with Myles's card) after they left the restaurant, occasionally and purposely sweeping the broom over his feet and earning heated glares from him.

When Jackie finally got her fill of telling him off, she stepped out of the shower, pushing Myles out of her way with both hands and stomping out of the bathroom.

Moments later, the front door slammed so hard it sent Mollie's cats running over to them, spooked from their peace being disturbed.

"I knew I liked her," Mollie commented, nudging her pink bath mat back into place with her toe, the dustpan full of the fake ashes in her hand. "Plugged-ass imbecile. That's good. I've gotta use that one."

"I don't even know what to say," Myles muttered, finally finding his voice. "This isn't part of the joke, is it?"

"No, you nut. The ashes were the joke. As far as Jackie, you actually messed up. And it's gonna be a while before I let you forget this one. Damn, I should've filmed this!"

Myles just stood there as if he was unable to move his feet from that spot. The more he thought about it, the more ridiculous he felt.

Maybe he really *was* a plugged-ass imbecile.

Jackie called Ringo and asked if she could come over, not wanting to be alone. She was still steaming over that whole scene.

She had to put up with a lot of crap. Growing up in the projects, from her nagging mother, in the corporate world, and especially since she opened her garage. And as frustrating as it was, such is life; she could deal with it.

But *this* was a first. No man had *ever* just assumed she was a lesbian simply because she worked on cars for a living. The mere fact that Myles hadn't at least had the courtesy to ask her first, to make sure...it just irked her to no end.

Did other men make that assumption? She hadn't even considered how her career change would affect her love life because she didn't think men would care that much. Some were surprised, some were amused, some were impressed; only one had been outwardly turned off. But now she was wondering if they somehow had equated her career to her sexuality. As ridiculous as that was to have to think about, clearly it was a thing; Myles had proven that.

She wasted no time venting when she arrived to Ringo's, going into her rant as soon as she was over the threshold. Ringo just got her a beer – since he didn't have any of her preferred rum – and listened, perching himself on the arm of his orange couch and giving her his full attention.

"This is some bullshit," Jackie mumbled, pacing in front of Ringo in her bare feet, respecting his no-shoes-in-the-house rule. "I have never encountered anything like this before and I'm still wondering if I'm being pranked. Hell, for all I know, both him *and* his damn sister are fucking with me."

"If they are, that's on them," Ringo finally spoke up, shrugging a muscled shoulder. His locs hung loose around his face. "I hope you're not letting *one* man's ignorant assumptions start to make you feel any kind of way about yourself, Jacks."

"No! I mean, I'm pissed but..." She sighed, cracking her knuckles as she continued pacing. "Look, there's nothing wrong with lesbians; I'm just not one. And it just ticks me off that he would jump to such a conclusion just because I'm a mechanic. It's not even about the lesbian part; he had no business assuming *anything* about me. And this was *after* he already made a shitty first impression, thinking I couldn't handle my job simply because I'm a woman. I tried to give him the benefit of the doubt after that shit but clearly, I shouldn't have."

"Jacks, don't let this shit get to you." Ringo stood, grabbing her wrist as she began to pace by him for the hundredth time and pulling her closer. "I get it; it's frustrating. But let him be ignorant by himself. You know who you are and what you're about, and so do the people that are important to you. That's all that should matter."

Taking a deep breath, Jackie felt her angst slide down a few notches. She looked at Ringo, whose caring eyes were fixed on hers. "You're right."

"He's just some random that you don't even have to see again. This guy – what was his name, Myles? – apparently has issues that are for *him* to deal with. It's not your problem. So don't stress over this shit." He placed both hands on her shoulders, rubbing them the way he knew she liked and earning a soft moan from her. "All right?"

Jackie didn't answer for a moment, enjoying what Ringo was doing to her. Her eyes slid closed and her head fell back slightly. All of her thoughts and irritation about Myles and her failed blind date vanished into nothing.

"You always know how to make me feel better," she finally muttered, rolling her head to the side. When she opened her eyes, Ringo was smirking at her. His fingers slid up to massage the back of her neck and Jackie felt sections of her body wake up as if something was going through and turning on the proverbial arousal lights in each one. Her hands gently rested on his defined obliques. "I so needed this..."

"I could tell." Ringo's voice was low as he continued to massage her tension away. He drew in a breath at her reactions, biting his bottom lip and willing his body to stay under control. "I know you, Jacks. And I've still got your back. Nothing's changed about that."

"So you know what I want right now, then."

Ringo's breathing deepened, his hands slowing into a more sensual caress along her neck and shoulders as Jackie slid her hands up and down his sculpted abs and pecs, not even trying to hide the lust that had overtaken her frustration. She recognized that look in his eyes; he wanted her, too. She just hoped he didn't prolong things by trying to deny it.

"Jacks..." His hoarse whisper was followed by groans when Jackie slid her hand between them and ran her finger along his hard erection through his sweats.

"Keep making me feel better, Ringo."

He drew her closer, one hand now on her round bottom, which he had always loved. It was way more than a handful and one of his favorite parts of her body, along with her ample breasts and plump lips that he was aching to kiss right then. Despite them having been broken up for years, Jackie still had an immense effect on him, and sometimes he could resist it, but this wasn't looking to be one of those times. And really, he didn't want it to be.

Suddenly gripping the back of her neck, he snatched her so close that his lips brushed hers when he asked, "You sure?"

Jackie immediately nodded, panting in anticipation.

Now his lips were at her ear. "Tell me what you want me to do to you."

"I want you inside of me," she breathed, her fingertips clawed into his back. Every inch of her was on fire. "I want you to fuck me so good and so hard and so deep that I forget about everything else. I want your tongue on my clit. Everything...I want everything, Ringo. Now."

His firm hold on her neck tightened as he trailed his tongue from her ear to her mouth, taking a kiss that immediately escalated to a tongue-dominate, erotically sloppy appetizer. Her hands tangled in his long locs as she returned his kiss with equal intensity and eagerness, wishing their clothes could somehow vanish into thin air so they wouldn't have to waste time removing them. Ringo had her ready to explode already, as usual.

"Go get on the bed," he ordered, gently biting her bottom lip. He turned her around and took both her breasts in his hands, squeezing and kneading them as he pressed his erection against her backside. Her head fell against his shoulder and she reached back to grab the back of his thigh, winding against him. "And be naked by the time I get in there."

Jackie wasted no time following his instruction, leaving a trail of her clothes from that spot to his bedroom door. A delicious grin spread across her face when he entered the room a few minutes later armed with a bottle of caramel sauce, a small paintbrush and some chopped nuts.

"I hope there's enough for me to use on you, too," she stated, sliding her legs open wider. "And you know how greedy I am."

His eyes were locked on hers as he kicked the bedroom door closed with his foot and advanced on her. Her anticipatory smile grew with each step.

"Jacks, you already know. You won't have room or energy for anything else by the time I'm done with you."

Jackie had no idea what time it was.

She was laid out across Ringo's bed, feeling like she was sinking into it. Her body felt heavy and appreciatively achy, still tingling from everything Ringo did to her.

When she felt him shift beside her, she managed to lift her head and turn it towards him, her lips curling into an automatic smile. Her hand slid over to touch him.

She knew she didn't want to leave. This was what she wanted. Her heart picked up speed when his hand closed around hers and briefly lifted it to his lips.

"Can you move?" he asked, his voice low in the dark room.

"That depends. Are you trying to go another round or are you about to ask me to leave?"

His head resting against the headboard fell slightly to the side as he chuckled, his gold tooth gleaming through his crooked grin. "Shouldn't matter, Jacks."

Summoning her minimal energy, Jackie pushed up onto her elbows, looking at him from where she was lying next to him on her stomach. "It does, though. Because I don't want to leave."

"You can crash here if you want to."

"I don't just mean tonight, Ringo. And I think you know that."

His smile fading, Ringo rubbed his thumb and forefinger across his eyes for a moment as if gathering his words. "We've had this discussion, Jackie. We broke up for a reason. And you know I'm in a situation now."

"We might've broke up for a reason but it was also years ago; I'm not on the same bullshit now that I was then. And as for your situation..." She slid her hand along his thigh, avoiding what they both knew she wanted to touch, "You can't tell me you're satisfied with some long distance arrangement where you only see each other every few months. Are you even in love with her?"

"That's for me to know."

"Whatever, but you know what we *both* know? I'm not out of your system. You're damn sure not out of mine. And whether or not you say it, you still love me. I'm right here, Ringo. I'm not sure why you wanna waste time on somebody who isn't."

He shook his head, looking away. "I've never known you to beg a man for anything. Just because we got down doesn't mean we need to take it back to a relationship, Jacks."

"I disagree. And nobody's begging; I'm just stating the obvious." She crawled over and snuggled up to him, draping her leg across him and helping herself to his neck, her fingertip circling his nipple. He cursed under his breath, automatically reacting to her. His eyes closed and he gritted his teeth in frustration, hating that she got to him so easily.

"You know you want me back, Ringo," Jackie taunted in his ear. "Let's just quit playing and make it happen."

His hand slid to her juicy thigh and she started slowly winding against him. She grabbed his chin and turned his face to hers, kissing him deeply and feeling encouraged when he immediately responded to her. She started to ease on top of him when he suddenly stopped, moving her off to the side and sitting up.

"I'm not going there with you again, Jacks," he grunted, running a hand down his face. "Us being friends, occasionally getting down...that's one thing. And you know it took me a while to even get to *this* point with you after we broke up. I just think we need to leave well enough alone."

Jackie couldn't believe her ears. His attitude almost had her as affronted as that whole scene with Myles earlier.

"So we can fuck, but we can't get back together?" she verified angrily, crossing her arms over her chest.

"Don't even try that shit," Ringo immediately warned, turning to glare at her. "Because I wasn't even trying to go there with you. *You're* the one that insisted you could handle a friends-with-benefits situation, and stayed on my damn back about it. Yeah, I gave in, but it was only after you swore you wouldn't try to switch shit up down the line. And clearly, I was wrong to believe you on that."

"Things change, Ringo. People change." Jackie moved to where she was directly next to him, sitting on her knees while he sat on the side of the bed, his hands braced beside him. She tried to ignore how sexy his arm muscles looked in that locked position. "Yeah, I know what I said before, and at the time, I meant it. But I'm not gonna apologize for wanting you back, or making it known."

"And I'm supposed to just forget about my situation and get back with you like everything is everything, huh?"

"Why not? Hell, you can't even call the woman by her name; you just refer to her as your 'situation.' Real romantic. Doesn't sound like anything all that serious to me."

He sighed and shook his head before letting it hang, his eyes on the dark hardwood floor. Jackie wondered what was going through his mind, and if she was finally making some headway with him. A trickle of nervousness weaved through her, crisscrossing the one of dread that was doubling in speed.

He turned his head in her direction, not quite looking at her. "You really think it'll work this time?"

She puffed a relieved breath that he seemed to be coming around and leaned forward to plant a kiss to his shoulder. Inching closer, she rubbed his back, feeling the excitement budding in her belly. "I do. I really do."

A few quiet moments passed before he finally sat up, looking at her. His eyes roamed her face. "I *do* love you, Jacks. That never stopped. And I admit, sometimes I do miss what we had..."

"I miss it every day." She slid onto his lap, draping her arms over his shoulders. "And you *know* I love you, too. Let's just..." She took hold of his handsome face, seeing the lingering hesitancy. "Let's just leave the past in the past. We're not the same people we were before. We can be even better together now. I want a second chance. I *deserve* a second chance."

She leaned forward and kissed him, gently at first. He slowly responded to her, their tongues easing together to meet. His hands slid to her butt and up her back, the grip steadily increasing in strength. When she reached down and grabbed his rejuvenated erection and slid down on it, he didn't stop her. They just kissed hungrily but quietly as she rode him, his hands guiding her, their moans in tandem.

Jackie felt like the happiest woman alive. She finally had Ringo back. Knowing he was hers again wiped out any lingering fatigue she had, juicing her with an eager energy. He still had to take care of his 'situation', but that was a formality. As crazy as it was, part of her actually wanted to thank Myles because his infuriating actions led her right back to who she was meant to be with.

"Ringo, baby..." she whispered, overtaken. She gasped when he sucked her nipple into his warm mouth. "Tell me this is it. That we're back together. I need to hear you say it."

His eyes lifted to hers. Before he could respond, though, his phone rang. He glanced to where it was sitting on the nightstand, his body still moving in rhythm with Jackie's. To her relief, he let it go to voicemail, but it immediately rang again. When he stopped moving and patted her bottom, she frowned.

"I know you're not," she snapped at the clear hint that he wanted her to get up.

"I need to take this, Jacks. Just...give me a minute."

Her face cleared in realization. "Is that her?"

He arched a warning brow at her before moving her off his lap. "Don't start. I'll be right back. Stay here."

"Fine. Go ahead and let her know what the deal is so we can be official when we get back to what we were doing."

Not acknowledging her comment, Ringo grabbed the phone and quickly headed out the door, answering it as soon as he stepped into the hallway. He only partially closed the door behind him before heading to the living room, talking in a low voice. Jackie couldn't make out what he was saying, but she told herself to just chill out and be patient. She imagined Ringo would probably want to let 'situation' – whatever her name was – down easy, so she'd give him a few minutes.

But when a few minutes stretched into almost a half hour, Jackie's forced patience disappeared. She could still hear Ringo's voice in the living room and if she didn't know better, she'd think he forgot she was back there waiting on him. That alone frustrated her, but when she heard him actually laugh, she became incensed. What did they have to laugh about? He was supposed to be breaking up with her. It was one thing to let her down easy and another to drag it out and string the woman along.

"Fuck this," she muttered, sliding off the bed and going straight for the door. She didn't cover herself or even try to step lightly on the hardwood floors as she stalked out of the room. Clearly Ringo needed help giving this woman her walking papers. Jackie certainly wasn't going to waste time beating around the bush.

She headed straight for the living room, finding Ringo on the couch, one arm casually stretched across the back of it like he was prepared to sit there all night. At some point he'd put his sweats back on. Jackie's nostrils flared in anger that he was keeping her waiting, but she grinned like a kid on Christmas when she noticed he was on a video call.

"Baby, what's taking you so long? Did you forget I was in your bed waiting on you to get back inside me? You were fucking me so good and we're damn sure not done!"

Ringo's head whipped around at her statement, no doubt taking note of the extra volume in her voice. His eyes widened then narrowed in anger upon seeing her head over to him, naked and determined.

"Jacks!"

"Ringo, what the hell? Who is that??"

It was a woman's voice, but one that sounded immediately familiar to Jackie. She finally focused her eyes on Ringo's phone screen. He snatched it out of view, but not before Jackie got a glimpse of who he'd been talking to. She felt her entire body go cold and she instantly crossed her arms over her breasts, horrified at her mistake.

"Mama, I need to call you back," Ringo muttered at the shocked woman, his back turned to Jackie. There were a few more hushed exchanges before he finally ended the call, shooting off the couch and turning to Jackie, looking angrier than she'd ever seen him.

"Ringo, I am *so* sorry!" she exclaimed, both hands on her head. "I...it's just that I thought you'd forgotten about me and-"

"Get your shit and get out of my house, Jackie."

"Ringo, I'm sorry! I thought you were talking to your girl!" Jackie took a few steps towards him, humiliated tears stinging her eyes as the realization of her stunt hit her. "Why didn't you tell me it was your mama that called??"

"Hell, should it matter??" Ringo exploded, throwing his phone to the couch. "Regardless of who it was, you bringing your naked ass in here to try to call me out is some childish bullshit!"

"I know, I'm s-"

"Don't keep saying you're sorry, 'cause you *wouldn't* be if it was who you thought it was on the phone! There's nothing you can say to justify this, Jackie. What happened to all that shit you were saying about how you've changed and you're not on the same bullshit anymore? Huh? 'Cause this is exactly the kind of nonsense that had me sending your ass packing the first time!"

"I made a mistake," Jackie cried, pressing her hands to her chest. "I was wrong. I own that. But I still meant everything I said to you earlier."

"Uh-huh. You meant it until you felt threatened, then you resorted right back to the same young-ass bullshit."

She winced, knowing he was right. "Ringo-"

"And to think I almost fell for the okie-doke." He chuckled sarcastically, shaking his head at himself. "You almost had me, Jackie, I admit it. But thank you for saving me from that mistake. I'd rather keep Sharonda – or as you know her, my 'situation' – and deal with the long distance than put up with your petty bullshit. Now get the fuck out. And while you're at it, lose my number."

Jackie wanted to stay and fight and try to wear him down until he listened to reason, but the look in his eyes told her to quit while she was ahead. She numbly turned and went to get dressed and get her things, not believing what was happening. The fact that she'd let herself do something so incredibly stupid weighed her down with shame.

Ringo didn't even look at her when she finally emerged from his bedroom. He just opened the front door and waited, his eyes boring a hole in the floor. His tight expression and the vise grip he had on the doorknob made it clear his anger hadn't budged. Jackie eyed him hopefully as she eased by him, but he ignored her. She was barely outside before he slammed the door behind her, and the tears resumed when she realized he was probably slamming the door on their friendship, too.

Chapter 8

Myles was swimming in his own vat of shame and embarrassment.

He'd been wrong about Jackie, putting his foot in his mouth with her yet again. His mind replayed how she looked when she jumped out at him at Mollie's apartment, looking justifiably furious. Of course, Mollie was still teasing him about his blunder days later, which didn't help his sour mood.

And he should've known he'd get the same from Ethan when he finally admitted what happened to him. But at least Ethan mixed his clowning with scolding.

"I really cannot believe you," he muttered, looking at Myles as if he had two heads. "Are you really that dense? What did Jackie do or say to make you jump to the conclusion that she was a lesbian?"

"Nothing," Myles admitted. He didn't have the energy to go into his line of thinking because in hindsight, he knew it made no sense. "I suppose I just thought that..."

"What, because she works with cars, she has to like women?"

"I..." Myles huffed, dropping his hand to his desk with a thump. "Look, I've never met a woman that was a mechanic before, all right? I admit I was wrong but it's not *that* unreasonable an assumption..."

"That was weak, Myles. I heard it in your voice. Even *you* know better than that but for whatever reason, you're trying to defend your ignorance. Just admit you were a dumb ass and leave it at that."

Myles didn't appreciate his friend's comment but felt he had no leg to stand on at the moment. He just grabbed his pen and scribbled random words on his notepad.

"I feel bad enough as it is," he finally mumbled. "I don't need you piling on."

"How do you think *she* feels? You should know better than this, man. How many times have people made assumptions about *you*? Because you're Black, because you went to an Ivy League school, because you carry yourself a certain way, because you play racquetball. Hell, folks have preconceived notions about your folks, thinking they're snobs just because they're rich and influential, when they're the furthest thing from it. It always made you feel some kind of way."

Myles dropped his pen. He sat back in his chair, his jaws clenching. "I know."

"I get that you were trying to do a nice thing but you could've at least asked her."

"I made a mistake. I get it, Ethan. I'm already thoroughly embarrassed so I hope you're done with the scolding and we can move on to what I need to do from here."

"You know what to do," Ethan stated, taking a seat in the chair facing Myles's desk and crossing an ankle over his knee. "Apologize to her."

"As if she'd listen to anything I'd have to say now."

"If she's still pissed, it's understandable. You can't control whether she stays mad at you or not but you can at least let her know you're aware of your blunder and apologize for it."

"She'd probably try to run me over with a car or something if she saw me. No thanks. I can write her a letter and have it messengered over, perhaps with a gift of some kind."

"I think we've established that you're not good at guessing what she likes."

Myles grunted, then his eyes brightened in realization. "Maybe *you* can go talk to her for me!"

"What are we, in high school? You don't need anyone to speak for you, Myles. And I'm sure she wouldn't buy any apology you sent someone to give on your behalf."

Knowing he was probably right, Myles ran a hand down his face. "I'm not sure what to do to make this right, then."

"All you can do is humble yourself, go to her, admit you were wrong, and leave it at that. Don't try to butter her up or justify your mistake. Just a sincere apology. It's really that simple."

Myles didn't feel like that would be enough but he could see the merit in Ethan's advice. If he'd kept it to a simple apology the first time instead of trying to go above and beyond by setting her up on a blind date, he wouldn't be in this situation.

Once Ethan left his office, Myles tried to get back to work but his mind kept straying back to Jackie. As bad as he felt, part of him was surprised at the level of guilt that came with it. He'd certainly made mistakes with women before, but his reconciliation attempts usually only went so far. And if the woman was being stubborn or trying to make him sweat, his remorse would fade into apathy and he'd just move on with his life. But it was strangely important to him to earn Jackie's forgiveness. He knew he owed her (another) apology, but the idea of facing her made him legitimately nervous.

Recalling what Ethan said about remembering Jackie from her previous career, Myles looked her up. It wasn't hard to find information about Jacqueline Malone. She was a COO for Joswell International when she resigned, the youngest in the company's history and a higher position than Myles currently held. Joswell was worldwide, and a company that even Myles had on his wish list after he graduated college before he was hired for his current company. His eyebrows shot up when he read about Jackie's awards and accolades. She'd accomplished so much and just walked away from all of it. Did something happen or was it simply about her following her heart and doing what she loved? The more he scrolled and clicked, the more curious Myles became. He found himself wanting to know more about Jacqueline - or Jackie - Malone.

He was still poking around when a meeting maker popped up on his screen, making him jump out of his seat. He'd forgotten all about it; usually, he'd have been in the conference room already.

There were a few people milling around the room when he arrived and he snagged a seat, hoping that this wouldn't take too long. Myles usually enjoyed his job and often had to actively stop himself from working, having no qualms about staying late at the office or taking work home. But he didn't have the same energy for it today, and he knew it was at least partially because his mind was still so consumed with the Jackie situation. That frustrated him; he'd never let a woman distract him from his work before and here he was doing exactly that over a woman that didn't even like him.

Thankfully, the meeting began promptly and there was no time-wasting chatter or small talk about anyone's previous evening. Myles managed to (mostly) pay attention during the presentations about mergers and projections, staying alert enough to be able to respond if he was addressed. He breathed a sigh of relief when it turned out to be a shorter meeting than expected and they wrapped in under an hour. He quickly stood, gathering his things so he could get back to his office.

Yawning, he grabbed his favorite Harvard mug, knowing he'd need a jolt to get through the rest of the day. He wasn't a huge coffee drinker, but he did have a Keurig in his office for the rare cravings. When he realized he was out of creamer, he grunted and headed to the break room. His associate, Davina, was in there perusing the options of the vending machine.

"Great presentation today, Davina," he commented politely, crossing over and grabbing the vanilla creamer.

"Thanks, Myles." She turned and smiled at him over her shoulder, her auburn natural hair smoothed into a tight bun on top of her head. He didn't think he'd ever seen her hair any other way since she'd been working there. "I was so nervous about it; being front and center really isn't my preference."

"Well, you hid your nervousness well. Everything went smoothly."

"Would you tell on me if I said that I took a couple of shots before the meeting?"

Myles looked over at her, alarmed. "Are you serious?"

Giggling, Davina punched a couple of buttons on the vending machine and watched a Snickers bar drop. Her raisin brown knee-length skirt strained against her wide hips and thighs as she bent down to retrieve it.

"I'm kidding," she finally confirmed, standing. Unwrapping the candy bar, she took a satisfying bite, moaning in pleasure. "This is actually my vice right here. I love these things. I actually keep some in my desk but I ate the rest of them before the meeting started."

"Hey, whatever works."

"I'm really trying to step out of my comfort zone around here; I realize I can't get very far just staying holed up in my office. I've been super-focused lately so I can finally start to advance and get out of this mid-level position I've been in for the past few years."

"I'm sure you will," Myles commented, blowing on his coffee a bit before taking a sip. He added a smidge more creamer before swirling a stirrer around the steaming brown liquid. "Your efforts aren't going unnoticed."

"I'd hope so but I've started to have my doubts. While most people around here seem cool, there's an unmistakable 'boys club' undercurrent in this office. Some of the conversations I've overheard at times are cringe-worthy. And it's not like there's a lot of women in higher positions around here."

That immediately made Myles think of Jackie. "True. But if today is any indication, you can be one of the ones to change that."

They chatted for another few minutes, with Davina semi-venting and Myles giving her encouragement, before she headed back to her office. Myles hung out in the break room, finishing his coffee while texting his mother to ask how she was feeling. She quickly responded letting him know she was fine, and was on her way to a candy-making class. Myles couldn't help but chuckle.

Myles finished his coffee, washed out his mug, and headed back to his office. He approached the conference room where the earlier meeting was held and heard a couple of people talking. Without even seeing them, he recognized their voices. Morton and Dennis. Educated men who behaved like a couple of mischievous adolescents when they thought no one was watching or listening.

"I'm telling you, I thought she was gonna bust outta that skirt," Dennis said in a hushed voice. "It's a good thing I was sitting at the table because my interest was surely *rising*, if you know what I mean."

Myles frowned in disbelief. *Seriously?*

"Oh, I know what you mean, all right. It's ironic that Davina is always eating all those Snickers 'cause that's damn sure how thick she is," Morton replied. "I don't even know what she was up there yapping about; my mind was on bending her over this table."

"Hmph. Maybe I'll find an excuse to go by her office...take her some candy bars or something. Hopefully she'll be especially appreciative and thank me. Repeatedly."

The men shared a laugh before Morton continued. "I'm just glad we have some decent eye candy in this office. The other women here are nice but I wouldn't want to wake up to them. Now *Davina* on the other hand-"

Myles cleared his throat, hearing enough. He could hear the automatic scrambling and sudden switch in tone, their voices going from catty to corporate in seconds. When Myles finally passed by the room, they actually looked relieved that it was just him, flashing him bright smiles and mock salutes. Myles just continued on to his office, not acknowledging them or their disrespectful comments.

Between that whole scene and still not knowing how he was going to approach Jackie, the rest of Myles's day slid downhill considerably. Part of him regretted letting Morton and Dennis slide with the disgusting things they said about Davina. He couldn't help but wonder if Jackie had to put up with that kind of thing when she was still in the corporate arena. But he remembered she still had to put up with nonsense thanks to men like him even now that she was out of it.

Not in the mood to cook, he headed to a restaurant he enjoyed, Tarin's, to get some dinner. He immediately ordered a scotch and soda, downing half of it before his food came. A couple of messages came in from Mollie, but he dismissed them for later when he saw they were nothing but memes and a clip of some skit she did for social media. He tried to clear his mind of the day as he read some news articles, enjoying his grilled steak salad.

He had just requested his check when he happened to look across the room and see Jackie sitting at a table alone.

Being in her presence again had him nervous, which felt silly; she might not have even seen him over there, and if she had, likely opted to pretend she didn't. He noted that she didn't seem like her usual spunky self; she actually looked sad. Her eyes barely moved from her plate of food or her glass of some kind of brown alcohol.

Once Myles paid his bill, he started to just leave but his feet seemed to take him over to Jackie's table all on their own. She didn't even notice his approach, as she was so lost in her thoughts. It wasn't until he was standing over her and cleared his throat that she looked up. To his surprise, she didn't instantly frown or go off upon recognizing him.

"Good evening, Jackie," he greeted politely.

She just stared at him a moment before returning her attention to the half-full plate of blackened catfish with red beans and rice she'd been picking at. "Hey."

He rubbed his hands together before sliding them into his pockets. "You, um...are you all right?"

Her shoulder lifted briefly. "Uh-huh."

Just leave, he told himself. *She clearly isn't in the mood to talk.*

But he found himself asking, "May I join you?"

She glanced back up at him, her expression a mix of confused and bothered. When she took her time responding, Myles started to recant his request and slink away, figuring he'd try to apologize to her another time. But she finally replied, "Sit on down, if you want to."

Both relieved and anxious, Myles pulled out the chair across from her and sat. Jackie put down her fork and leaned back in her chair, looking at him expectantly. Since she was evidently leaving it to him to lead the conversation, Myles figured he might as well just jump right in.

"You look lovely this evening." He smiled.

Her eyes widened slightly and she crossed her arms over her chest, pressing her lips together for a moment before giving him a clipped, "Thank you."

Myles remembered Ethan's directive to not try to butter Jackie up and just say what he needed to say.

"Look, Jackie, about the other night..." His clawed hand hovered over the table as he tried to find the right words. "I apologize for the assumption I made about you. There's no excuse."

"True."

"The more I thought about it since, the more embarrassed I got. I should have asked you instead of jumping to my own conclusions. Definitely not my proudest moment."

She was still giving him something of a strange look. "Right."

"It seems I just keep putting my foot in my mouth with you. I can only imagine what you think of me."

She actually chuckled a little at that, to Myles's surprise. Briefly pressing the side of her hand to her mouth and composing herself, Jackie cleared her throat and re-folded her arms. "Seems so, yeah."

Mildly encouraged since she seemed to be loosening up some, Myles forged ahead. "It may seem trite, but I'd really like to make this up to you somehow. I'm really not a bad guy. Can I pay for your meal? Order you some dessert? They have great bread pudding here."

"That's, um," she coughed, "That's nice of you but it's really not necessary."

"Okay. Um...do you have any siblings? I can't say why but you strike me as an only child. I don't mean that in a bad way or anything," he quickly added, holding up a hand.

The waitress came over and asked if they needed anything else, and Myles politely declined with a smile. She stared at him for a moment as if stumped before scurrying off. Jackie's lips curled in, watching.

"I *am* an only child, actually," she replied, resuming their conversation. Her chin quivered slightly before she covered her mouth with her curled fingers. She looked like she was trying to compose herself but Myles couldn't imagine why she would be losing her composure in the first place. "And you just have the one sister?"

"Yes. My parents were unable to conceive after me; my mother has a myriad of health issues. They were extra thankful for Mollie since they didn't want me to grow up without companionship; I didn't have many friends growing up."

Myles didn't know why he was telling her all of this but he couldn't seem to help it. The fact that she was sitting there actually looking amused was starting to make him regret being so forthcoming, though.

"Okay, I have to ask...is there something going on?" He looked at her, noting that she seemed to be almost vibrating in her seat. "You seem to be acting strangely and, I must admit, it's making me a little uncomfortable."

Jackie was giggling outright now, unable to hold it in any longer. She clamped a hand over her mouth, dropping her head as her shoulders shook with laughter. Myles felt his annoyance ignite. All he was trying to do was make amends and get to know her; he'd even shared a semi-vulnerable moment, and she was mocking him. He didn't appreciate that one bit.

"Okay, well, I can see that you're not in the mood to talk. At least, not to me," he said, his voice clipped. He'd apologized, sincerely and to her face, so they had nothing else to talk about. His penance was paid. "I'll leave you alone, then."

"Oh, sit down." Jackie waved a hand at him when he started to stand. She pressed her hands to her face before straightening in her seat, clearing her expression best she could. "My bad for laughing but I honestly couldn't help it."

"I'm not sure what I said that was so funny."

"It wasn't anything you *said*. You..." She bit her lip. "You have spinach in your teeth."

"What??" Myles's hand flew to his mouth, feeling his face flame. Part of him didn't believe her, but he *did* just eat a salad loaded with spinach. How did he always come out feeling ridiculous around this woman?

"Thanks for letting me go on and on without letting me know," he muttered behind his hand. "I guess this is your payback for what I did, huh? Letting me humiliate myself?"

"Oh, loosen up. You're just always so put together and buttoned-up, it was a trip seeing you sitting there like that. I wanted to point it out but I admit I couldn't resist."

"You could've tried harder. I'm legitimately embarrassed, here."

"Okay, okay. Sorry. All right?"

Myles glared at her, but he noticed she was smiling at him, a genuine smile. He felt his irritation slowly disappear like water down a drain.

She didn't seem to be in a hurry for him to leave, so after a quick trip to the men's room to de-spinach his teeth, Myles rejoined her at the table and they eased into conversation. The nervousness he felt when he initially approached her was nowhere to be found as Myles realized he actually enjoyed talking to Jackie. She was intelligent, but not in a stuffy way; her sense of humor was (mostly) endearing. He wasn't even thinking about the time as they chatted about things like developments happening around Brodence and even trading stories from their childhoods. Lo and behold, he was actually enjoying her company.

Jackie was equally as surprised. She felt better than she did when she arrived at the restaurant, which she had only gone to because she was still smarting over what happened with Ringo and didn't want to be home alone with her thoughts. But Myles had made her forget all about that, however temporarily. Yeah, the spinach-in-the-teeth thing might have broken the ice for her, but she found that he actually wasn't terrible to talk to. Maybe a little formal for her tastes, but not so much that it turned her off.

Her appetite renewed, she did take him up on his offer for dessert, and they shared a huge hunk of caramel cake. When she glanced at her phone, she was surprised to see so much time had passed. Her eyes fluttered up to his face, eying him thoughtfully.

Myles signaled for the waitress when he noticed Jackie checking the time, sensing he was about to be bid goodnight.

She had indulged him longer than expected, and it was nice. But he figured it was time for each of them to get on with their evenings. He had to get up early the next morning, anyway.

So he was utterly floored with what she said next.

"Come home with me, Myles."

Chapter 9

What was happening?

Jackie hadn't planned on inviting Myles back to her place. But when he started to reach for his wallet, she figured he was about to wish her good night and she realized she wasn't ready for their time to end just yet. There was something about Myles Cornwall that intrigued her, and figuring out what that was would be a good distraction from the other things plaguing her mind.

Myles had been momentarily stumped at the invitation, but it surprised them both at how quickly he said yes when he recovered. His head was swimming as he followed her to her house. This certainly wasn't how he imagined his evening going. He was nervous, but it was a different brand than the kind he had when he first approached Jackie at her table earlier. This kind was more anticipatory. He wasn't sure exactly why she wanted him to come over, and he admittedly hadn't had the nerve to ask, but he realized he was eager to find out.

She excused herself to quickly change clothes, emerging in a large t-shirt that stopped mid-thigh. Myles tried not to stare at her smooth legs or blue-painted toenails, but he wasn't doing the best job.

"I hope this doesn't make you uncomfortable," Jackie said, noting he'd momentarily gone mute. She poured them both glasses of rum. "I just had to get out of those clothes and this is closest to what I usually wear when I'm home alone."

"What do you usually wear?"

"Nothing."

She almost laughed at the stricken expression on his face. He wordlessly accepted his glass, his Adam's apple bobbing with a nervous swallow.

"Oh..." He cleared his throat.

"Yeah. I like being naked when I'm in my space. But you're not ready for all that."

Myles didn't say aloud that she was right. If Jackie had walked out of her room naked, he probably would have melted right on the spot. People actually walked around their homes nude? He thought that was only a fallacy.

"Right. Well..." He cleared his throat again before taking a sizeable swig of rum. "What do we do now?"

Jackie glanced over at him and laughed. He was standing near the couch as if rooted to that spot, back as straight as a board, as if he was scared to move or touch anything. She couldn't decide if she wanted to mess with him or try to put him at ease.

"What would you *like* to do, Mr. Cornwall?" she teased, setting her glass on the end table.

He eyed the movement. "You don't use coasters?"

Jackie glanced down as if that hadn't occurred to her and shrugged. "I don't even have any. It's just a table; it's not all that precious."

Myles couldn't imagine. He kept coasters on every surface and anyone who didn't use them felt his wrath.

"How old are you, Jackie?" he suddenly asked.

When her head whipped around with an amused glare, he quickly held up a hand.

"I apologize; I don't know what I was thinking," he amended, silently kicking himself. "I know it's improper to ask that of a lady."

"I'm improper probably eighty percent of the time. Decorum isn't my concern." She moved closer to him, eyes on him as she sipped her own drink. "I'm just curious as to how old you *think* I am."

"Oh no, I'm not falling for that one." Myles shook his head, mildly surprised when Jackie busted out laughing. "If I guess wrong then you'll get offended and incensed and probably curse me out. No thank you. Just tell me, please."

"Oh, come on..."

"No ma'am. I might not be an expert on women but I can just *hear* my mother and my sister in my head telling me not to fall for this."

"Okay, okay, how about you guess the age range, then? Twenty-five to thirty? Thirty to thirty-five? Thirty-five to forty?"

Myles started to respond, then his eyes narrowed. "No, because if I guess the incorrect range, you won't like that, either."

Jackie laughed again, plopping onto the couch with a leg tucked underneath her. Myles had to move his eyes from her legs again. "I promise you, Myles, I am not that sensitive. Age is just a number, not a definition. You have my word that I won't rip your head off if you guess wrong."

"All right." He was still mildly wary but chose to take her at her word. "Thirty to thirty-five."

"Is that your real guess or are you trying to flatter me?"

"Umm..."

"I'm thirty-eight, Myles," Jackie put him out of his misery with a good-natured smile and shake of her head. "A loud and proud thirty-eight."

"Wow. You've accomplished a lot," Myles noted, moving over to the bookcase that held her diplomas and awards, a couple of which he wasn't aware of. His eyebrows rose slightly when he noticed pictures of her with notable executives, and even a couple of celebrities. It still floored him to see her in business suits and jewelry and makeup. He couldn't help but smile at the picture of her in front of her garage, her arms spread wide and a huge grin on her face. He could see the 'grand opening' sign over the door behind her. The joy on her face in that picture radiated; the smiles she wore in the other pictures of her corporate life didn't have nearly the same exuberance.

"I guess, yeah." Jackie shrugged. "Most of that stuff you're looking at is from what seems like a whole other lifetime, though."

"But I imagine you're still proud of it, though, right?"

"Sure. But it didn't make me happy. Being good at something doesn't mean it's what you were meant to do."

"So if you don't mind my asking, why did you do it? I mean, you got to a pretty high level so-"

"It wasn't by choice. My mama *stayed* on my back about 'being the best.' Grades were never an issue for me; it was evident early on that I was smarter than most my age and she hopped on that shit, putting me in 'gifted' everything. I skipped a couple grades, took advanced classes, accelerated programs, all that," Jackie revealed with a dismissive wave, as if it was no big deal. "After so many years of her nagging,

I was basically on autopilot and just going through the motions. But I never really enjoyed it. It wasn't me."

"Oh...and your mother never knew this?"

"She didn't give a damn what I wanted. All she cared about was molding me into something she could brag on to her trifling friends. It took years but thankfully I snapped out of the trance she had me under and decided to live my life for me. She's had no more words for me since."

Myles's eyebrows shot up. "Your mother stopped speaking to you simply because you changed careers?"

"Because I stopped doing what she wanted me to do, yeah. Telling folks her daughter owns an auto garage wasn't as clit-tingling as bragging that I was a COO for an international corporation. Especially since she never did anything nearly as noteworthy in her own life. Once I stopped letting her use me to live out her dreams, she had no more use for me. Or my dad, since he's supported me since day one. I have no idea where she is and I don't give a fuck."

Myles eyed Jackie, feeling a pang of empathy for her. He'd been blessed with such loving and supportive parents that he couldn't imagine a mother willingly disassociating from her daughter simply because she chose to forge her own life path. He wondered if that was why Jackie acted as tough as she did.

"I'm sorry to hear that, Jackie," he said, hoping she believed him.

"It is what it is," Jackie shrugged again. "Her loss."

"True." Myles joined her on the couch, taking another sip of his rum before moving to put it on the coffee table in front of them. He hovered the glass over the wooden surface, remembering there were no coasters, before pulling a car magazine closer and setting the glass on top of it. Jackie just eyed him with amusement. "Even if it wasn't your heart's desire, you still excelled. And you have everything displayed so it must still be important to you. I have to say, I'm rather impressed, especially after hearing your backstory."

When Jackie didn't speak for several moments, he looked over his shoulder at her. She was eyeing him thoughtfully and he immediately wondered what he could have possibly said wrong.

"What?" he finally asked.

"Why couldn't you be impressed when you thought I was just a mechanic?"

"I, uh...what?"

"Before you found out about all that," Jackie waved a hand towards her bookcase, "You weren't impressed that I'm a woman that opened her own business doing something she loves? A business that's doing very well, I might add, in a male-dominated industry?"

"Jackie, I..." Myles adjusted his glasses and shifted in his seat. "I was giving you a compliment."

"And I'm asking you a question. Why did it take seeing me all suited up and hobnobbing with famous stuffed-shirts for you to give me a damn compliment? I didn't deserve your respect until you saw my degrees and awards and association with certain people?"

He frowned. "That's not what I said."

"But that's what it is." She untucked her leg and sat forward, her big brown eyes challenging. "It's like your dick got hard at seeing me in 'Jacqueline' mode, because of course you've already shown what you think about dirty ol' mechanic Jackie. You don't respect what I do. Just admit it."

"Yes, Jackie, I respect what you do. My being impressed by your former accomplishments doesn't mean your current ones are invalid."

"I sure can't tell."

"Please don't put words in my mouth, Jackie."

"I didn't have to put anything in your mouth. You said it. Yet I never heard any praise before you saw all that shit on my bookcase. Or do you pity me now because of the shit I told you about my mama?"

"No, I do not pity you. I empathize and I feel for you but I don't pity you."

"Right. So it's just about those bullshit accomplishments you were just drooling over, huh?"

Myles thought it smart not to mention that he'd already done some snooping on her before even seeing that bookcase. His own ire now riled, he turned towards her, frowning almost as intensely as she was. "Why do you care what I think, anyway?"

"I *don't* care," Jackie immediately snapped. "Just because I'm pointing out what a pretentious jackass you are doesn't mean I give a damn what you think."

"Clearly, you're still upset about the mistakes I've made with you before. I suppose it was foolish of me to believe that your acceptance of my apology was sincere. I can tell dealing with you would be like treading a minefield. Is this why you invited me over here? So you could continue berating me on your turf?"

"Oh, don't try to make me out to be the bad guy, here. Don't put this on me."

"You started this ridiculous fight, Jackie. I'm not sure *why* I agreed to come here, but it surely wasn't for this." He pinched the bridge of his nose under his glasses before taking a breath. "This is ridiculous."

Jackie folded her arms, still glaring at him.

"Look, if I've somehow offended you yet again, I apologize. It wasn't my intention." Myles grabbed his glass and downed the rest of his rum before returning it to the magazine. "Have a good night, Jackie."

He moved to stand, but Jackie grabbed his arm. His eyes fell to her hand before lifting to her face, his surprise and curiosity evident.

Jackie didn't have a plan. It looked like he was about to leave and she jumped. It shocked her as much as it did him. She was annoyed with him but wanted him to stay. She couldn't quite pinpoint why that was and it both intrigued and frustrated her.

"Yes?" Myles finally murmured. He looked at her expectedly, clearly waiting for an explanation.

It was a rare time that Jackie didn't know what to say. She looked at the floor, noting his brown wingtips, letting her eyes travel up his legs that now seemed longer than before. His cologne that hadn't even registered to her before was now enticingly potent. Her breathing deepened slightly as her hold tightened on his arm.

"Jackie, I-"

She lunged forward, pressing her lips to his. Part of her expected him to immediately push her away, but he didn't.

The kiss lingered for several moments before she eased back a bit, still in his personal space, eyes on his.

Myles was stunned. The kiss had totally caught him off guard, and he was rendered momentarily immobile as she kept her mouth on his. His lips stayed put and so did his hands. When she pulled back and looked at him, as if silently asking for permission or reprimand, he could do nothing but stare back. Why did she kiss him? Just moments before, she was biting his head off. He'd been about to leave. Was this why she invited him over?

His silent musings were paused when she kissed him again, this time more aggressively. This time, he responded, and returned her kiss with an almost equal energy. It was both exploratory and eager, and she let out a satisfied moan as her hand slid to his face. Her body moved closer, her soft breasts pressing to his chest as she eased him onto his back on the couch. Myles felt long-dormant parts of him wake up as Jackie slid on top of him, their tongues now stroking each other's as if they'd been waiting to do so all evening.

Jackie's body on top of his felt amazing. Lush and soft. And she smelled like cotton candy. Myles's hands eased to her back then sprang away when he realized how close they'd landed to her butt. He awkwardly grabbed the back of the couch with one hand while the other one just hovered, not wanting to overstep despite them making out with such intensity.

"You can touch me," she whispered. She grabbed his hand and put it on her lower back, holding it there when it felt like he was going to ease it away again. "Don't be a gentleman right now."

His fingers flexed, and he was surprised at the urge to slide his hand under her shirt. "What are we doing, Jackie?"

"We're kissing." She gave him a small smile, trailing her finger along his jawline. "Are you enjoying it?"

Swallowing, Myles tried to calm his racing nerves. As crazy as what they were doing felt, he realized he wasn't ready for it to stop. "Yes."

"I can tell." She began to grind on him, earning a gasping groan from Myles. "I am, too."

"Where is this leading, Jackie?"

"Stay in the moment, Mr. Cornwall." She leaned down to flick his earlobe with her tongue and he sucked in a breath. She moaned when she felt him flinch underneath her. "Don't think." She kissed her way back to his lips. "Just feel." Kiss. "Feel this. Feel *me*." Her tongue trailed his bottom lip. "I want you to."

Her words seemed to embolden him, and his arms slowly began to slide around her body. Jackie's hips wound more intently as their kisses deepened again, breaths and moans escaping between them. Myles shifted so she could bring her body more flush with his, totally caught up in the moment. His mind clicked off, relieving him of the mental questioning of whether or not this was a smart thing to do.

"Should we lose the glasses?" she whispered.

Wordlessly, Myles removed his glasses and blindly tossed them towards the coffee table, almost not caring if they landed there or not. Their making out resumed, Jacking grinding on him, driving him crazier than he'd felt in recent memory. His hands itched to slide underneath her shirt but his hesitancy remained, despite her earlier permission. He wondered if she was going to expect sex from him, and what he'd say if she did. His body wanted to, but he barely knew her. He wasn't even sure if he *liked* her. But he couldn't deny how amazing she felt on top of him and how much he was enjoying kissing her.

They continued going at it on the couch, each of them surprised at just how good the other felt and how they weren't in any hurry to stop. They eventually shifted to where Jackie was straddling him as Myles sat up on the couch, Jackie's arms wound tightly around his neck as she leisurely wound her hips. Myles's hands slid around her back, unable to keep them still, squeezing her like she was squeezing him. He finally allowed himself to grip her bottom, already hooked on how his fingers sunk into the softness of it. He'd never experienced a woman of her curves.

God help him, he wanted her.

As if she was able to read that mental realization, Jackie pulled back and looked at him, her hands still framing his neck.

"Myles."

"Yes?" His response was almost embarrassingly eager.

They were both breathless and panting, staring right at each other. Myles both anticipated and dreaded whatever she was about to say.

"We're gonna have sex."

His body loved that decision. But his brain was telling him to pump the brakes. Before he could respond, though, Jackie placed a finger to his lips.

"But not tonight."

"Oh." He blinked, startled. "Um, okay..."

"You're not ready for me yet," she declared. "And I want you to be as ready as I am when we go there." She leaned forward, giving him a gentle peck. "This is enough for now."

Myles didn't have time to decide how he felt about Jackie making such a decision on his behalf because when she eased her tongue between his lips and pressed herself closer to him, all thoughts disappeared.

When Myles woke up the next morning, he wondered if the previous evening had all been a dream; running into Jackie at Tarin's, her inviting him to her place, them arguing, her kissing him. He didn't even know how long they were going at it but he knew it was rather late by the time he finally made it home. His body maintained the tingles from Jackie's touch even after he took a shower and got into bed, surprised that part of him hated that he was getting in alone.

His work day was just filled with more reminiscing and analyzing. He wondered what Jackie's deal was. She didn't seem to like him very much yet she made a move on him. Everything he did seemed to tick her off, but she hadn't wanted him to leave when he started to. They were not each other's type, but she had already claimed they were going to sleep together at some point. Myles still wasn't even sure how he felt about that; casual sex had never been something he participated in. And who was Jackie to determine that he wasn't ready? What did that even mean, that he *wasn't ready for her*? True enough, he'd been mentally battling whether he should go there with her or not, but it certainly wasn't a question of desire. She probably thought he was inexperienced or couldn't 'handle' her, which was silly. Myles had never been one to brag on his sexual abilities, but he had no doubt that he could handle Jackie Malone in the bedroom if the opportunity arose.

Getting any work done was a task. His mind kept straying back to him and Jackie locked together on her couch. Part of him was embarrassed for losing control like he did, even though things really didn't go that far; all they'd done was kiss and do some semi-heavy petting and grinding. No clothes were removed. Mouths stayed above the shoulders. But if that had been Cynthia or any other woman he wasn't that fond of, he'd have shut it down immediately. But the thought hadn't even crossed his mind with Jackie, despite them having just argued moments before. Yeah, he was a little hesitant, but that was only because her one-eighty attitude change had thrown him.

If Myles was honest with himself, he knew that the frustration from Jackie doubting his readiness and the embarrassment from him losing his head was greatly outweighed by intrigue. Rather intense intrigue, at that. Despite all of the reasons it wasn't a good idea, and all the indications that he should leave her be and go about his business, Myles couldn't help anticipating what might come next with Jackie. She irked him, but he also felt a pull towards her. He'd made two major blunders with her, and it had become strangely important to him to get her forgiveness.

And now that he'd gotten to kiss her and touch that luscious body of hers, he knew just putting her out of his mind wasn't going to happen.

Figuring he needed to move in order to stop fantasizing about Jackie, Myles decided to go on a coffee run, though he didn't bother asking anyone else if they wanted anything. He just told his assistant he was going out for a little while and left, heading to Lula's Cup.

"Is that my sweetie pie Myles coming in here?"

His grin was automatic. Myles turned to see Ms. Lula rounding the front counter with a huge grin and her arms open wide for a hug, which he gladly obliged. She was a woman in her upper sixties, though her teak brown skin held few wrinkles. Her mostly-gray hair was pinned up in a casual French roll, a few wisps framing her face. A red printed scarf was tied around her head, the material matching her airy cotton blouse that was tucked into a long denim skirt. White thick-soled sneakers adorned her feet. They held onto each other for several moments, Ms. Lula lovingly rubbing his back, before they separated.

"How are you, Ms. Lula?"

"I'm good, baby. Surprised to see you in here in the middle of the day."

"Yeah, I just needed to get out of the office for a while." Myles had no plans to divulge why. "You have a minute to talk?"

"Yeah, I've got a few minutes. Just have a seat and I'll be right back. You want anything? A cappuccino or some sour cream pound cake?"

Myles loved her pound cake but he made himself resist. "Just the cappuccino would be great."

She scurried off to the back and Myles took a seat at one of the dark wood round tables, choosing one near the window. The afternoon lull had hit, as there were only a few customers milling about. Mornings were the busiest, usually with a line stretching out the door. It didn't calm down until around eleven a.m., remaining steady until closing time.

Ms. Lula approached the table, Myles's drink in one hand and a small clear to-go container in the other. Myles shook his head. He should've known she'd bring him the cake anyway.

"Don't give me that look," she said at his playfully admonishing expression, sliding the cake over to him. "I bet you'll be glad I gave this to you later on tonight."

Knowing she was probably right, Myles just gave a conceding nod. "Thank you, Ms. Lula. I'll pay for all of this before I leave."

"No, you won't."

"We're not doing this, Ms. Lula. I love you for being so generous but you know I'm not going to accept anything for free. You're running a business."

"And you've *helped* my business by getting people through the door, blessing me with that fancy new refrigerator when mine broke, and bringing me employees. So let me spoil you a little bit."

"I've been meaning to ask you how Gloria was working out. Has she been helpful?"

"Oh my, yes! You sending her here was right on time; my cashier had just quit and the child I'd hired to replace her wanted to get paid for hardly doing anything, not to mention being late more times than she wasn't. That Gloria has been a godsend. A *huge* help."

"I'm so glad to hear that." Gloria was a homeless woman that Myles had encountered several months before, when he was out running some errands. Seeing his suit, she'd asked if he knew of any job openings, explaining that she used to own a day care center before a hurricane of bad luck that consisted of crooked employees, an abusive ex, and uncaring parents left her on the street with all of her belongings in a pilfered shopping cart. Myles had promised to keep an eye out for her, and when Ms. Lula mentioned needing a new cashier, Myles suggested Gloria, being transparent about her circumstances. Ms. Lula wasn't fazed, and insisted he bring Gloria by. When he did, the ladies bonded immediately, and Gloria had cried almost uncontrollable tears of gratitude when Ms. Lula offered her the job and a room to stay in. Myles's heart tugged at the scene, watching Gloria hug Ms. Lula tightly, clinging to her, thanking her for giving her a chance. Ms. Lula just held her head to her shoulder as she rubbed her back and assured her that everything was going to be all right.

"Is she working today?" Myles asked, his eyes sweeping for a glimpse of the twenty-something biracial woman.

"She's out getting things situated with the room she's renting. She'll be in later. You'll be back at the office by then but I'll be sure to tell her you stopped by."

"Good." Myles took a sip of his drink before glancing around and leaning forward slightly. "Are your other employees aware of her...situation?"

Ms. Lula flicked her wrist. "Her *former* situation, you mean? If they are, they didn't hear it from me. I told her it was up to her to let folks know about that or not. But I also told her that I didn't think it was any of their business. You know how some folks can be."

"Unfortunately." Myles was glad to hear that things with Gloria were going so well and she was getting back on her feet. It only made him want to help even more of the homeless he came across.

He and Ms. Lula chatted for another couple of minutes, their conversation occasionally pausing when someone came over to speak to Ms. Lula. Myles was glad he'd come by, feeling better from soaking in the kind coffee shop owner's welcoming spirit, but the good vibes screeched to a halt when she mentioned greedy developers hounding her.

"Are you serious?"

"I wish I wasn't." Ms. Lula sighed. "Some woman has been in here almost every week, trying to sweet-talk me into selling."

"Do they not know this shop has been around for over forty years? This is a Brodence landmark."

"I don't think they care, baby. History doesn't mean much to those people. They want what they want. And it seems they're gonna try to wear me down until they get it."

Myles scowled, turning his face to the window. The thought of someone trying to get rid of Lula's Cup infuriated him. He'd heard about developers poking around at other places, which was bad enough, but he didn't know they were after Ms. Lula's shop, too. His mind began whirling as to what he could do.

"Hey," Ms. Lula's hand gently shook his arm, waiting for him to turn back to her, "I'm gonna be just fine, all right?

Don't start worrying yourself over this. It'll all work out like it's supposed to."

Myles placed his hand over hers, giving her a tight smile. He wished he shared her optimism. He was familiar with how land developers were. They had a job to do and wouldn't just go away because they got on people's nerves.

He headed back to work a little while later, still fuming. He almost didn't see Ethan when he brushed by him on the way to his office, and was surprised when his friend grabbed his arm, stopping him.

"Hey, what's going on with you?" Ethan asked, concerned. His eyes dropped, then brightened. "And is that pound cake?"

"I've just got something on my mind, is all," Myles muttered, not addressing the second question.

"You need to talk?"

At Myles's shrug, Ethan motioned for Myles to follow him to his office. Once they were inside, Myles relayed what Ms. Lula told him about the developers hounding her about selling, getting riled up all over again. Ethan wasn't any happier to hear this news than he'd been.

"I'm unfortunately not surprised." Ethan leaned back in his leather desk chair, linking his hands behind his head. "Chanel James can be relentlessly persistent. I've heard of them doing the same stuff over in Terston and Brina Falls."

Myles shook his head. "It just seems...almost *evil* that anyone would want to get rid of Lula's Cup. Ms. Lula has done *so* much for the people around here."

"I know, buddy. But don't stress; there's a solution for just about every problem. We just have to find it."

Needing to change the subject, Myles asked how things were going with Eniah, the lady Ethan had recently started dating. Upon hearing her name, Ethan broke out into a large smile, which Myles couldn't help but chuckle at.

"Things are great," Ethan confirmed, picking up his pen and scribbling something on a nearby notepad.

"Doodling her name already?"

"I am not." Ethan dropped the pen, though the color in his cheeks gave him away. "But we've been seeing a lot of each other recently and...I'm enjoying where it's headed. I have a date with her tonight, actually."

"Well, good for you. It's been a while since I've seen you actually blush over a woman like this. I guess that atrocious salmon-colored shirt you bought for your first date paid off. Perhaps you should have it framed because if she still wanted to see you after *that*..."

"Haha. You should go on after Mollie one night."

"No, but seriously. I hope things continue to go well for you two."

"Thank you. And thank you for introducing me to her. I owe you a steak dinner for that."

"No thanks necessary. I knew when I met her at that fundraiser my parents hosted that she'd be a good match for you, even though I sensed Mother had invited her there for my benefit."

Ethan leveled his gaze on him. "Still no new developments on the dating front, then, I take it?"

Myles immediately thought of Jackie and he fought to keep his face even. Part of him wanted to get Ethan's take on what happened with Jackie the night before but the other part was wary. Ethan would probably just gloat, since he'd mentioned how attractive Jackie was up front and Myles had claimed not to notice. And at the time, he hadn't. But he surely did now.

He decided to keep it to himself for the time being. It was all still so fresh and he needed to wrap his head around it first.

"Not really," he replied, proud of how believable he sounded. "You know I've had my finger on the pause button when it comes to dating."

"And you're not tired of that yet?"

Myles shrugged, glancing at his watch and standing. "I'm sure I will be soon enough. Look, I need to get back to work; I didn't have a very productive morning. Thanks for listening, regarding Lula's Cup."

"Of course."

Myles headed back to his office, feeling he'd dodged a bullet. He knew he'd divulge what happened with Jackie to Ethan at some point, but he just wasn't ready yet. And what he'd told his friend was true; dating *was* still paused for him. His evening with Jackie happened by chance. It wasn't a date. He didn't know *what* to call it, but it wasn't a date.

And when his phone buzzed with a call and he saw Jackie's name on the screen, he didn't let himself question the instant surge of excitement that shot through him.

"Good afternoon," he answered the call, making sure his office door was good and closed.

"Mr. Cornwall, what's up?" The smile in her voice was evident, and it actually made him blush that she seemed happy to talk to him. "How's your day going?"

Myles winced when he heard her pop her gum. It was just as grating as the first time he'd heard it. And just as annoying.

"Just fine, thank you," he replied, holding his tongue about it. "And yours?"

"I'm managing to get things done despite thinking about what we did on my couch last night every other minute."

Myles almost missed his chair when he tried to sit at his desk. Thank goodness no one else was in his office. His face was on fire now. "Are you serious?"

"I'm very serious. Has it been on your mind at all today?"

Only the entire morning. Myles didn't want to admit just how much their makeout session consumed his thoughts. It was the reason he'd barely been able to get anything done. "It's crossed my mind."

"Crossed your mind, huh?" She chuckled, as if knowing he was full of it. There were people talking and the sounds of tools in the background, and Myles figured she called him on a break. Which was also strangely flattering. "Well, we're both busy people so I'll get to the point of this call. I was wondering if you wanted to hang out again."

"Hang out?"

"Yes," she replied slowly, as if he should know what that meant. "I'm asking if you want to get together. If you're not ready to be seen in public with me or something, we can keep it simple and have dinner at my place."

She said it as a joke but Myles sensed there was an undercurrent of doubt about him that belied her attempt at playfulness. It didn't make Myles feel great. Did she really believe he'd be ashamed to go out with her in public? They'd spent time at the restaurant together, even though it had been by happenstance. Was that the kind of man she thought he was?

"I'd like that, Jackie," he assured. "Be it at your place or anywhere else."

"Good to know. How about tonight? Eight o'clock?"

He blinked in surprise. "So soon?"

"What are we waiting for? You'll learn soon enough that I'm rather impatient and I don't waste time being coy. I don't like to waste time, period. We're interested in each other, not to mention our clear physical attraction. Why not just go ahead and jump in with both feet?"

Myles had never been the jump-in-with-both-feet kind of man. He was more cautious, preferring to dip his toes in, access then reevaluate, weighing all the pros and cons before making a decision and then easing into it. Jackie seemed to be the complete opposite of that, the kind that would cannonball right in and not care where the splashes landed, and he again wondered what in the world had him so intrigued by this woman.

But he couldn't deny that seeing Jackie in a matter of hours was more appealing than going through his usual overanalyzing, which could take days. Now that the invitation was out there, he felt himself anticipating it. He wanted to see her. Apparently, it could be as simple as that.

"I'll see you at eight."

"Great!"

Myles felt his smile grow. He glanced at the time on his computer, already wishing for it to move faster.

He was jumping into whatever this was with Jackie with both feet. He just hoped he remembered how to swim.

Chapter 10

"Wait, so you and Corny Cornwall are a *thing* now?"

Jackie rolled her eyes at Cassidy's nickname for Myles. "I'm not sure why you're so astonished. You said yourself he was handsome. And I don't like that nickname."

"Come on now, Jackie. You know that man is corny. Admittedly handsome, yes, but corny as hell."

Jackie didn't want to admit out loud that she agreed with Cassidy. Myles *was* a little corny, which was usually an automatic turn-off for her. But on him it was strangely endearing.

"Whatever. Don't be calling him that."

"Oooh, standing up for your *boo* already, huh? I was the one that had to shame you into even listening to his apology and now you're biting my head off about him. I mean, I'm seriously trippin' right now...you and *Myles*??"

It was after closing time at The Auto Loft and Jackie and Cassidy were hanging out, having some girl talk. Jackie was eager to tell her bestie about her surprisingly amazing evening with Myles the night before, and Cassidy had sat there with her jaw practically on the floor the whole time. At first she thought Jackie was playing with her, but once Jackie insisted she was a hundred percent serious, Cassidy went from being speechless to having a *lot* to say about it.

"I just...I honestly couldn't have seen this coming," Cassidy continued, pressing her hands to her cheeks. "You're actually dating that man??"

"Yes, Cassidy. Why are you acting so shocked? You were encouraging me to give him a shot, remember?"

"Yeah, but...still. I admit when I said all that I didn't expect for you to actually *do* it. Are you forgetting how he insulted you? Doubted your skills? Assumed you were gay?"

"No, I didn't forget. But he apologized for all that."

"And that's it? That's all it took for you to give up the draws?"

"We have not had sex, Cassidy." Jackie sighed, running a hand down the back of her head. The image of grinding on Myles's lap flashed through her mind. "But damn if I haven't thought about it."

"I mean, I get that I'm the one that thought he was going to be on the other end of the blind date he set up for you, but I never thought you'd *really* consider dating him. You two have nothing in common."

"Sure we do. We're both about our business. We're both...Black..."

"Wow."

"Okay, maybe we don't. But so what? It doesn't have to make sense. I like him," Jackie declared, her voice firm. "And anyway, I realized I'm really in no position to judge Myles for his dumb mistakes after the ones I've made recently."

Cassidy's expression melted into one of understanding. "You're talking about Ringo?"

"Yeah." Jackie heaved a deep sigh, the slight pang returning upon remembering their last encounter. "I still feel ridiculous when I think about how I acted that night. If I want Ringo to forgive me for that, I should forgive Myles for his shit."

"Is that what this is about? Are you latching onto Myles because you can't have Ringo?"

"No. This isn't a rebound thing. I *was* bummed, but...as bad as that situation at Ringo's was, I realized that it was probably for the best. Being with Ringo isn't good for me; I don't like the person I am when I'm with him. And anyway, I'm certainly not going to waste time pining over a man that kicked me out of his house in the middle of the night and told me to lose his number, even if his anger *was* justified."

"I get that."

"Trust, I'm just as surprised as you are that I like Myles that way 'cause believe me, I was *not* looking at him like that at first. I thought he was like an annoying wad of gum that you can't fully scrape off the bottom of your shoe and you still feel that tack every time you take a step."

"Sexy."

"But when he came over to my table last night, he just looked so...humble. Almost shy. Like getting my forgiveness meant something to him. And him having spinach in his teeth just kinda broke the ice. It was cute. And I started to see what you were talking about before with the sexy nerd thing."

"I did say that, didn't I? Okay. So you invited him back to your place and jumped him."

"I guess if you wanna break it down to the studs, yeah. But I didn't invite him over to seduce him; I really was just enjoying his company and wasn't ready for it to end. And even after we had that bullshit argument, I still didn't want him to go anywhere. Next thing I knew, I was tackling him. He's a damn good kisser..."

"Don't start getting all hot and bothered now," Cassidy teased, nudging Jackie's leg. "Save it for tonight."

"Speaking of which, I need to get out of here," Jackie jumped up from the loveseat she and Cassidy were lounging on. "Myles will be coming to my place in a couple of hours and I need to get home and cute up. Thankfully I ran out to get groceries earlier."

"I swear, part of me is still waiting on you to tell me that this is all a joke," Cassidy admitted, pushing herself up.

"I'll let you work that out for yourself. I already told you it isn't."

"I'm saying, though. You...and *Myles*??" Cassidy shuddered lightly as she headed over to the desk to get her things. "You're rushing home, getting ready to cook for him...hmph. Maybe next, meatballs will start falling out of the sky."

Jackie just ignored her as she went to her office. Cassidy didn't have to understand her attraction to Myles. There was something about him that Jackie liked and that was all that mattered.

As Jackie headed home a little later, though, she felt nervousness overtake her anticipation. What she hadn't told Cassidy was that as much as she was willing to explore things with Myles, there was still a small part of her that was wary. Cassidy had a point about them having nothing in common. And while that wasn't always a bad thing, Jackie wondered if it would become an issue at some point. She didn't forget about him complimenting what she did in her past more than what she was doing now. Maybe the novelty of their unexpected attraction would wear off and he'd remember that he was actually dating a mechanic, not a socialite. Never mind that she used to be a big-time executive; she'd left that life to spend her days hunched under car hoods. Myles probably kept a better manicure than she did.

She made herself shake those thoughts off. If she let herself go down that road, she might as well nip things in the bud now. There was more to her than her job. She liked him. He liked her. They were both interested in exploring that. Enough said. She couldn't waste time on things she couldn't control. And she certainly wasn't a psychic.

Her phone rang and she groaned. She was so not in the mood for this.

"Yes, Chanel?"

"Wow, don't sound so happy to hear from me," Chanel chuckled, her voice annoyingly loud and clear through the Bluetooth. "You're the one that gave me your number, remember?"

"One of my rare moments trying to be polite. Why are you calling me?"

"Have your fellow business owners been talking to you about me? Because I'm getting way more pushback than before. People actually cross the street when they see me coming or duck around a corner. It would be funny if it didn't make doing my job that much more damn difficult."

"I'm not sure what you want *me* to do about it."

"You're about the only one that doesn't seem to have a problem with me. Can you help me get these people on board?"

"Are you forgetting that I initially wasn't taking your calls, either?"

"But you don't treat me like the devil."

"Chanel," Jackie sighed. She regretted answering the phone. "If you're trying to get me to be your co-signer, you can forget it. I might not be as against the idea of selling as other people but that doesn't mean I'm gonna cape for your cause."

Chanel was quiet for a moment. "You want to sell?"

Jackie gritted her teeth, cursing herself for the slip-up. "I didn't say that."

"You said you're not against it."

"I said I'm not *as* against it as everyone else. Look...if you spout this to anybody else I'll deny it and if you happen to be recording this call, I'll beat your ass with a tire iron. My position is that I can build bigger and better somewhere else, so selling wouldn't be all that big of a deal to me. I like where I am, but the value is more practical than sentimental. I've already started scoping out locations, in case it should ever be necessary."

"*Finally*, someone who's on board! I'm so relieved that I'm gonna forget about you threatening bodily harm with a car part."

"Don't do that, because as I told you, this is between you and me. Most people around here want no parts of what you're trying to do, and I'm not going to be the sore thumb. Whatever the majority goes with, I go with. That is my official position."

"Hmm. The Jackie *I* know wouldn't be worried about ruffling a few feathers. Regardless of what you say, I think you've still got some corporate shark in you. You *have* to know that some of these changes would make sense for

Brodence. People need to learn to leave their feelings out of it and look at the big picture, like you're doing."

"That may be. But thankfully it's not my job to convince anybody. Now if you'll excuse me, I have to go."

Jackie hung up without waiting for a response. She gripped the steering wheel as she tried to tell herself that her little slip-up with Chanel wouldn't mean anything. The last thing Jackie needed was everyone thinking she was just a corporate shark in coveralls who still cared more about the bottom line than people. She'd left all that behind for a reason.

Arriving at her house, she put Chanel and all that development business out of her mind and focused on the man that would be coming over shortly. She couldn't help but smile, feeling that starting-up-with-someone-new giddiness wash over her and send her feet moving faster into the house. After a quick shower, she put on some leggings and a v-neck shirt, resisting the urge to just throw on another large t-shirt over her underwear like the previous night. She didn't want to give the impression that it was just a glorified booty call, although she hoped the night didn't end without *some* intimacy. The way Myles had kissed and touched her the night before had her squirming in her bed all night.

By the time Myles arrived, Jackie had taken all of the dinner ingredients out and turned on some Kendrick Lamar to groove to as she cooked. It was no surprise to her that he was right on time.

"Hey, you," she greeted him after she swung open the door. Her right foot rubbed the back of her left ankle as her gaze swept over him.

"Good evening, Jackie." Myles returned her smile. He had a bouquet of tulips clutched in a death grip.

A beat passed with them just smiling at each other before Jackie stepped back with a 'come on' wave of her hand. "Well, don't just stand there. Come in."

Myles stepped inside and Jackie immediately recognized his cologne. Dior Sauvage. Ringo had worn it. But it hit differently on Myles.

"These are for you." Myles held the flowers out to her, then retracted just as she reached for them. "Oh...I just realized that you might not like flowers. I shouldn't have assumed you would...I apologize. Um, I can go put them back in my car-"

"Myles." Jackie couldn't help but giggle at how flustered he was. "Chill out. I actually *do* like flowers. And these are really nice, so thank you."

He was clearly surprised as she took the bouquet from his hand. "Really?"

"Yes, Myles. I like flowers, I wear makeup, occasionally wear the color pink. Just because I like cars doesn't mean I don't like girly stuff, too. Assuming that I don't like certain things is almost as bad as assuming I do. My job doesn't determine everything about me; it's just my job."

Sufficiently humbled, Myles pursed his lips and nodded. "I stand corrected. And thoroughly reprimanded. Thank you for having me."

"Thank you for coming. I was just about to get dinner started. Get comfortable; make yourself at home."

"Should I remove my shoes?"

Jackie shrugged, heading to the kitchen for a vase. "If you want."

"This is...interesting music."

"Not a fan of rap, huh?"

"It's admittedly not my go-to."

"You want me to turn it off, don't you?"

He hesitated only briefly before forcing out, "No. No, of course not. It's your house, after all."

Jackie left it at that. It was clear he didn't like rap but she was glad he didn't make an issue out of it. She would have felt some kind of way if he'd asked her to turn it off or change it to something like classical, which she could totally imagine him choosing. She figured their taste in music was just another thing they didn't have in common, because she loved rap and hip-hop.

Myles eased further into the living room, anxiously rubbing his hands together. Jackie eyed him as she filled the vase with water. He was dressed like he was going to a business meeting; she wondered if he'd come straight from work or if he'd chosen to wear a suit for a dinner at her house. He looked good in it, but still.

"Did you have to work late?" she couldn't resist asking.

"Oh, no." He turned towards her, sliding his hands into his pants pockets. "I went home to change first."

"And...that's what you put on?"

He glanced down at his outfit. "What's wrong with it?"

"It's a little dressy, isn't it? I would've thought you'd loosen up for a date at the house."

His expression flattened slightly. He looked away, pretending to be interested in her Peace Lily plant. "It's just what I prefer to wear. I didn't realize it would be a problem."

Jackie's hands slowed putting the flowers into the vase, sensing she'd struck a nerve.

"It's not a problem; was just making an observation, that's all." She kept her voice light, trying to buoy the vibe. She didn't want them butting heads two minutes in. "So how did the rest of your work day go?"

She was grateful when he seemed to let the suit thing go and engaged in conversation with her. He told her about an irritating meeting he had towards the end of the day; she told him about an irritating customer that resulted in more money being added to her and Cassidy's Disrespect Jar. When Myles heard about that, he actually cringed.

"Did any money go in there because of me?"

"Oh, baby, your visits paid for our flight upgrades." She gave him a playful wink over her shoulder. "We almost hoped you'd come back so we could spring for the good beachside hotel."

"And I thought my sister was the comedienne."

"I do want to go to one of her shows one day soon."

"I'm sure she'd love that. She always wants me in attendance even though I'm *really* not her target audience. I'm mostly just a glorified seat filler."

"Hmm. Well...maybe you and I could go together," Jackie suggested, her back turned to him as she washed her hands. "It might be more fun if you have someone sitting there with you."

Myles was quiet for a moment and Jackie wondered if he was going to decline. She released a small breath when he finally replied, "Yeah, perhaps. Do you need any help?"

"No, I've got it."

"What are you making, if I may ask?"

"Stir fry. I'm still deciding which protein I wanna use, though. I have some yeast rolls, too."

"Sounds delicious. You know, I happen to make a rather delectable stir fry, myself."

Jackie put down her knife, turning to look at him with a sly smile. "Is that right? I somehow can't imagine you in the kitchen."

"Why is that?"

"I don't know. Cooking can get rather...messy. And you don't strike me as the type that likes that. I actually imagined you having a personal chef."

"My parents have one of those, not me. And they only do so because my father can hardly boil water and he doesn't want my mother expending what energy she has in the kitchen. I'm self-sufficient enough to prepare my own meals. And as for getting messy..." He hunched a shoulder. "That's what showers are for, right?"

I bet he looks sexy in the shower...

The thought came automatically and Jackie had to keep her smile from erupting like it started to. She bit her lip and pretended to adjust the temperature on the oven, knowing her face was flushed a little bit. The amount of lusty thoughts she was accumulating about this man was flooring her.

"Yeah..." She cleared her throat. "Well, that's good to know. I like a man that knows his way around a kitchen."

"I can show you right now, if you like."

He started walking towards her and she felt her nipples harden; thank goodness she'd put on a bra. What was it about this slightly-uptight man that was getting to her so much? It wasn't like it had been a while since she'd had any; she'd just had sex a week ago. But Myles had her reacting as if it had been years.

"Wh-what do you mean?" she stammered, eying his approach.

He was standing in front of her, his presence and cologne now even more potent. His eyes roamed her face behind his glasses.

"Let me help you cook."

"Oh." Jackie felt a little silly for getting so flustered; it should have been obvious what he meant. "I really don't mind doing it myself but if you insist..."

"I do." He removed his suit jacket, draping it over a kitchen chair and removing his cufflinks before rolling up his shirt sleeves. Jackie couldn't resist eyeing his forearms as he did so. He moved over to the sink to wash his hands. "I don't want to stand around while you do all the work."

"Whatever you say."

They tried to divide and conquer, but it didn't take long for them to disagree on ingredient choices and amounts and technique and seasonings. Myles was making so many suggestions (and gentle critiques) on what she was doing that Jackie suggested they have a cook-off and see who made it best. It wasn't lost on either of them that she mainly did that to squelch another potential argument before it sprouted.

"Challenge accepted," he stated, smirking.

They proceeded to each make their own versions of the dinner for the evening, with plenty of smack talk. Jackie couldn't resist ribbing Myles on just about everything, and he surprisingly gave as good as he got. She honestly didn't think he had trash talk in him.

"Was your amateur knife skills the reason you bought so much extra produce?" he asked, eying her as she chopped the bell peppers. "That would explain why you happen to have enough for both of us to prepare full meals. You needed to ensure you were covered in case you butchered things beyond recognition, correct?"

Her jaw dropped. "Excuse you. There is nothing wrong with my knife skills."

"Sure." He continued chopping mushrooms as swiftly and evenly as a television chef, eyes on her. "Whatever you need to tell yourself."

How did he do that??

Jackie hated that she was even more turned on by his brand of cockiness as well as his skill. She couldn't deny that he looked like a professional with how he chopped vegetables and herbs, broke down a chicken with ease, and even how he cooked some of the seasoning before use. But she wasn't about to admit that to him.

"Just hush and keep your eyes on your own work. You can have all the fancy techniques you want, but it's all about how it comes together in the end. And I just hope you're willing to be honest when it becomes clear that my shit turns out better than yours."

"It's cute that you think that, Jackie. But I'll have no problem giving you your just due...if it's deserved."

"Oh, it'll be deserved, buddy."

Myles chuckled, shaking his head at her.

They continued cooking and teasing, working around each other in Jackie's decently-sized kitchen. Once everything was done, plating became another part of their impromptu competition. Jackie hadn't even planned on using her 'good' plates, but she wasn't about to have Myles cracking on her plastic plates, too. She got them for a buck apiece and used them often, since she lived alone and had no one to impress, usually. But she wanted to break out the good stuff for Myles.

"Moment of truth, Mr. Cornwall," Jackie hedged with a smile once they were seated at the table, rubbing her hands together. Plates of each of their versions of the meal sat in front of both of them, ready to be tested and critiqued. "You ready?"

"Absolutely." Myles nodded at her, picking up his fork. His moist lips stretched into a wide smile. "Let's dig in."

They eagerly tasted the other's dishes, their eyes floating to the ceiling as they took their time accessing the flavors and textures. It was like they were actually judging and real prizes were at stake, but it was all about the bragging rights. To Jackie's surprise and slight disappointment, though, Myles's food was superb. Like, restaurant-quality superb. Even with how he'd been showing off earlier, she hadn't expected it to turn out *this* good.

"What do you think?" he asked her, taking a swig of the wine she had on hand in case he wanted it. Jackie had never been a wine drinker and was having her usual rum.

She eyed him, still chewing. "You first."

"I can't deny, your food is very good," he admitted easily. "The steak is tender and well-seasoned, the rice al dente, the sauce is balanced. Everything pairs together very well. I'll likely clean my plate."

Jackie grinned, feeling a silly amount of pride at his approval. "Told you I knew what I was doing."

"Well, now I believe you. So what do you think of mine?"

Jackie was tempted to lie, but she knew she had to go ahead and give him his props. "Everything is dope. Like, *extremely* dope."

He blinked. "And 'dope' is good, right?"

Jackie burst out laughing. "Yes, Mr. Cornwall, 'dope' is good. If I'm being all the way honest, I'm greatly underselling it. I almost hope there are leftovers so I can take them for my lunch tomorrow and experience this again. You have some serious skills. I'm actually impressed."

"And surprised, right?" he challenged with an arched brow.

Fighting to keep her smile in check, Jackie took her time chewing before taking an extended sip of rum. But she finally conceded, "Yes, I admit I'm surprised. You got me."

Looking pleased, Myles sat back in his chair. "I've always liked proving people wrong."

They continued chatting as they ate, sharing stories about their backgrounds in between good-natured teases and jokes. Jackie was surprised at how much Myles laughed; just like she hadn't expected his cooking skills, she didn't expect him to have such a sense of humor. He was sitting in the kitchen in his shirt and tie, still thankfully showing off those sexy forearms, laughing and joking with her as if it were the most natural thing in the world. Jackie was glad she invited him over because she was enjoying their evening even more than she expected to.

Myles was having an equally good time. He'd been nervous when he showed up at Jackie's door, armed with the conventional gift of flowers. It was a thoughtless gift that surprisingly didn't blow up in his face, since Jackie squelched his assumption that she wouldn't appreciate them. Myles knew he had to get out of his own head, and also, put the fact that Jackie was a mechanic on the backburner. She was still a woman. A woman that looked damn good in leggings.

And who could make a simple cotton v-neck shirt look like the sexiest garment in creation.

He honestly couldn't remember the last time he'd laughed so much, or enjoyed such an easy rapport and banter with a woman. None of the ladies he'd dated previously had much of a sense of humor; the prim and proper women he was accustomed to weren't exactly known for letting loose. But Jackie had no qualms about being silly, and while Myles oftentimes found that off-putting, that wasn't the case now. She wasn't being crude for the sake of it or nonsensical to the point where he wanted to roll his eyes. And he could tell she wasn't *trying*; she was just being herself. And he found himself endeared to that.

After they ate, he wanted to go ahead and clean the kitchen but Jackie insisted it could wait, grabbing his wrist and pulling him to the living room. She released him once they were near the couch, and flashbacks of their heated kisses from the night before sent heat up the back of her neck.

"Do you have to leave?" she asked him, sliding her hands to her lower back. "How much longer do I have you for?"

He glanced at his watch but really didn't register the time. "I wasn't planning on leaving just yet. Unless you-"

"Good." She stepped forward and wrapped her arms around his neck, pressing herself to him. She realized they hadn't hugged or really touched much at all since he arrived and she was done depriving herself. She inhaled his cologne and smiled when he hugged her back as firmly as she was holding him. "'Cause I'm not ready for you to leave."

Myles's fingers flexed on her waist before he eased back slightly, looking down at her. "Then we're on the same page."

Her bottom lip disappeared between her teeth as she grabbed his tie and gently pulled him closer. When his face was hovering above hers, she asked, "About this, too?"

She lifted her lips to his, her free hand clamping the back of his neck. Myles responded to her immediately, stepping closer and sliding his arm back around her. The kiss was deep and probing, lasting several delicious moments before they each pulled back. Jackie gazed up at him, battling with herself as to whether she should just lead him back to her bedroom like she wanted to do. She was intensely eager to see if his skills in the bedroom were as good as his skills in the kitchen.

Resisting the temptation, she forced herself to calm down. She still didn't feel Myles was ready to go there with her yet, despite the heat she could clearly see in his eyes.

"What are we going to do now?" he asked in a low voice. His gaze kept dropping to her mouth and his hands remained lingering on her hips.

Licking her lips to keep from saying what she really wanted to say, Jackie took a beat before taking another step back, causing Myles's hands to fall. "I'll show you. Be right back."

She scurried off to her bedroom and Myles eyed her until she was out of sight, then removed his glasses and ran a hand down his face. He turned away, trying to will his hardening erection back to sleep. Jackie had such a potent effect on him that he almost didn't know how to handle it. He wasn't accustomed to such intense reaction to a woman he didn't know that well. Part of him was disappointed that she hadn't tackled him again like she did the night before.

When she returned a couple minutes later, Myles's eyebrows shot up when he saw she was holding a couple of board games.

"Umm...what is that for?" he asked, eyeing the games with an arched brow.

"What do you mean? We're gonna play."

"Really, Jackie? Board games?"

"What's the matter with board games?"

"It's silly."

"So?" She set the games on the coffee table and looked at him with a challenging glare and both hands on her hips. "Too stuffy to get silly?"

He pursed his lips, recognizing the challenge for what it was. This wasn't what he thought he'd be doing when he came to see her for what was essentially their first official date, but he could only imagine the ribbing he'd get if he resisted. He'd never been into board games but he wasn't about to be shown up.

"Fine," he clipped. He sat on the couch, smoothing his tie and poking the game boxes with his fingertips. "Let's do it, then."

Jackie grinned triumphantly as she joined him on the couch, grabbing the box of Monopoly. She started to give him a brief rundown of how to play but he insisted he could figure it out as they went, saying it couldn't be all that hard. Jackie just shrugged and started pulling out game pieces.

They proceeded to play Monopoly and then Scrabble, the vibe not quite as lighthearted as when they were cooking and eating since Myles was mainly just playing out of spite and wasn't as eager to banter. But Jackie ignored his change in attitude, mainly because them playing games kept her from jumping him like she *really* wanted to.

After about an hour, though, Myles looked at his watch again and stretched. "I suppose I should be getting home. It's after eleven."

"You don't have to go home."

He looked at her, mildly surprised. "Don't you have to get up early?"

Shrugging, Jackie rubbed a hand back and forth along her thigh. "It'll still be early if you're here or not. If you don't mind having to go home to change before work..."

"You...really want me to spend the night?"

"Yeah. That's if you're done pouting about playing the board games."

"I was not pouting. And I played, didn't I?"

"Grudgingly. But whatever. If you want or need to leave, I get it, but I'm telling you that you can stay." Her other hand inched closer to his on the couch between them. "I've had a good time with you tonight, Myles. Call me greedy but I'm not ready for it to be over with just because it's a week night."

His chin quivered with a smile. Closing the distance between their hands, he took hold of her surprisingly smooth fingers, noting the midnight blue polish on her short nails. It flattered him that she seemed to enjoy his company so much, even if it baffled him. His rational brain told him to just end the evening where it was and go home to get in his cold bed alone.

But whenever he started to tell her he should go, he couldn't make his mouth move. The next day was Friday; he wouldn't have a ton going on at work. He paused, trying to recall what he had on his calendar.

Mistaking this for hesitancy, Jackie eased her hand from his and stood, snatching up the game boxes. "Never mind. I was just putting it out there but if you have to go, then go."

He blinked at the sudden change in her attitude. "What? Jackie, I-"

"Forget it, Myles." She stomped off towards her room. "I just saved you from having to figure out how to let me down politely, like you were apparently trying to do. Just give me a call tomorrow. That's *if* you have time."

"What the..." Myles sat there, befuddled at how things had taken such a turn. Jackie sounded ticked off; almost insulted. The fact that she had jumped to conclusions and acted like he'd done something wrong irked him. Jackie's attitude was going to be an issue and he had to wonder how eager he was to put up with it.

When it was clear she wasn't coming back out, Myles stood and stalked back to her bedroom, half expecting to find the door closed and locked. Surprisingly, it was ajar, and he hesitated only briefly before slowly pushing it open. He wasn't usually in the habit of entering a woman's bedroom uninvited, but this was a necessary anomaly.

"Jackie?"

She was sitting on the side of her bed with her arms folded, and swung her face to the opposite wall when she heard his voice. "I thought you had to go."

"I never said that." He stepped into the room, barely taking note of the heavy blue-gray curtains framing gauzy white ones, the pale gray walls, and the various paintings of faceless Black people that hung on the wall above her queen-sized canopy bed. His hands slid into his pockets as he looked at her, unmoved that she was refusing to do the same. "*You* said that. Because apparently you can read my mind?"

Sucking her teeth, she cut her eyes at him. "You got jokes?"

"I'm not joking. But I'm hoping *you* are with all this."

"Look, this isn't necessary. It doesn't have to be a big deal. You said it's getting late so I said you can just go-"

"Are you always prone to tantrums when you think you're not getting your way?" Myles stepped closer to the bed, his frown deepening slightly. "Is jumping to conclusions your usual behavior? Because I must say, Jackie, I'm not a fan of that."

"This is not a damn tantrum." Jackie shot off the bed and stalked over to her dresser, mindlessly picking up a comb and tapping it. "I extended an invitation and you were clearly hesitating. I'm not a fan of *that*. If you're still not sure about me-"

"My *hesitancy*, as you call it, was me recalling my calendar for tomorrow morning. Which I would have gladly relayed to you if you hadn't flown off the handle. I actually wanted to stay, Jackie."

The tapping stopped and Jackie looked over at him, her eyes going from annoyed to regretful like a switch had been flipped. "Oh..."

"Yeah."

She sighed, turning to him with a hand on her belly. "Well, I feel ridiculous."

"You should."

"I'm sorry for assuming, Myles." She lifted a hand before dropping it, shaking her head as if her actions were finally hitting her. "That was...well, it was childish. And I'm not gonna try to make an excuse. Guess I have to check myself."

"I agree. Jackie, whatever it is we're doing...I'm enjoying it. I'm intrigued by you, despite our many glaring differences. But I don't want to constantly butt heads with you, especially over trivial things. If we're going to do this, can we agree to do better about communicating?"

"That's fair." She crossed over to him, wanting to take his hand but they were both still stuffed in his pockets. "I'm enjoying this, too. And for the record, 'what it is we're doing' is dating. Building a relationship. We're having some bumps in the road, that's all."

Myles didn't speak for a moment. "That's all, huh? You don't think this is crazy of us to even try this? I'm sure it's not lost on you that we're not an ideal match. Yes we're attracted to each other but...I'll be honest, Jackie, as recently as yesterday I was trying to decide if I even *liked* you, despite my attraction."

Jackie couldn't help but laugh at that. "I'm not mad at that 'cause I was having similar thoughts. I mean, this might *be* crazy but I realized I like you more than I care about that. It might work, it might not. But I'm willing to try it and see. If you're not..." Her eyes flitted briefly to the ground. "I get it."

A few quiet moments passed and Jackie had to remind herself to just wait. It made sense that he needed a minute.

Finally, he gently grabbed her hand and brought it to his lips, stepping closer so their bodies were barely touching. "I'm willing to try, too. Whether or not I should, I'm not ready to walk away from you yet."

Her smile spread instantly at his words. "So...we're dating?"

"We are dating."

"Exclusively? Or do you want to see other people?"

"I'm not currently interested in that. If that changes, I'll tell you. Do you?"

"Not as of right now. I'm typically a one-man woman. But we can save the titles for after we've tested the waters for a while...so we're not putting unnecessary pressure on things from the jump. What do you think of that?"

"You make a good point. I'd rather not add labels this early on, either. So I suppose that means we're seeing each other exclusively, though unlabeled, until such time one of us decides they want to either see someone else, declare ourselves in a serious committed relationship with boyfriend/girlfriend titling, or end it altogether. Agreed?"

"Agreed, you hot nerd. Now kiss me and make it official, Mr. Cornwall."

Chuckling and shaking his head, Myles cupped her chin and claimed her lips, and she immediately slid her arms around his neck, her tongue searching for his. They stood there making out for several long minutes, in no hurry. Now that they had put it out there that they were dating and in a budding relationship, the kisses felt different. The caresses were more intentional and the moans more concentrated. Their relationship didn't feel as new as it was when they were in each other's arms.

Myles ended up spending the night, as they both wanted him to. After going to clean up the kitchen together, they freshened up (Myles kept a toiletry kit in his car), then slept together in her bed, clothed. Jackie resisted the urge to sleep naked like she usually did. Myles removed his button-down shirt and tie and his pants, mostly because he didn't want them to get wrinkled, and he took the time to meticulously fold and set them aside before getting into bed. But Jackie didn't care. She was more than happy to have him in her bed in his t-shirt and boxer briefs. And socks, which he insisted on keeping on.

They didn't have sex but there was plenty more making out before they finally dozed off for the night. They started out cuddled up but eventually drifted to opposite sides of the bed, the separation comfortable and unstrained.

Incessant doorbell ringing woke them up before Myles's alarm had the chance to go off. He sat up first, frowning in the direction of the door before gently shaking Jackie awake. She sat up with a jolt, rubbing her eyes and squinting.

"What the hell is that??" she practically shrieked.

"Someone is at the door."

"Shit...what time is it?"

Myles reached over for his watch that was on the nightstand, simultaneously slipping his glasses on. "It's almost six. Were you expecting someone?"

"At six in the morning? Hell no." Jackie briefly checked her phone for any possible messages from the unwanted visitor before she flung the covers back and swung her legs over the side of the bed, cursing under her breath. She didn't know who could possibly be at her door this time of morning, and for what. Cassidy hated getting up early unless she absolutely had to. Her dad lived out of state, and wasn't one for surprise visits. The only other person she could think of with this kind of nerve was Chanel, and if it was her, Jackie wouldn't even try to stop herself from going off. And possibly throwing hands.

Myles had hurriedly pulled on his pants and followed her, not wanting to leave her alone with whoever this was that showed up uninvited first thing in the morning.

"Don't judge me for the indelicate language you'll hear me use on whoever this is," Jackie warned him over her shoulder right before she reached the front door. She adjusted the purple silk scarf covering her short hair. "I'm not a fan of pop-up visits during the day so they especially piss me off at the crack of dawn."

"I won't hold it against you. I'm not supposed to be up for another hour so I'm almost as annoyed as you are."

"Good." But some of Jackie's ire instantly cooled when she checked the peephole and saw who was standing there. She whirled around to Myles, who was looking at her curiously.

"Someone you know?" he asked, noting how stricken she suddenly looked.

"Yeah." She scoffed, not believing this was happening. "Yeah, I know him, all right."

"Him?"

Jackie swung open the door, finally putting an end to the constant doorbell ringing. With a hand on her hip, her eyes were anything but welcoming when she demanded, "What the hell are you doing here, Ringo?"

Chapter 11

Myles had never gotten dressed so fast.

He didn't know what to think, seeing a man show up at the door of the woman he's seeing first thing in the morning. In his mind, this Ringo gentleman would only be comfortable enough to do that if he and Jackie were close. And with the look Jackie had in her eyes when she realized who it was, Myles couldn't help but assume they were.

"Myles!" Jackie exclaimed as he brushed by them, fully dressed and keys in hand. "Myles, you don't have to leave. This is not what it seems like!"

Myles didn't respond, because he couldn't. His head was spinning. This was new to him and he didn't know how to properly react or handle it, so he felt it was best he just leave. His hands were actually shaking.

"Myles-"

"I have to go, Jackie," he mumbled when he was at the door. The unwelcome visitor, Ringo, just picked up a magazine from the end table like he didn't hear what was going on, his long wavy locs pulled into a ponytail. He wore a leather jacket, a skintight black t-shirt, gray sweatpants, and white Air Force Ones. It was like he just threw on something and came over, and he didn't seem intent on leaving until his purpose was fulfilled.

"I'll leave you to handle...whatever this is," Myles said to Jackie, his voice slightly lowered, jerking his head in Ringo's direction. "I can't..."

"What did we say *just* last night about jumping to conclusions and communicating?" Jackie hissed, grabbing his arm. "Ringo is my ex. I have no idea what he's doing here. But don't let him run you off!"

"You didn't try very hard to make him leave," Myles noted, his tone now biting. "He came right in and seems to be making himself at home. And I didn't hear any of the *indelicate language* that you were going to unleash on whoever the unwanted visitor was, so that only makes me think he's not that *unwanted*."

"Myles-"

"Jackie." Ringo called out, tossing the magazine back to the end table and sliding his hands into his pockets, unbothered by the trouble he was causing. "You and me got shit to handle."

Her face screwed in angry confusion. "What are you talking about? We don't have any-"

Myles pulled his arm free and hurried out to his car, barely even glancing at her as he got in and pulled away. Jackie stood looking after him for a moment in disbelief before she stepped back inside and slammed the door shut, turning and glaring at Ringo with a look that could melt steel.

"What the fuck, Ringo??"

"We need to talk, Jacks."

"I have a damn phone. I'm sure you still have the number despite telling me to lose yours. You put me out of your house and then show up at mine this time of morning unannounced. Somebody better be dead."

"Jacks-"

"It's Jackie to you."

He paused, rearing slightly. "It's like that?"

"You made it like that."

"Look," he blew out a frustrated breath, "I told Sharonda I wanted to be with her for real, in the same place. Offered to help her move out here."

Jackie paused and crossed her arms, hunching a shoulder. "Yeah, so?"

"I didn't want any secrets so I told her all about us; my history with you and how we've fooled around since me and her got together. She got upset and said she needed some time. Then late last night, she called and ended it. Said she wasn't surprised and suspected I wasn't keeping it in my pants all this time we were apart but now that she knew, she couldn't deal with it. She actually wished I hadn't told her about it."

Jackie just stared at him. "And what the hell does that have to do with me, Ringo?"

"You don't think you owe me? I lost my relationship because of you."

"You lost your relationship because of *you*. I wasn't in a relationship with her; you were. You chose to sleep with me; I didn't force you to do a damn thing. So whatever happens between y'all is between y'all."

"Jacks-"

"Jackie."

His nostrils flared. "Jackie, I came here to tell you we can do this now. Be together, for real. I'm not attached to anybody so there's nothing stopping us."

"I'm good."

" What you mean, *you're good*? I'd think you'd be happy to hear about this, since you were on me about getting back together."

"I like your damn nerve, Ringo. From one, you're the one that left me in the first place. I admit I showed my ass and can't really blame you, but still. Then you got with her not even two weeks later. Two, I am not some consolation prize. If you wouldn't leave her for me then, don't come running to me 'cause she's left you now. And three - and most importantly – I am not available. I'm seeing someone."

"Not that suit that I sent running out of here?"

"Yes, him. Suit or not, I'm feeling him and you'd better hope that he's not thinking the most about your coming over here telling me this bullshit. But even if he decides to walk, I still wouldn't get back with you, Ringo. Clearly, you and I don't work. What happened at your house proved that. We don't exactly bring out the best in each other and that's not the kind of relationship I want."

"Are you seriously acting like you want that corny-looking dude over me and all the history we have?"

"I'm not acting."

"Wait a damn minute...Myles? Isn't that the asshole that tried to set you up with his sister 'cause he thought you were gay? Now you're fucking around with him? I've never known you to be desperate, Jackie. You don't have to stoop this low to get over me."

Jackie chuckled sarcastically at his nerve. "You arrogant asshole. I haven't reached out to your ass *once* since you kicked me to the curb after cussing me out and telling me to lose your number, yet you ran over here in the wee hours trying to get *me* to take *you* back 'cause your dick deflated after getting dumped. So it sounds like there's only *one* desperate muthafucka up in here and it sure as fuck ain't me."

"Jackie-"

"And as for who I'm fucking around with and why, don't worry about all that. Just like you used to tell me regarding your *situation*, it's not for you to get."

Ringo sighed. "Look... I get it. Be pissed at me. But the way I see it, Sharonda calling it quits just means we're supposed to give this thing another shot."

"That's not what it means. You just don't like being alone; you never have. That's why you got with her so quick after we broke up in the first place, and you chose someone in a whole other state so you could feel single while technically still being linked up. I'm not interested in being your crutch, Ringo, and that would be the case whether Myles was in the picture or not."

"You don't even like corporate dudes like that. He doesn't even look like your type."

"That's what I like about him. But regardless, it's not your damn business. So find you another warm body at one of your revues or something to cling onto because I am no longer available, to you or anyone else that's not the man I woke up with this morning. Now that *that's* settled," Jackie moved over to the door, "Get the fuck outta my house."

As Jackie figured would happen, Myles was dodging her. She knew he'd gone to work, but he only spoke to her for a few minutes before muttering something about needing to rush off to a meeting. She didn't even get a chance to explain about Ringo.

She had a full morning at the garage, but when an afternoon appointment cancelled, Jackie told Cassidy that she needed to make a quick run and rushed to her car, wanting to see Myles. She hated that she didn't have time to change into something more presentable, but it couldn't be helped. With the way he had run out of her house that morning and how he was avoiding her now, she wanted to make sure they were okay. A teeny part of her was affronted that he'd fled like he did instead of staying and dealing with it, but she told herself to give him the benefit of the doubt. She could imagine that this was a scenario he hadn't dealt with, with the kind of women he'd told her he was used to dating.

Jackie arrived at Myles's office building and checked her appearance in the visor mirror, removing the scarf covering her short hair and grabbing a wet wipe from her dashboard to clean any dirt from her face. Aside from smearing on some lip gloss and throwing a jacket over her coveralls, she figured that was the best she could do, as far as her appearance.

Before getting out of the car, she tried to call Myles one more time. When it went to voicemail, she sucked her teeth in frustration. They were going to have to have a talk about how to handle intense unexpected situations, because this wasn't it.

Jackie told herself to think positively as she headed inside the building, hoping that Myles wasn't swamped with meetings or something and would be willing to talk. Part of her warned that it wasn't the best idea to ambush him at his job like this, but Jackie had never been known for her patience. She wanted to work this out and make sure they were still good; their relationship was just getting off the ground and she didn't want a misunderstanding to cause a snag in it not even twenty-four hours in.

"May I help you?" the lady at the welcome desk in the lobby greeted Jackie when she approached. She smiled politely as her eyes subtly swept up and down Jackie's coveralls.

"Hey, good afternoon. I'm here to see Myles Cornwall; he's on the tenth floor." Jackie recalled him telling her that when they were at the restaurant a couple of nights earlier, though she couldn't remember how it had come up.

"Is he expecting you?"

"He surely is." The lie rolled right off Jackie's tongue.

"May I have your name, please?"

Jackie hesitated only slightly, wondering if the woman was going to call Myles and catch her in a bold-faced lie. "Jackie Malone."

The woman nodded and punched a few buttons on her computer, apparently pleased. "Ms. Malone, if you could just sign in right here, I'll give you a visitor access badge and you can go right on up."

Jackie breathed a sigh of relief as she scribbled her name and check-in time in the sign-in book, then accepted the laminated card showcasing her visitor status that would also allow her to access the elevators. After a couple of quick directional instructions from the receptionist, Jackie thanked her and headed towards the elevator bank. A couple of people in business suits passed her and gave her curious looks, and Jackie questioned her decision to come there in her work coveralls. Even with a jacket over them, she looked extremely out of place in this sea of marble and glass and business formality.

"Oh well, I'm here now," she muttered, stepping onto an elevator and pushing the button for the tenth floor. Rubbing her hands together before linking them in front of her, she eyed the digital number showing the ascending floors, her mind on what she was going to say to Myles.

The doors slid open to plush pale gray carpeting and a large curved desk with an elevated platform straight ahead sitting in front of a quiet waterfall that the company name protruded through in elegant silver block letters. A Black woman with a dark burgundy braided updo sat at the desk, smiling as Jackie approached. Like the woman in the lobby, she clearly took note of Jackie's attire.

"Welcome to J&M Unity Financial. How can I help you today?"

"Good afternoon. I'm Jackie Malone; here to see Myles Cornwall. Love the hair, by the way."

"Thank you!" The woman, whose nameplate read Dandria, blinked and tilted her head slightly, her gaze shifting from polite to pondering. "Have we met? You look familiar."

Now Jackie was looking at her with the same curious gaze, her own head tilting. "Um, not that I'm aware of..."

"Oh yes, I remember!" Dandria snapped her fingers, pointing a long red-painted nail. "Jacqueline Malone! You used to work over at Joswell International, right?"

Floored, Jackie nodded. "I did, actually. You worked there, also? Forgive me for not remembering..."

"Oh no, I don't expect you to remember. I was an executive assistant in another part of the office; we didn't deal with each other," Dandria insisted with a wave of her hand. "But I certainly knew who *you* were. You were the HBIC over there before you left."

Jackie couldn't help but grin. She didn't miss her previous work life at all but it still gave her a surge of pride that anyone thought of her as the Head Bitch in Charge. Technically, she would've had another level or two to go to reach that status, at least as far as job title.

Now, she *was* the HBIC for her own business. The thought made her grin spread even wider.

"I did my thing," Jackie replied humbly. "I see you left there, too...are you liking it better here?"

"Absolutely. That place became a cesspool for nonsense and confusion after a while, once that new CEO took over. Believe me, you and I aren't the only ones that left. You changed industries, right?"

"I did. I'm a full-time mechanic now. My garage is over on Lynn Boulevard; The Auto Loft."

"Oh okay!" Dandria nodded, Jackie's appearance apparently now making sense. "That is amazing, though I admit I never would have guessed you'd go into that in a million years. That's a far cry from the high-level executive track you were on. But I admire you for going for yours." She sat up straight in a snap and glanced around, as if remembering she was at work and not out gossiping with a girlfriend. "You said you're here to see Myles Cornwall, yes? Let me call back and see if he's available. One sec."

Jackie waited as Dandria made the call, her voice morphing back into warm formality as she informed someone that Myles had a visitor. She gave Jackie's name, said a couple of 'yes' and 'all right' and 'that's correct' responses, and let the person know that it was important, which Jackie hadn't told her but still appreciated nonetheless. Dandria hung up the phone and smiled.

"He's in, right?" Jackie asked, wondering if she sounded as eager to Dandria as she did to herself.

"He is. He has someone in his office currently and there's one other visitor waiting for him, but if you're not in a huge hurry, I can take you on back there."

Jackie hesitated, checking the time. She did need to get back to the garage, but she figured Irv and Jimmy could handle things until she got back. She'd send Cassidy a text to let her know she got held up. "I have some time."

"Excellent! Follow me."

Dandria stood and smoothed down her black and white pinstripe crew neck dress with a tie at the waist before stepping towards a side hallway. Jackie followed, unable to resist eying Dandria sauntering in front of her in the knee-length dress and black peep-toe pumps. She tugged the sides of her jacket closer around her coveralls, suddenly feeling even more out of place.

The area Dandria led Jackie to housed Myles's office along with one other on the opposite side, both sporting frosted glass walls and stylish metal doors. Each had a desk sitting perpendicular nearby, where their personal executive assistants sat guard. Dandra veered towards the one on the left, speaking to her before briefly introducing Jackie and heading back to her own desk, wishing her a good day.

"It shouldn't be too long, Ms. Malone," the assistant said politely. "Mr. Cornwall's phone is on Do Not Disturb at the moment because he's in a meeting but it should be wrapping up shortly. Would you like some water or coffee while you wait?"

"No thank you; I'm good."

"You can have a seat right over there, and I'll let him know you're here as soon as his meeting is done."

"Thank you."

Jackie moved towards the cushy chairs that lined the wall between the two offices, not missing the assistant's curious perusal of her outfit when she thought Jackie couldn't see her. She made herself ignore it as she took a seat a couple chairs down from a woman who looked like she was heading to high tea in her vintage floral midi dress and white t-strap heels. She held her quilted white purse in her lap, occasionally tapping her manicured pale pink nails impatiently on top of it. Her long black hair was pulled into a low ponytail and secured with white silk ribbon. When Jackie sat near her, she glanced over, not even trying to hide her distaste for Jackie's coveralls and work boots. Jackie ignored her, though part of her itched to ask her who the hell she was looking at like that.

Be good, she told herself. *This is not the time or place for you to show your ass again.*

After fifteen minutes, Jackie checked the time again and contemplated letting Myles know she was out there waiting for him. She had already texted Cassidy to let her know that she was running behind getting back, and 'forgot' to respond when Cassidy asked what she was doing. When another few minutes passed, she did go ahead and text Myles to let him know she was in the building, hoping that would give him a nudge. She again questioned her decision to just show up unannounced; she had no idea of his schedule and realized he might not have any time to spare, although she'd hope he would carve out a couple of minutes for her.

Finally, Myles's office door opened. Jackie sat forward immediately, and noticed the prim and proper woman near her did, too, looking just as eager.

Is she here to see Myles?

Before Jackie's imagination could run amok, Myles stepped out, followed by Ethan. They were still talking amongst themselves in low voices, Myles's back turned to the waiting area. Neither of them glanced in Jackie's direction.

"Mr. Cornwall, you have visitors."

Myles just held up a hand indicating to give him a minute, not yet turning around as he continued talking to Ethan. Ethan noticed Jackie first, his eyes showing clear but pleasant surprise. They dimmed slightly, though, when they slid over to Ms. Prim and Proper. He cleared his throat and nodded his head in their direction, causing Myles to finally turn around.

To say Myles was shocked was an understatement. He was momentarily paralyzed, as the last thing he had expected was to see Jackie sitting outside of his office, and in her coveralls, no less. His face and neck flushed with heated embarrassment.

"Jacqueline," he greeted her, his voice thick with forced civility. "I wasn't expecting you."

"I know." She stood, forcing herself to ignore that he didn't exactly look happy to see her. "I apologize for just stopping by but I need a minute, if possible."

"Hello, Myles, darling."

Myles's face tightened. Jackie looked over at the other woman with a clear frown that only deepened when she stepped closer, and he prayed that Jackie didn't go off and cause a scene.

"Cynthia." His voice was clipped. "Why are you here?"

"We have things to discuss. This silliness of you not talking to me has gone on long enough. Shall we go in your office?"

"No," Myles stopped her as she started to head in that direction. "This is not the time or place, Cynthia, and I believe I severed whatever ties we had already."

"You couldn't have possibly meant-"

"Jackie, it's so good to see you again!" Ethan interjected, stepping in front of Myles with a warm smile. When she placed her hands in his outstretched ones, he leaned down to kiss her cheek. "You surely are a sight for sore eyes this afternoon."

"Aww thank you, Ethan," Jackie beamed gratefully. "That's so sweet of you. It's good to see you, too."

She didn't even care if he was putting on. His warm welcome was enough to put her at ease, especially since Myles hadn't exactly greeted her with open arms and there was another woman there that clearly wanted his attention, too. Jackie wondered if she was one of Myles's exes or if there was something he hadn't told her. But Myles's expression didn't look caught; it looked perturbed.

"Myles, why don't you take Jackie on into your office?" Ethan offered, placing a warm hand on Jackie's shoulder and looking at his friend pointedly. "We can continue our conversation later."

Myles didn't look pleased with that suggestion. "I'm not sure this is the time to-"

"Myles, what is going on? Who is this?" Cynthia demanded, glaring at Ethan before her affronted frown landed on Jackie. It wasn't lost on any of them that Ethan hadn't acknowledged her. "Is this one of your homeless people that you like to try to help? Since when do you let them just show up at your office?"

Jackie's mouth automatically opened to respond but Myles hurriedly held up a hand and said, "Not that it's any of your business, Cynthia, but no, she is not. Far from it. Jacqueline is a good friend of mine and a successful entrepreneur."

He could feel Ethan's eyes boring into him and Jackie didn't look too pleased, either, but he kept his eyes trained on Cynthia, who looked at Jackie in a renewed yet still skeptical light.

"Is that right?"

"Jackie is a little more than *that*, though, Myles, right?" Ethan pressed.

"Oh, is she?" Cynthia's eyes darted between the three of them curiously. "That's interesting. I've never heard you mention a Jacqueline before. Exactly who else is she to you, Myles?"

Myles hated being put in this position. He felt like all three of them had put him on the spot, and it angered him. He had already spent the better part of the morning venting to Ethan about what happened with Jackie the previous night and early that morning with her unexpected visitor. He was still trying to wrap his brain around that, which was why he hadn't yet returned her calls. He had every intention of doing so later, but she just couldn't wait and had to show up at his office. And it was just his luck that Cynthia also decided to do her own unannounced visit at the same time.

Jackie stared at him, feeling more ridiculous with every silent moment that ticked by. But now it had nothing to do with her out-of-place attire. Here she was so concerned about Myles and wanting to make sure they were good, and he wouldn't even acknowledge the true nature of their relationship. He called her Jacqueline, and spoke to and of her like she was some colleague and not the woman he'd spent the previous night cuddled up with. He wouldn't even look at her. Jackie didn't know if he was embarrassed of her simply because of how she was dressed or if he was just embarrassed of her, period. He'd apparently told Ethan about the change in their relationship, but he clearly didn't want whoever this woman was to know who she was to him, since he still hadn't spoken up.

Over it, she scoffed and shook her head, turning to the woman fully. "Jackie Malone. I'm not anyone important." She spun around to Ethan, flashing a sad smile. "It was good to see you, Ethan. And thank you for the warm welcome."

"Jackie, you don't have to leave," Ethan insisted, again looking pointedly at Myles. He didn't understand why his friend had suddenly gone mute. "I can walk Cynthia out so you and Myles can discuss things alone."

"It's okay, Ethan," Jackie replied, her voice softening slightly. Sadness overtook her momentary anger at Myles's behavior, and she gave a disappointed chuckle. "Mr. Cornwall clearly doesn't have time. This was my mistake; I'll get out of the way now."

Myles's head snapped up at her words, his eyes meeting hers briefly before she turned and hurried towards the elevator. He started to go after her, but by the time he got his feet to finally move, she was already gone.

"Why do I feel like I'm in the middle of some kind of soap opera?" Cynthia mused with a hand to her chest. "Myles, why was that woman here?"

Myles glared at her, as upset at her as he was with himself. He knew he messed up.

"Good day, Cynthia," he snapped, stalking towards his office and closing the door behind him.

Unsurprisingly, Ethan wasted no time storming back into Myles's office. Barely five minutes after Jackie left, he knocked on Myles's door, not waiting on an invitation to barge in.

"What the hell, Myles?"

Myles pinched the bridge of his nose under his glasses before taking them off altogether and placing them on his desk. "You don't have to tell me I handled that poorly."

"'Poorly' is a *nice* way of putting it. What the hell is wrong with you?"

"Look, I know that I should have been more vocal out there but...I froze. All three of you put me on the spot."

"And? You act like you're never put on the spot any other time. It's practically a daily thing here at work."

"Work is one thing, my personal relationships are another. Jackie showing up here out of the blue, and dressed like she was...it threw me."

"So, what, you're ashamed of her? You two just started dating; I thought you were over the hang-up of her being a mechanic."

"I am."

"Just as long as she doesn't look like one, right?"

Myles huffed a frustrated breath. He grabbed his cell phone that he hadn't bothered to check in the past couple of hours. "I didn't know she was coming here. I can only imagine it was to talk about our situation, which she should know better than to do. She might not work in this arena anymore but I'm sure that doesn't mean she's forgotten about executive decorum."

"Oh don't give me that crap," Ethan spat. "You were too embarrassed to admit who she was to you because she was in her work clothes. Just admit it. That's bad enough, but it was your ex you couldn't admit it to. How does *that* look? Do you want Cynthia back?"

"Absolutely not."

"Then why couldn't you tell her that Jackie is who you're seeing now? Why do you care what she thinks about it?"

"I..." Myles couldn't answer that question. He wanted to say he *didn't* care what Cynthia thought, but his actions had indicated otherwise. It hadn't occurred to him in the moment how his hesitancy would come across, not only to Jackie but to Cynthia. Now if she ever did find out he and Jackie were together, she'd know he was initially ashamed to admit as much to her. That was if Jackie even wanted to keep seeing him after all this.

Ethan just looked at him with clear disapproval and Myles wondered if he was again questioning their friendship. Myles could admit that whole scene hadn't been his proudest moment, but he couldn't let go of the notion that Jackie had added to it by showing up unannounced at his place of business in dirty coveralls. He didn't want to ask himself how different his reaction would have been if she'd been wearing regular clothes; he knew the answer and it didn't make him come out looking any better.

"I don't even know what to say about you, man," Ethan muttered. He turned to leave, his hand on the doorknob. "You really need to get your shit together. And if Jackie leaves you alone over this, I won't blame her."

He left, and Myles stared after him before sucking his teeth and putting his glasses back on. He refused to be the only one at fault for this. Jackie had kicked it off when she welcomed some other man into her house in the wee hours of the morning instead of sending him away. Then she showed up at his job wanting to talk about it. He couldn't imagine she would have been much more receptive had the roles been reversed.

But the look on her face before she left cooled some of his stubborn ire, not to mention her parting words. He could only hope that wasn't some subliminal passive-aggressive way of ending things. He didn't want that, despite his frustration. And when he finally checked his messages and saw how many times she'd tried to call and text him, including one shortly before he saw her letting him know she was there, he felt even less indignant. If only he'd checked his phone. Hell, if only he'd just told her they'd talk about everything later during the brief time they spoke earlier. But he'd been too in his feelings to do that.

The way that man showed up at Jackie's and walked in like he was entitled stuck in Myles's craw. Not to mention the fact that the man was so vastly different from him. He could totally see him – Ringo, was it? – as being Jackie's type. She said he was her ex...was he there to get her back? Part of Myles hated that he had run off instead of staying and demanding some answers. That's what Ethan thought he should've done. And Myles now realized how it made him look that he didn't.

Frustrated thinking about all of this, he tried to get his focus back on work. He had too much on his plate to sit stewing over relationship issues, and he had frittered away enough time already. He'd deal with Jackie later.

Myles managed to keep his mind on work for the next few hours. He had a call with Veronica, the woman he'd met at the charity gala he attended with Cynthia who wanted to start a foundation for the homeless. She caught him up on how things were progressing, and he told her about the project he was working on to get houses converted into shelters, along with his plan for a job training program. It was encouraging how excited Veronica got about his ideas, and asked him to consider being on her foundation board. Myles didn't have to consider it; he accepted on the spot.

At least something positive had come of his afternoon. As excited as he was about the foundation, the issue with Jackie still lingered in the back of his mind. Of course she hadn't reached out to him since she left earlier. Myles knew he should make the first move, but he wasn't sure what to say, especially since part of him hadn't let go of his frustration over what he felt was Jackie's part in everything. But he figured telling her that wouldn't go over well.

Maybe this was a sign that they just weren't a match. They were *so* different, and he clearly still had some hang-ups he hadn't realized. Myles could see it just becoming a bigger issue the further they progressed. He figured Jackie would likely agree that they should just nip things in the bud now, before they totally slid back to the disdain they previously had for each other. Jackie might have been there already, for all he knew.

He popped a couple of Tylenol for the lingering headache he'd been trying to ignore and got up to head to the break room for a snack. He had a mini fridge in his office that he kept fruit and bottled smoothies in for when he felt peckish during the day, but that wasn't going to cut it this time. He wanted something sugary, so to the vending machine he went.

When he saw Morton and Dennis sitting in there eating some takeout from a nearby café, Myles groaned out loud. Neither of them seemed to notice, though, barely acknowledging him with nods before going back to their conversation. Myles just headed to the vending machine, even more intent on getting his snack as quickly as possible and getting back to his office.

"I'm telling you, man, that broad I went out with last night better be glad I was in such a good mood 'cause I spent a *grip* on her," Dennis groused, shaking soy sauce onto his beef fried rice.

"Where'd y'all go?" Morton asked.

"That new steakhouse across town. Man, she wanted appetizers, the biggest damn steak on the menu, dessert, *and* drinks. After all that, she knew what the deal was. We went straight back to my place."

"I thought you said you weren't really feeling her."

"Oh, I was *feeling* her all right, especially after all that money I spent." Dennis jabbed a forkful of rice into his mouth, several kernels dropping into his lap. "After she ran up the bill like that, she owed me. And I made sure I got more than my money's worth."

Myles frowned in disgust. This was a grown man talking like this?

"I'll tell you someone I wish owed *me* something like that," Morton commented. "Did you see that chick that was here earlier?"

"Who?"

"I don't know her name or who she was here to see, but she had super short hair and some lips that I'd bet can do some *thangs*. She had on some coveralls like she just crawled out of a cave or out from under a car or something."

Myles shot up from where he'd knelt to try to determine the freshness of the honeybuns at the bottom of the vending machine, knowing Morton was talking about Jackie.

"I didn't see her," Dennis commented. "She was hot?"

"Man...those dirty coveralls couldn't hide all that body. Titties and ass for *days.* I actually wondered how I could get her in the elevator and then get us stuck in there together. When I tell you, the shit I would do to her-"

"I would advise you to watch what you say, Morton," Myles interjected, whirling around. "You are treading on *very* thin ice right now."

"What are you talking about?" Morton asked, rearing. Both he and Dennis were looking at Myles in surprise, as they'd never heard him sound so menacing or look so angry. His fists were actually clenched. "I'm talking to my boy; this doesn't have anything to do with you."

"Oh, but it does. Because the woman you're degrading happens to be with me."

Both men looked utterly floored.

"You??" Morton exclaimed. "I don't think we're talking about the same woman, dawg. I've seen some of the chicks you've been with and this one isn't even on your level. Fine as she was, she came up in here looking like somebody pulled her out of a-"

"I said *watch it,* Morton." Myles stalked over to their table, standing over Morton with a glare that meant business. "You two are nothing more than children in men's bodies and I've listened to the both of you say some of the most disrespectful things about women, and I was wrong for not calling you on it before. But now you're talking about *my* lady, and I will not stand for it. Say another word about her and I'll be meeting you outside before the day is out. I know what car you drive."

Both Morton and Dennis were rendered speechless. Myles's hazel eyes were almost catlike, and locked unwaveringly on Morton's as he leaned into his personal space. The look of concentrated venom was unmistakable and more chilling than any scowl.

Morton's hands lifted slightly. "My bad, man...I didn't know she was with you."

"It shouldn't matter who she's with. The way you two talk about women is embarrassing and disgusting. Both of you need to grow up and learn some respect instead of behaving like some horny and desperate adolescents."

Dennis sucked his teeth. "What are you gonna do, Cornwall, report us or something?"

Myles's glare slid to him. "I know your car, too."

No longer caring about his snack, Myles headed for the door, leaving the two men sitting stumped at the table. He was surprised to see Ethan standing just outside the entrance.

"Well, that was impressive."

Myles rolled his eyes and headed to his office, still too keyed up. Ethan caught up to him and clamped a hand on his shoulder, stopping him.

"What?" Myles snapped, whirling around.

"You know they can go report *you* now, right?"

"I don't care."

"Which is just what I figured. You wouldn't be this incensed over what they said about Jackie if she didn't matter to you. Hell, I've never seen you this pissed about *anything*, especially to the point of threatening people."

"They pissed me off."

"I know, and I get it, but if it had been about any other woman, excluding your mother or sister, would you have had such a strong reaction?"

Myles looked away, knowing he wouldn't have. He didn't say a word when he overheard the things they'd said about their coworker Davina a couple weeks earlier, despite how disgusted he'd been.

Ethan stepped to where he was in front of Myles. "You called her your lady, man, and I know you didn't just do that for those idiots' benefit. You want her. So do whatever you need to do to fix things. Don't let her get away, buddy. I think it's pretty clear that's not what you want."

Myles rubbed his throbbing temples as Ethan walked away. He did care about Jackie, and the look that she gave him before she left earlier still burned in his chest. But he still wasn't sure if that meant they needed to be together. He was going to have to slink back to her with yet another apology; how many times would she forgive him for his stupid blunders before she decided he wasn't worth the trouble? The fact that Myles kept screwing up with her was indicative enough, because while he wasn't the smoothest man on the planet, he was never *this* inept with women.

He trudged back to his office, not knowing what he was going to do.

Chapter 12

"Why are you looking like somebody stole all your sheep and oranges?"

Myles cast a brief confused frown at Mollie before shaking his head, deciding he didn't have the energy to ask what that meant. "I'm fine, Mollie."

"You are not. What, did some work deal fall through or something?"

He leaned back on the couch, closing his eyes and sliding his fingers back and forth across his forehead. "No."

"You get demoted?"

"No."

"Fired?"

"No."

"Castrated?"

"Mollie."

"I'm just trying to get you to tell me what's wrong with you. You've been pouting ever since I got here."

"I am not pouting. I'm just not in the mood for conversation." His eyes opened briefly, flitting to where she lounged on the opposite end of the couch. "Or company, for that matter."

"Well, too bad, 'cause I'm here now. You shouldn't have let me in."

"I didn't want to. But I knew you'd tell on me or pull some kind of childish prank if I didn't."

"You know me so well."

"Mollie..." He felt yet another headache coming on. "If you're going to be here, I need you to at least be quiet and respect that I don't want to talk about what's on my mind at the moment. If you can't do that, please leave."

She didn't say anything for a moment and Myles waited to see if she'd try to press some more or make another joke. Thankfully, she did neither.

"All right, I'll just sit here with you, then," she finally conceded, her voice uncharacteristically serious. "Just so you're not by yourself. Do you mind if I watch some TV, though?"

Myles just shrugged, throwing up a hand indifferently that landed back on the couch with a plunk. He closed his eyes and tried to pretend that he was alone, doing his best to drown out the voices from what sounded like some kind of reality show. Myles certainly never watched those, so having to expend energy to ignore it didn't help his agitation.

"You hungry?" Mollie finally asked after a while. "I can fix you a sandwich or something."

Myles's eyes stayed closed. "*You* just want a sandwich, Mollie. I can hear your stomach growling."

"Well hell, I'm low on groceries and only had a couple of cereal bars today. And a pack of Starburst. At least I'm trying to include you and not be greedy *and* selfish."

"How many times do I have to tell you to just ask if you need money? You don't need to be going around hungry when you have family that's more than willing and able to help you."

"And I love y'all for it but let's save the handouts for when things get dire. I'll appreciate these lean times when I hit it big and my name is in lights. For now, though, about that sandwich..."

Sighing, Myles threw up a tired hand again. "Go ahead, Mollie."

She hopped up and scurried to the kitchen, humming to herself as she made something to eat. Myles resisted the urge to check his phone yet again for any messages from Jackie; he knew there weren't any. They hadn't communicated since she left his office two days earlier, and Myles figured it would be on him to make the first move, if there were any to be made. The stubborn part of him still didn't think he deserved a hundred percent of the blame for their situation, but he knew the bulk of this was on him. Just like he knew he should've reached out by now, but was hesitating. Partially because he didn't know what to say, but mostly because he feared what she would say to him...namely that she was done.

Myles didn't want to hear that from her, and that fact surprised him. They hadn't known each other long enough to form any deep connection. Their budding relationship was only a few days old and not too long before that, they couldn't stand each other. It should've been easier to just cut his losses and walk away. But try as he might, he couldn't. Jackie had somehow wormed her way into his heart before he could decide if that's what he really wanted or not.

"Here."

Myles opened his eyes to Mollie standing in front of him, holding out a plate with a smoked turkey BLT. He wordlessly accepted it before Mollie plopped onto the loveseat near him and tucked her bare feet underneath her, already picking up one of the two sandwiches she made for herself.

"Sorry I had to mess up some plates," she commented, taking a huge bite. "I'll wash 'em when we're done. I couldn't find your paper ones."

"I don't buy those."

"Oh yeah, I forgot. What was I thinking."

Choosing not to respond to her sarcasm, Myles just began eating his own sandwich. He kept to himself how he would've toasted the bread. Seasoned the tomatoes. Heated the turkey bacon. Whipped up a quick aioli. He thought of his and Jackie's impromptu cooking competition and wondered if she would have made the sandwich as he would have. He couldn't deny that he missed her.

"I know you don't feel like talking, but I have to remind you about the anniversary party," Mollie spoke up after several moments. She popped the last bit of her first sandwich into her mouth and continued, "For whatever reason, Mama and Daddy are having some big formal thing for it this year."

"It's their fortieth; that's the reason. And please stop talking with your mouth full."

"*Anyway*, in other announcements, I have a comedy showcase coming up. And I want you there, even if you do pout about it. I need all the support I can get. A lot of network bigwigs will be in the house. And just so you know, I'm inviting Jackie."

Myles's eyes snapped to her. "You what?"

"Don't trip. We've stayed in touch since your failed blind date attempt. I know y'all aren't cool but it's not like you have to sit together."

Putting down the rest of his sandwich and placing the plate on the coffee table in front of him, Myles mindlessly brushed bread crumbs from his hands. He briefly debated whether or not to say what was on his mind and figured there was no point in hiding it. "We actually started dating recently."

Mollie started to shoot up from her seat, then remembered the plate on her lap. "Hold the phone! You and Jackie are *dating*? Since when??"

"Recently."

"How, sway?"

"I don't know what that means."

"She couldn't stand you. She told me so herself. How did you manage to charm her? I didn't know you had game like that."

"We just realized there was an attraction. There were no games involved."

"I would actually use one of my three wishes on getting you out of being such a square. That's *not* what I meant. But anyway, I'm pleasantly surprised; I'd never imagine you'd go for someone as real and down-to-earth as Jackie and I'm here for it. How are things going?"

Myles didn't want to admit to the latest screw-up with Jackie. He'd just gotten Mollie to stop teasing him for the last one.

"They're going," he replied, managing to keep his voice even. "But since we're on the subject of relationships, have you ever been in one where the person you were with was...ashamed of you? Or acted like they were?"

Frowning slightly in thought, Mollie slowly shook her head. "Not really. They might not have loved my delightful jovial nature but I can't say they acted *ashamed* of me. Embarrassed, maybe, but not ashamed. Why?"

"Isn't embarrassed just as bad?"

"Guess it depends on the details. Not liking something I do or say in a moment isn't the same as being put off by me as a person."

Myles considered that. "I suppose."

"Why are you asking?"

"Just a hypothetical. It just occurred to me to ask, for whatever reason."

He picked up his sandwich and made himself eat the rest of it, knowing Mollie was giving him a weird look. Even though part of him was tempted to ask his sister for advice, it wasn't worth the price of the teasing torment that would come with it.

Really, Myles didn't need any input from anyone; he knew what he needed to do. He just had to grow the balls to do it.

"So you agree with me, Dad, don't you? I'm wasting my time, right?"

Stephen Malone, Jackie's father, chuckled. "I wouldn't be surprised if you ended up marrying that man, girl."

"What? Didn't you hear any of the stuff I just said?"

"Yeah, I heard you. Damn near thirty minutes of fussing. I missed my show listening to you."

"Dad, whatever show it is, you can probably watch it on streaming tomorrow."

"You know I don't have none of those fifty-'leven streaming things. That's not my point, anyway. I've *never* heard you sit and fuss this much over one man, which means he's got his hooks into you."

"It doesn't have to mean that. Maybe he just gets on my nerves."

"You wouldn't care one way or the other if you didn't care nothing 'bout him."

Jackie hated to admit he had a point. So she didn't. "Dad, you're supposed to be helping me, here."

"Help you with what?"

"Tell me what to do about Myles."

"You know that don't even sound right," Stephen's gravely voice sounded amused. "Like you ever ask anybody to tell you what to do about anything. You just want me to co-sign you running. Not gonna happen, slick."

"So you think I need to keep spending time with a stick-in-the-mud that acts ashamed of me?"

"You mean when you showed up unannounced to his office covered in car oil to talk about your personal business? A conversation that could've waited until *after* business hours?"

"You're taking his side??"

"Nope. Just *telling* you his side. Look, girl, I don't know this Myles fella but I like him already just because he's taking you out of the same box you've been in for years when it comes to men. All I've ever seen or heard about you dating is men like Ringo, and you never got so up in arms about him to me. Not even after he dumped you."

"Dad!"

"Well, didn't he? All I'm saying is, give this Myles a chance to explain himself. It sounds like he's fumbling because he's not used to a woman like you any more than you are to a man like him. But don't go running just because he's different. You picked a fight then seduced him for a reason."

"That's not what I did!"

"That's what you told me."

"I didn't pick a fight for *no* reason. And 'seduce' is strong. All we did was kiss."

"Right. Your fast tail just kept it at kissing. Why are we doing this when we both know better?"

"Dad!"

"Because he didn't compliment you exactly like you wanted him to. Shame on him."

"Fine, I acknowledge that I kinda blew it out of proportion but I still maintain that my main point was a valid one. *Anyway...*"

"You gonna call him?"

"Hell no. He's the one that needs to call *me*."

"I've never known you to just sit around waiting for stuff to happen but all right. Hopefully he'll call soon, then. If he doesn't, though, wait until my show isn't on to call and fuss about it."

"Thanks a lot, Dad."

Jackie knew her dad was just messing with her, at least partially. As much as he supported her, he'd never been one to coddle or pacify her just because she was his daughter and instead of resenting that, Jackie appreciated it. He kept her from getting too full of herself, which was an accusation that had been pinned on her more than a few times.

She might not have said it to him, but Jackie could see her dad's point about the scene with Myles at his office. Yeah, it stung when he didn't jump to claim her, but once she was thinking rationally again, she could concede that she could've in fact waited until they got off work to talk about their relationship instead of just showing up at his office in the middle of the day. *And* looking like she did. She hadn't known Myles all that long but she knew his type, and he was about his business. Optics mattered to him. It simply wasn't the place for such a conversation, and Jackie realized that.

And it wasn't like they'd been dating that long. It hadn't even been a week. If they'd been together for months or years and he'd behaved like that, then she'd have more of a right to get upset. But she couldn't expect him to shout her out from the rooftops after a few days. They weren't even official yet.

She still wasn't calling him, though.

Maybe this was it for them and they were over before they really got started. Jackie might've been a little annoyed with Myles, but she couldn't make herself believe that she wanted nothing more to do with him. Her dad might have been right about Myles not being used to a woman like her. If the woman that had been waiting for him at his office that day was any indication of his type, then Myles was probably going through romantic culture shock dealing with Jackie.

When her phone finally rang with Myles's call, Jackie was surprised at just how much relief she felt. Her chest thumped a little harder as she answered the call, reminding herself to keep her cool no matter what he said.

"Mr. Cornwall."

"Good evening, Jackie." He cleared his throat, his nervousness evident. "Are you, um....is now a good time?"

"Depends on what the time is for."

"Oh. Well, I wanted to call, to...hmm. I've been meaning to reach out and let you know how I, I mean, to apologize. I want to apologize."

"For?"

"For..." He sighed. "You're going to make me work for this, aren't you?"

"Whatever do you mean, Mr. Cornwall? I figured you knew what you were going to say before you decided to call me."

"I did. At least, I thought I did. Jackie...I admit I still don't know how to handle the affect you have on me."

Jackie smiled at that. It eased her mild worry that Myles hadn't called because he was just no longer interested. And she actually found his nervousness cute, not to mention touching. Well-spoken Myles fumbling his words meant that he cared about getting them just right. That was like a salve to her mildly-bruised ego. "So is that why you acted like you did the other day?"

"I don't have an excuse for that. Yes, I was caught off-guard when you showed up at my office...dressed as you were...but that shouldn't have stopped me from answering when asked who you were to me. It made it seem as if I'm ashamed of you and that's *not* the case. I'd understand if you don't believe that but I hope that you do."

Her smile grew a little more. "That's good to know. I'll admit I was feeling some kinda way when I left there. *And* when I didn't hear from you afterwards..."

"I can admit I was being stubborn. As soon as you left I knew I had screwed up again, but there was a part of me that still felt as if I was at least marginally justified in my behavior. I'm sure it wouldn't be a shock to hear that I'm not exactly used to women accosting me at my place of business like on one of those reality shows my sister likes to watch."

Jackie couldn't help but laugh at that. She felt warm, talking to Myles again. He might've been outside of her comfort zone but damn if she didn't like him, anyway.

"I can understand that," she finally admitted, figuring she'd stop making him sweat. "In hindsight, I could've handled things better, myself. You know I'm impatient, and I had it in my head that I needed to talk to you immediately to make sure we were okay. But just popping up at your job unannounced in my dirty coveralls wasn't the move."

"Well, maybe you wouldn't have felt the need to do that if I'd been more mature about that man showing up at your house first thing in the morning," Myles countered. "Another new situation that I mishandled."

"You weren't wrong for being upset about that, Myles. Hell, *I* was upset about my ex showing up like he did, and I let him know it. He and I are over, though...he's trying to spin the block only because his girlfriend dumped him and he hates being alone. And I'm a familiar place for him to land. It's certainly not because we're right for each other."

"I see. And I'm going to infer that 'spin the block' means resuming your previous relationship. Is that correct?"

Chuckling slightly, Jackie confirmed, "Yes, Myles."

"If I may ask, why did your relationship end in the first place?"

Jackie hesitated. She wasn't thrilled to admit to how she behaved with Ringo but lying wasn't an option. If she and Myles were going to make a go of things, she had to keep it real, regardless of the light it painted her in.

"I got a little too possessive," she admitted. "Ringo is an exotic dancer and it would make me crazy to see other women pawing all over him. Well, one night I got a little *too* crazy with this woman when I thought she was trying to grab his...well, I thought she was going too far with the touching. I snatched off her wig and slapped her around with it before pushing her into the table nearby, causing quite a mess. And I wasn't exactly being quiet or censored during this; my yelling was drowning out the music. Ringo dumped me that same night."

Myles sat speechless for a moment. "You assaulted a woman?"

"I...okay, I guess there's no way to pretty it up. Yeah, I did."

"Did she press charges?"

"Thankfully not. They certainly called the police and I thought my goose was cooked, but ultimately I just had to pay for whatever damages I caused and was banned from going back. By then I realized the enormity of what I did and was apologetic and cooperative, and the owner decided he didn't care enough to do all that. It wasn't like that was the first time women got to fighting over a man there."

"What about the woman? She just let it go?"

"She was half-hammered and didn't even wanna stay until the police got there. I heard her say something to her friend about some warrant that was out on her. She wasn't going to risk it."

"Wow, Jackie."

"Look, I'm not proud of it...I was an ass and I know it. And since I'm telling my truths, Ringo and I were together fairly recently and I took things too far yet again, this time humiliating myself in front of his mother. She was on a video call, but still. After that, I realized that being with Ringo just isn't good for me."

Myles blew out a long breath, taking his time to respond. Jackie wondered what he was thinking about her now and if her honesty was turning him off. Maybe this would just be too much for him.

"You ready to run?" Jackie asked, unable to wait for him to get his words together. "Not feeling me anymore?"

"I didn't say that," he quickly retorted, though unconvincingly. "I get that we all have pasts and I shouldn't judge but...I wasn't expecting *that*."

"Like I said, I'm not proud of it. But what you said is exactly right; that shit is in my *past*. So is Ringo. He is not a factor. I am a one-man woman, Myles, and the one man I'm interested in is you."

A beat passed before Myles finally replied, "I'm interested in you, too. God help me."

Jackie burst out laughing. The brief moment of tension lifted as Myles chuckled along with her. "Hey, it's not exactly a picnic dealing with you either, buddy. We're *both* gonna have to learn to give each other some grace. We're clearly anomalies for each other and that's gonna require a certain level of patience. I'm willing if you are."

"I am," Myles wasted no time responding, causing Jackie to full-on grin. "I'd like to see where things can go with you, Jackie. You've already bonded with my sister, which I feel is a good sign since she's never liked any other woman I've dated."

"Mollie is good people. And some of her skits online had me cracking up. I can't wait to go to one of her shows and see her live."

"Funny you should mention that. She has a comedy showcase and mentioned inviting you. And now I'd like to invite you to accompany me there. As my date."

"It's about time you asked me out," Jackie joked with a grin. "I'd love to go with you. When is it, again?"

"I'm not sure exactly; I imagine in a few weeks or so."

"Well, call me impatient but I'm damn sure not trying to wait that long to see you again."

"I concur." The smile in Myles's voice was evident.

"So what do you say we meet up later tonight? Around ten o'clock. There's a diner over near the airport that has some of the best fried chicken you'll have in your life."

"A diner? And you're suggesting *arriving* there at ten??"

"Staying up past your bedtime once in a while won't kill you, Mr. Cornwall. And yes, a diner. Yes, arriving at ten. I get that it might not be your speed but so what? The main point is us hanging out together, I'd say."

"Hmm. You know...you're right. Let's do it. If I'm a little tired tomorrow, that's what coffee is for."

Chapter 13

Two months after their late-night diner date, Jackie and Myles were still dating. Just about everyone marveled at the fact that what at first seemed like some kind of curious experiment had blossomed into an actual relationship.

Jackie might have teased Myles at times about his stuffiness, but she'd seen flashes of his edgier side when they encountered a rude cashier while out grabbing a birthday gift for Cassidy's husband, Orion. After one too many snippy comments, Myles demanded to see the manager and proceeded to take the cashier down several pegs in front of the line of customers that had formed, all without using the slew of curse words that Jackie would have (and started to). By the end of it, the rude cashier was near tears and forced to apologize, the manager apologized profusely, and the other customers were commenting on how well Myles handled things. Jackie had gotten so turned on standing there watching him that she dove on him as soon as they were back in the car.

Myles realized he actually respected Jackie's fiery nature; it was a welcome change from the relatively docile women he was used to. Or at least, they were docile in public but totally different people once they got away from judgmental eyes. Jackie was who she was in public or private, and Myles appreciated not having to guess which version of her he was going to get.

He also got to see a softer side of her, though. She liked to volunteer at the animal shelter when she could. Even though she left and detested the corporate life, she was still more than willing to listen to him vent after frustrating work days or about the pressure he was under with the big Morlock account, and even offer advice. She liked to curl up in his lap and nuzzle his neck, purring at how good he always smelled. He'd never been with a woman as affectionate as Jackie; she loved touching him. And he loved letting her.

They still hadn't slept together. Lots of kissing, heavy petting, and nights in each other's beds, but Jackie still didn't think Myles was ready for sex and Myles was letting her continue to think that. He wasn't in a rush to get her into bed, but he still didn't love her taking it upon herself to determine his readiness. The one discussion they had about it was starting to morph into an argument after Jackie held onto her insistence that she would know when Myles was ready for sex more than he would, and he had to force himself to just clamp his mouth shut and let it go. He didn't want to argue with her about something like sex, though he did tell her she was wrong for making assumptions.

Not that they didn't butt heads about other things. Their still officially un-labeled relationship was anything but smooth sailing, but usually one of them was able to catch themselves whenever their differences sparked a disagreement and cool things down. Like when Jackie nagged him about always dressing so formally or when Myles corrected her grammar. Things that were annoying in the moment but overall, not terribly big deals. Recognizing what was and wasn't worth spending time going back and forth about was an ongoing lesson for them. But they liked each other enough to be willing to learn.

And Jackie's latest affirmation that she'd written on her board after reconciling with Myles gave her a rush every time she looked at it:

This one feels different. Don't mess this up.

Myles and Ethan were taking an extended lunch one afternoon after getting out of a meeting that took up most of the morning. Ethan took the opportunity to gush about his growing relationship with his girlfriend, Eniah.

"I think she's it," he admitted, sprinkling red pepper flakes onto his pork ramen and stirring them in. The smile hadn't left his face since the discussion started. "Eniah is everything I've said I wanted in a woman. Not to mention how much we have in common; it's almost freaky, when I think about it. I've never been so in sync with a woman. You know?"

"Not really," Myles admitted. He dragged his steak through the smear of peppercorn sauce on his plate. "I can't say I've been that in tune with any of my past love interests. Any commonalities we shared were usually surface-level and meaningless. And I *certainly* don't have that with Jackie; we hardly have anything in common."

"I can't say I'm too surprised about that, man. I like Jackie a lot but I wouldn't have put you two together in a million years."

"I don't blame you. Jackie is by far the most challenging woman I've ever dated. In a lot of ways."

"That's a good thing, though," Ethan commented, leveling a gaze at his friend. "You need someone to keep you on your toes and that isn't afraid to challenge you. All of your exes seemed to just want you to help complete their live version of a Normal Rockwell painting, basically."

"True enough. It's something I don't think I realized until Jackie and I began taking interest in each other; just how empty my past romantic life has been. I've dated plenty but none have made me want to look into a future with them."

"And you want to do that with Jackie? Because I absolutely do with Eniah."

Myles glanced at his table setting. "I can admit I've pictured myself with Jackie in certain scenarios that I haven't with other women." He cleared his throat. "But I think it's still too soon to think of such things."

"Who says? Man, when you know, you know. And there's no set amount of time for that."

"Hmm."

"Myles," Ethan put down his fork and sat back in his chair, wiping his hands on a linen napkin. "Have you ever been in love, man?"

Pausing, Myles considered the question. His eyes wandered to an abstract painting on the far wall.

"If you have to think about it that much, you haven't," Ethan concluded.

"I've been deeply infatuated with women," Myles stated. "But I'm not sure I can say I've truly been in love. It's something I never realized until now, funny enough."

"Can you see yourself falling for Jackie?"

"Stranger things have happened."

"Would you admit it if you did?"

"I'd like to think so. I've admittedly had some slip-ups with Jackie but I never ran from my interest in her. If my feelings evolved into love, I'd welcome it. I already care about her more than even I can believe. She's important to me. Though there are some things about her that I'm still getting used to."

"Such as?"

"She has no filter. I never know *what* will come out of that woman's mouth and at times, it can be off-putting. And she's quite...uninhibited."

"In what way?"

"She has an affinity for being naked when she's at home," Myles revealed, hoping he wasn't saying too much. But knowing Jackie as he did by then, she wouldn't have cared about Ethan knowing that about her. "She told me that up front but the first time she actually walked out nude in front of me almost had me tripping over my own feet."

Ethan laughed at that. "I can just imagine how it is between the two of you behind closed doors. I would almost pay to be able to watch you two spend an evening together. Pure hilarity."

"I don't think it would be *that* funny," Myles muttered.

"I'm just saying, Myles...you know I love you like a brother but let's face it; you can be a little stuffy. And Jackie sounds like anything but. The fact that the two of you are even attracted to each other at all is a marvel in and of itself but I can just imagine how it is when one of you tries to bring the other into unfamiliar territory or when you butt heads. Jackie seems plenty fiery when she's *not* pissed off. Has she had to tear you a new one yet? Sent you to bed without any dinner after you ticked her off?"

Myles couldn't help but take offense to that. Ethan was making it sound like Myles was the *only* one that ever messed up in his relationship with Jackie. And that Jackie scolded him while he just sat and took it like a meek, humbled child.

"I'll have you know, Ethan, that despite how *stuffy* I may be, I more than hold my own with Jackie," Myles snipped. "Yes, she is a strong woman and I like that about her. But don't ever forget that I'm just as strong of a man, regardless of whether I present my strength in the same way or not."

Ethan's smile faded, noting the seriousness on his friend's face and the bite in his voice. It was clear he'd struck a nerve.

"I was just teasing, man," he assured. "I didn't mean to imply that Jackie runs you or anything like that."

Myles glared at him for a moment before picking up his fork and jabbing it into his last morsel of steak. He silently told himself to calm down but couldn't resist saying, "Harmless japes are one thing; insulting my manhood is another. And I've gotten enough of that in the past from strangers without having to put up with it from my friend, as well."

"I apologize. That wasn't my intention," Ethan insisted, sincere. "I'm well aware that you can handle yourself. And I know you well enough to know that you wouldn't entertain a woman that disrespected you, regardless of how attractive she is."

"Damn right."

Ethan blinked in surprise. Myles didn't typically use such language, as tame as it was in the realm of indelicacy.

He changed the subject, to both of their relief. Myles's momentary ire eased as they began talking about Myles's project for the homeless and the latest in the land development rumors. Despite himself, though, Myles couldn't help but wonder if Jackie shared Ethan's idea – joking or not - that she had the upper hand in their relationship. She was already dictating when they would sleep together, which was only a big deal because it wasn't that she wasn't ready for it, but because she had determined that *he* wasn't. It was something he didn't press because he didn't want to argue, but maybe they needed to have a talk about that. It had irked him from the first time she said it, and he didn't need to get into the habit of suppressing his feelings just to appease hers.

Not to mention, if she would do that about sex, what would stop her from making decisions on his behalf about anything else? As much as Myles liked Jackie, he wouldn't tolerate being bulldozed. If their relationship was going to have any shot, they were going to have to get some things straight.

It was the night of Mollie's comedy showcase, and try as he might, Myles could only scrape up marginal enthusiasm for it. He was excited for Mollie because he knew it was a big opportunity for her, but he wasn't looking forward to hearing her crude jokes any more than he usually was. Jackie, on the other hand, was as giddy as could be.

"I am *so* looking forward to this," she gushed as she put on her hoop earrings in the vanity mirror. Myles was perched on her bed, waiting for her to finish getting ready and trying to resist the urge to look at his watch. "Things have been so crazy and frustrating at work; a night of letting loose and laughing my ass off is just what I need."

Myles was well aware of how crazy and frustrating things had been for her at work; she'd been venting to him plenty over the previous several days. Which was why he still hadn't broached the subject about her perceived dominance in their relationship. Myles had asked himself many times since Ethan made his little jab if he was overreacting; if maybe he was creating an issue out of nothing. Jackie hadn't done anything outright emasculating or disrespectful. He didn't want to insult her by being unfairly accusatory.

But at the same time, he didn't want to invalidate his own feelings, and this was bugging him for a reason. He wasn't inherently insecure. He needed to broach the subject; he just needed to be mindful of how he did it so as to not start an argument. There just hadn't been a good time to do so.

"It should be an interesting evening," Myles commented, doing his best to sound positive. He didn't want to always seem so surly when it came to his little sister's performances, despite how he felt about her material. "How much longer will it take for you to finish getting ready? I'd rather not be late."

"We won't be late, Myles; we've got plenty of time. Chill out."

"You know how traffic can be."

"Even if we *are* a couple of minutes late, it won't be a big deal. Try to loosen up tonight, will you?"

Pursing his lips, Myles sighed. If he had a dollar for every time she'd told him that since they met. "Do you want to have dinner after the show?"

"Sure, we can do that. I ate a while ago but I'm sure I'll be good and hungry by the time we leave there." Jackie turned and looked at him as she finished securing her second earring, dropping a hand to her hip as her eyes roamed over his suit. "I should've known you'd wear something like that."

His nostrils flared slightly at another thing she often commented on. "There's nothing wrong with what I'm wearing, Jackie."

"It's not that there's anything wrong with it in general, but we're going to a comedy club, babe. Here I am with the sexy-casual vibe in my cute booty-hugging jeans and fuzzy top and boots and you're looking like you're headed to some kind of conference. There's nothing wrong with toning it down every now and then. Do you even own any jeans?"

"I do not. But you have plenty, as evidenced by the *still*-unfolded laundry over there in the basket from three days ago."

"What the fu-"

"Jackie, I do not want to have this particular discussion with you yet again. I wear what I like. What I like is suits. At the risk of sounding arrogant, it's not like I don't look good in them. I'd think you'd be *glad* to be on the arm of someone who puts such care into their appearance."

"I'm more than glad to be on your arm. But why does that arm always have to be draped in a fancy suit no matter where we're going? That's all I'm saying."

"Why is it such a big issue for you?"

"It's not an *issue-*"

"It seems like it is. Seeing as how you constantly nag me about it."

She frowned slightly. "I'm not nagging you, Myles."

"You *are*, Jackie. You always make your little comments about my clothing and I have to tell you, I'd rather you didn't. You wouldn't love it if I was constantly critiquing everything you chose to wear. You'd likely curse me out."

"You've asked me to put on dresses before, Myles."

"That was specifically because where we were going had a dress code. I don't make a habit of commenting on your outfits like you do mine. So don't even try that."

"Why are you getting so defensive?"

"The same way you would be if I commented on how you're always popping gum in my ear whenever we talk while you're at work. I hate it, by the way, and wish you would stop."

Jackie folded her arms. "Oh really?"

"Yes, really."

"And how long have you been waiting to tell me *that*?"

"Since the first conversation I had to endure it. And let's not act like you would've loved hearing me say that, no more than I love the constant nitpicking about my choice of attire. I don't need fashion advice from you, Jackie." He stood from the bed, tugging the sides of his tailored suit jacket as he looked square into her eyes. "If I want your opinion, I'll ask you. All *I'm* saying is, I don't try to tell you what to do; I'd appreciate it if you'd extend me the same courtesy and stop trying to change me into something you'd like for me to be."

Her jaw dropped. "Where the hell is all this coming from? That's not what I'm doing!"

"Right." He glanced at his watch. "Please hurry and finish getting ready. I'll wait in the living room."

"Myles!"

Ignoring her, he stalked out of her bedroom, part of him tempted to continue on out the front door and go home. He was in even less of a mood to go to a comedy showcase, but he knew he couldn't skip out on Mollie's night. Nor did he really want to have his and Jackie's date night ruined over a silly disagreement about clothes.

Jackie emerged from her bedroom a couple of minutes later and they left, the noticeable tension still in the air. Myles had managed to calm himself down, though he still didn't have a lot to say. Jackie was quiet herself, and she kept stealing glances at him as he drove. When she reached over and rested her hand on his thigh, he glanced down at it silently. It was several moments later when he finally lowered his hand on top of hers, squeezing it slightly. Jackie's face stayed turned towards the window but she couldn't resist the smile that erupted at his acceptance of her silent olive branch.

They arrived to the club, their hands joined as they headed inside. They still hadn't spoken, but had seemed to come to a silent agreement to press pause on their issues for the time being.

Myles and Mollie's parents had already arrived, seated at a table front and center. When Hampton saw them come in, he stood and waved them over, the smile already plastered on his face. Myles led Jackie over to them, snaking around the tables with Jackie's hand still encased in his. His parents noted this with interest, their eyes dropping to the joined hands before flitting to each other's in silent communication.

"Dad, Mom," Myles greeted, giving them each hugs and treating his mother Agatha to a kiss on the cheek. "How are you feeling? Are you sure you should be out tonight?"

"Now you know your father would not have let me out of the house if I was feeling anything other than tip top," Agatha reminded with a smile, placing a brief loving hand to her son's cheek. "I'm just fine."

"You know I have to ask."

"I know, I know." Her eyes turned to Jackie. "And who is this beautifully adorable woman you have with you?"

Jackie grinned as Myles gently tugged her hand, pulling her closer.

"Mom, Dad, this is Jacqueline Malone," Myles introduced. "Though she prefers to be called Jackie. Jackie, these are my parents Hampton and Agatha Cornwall."

"A pleasure to meet you, Jackie," Hampton greeted, taking her free hand and bowing slightly at the waist. "You are lovely, indeed."

"Thank you so much," Jackie beamed. "It really is an honor to meet you both; I've heard the names since I moved to Brodence but never thought I'd actually get to meet you. It floored me when I realized you were Myles's parents."

"That's so nice of you to say but we're just people," Agatha insisted with a wave of her hand. "We're happy to meet the lady friend of our son, here; he doesn't usually make a habit of bringing them around us."

"Well I feel pretty special, then," Jackie teased, gazing up at Myles and trying to hide her amusement at how uncomfortable he looked all of a sudden. "I'm surely glad to be here with him."

Myles felt his face flush. All three of them were looking at him and he wished someone would suddenly appear on stage and announce that the show was starting.

"Yes, things are going well," he finally commented, clearing his throat. He wasn't about to let on about their earlier disagreement; that was something they'd deal with in private. He turned his eyes to hers. "I've definitely been enjoying my time with Jackie."

"We love to hear it," Hampton commented, nudging his wife at the looks Myles and Jackie were sharing. "It's great of you to come and support our baby Mollie. I think she's up second, she said. Have you had a chance to meet her yet, Jackie?"

Jackie tore her gaze from Myles. "I have, yes. She's a trip. I'm excited to see her do her thing in person."

Myles had instantly tensed when his father asked if Jackie and Mollie had met but he relaxed when it seemed that Jackie wasn't going to reveal how they had. Really, Myles was a little surprised Mollie hadn't already told them the whole humiliating story of his blind date hookup blunder. He could only imagine how they'd come down on him if they knew about it.

They all took their seats, Hampton ordering drinks for everyone (and declining when they were offered on the house) before the show got started a few minutes later. The MC came out and warmed the crowd up a little, telling a few jokes of his own before introducing the first comedian, who Myles didn't even pretend to listen to. His eyes might have been on the stage but his mind was on the things he needed to get done for the foundation and the orders he needed to put in to replenish his care kit supplies, as well as the latest developments on the Morlock account he was busting his behind on. He also wanted to check in on Ms. Lula at the coffee shop to make sure she was okay, since he was sure the greedy land developer was still sniffing after her location.

When Mollie took the stage, Myles cleared his mind and gave her his attention. Jackie was grinning excitedly and his parents were practically buzzing with anticipation. Even though he wasn't feeling nearly the same level of excitement, he tried to fix his expression to where it at least looked like he was.

Mollie did her customary skip to the microphone, giving everyone a twirl before snatching the microphone from the stand and setting the stand aside, placing herself front and center with her fist planted to her hip.

"How the hell are ya tonight?"

Most of the crowd shouted out in response with various answers, and Myles's eyes widened in shock when some guy yelled something about having blue balls. Mollie chuckled, Jackie cracked up, and Hampton and Agatha giggled amongst themselves. Myles just hoped the rest of the act didn't involve audience participation.

"Well, I hope you get someone to help you out with that, buddy," Mollie quipped, throwing a wink in the guy's direction before sweeping her narrow eyes among the rest of the crowd. Her expression brightened slightly when she got to her family's table. "I certainly can't relate to your frustration 'cause I just got some an hour ago. Some good dick is better than any damn liquor you can think of, I'll tell you *that*. My dress isn't on backwards, is it?"

Everyone laughed as Mollie playfully checked her clothes, actually spinning around in a circle as she pretended to try to see the back. Myles could only hope her declaration was a joke but he didn't put much past his uninhibited little sister.

His hope that maybe her act wouldn't be another barrage of sexual and crude material vanished when Mollie launched into a spiel about 'blow job etiquette'. Not only did Myles not find her material funny, but it also made him a little uncomfortable. Maybe he was a prude, but he just didn't enjoy this kind of humor, even if it was his sister delivering it. Or especially *because* it was his sister delivering it.

He was definitely in the minority, though, because everyone else loved it. Jackie was crying, she was laughing so hard. And Myles's parents had let out more than a few guffaws. The crowd surely seemed to enjoy it. Myles was the clear fly in the ointment. He barely chuckled once.

When her set was over, Mollie thanked everyone for feeding her ego and blew kisses as she pranced off the stage. Myles might not have loved her material but he couldn't help but be proud of her for the reception she got. Even if he didn't like it, plenty of other people did.

They sat through the rest of the comics before the showcase was over. Mollie finally came over to her family after speaking and taking pictures with several people.

"Thank y'all so much for coming!" she exclaimed, giving them all enthusiastic hugs one by one. "It made a girl feel all warm and fuzzy to see you sitting out there."

"You know we wouldn't have missed it," Hampton commented. "Though I do need to be getting your mother home soon. It's getting late."

"I don't have a curfew, Hampton," Agatha snapped, though she was smiling. "I told you I feel fine. Today is a good one."

"Still. We don't need to push it."

"Yeah, Mama, you came, you laughed, we hugged; that's the trifecta I wanted," Mollie added. "Go on home and get some rest."

Agatha tsked. "Don't *you* start fussing over me, too."

"Jackie, I am so glad you came!" Mollie exclaimed, giving her another hug. "I really thought Myles was messing with me when he told me the two of you were dating. Part of me is still wondering if you lost some kind of bet."

"Thanks a lot, Mollie," Myles muttered.

"I'm just playing. Kind of. Anyway, Jackie, I'm going to be calling you soon; I need to bring my car in for you to work your magic. Ol' Bertha's been acting up this past week."

"Why am I not surprised you named your car Bertha?" Jackie chuckled. "But yeah, just let me know; you know I'll do everything I can for you."

"Oh, you're a mechanic?" Hampton asked, intrigued.

"Yep, she owns her own garage over on Lynn Boulevard; The Auto Loft," Mollie replied with a proud grin, slinging an arm around Jackie's shoulders. "Myles's boo is a fierce sexy Black entrepreneur, doin' the damn thang."

"That's wonderful!" Agatha gushed, taking one of Jackie's hands in both of hers. "I *love* to see our young women step out on their own, and in male-dominated industries, to boot. I'll surely be coming by to visit, if that's all right."

"Of-of *course*!" Jackie sputtered, uncharacteristically. "Come by whenever you like."

"How long have you been in business?" Hampton asked.

"Almost three years. Best decision I ever made was to leave corporate America and go into business for myself. I absolutely love it."

They all stood around discussing Jackie's business before Mollie introduced her parents to a few eager fellow comics, and Jackie passed out business cards to some people who overheard their conversation about her being a mechanic. Myles stood by, patient and practically silent, waiting for her to finish networking so they could head home.

When they finally said their goodbyes and headed out, this time not holding hands, some of the earlier tension returned. Though this time, it wasn't totally for the same reasons as when they arrived.

They went to get a bite to eat, their conversation minimal and polite. They were back at Jackie's before she finally said what was on her mind.

"I noticed you were pretty quiet this evening."

Glancing at her in mild surprise, Myles shrugged. "I've told you that I'm not Mollie's target audience."

"Oh, I know. I'm not talking about during her set, which I thought was hilarious. I meant after."

Sensing there was more to her statement than she was letting on, Myles sighed. He'd hoped they would be able to close out the evening on a pleasant-enough note but it looked like he might not get his wish.

"Just say what you're getting at, Jackie," he droned. "I'm not in the mood to pull it out of you."

"Why weren't you saying anything when we were all talking about my business?" Jackie inquired, placing her hands on her hips as she faced him. "Mollie was riding hard, hyping me up. Your parents were interested and asking questions. Even total strangers were poking their noses in and getting information. And you, the man I'm dating, just stood there mute."

"What was it I was supposed to say?"

"Hell, *something*!" She threw up her hands. "It would've been nice if you'd given *some* indication that you're proud of me to your folks but you didn't say a damn word, Myles. Or are you still embarrassed by what I do?"

"No," he quickly insisted, his defensive stance cracking. He moved closer to her. "I told you, I've moved past that."

"I can't tell."

"Well next time, be sure to give me my script before we arrive somewhere so I'll know exactly what to say to appease you and we can avoid this confusion."

Jackie's expression morphed into an incredulous frown. "You trying to be funny? This is *not* the time for you to be a dick, Myles."

"I'm not being...that. But I'm also not trying to be dictated to, either."

"How is me wanting my man to have my back 'dictating'?"

"Jackie. With you I'm always seeming to say or do the wrong thing. Some of that is on me and I acknowledge that, but a good bit of it is you expecting me to adhere to your preferences. Remember biting my head off the first time I came over here because I complimented your past accomplishments?"

Jackie's own defensive stance waned. "I acknowledge that I could've handled that better. But I don't like or appreciate the implication that I'm controlling."

"No? Well, what do you call it when you get incensed when I don't say exactly what you want me to say? Or when I wear what you don't think I should wear? Not to mention all of your 'suggestions,' like when you tried to convince me to get contacts. Or when you hounded me into eating the soul food that I'd already told you I wasn't a fan of, simply because, according to you, it's something I *should* like." He stepped into her personal space, looking down into her intense brown eyes. "Or when you determine on your own that I'm not ready for sex with you without even asking me first."

Jackie's face flushed at the intensity of his gaze. Even through his glasses, she could see those hazel eyes of his boring into her. Her stomach clenched as parts of her began to tingle.

"That wasn't about me being controlling," she managed, breathlessness replacing the earlier bite in her voice.

Myles started walking forward, Jackie instantly backing up in step. Their eyes were still locked.

"Then what was it about?" Myles asked in a rumble. His hands were in his pockets, resisting the urge to touch her like he wanted to. He recognized the shift in her eyes and it did something to him. "Who are you to determine what I am and am not ready for?"

Jackie sucked in a breath, her gaze dropping to his lips. "Are you?"

Their slow walk stopped when Jackie's back hit the wall near the entrance to the kitchen. Myles stood as close as he could without touching her, his ache now spreading almost as fast as hers. Every beat and pulse in his body started accelerating. He was annoyed with her, but damn if she didn't turn him on. He leaned down, his lips barely grazing her ear.

"Among other things," he whispered, earning a shudder from her. "Yes."

Her chest starting to heave slightly, Jackie lightly gripped the sides of his starched button-down white shirt, glad that he'd removed his jacket when they got there. She wished the rest of his clothes were off now, too, because she wanted this man more than she wanted anything in that moment.

"What other things?" she breathed, her hands tightening.

She couldn't help the shaky moan that escaped when she felt Myles's tongue lightly trace her ear.

"I want you," his tongue trailed down her neck, ending with a lingering kiss at the shoulder junction, "In every possible way."

"Really?" Jackie's eyes slid closed as she enjoyed what Myles was doing and saying, the back of her head mashed against the wall and her hands now gripping his waistband. "Because I want that, too."

"So you're as ready to make this official as I am?"

Her eyes popped open. "Are you serious? Please don't play with me right now, Myles."

"You know me well enough by now to know better than that."

"So me and you..." She pulled his body flush against hers, unable to resist anymore. Feeling his bulge made her panties flood with desire and anticipation. "This is for real?"

"Yes, Jackie." His hand slid up her arm, along her shoulder, and up to the side of her face. "You drive me nuts and there are clearly some things we still need to work on so we don't kill each other, but when it comes down to it..." He gave her a brief but hungry kiss, leaving her whimpering when he pulled away, "I realize I don't want anyone else but you. I'd like to be yours." Another teasing kiss. "And I'd like for you to be mine. Are *you* ready for *that*?"

"Yes," she immediately panted, her lips aching for another kiss as well as the rest of her aching for everything else. "And you're right, we do still need to work on some things, none of which I want to worry about right now. Right now I want to take the rest of this designer suit off of you and finally enjoy this body I'm always feeling up."

Myles smirked, his other hand sliding down to her hip. He lifted her leg, pressing himself closer to her. He loved how she gasped in response. He loved to see that he could have such an effect on her and it only emboldened him. "Only if I get to do the same to you."

"Hell yeah, you can." Jackie wound against him as he took her lips again, this time the kiss longer and deeper. They moaned and moved against each other. "You have no idea what I want you to do to me, Myles."

"Care to join me in the bedroom and enlighten me?"

"With pleasure. But first," she grasped his face in both hands, some of the lust muting from her eyes as she looked at him with a serious expression. "I need you to know that I am *not* trying to change or control you, baby. I'm not about that. And I sincerely apologize if I made it seem like I was. You're clearly not the only one that has fumbled the bag in our relationship."

Myles had no idea what 'fumbling the bag' meant but he wasn't about to waste time asking. He could infer enough from context. "Thank you for saying that. And I, in turn, apologize if I've given the impression that I'm not proud of you. Because I am, Jackie. I'm both proud of what you've done for yourself and I'm proud to be with you. And I look forward to making that known at the next opportunity."

Jackie's arousal flamed like water on a grease fire. Not only at what Myles was saying but how he said it. She never thought she'd be so turned on by someone speaking so formally to her but Myles doing it drove her crazy.

She started unbuttoning his shirt. "So we've both established we're not perfect. We can deal with the rest of our issues later. Right now I just want to get naked with you."

Myles couldn't help but grin as she aggressively pushed his shirt open and over his shoulders. It remained bunched at the crook of his arms as he was too busy unbuttoning her jeans to let her fully remove it. He started peeling the tight jeans downwards, reminded of how generous her hips and ass were. He grunted in appreciation.

"And I you."

They continued undressing each other, their haste increasing as the moments ticked by. Myles only hastily folded his clothes and left them on the couch before Jackie grabbed his hand and quickly led him to her bedroom. She pushed him onto the bed and took a moment to openly admire his nakedness for the first time before climbing on top of him, Myles's arms immediately encircling her. They kissed wildly, rolling around as they took turns jockeying for momentary control.

"Jackie," Myles groaned tortuously as she reached between their writhing bodies and began stroking him. "Oh my *god*, Jackie..."

"You like that?"

"Immensely."

"This might not be the ideal time to talk about this but for the record," Jackie shuddered when Myles's hand gripped her breast, "My saying you weren't ready for sex wasn't about control. I just...ahh...a lot of guys mainly want me for my body and I liked you too much for it to be about that with us."

"Hmm." Myles kissed his way down to her heaving breasts, tongue-kissing one nipple while his fingers gently squeezed the other. "And you thought that was the best way to go about that, huh?"

"It probably wasn't." Jackie writhed underneath him, pleasantly surprised at just how much he was pleasing her. "Myles, baby, that feels so good..."

"You could've had it sooner if you hadn't been so stubborn."

"You're right." She reluctantly pushed against his shoulders, rolling on top of him and giving him a deep, tongue-filled kiss. "And I think it's time I made it up to you."

She slid down his body and settled herself between his legs, biting her lips at how strong they were. Myles truly had it going on underneath all those suits.

I had no idea playing racquetball could produce a body like this.

Jackie grabbed his thick, lengthy erection, stroking it as her mouth actually watered in anticipation. She started to lower her face towards it when Myles stopped her.

"Jackie, wait a second."

She glanced up, startled. "What's wrong?"

"I must admit that I, umm..." His head fell against the pillows as he searched for the least-embarrassing explanation. "This isn't something I..."

"Oh my god..." Jackie straightened, resting on her knees as she released her hold on him. "Please don't tell me you don't like getting head."

"No, that's not it," Myles quickly insisted. He sighed, knowing there was no other option than to just say it. "It's not that I don't like it. It's that I've never received it."

Jackie's jaw dropped in shock. She started to ask if he was joking but stopped herself, knowing better.

"How is that possible?" she marveled. "You've been in relationships before, right? Serious ones? That included sex?"

"Yes to the latter three questions. As far as how it's possible, none of the women I've been with wanted to do that or even offered to. And I certainly wasn't going to pressure them. So I just accepted that it wasn't going to happen."

Jackie couldn't believe her ears. What kind of prissy uptight women had Myles been dating that they didn't want to give their man head?

"Do you want it?" she asked, not wanting to assume anything. "Would you like for me to go down on you, baby?"

Her hands were rubbing along his thighs, and Myles twitched as his arousal reignited. The look in her eyes had him achingly hard.

"I would," he mumbled, his chest heaving as her hand returned to his manhood. He groaned as she began stroking him again. "Yes, Jackie, I want that."

"That's all I need to know. I've got you, baby...and you won't *ever* have to worry about going without anymore as long as you're with me."

He shuddered violently as Jackie slid her tongue along his shaft and around the head before her lips slid over him, his hips bucking all on their own. Myles instantly wondered how in the world he'd gone so long without this particular pleasure as his body jerked and his words got caught in his throat, letting this woman drive him crazy yet again. But this time, though, he welcomed it.

Chapter 14

Myles felt like he should've been embarrassed at the amount of time he spent fantasizing about Jackie and the things she did to him, but he wasn't. He enjoyed every delicious fantasy, regardless of what they interrupted or distracted him from.

Ever since the night she showed him what he'd been missing by gracing him with his first taste of fellatio, Myles was, in a word, hooked. He couldn't get enough of Jackie's mouth between his legs. Sex with Jackie was addicting overall; the ecstasy that overtook her face and the way she clung to him the first time he slid inside of her replayed through his mind on a bolstering loop. She was so expressive in bed, even more so than any other time, and Myles loved the affirmation. There was no uncertainty as to whether she enjoyed what he did to her or not like there had been with women of his past. Jackie was vocal, whispering dirty talk in his ear that would've made him blush in any other situation. Myles might not have been as vocal as she, but he was plenty expressive. There was just no way he could be quiet when Jackie's body was on his.

The level of attraction he felt towards Jackie actually floored him. He liked her plenty before they slept together, but now that they had – and she had shown him what he'd been missing – the idea of letting her go became less and less acceptable. They still butted heads occasionally and got on each other's nerves, but that was minor compared to the growing feelings that were developing between them. Myles never would have guessed when he begrudgingly walked into her garage months earlier that he and Jackie would end up together, but it was turning out to be one of the best decisions he'd made.

One morning before work, Myles headed to Lula's Cup to check in with Ms. Lula and get himself some coffee, and maybe a pastry. He needed the caffeine and sugar rush after the long night he'd had with Jackie the night before. They met up with Mollie and her date (a woman whose name Myles didn't bother retaining, especially after she kept calling him Niles), before Jackie talked him into a late movie. They actually agreed on what to see immediately, though Myles realized it was because Jackie didn't care about what was on the screen; she had grabbed his hand and eased it underneath her short jersey dress five minutes in. Myles had never before done anything so naughty in public, especially since there were other people in the theater with them, but he willingly obliged her. And of course she insisted on returning the favor. They were all over each other when they got back to his house, not falling asleep until the wee hours.

Trying his best to clear his mind of dirty thoughts, Myles entered the coffee shop, his eyes roaming for the owner. He waved to Gloria, glad to see that she was still working there and thriving.

"How's it going, Gloria?" Myles greeted with a smile when he made it to the front of the thankfully-short line. "You're looking great."

"Thanks!" Gloria beamed, her wavy brown hair pulled up into a messy bun and held back with a wide headband.

"I'm doing so great. I can't thank you enough for helping me get this job."

"You've already thanked me a hundred times, Gloria," he reminded, chuckling. "And you're more than welcome. I knew Ms. Lula would take care of you."

"She certainly has been. She's become like a mother to me, including fattening me up; I was *so* underweight when I met her but now, I don't look like a strong wind could knock me over anymore."

Laughing, Myles chatted with Gloria for another couple of moments as he placed his order. He stepped aside as more people started coming in, checking an email on his phone that had just come in.

"There's my handsome darling."

He looked up, grinning when he saw Ms. Lula standing in front of him with a warm smile and open arms. Stepping into them, he wrapped her in a tight hug.

"How are you, Ms. Lula?"

"I'm a little tired but I can't complain."

Myles pulled back in mild surprise. Ms. Lula was usually so upbeat and positive, it was jarring to hear anything outside of that. The usual sparkle was missing from her eyes. "What's going on?"

Hesitating, Ms. Lula pursed her lips and glanced around before grabbing Myles's wrist and leading him to an empty corner table. Once they were seated, she leaned forward slightly, taking a moment to gather her words before speaking.

"I'm just feeling a little worn out," she admitted, her voice low. "These developers have been turning up the heat and...I've begun wondering if it'll be easier to just give in to them."

Myles's eyes widened. "Are you serious?"

"I don't *want* to. But the young lady that has been hounding me is very convincing. And she made me a pretty generous offer. I wasn't planning on retiring just yet but maybe it's not the worst idea."

"This place has been in business for so long, Ms. Lula. Since before I was even born. It's a landmark here in Brodence. You really want to give it up just like that?"

"I'm tired, baby," Ms. Lula admitted, turning her eyes to him. "Running this place takes all the energy I have, and I still love it...I'm not sure I have the energy to do that *and* fend these people off, too. I've told her time and time again that I'm not interested but they're not willing to take no for an answer, hounding me day in and day out. It's just getting to be too much."

Myles hated the slightly defeated look on Ms. Lula's face, and he felt himself become incensed. He couldn't help but think that the developer was likely preying on Ms. Lula's age, enticing her with visions of not having to get up at the crack of dawn, being able to sleep in, spend her days doing whatever hobby pleased her, getting to travel. The coffee shop had been Ms. Lula's life for as long as Myles could remember; it would be one thing if she was ready to walk away from it on her own, but he couldn't stand for her being pressured into it.

"I hate that they're harassing you like they are," he commented, reaching over to take her hand. "And I get it; the constant pressure is undoubtedly exhausting. But can you please promise that you won't make a decision yet? I want to find a way to help you."

"You don't need to worry yourself about this, baby," Ms. Lula assured wearily, patting his hand with a grateful smile. "I know you've got your hands full with so much already."

"Don't worry about that. I just need you to promise me that you won't give up. Can you please do that for me?"

She looked at him for a moment before her face slowly brightened, as if his words had plugged in her energy.

"I can do that," she assured. "And I love you for caring so much. Now I think your order is ready; get on out of here so you can get to work. You don't need to be late for being in here fussing over me."

He just grinned, standing and leaning down to kiss her cheek. "I love you too, Ms. Lula."

"Hey, my hot nerd."

Myles couldn't help but smile. He couldn't believe he actually liked that nickname Jackie had given him.

"Good afternoon, Jackie." He didn't have any pet names for her; it was something he always felt silly doing, even in past relationships. Unless they were in the throes of passion, she was always 'Jackie' to him. Thankfully, she didn't seem to mind. "How is your day going?"

"Busy, but that's how I like it. It does and doesn't help that my mind keeps wandering to what you did to me before I left your house this morning. One of my mechanics has already asked me what I keep smiling to myself about."

Myles's grin widened. "Glad to know I bring you pleasure."

"Oh you most definitely do *that*. I never would've thought when I met you that you would be such an animal in bed. I'm getting kind of hooked on you, Mr. Cornwall."

"Is that right?"

"It is. And not just because of your sex game. I'm just really into you. In fact..."

Myles quirked a brow when she paused. "In fact..."

"I'm pretty sure I'm falling for you, Myles," Jackie finally admitted. "That's usually something I would prefer to tell you to your face but...I don't know, the thought hit me and I just couldn't hold it in. I had to let you know."

"I'm glad you did." Myles felt himself heat at her words. The good kind of heat. Every progression in his relationship with Jackie amazed him simply because it happened, because there was a part of him that still marveled over the fact that they were together at all. It might not have made sense, but Myles wouldn't change it. "My feelings for you have been deepening, as well. And I'm not simply being reciprocal because you said it; it's been on my mind for several days now."

"Why didn't you say anything?" Jackie asked, a smile in her voice.

"It admittedly freaked me out. I wasn't sure what to do with the feelings. I welcome them, but I surely wasn't expecting them. Especially at this intensity. And I wanted to be sure, since I've never really been in love before."

"I get that," Jackie admitted, to Myles's relief. He was afraid she'd be affronted. "I damn sure wasn't expecting to be sprung over you, either. I'm just glad you're not running from it. Or me."

"If I was going to run from you, Jackie, I'd have done so already."

She laughed. "I'm glad you're ten toes down, then. How's your day going?"

"Work-wise, it's fine. But I admit my mind is rather consumed with something else."

"What?"

"These blasted land developers," Myles spat, his voice hardening. "They have no shame or respect for the history of this city. You know Lula's Cup, right?"

Jackie hesitated briefly. "Yeah..."

"They've harassed the owner, Ms. Lula, to the point that she's actually considering giving up her business that's been there for over forty years. And not just hers, but several businesses around town. Ms. Lula has a special place in my heart, though, and I hate that they're bothering her like they are."

"Oh...yeah, that's not good," Jackie croaked, the usual zest missing from her voice. She cleared her throat.

"From what I hear, Chanel James is leading the charge. Either she doesn't realize or doesn't care that this doesn't only affect Ms. Lula; what about all of her employees? The vendors she works with? All of those people are going to be affected but I suppose that doesn't matter as long as Ms. James meets her quota."

Myles continued to vent about the situation, not noticing that he was pretty much talking to himself until a few minutes had passed without Jackie responding or doing more than giving acknowledging grunts.

"Is something wrong?" he finally asked when his tangent ended. "You're being unusually unresponsive."

"No reason. I'm just listening to you."

"And you have *nothing* to say? As an entrepreneur yourself, I'd think you'd be more incensed over this. Has Chanel approached you? I recall Ethan mentioning seeing you two chatting at the store a while back. Please tell me you aren't friends with her."

A beat passed before Jackie took a deep breath. "Myles, baby, there's something I should probably tell you-"

There was a brief knock on Myles's office door before his boss, Mr. Beck, poked his head in. "Myles, I'm sorry to interrupt but we need you in the conference room. There's a situation with the Morlock account and it's urgent."

"Of course." Myles stood as Mr. Beck ducked back out of the office, though remained just outside the ajar door as if to make sure Myles was expeditious. To Jackie, Myles lowered his voice and murmured, "I need to go; something has come up here. I'll call you later this evening."

"Okay." Jackie's voice sounded mildly relieved. "No problem. Talk to you later."

Myles hung up, sliding his glasses back on before grabbing his tablet and striding around the desk, joining Mr. Beck as they hurried to the conference room. Whatever Jackie had been about to tell him before they were interrupted was forgotten.

Jackie knew she dodged a bullet, however temporarily. She knew she needed to come clean with Myles about her affiliation with Chanel and her true stance on all of the land development hoopla. She couldn't imagine Myles would be glad to hear that she wasn't as against it as he was, and it wasn't something she looked forward to admitting. It wasn't that she'd done anything wrong, but this was something Myles clearly felt strongly about; the idea of upsetting him didn't thrill her.

But Jackie hated secrets, so she was going to suck it up and tell him before they got interrupted. It was a momentary relief, but she knew she had to get everything out on the table. She was sure that once she explained her reasoning for not opposing the land development offers, Myles would be understanding, even if he didn't agree with her.

Unfortunately, Myles ended up having to work late that night on whatever emergency had come up, so they didn't do much more than exchange a few texts before going to bed. Not wanting to drag things out, Jackie invited Myles out the following Saturday night, which thankfully was only two days away. She would have rather seen him sooner, but she'd already promised her Friday night to Cassidy, who'd been fussing about Jackie spending all of her free time with Myles. Jackie promised her a girl's night, which she usually looked forward to, but her mind was on Myles most of the evening. She wasn't kidding when she told him she was falling for him and her craving for him got more intense the longer they were together. Cassidy was utterly floored when she told her.

"You really think you're falling for him?" Cassidy exclaimed. They were in Jackie's living room, curled up in their pajamas, drinking rum and gorging on pizza. Cassidy had also brought over some homemade butter pecan cookies. "Did you actually just say that?"

"I thought we were past the incredulousness over me and Myles. We've been dating for a while now."

"Yeah, true. I guess I *should* stop tripping about that." Cassidy adjusted a fuzzy pink blanket around her waist. "You seem really happy with him."

"I am. And believe me, I still have my moments where I shake my head in disbelief, myself. But really, I don't care if it doesn't make sense. I don't need anyone to understand it. Myles is a handsome, educated, intelligent, deceptively sexy man. And he has me open. That's all that needs to be said."

"Well I guess you told me, didn't you? I get it...I wouldn't love it if you kept questioning my relationship with Orion. And it's not like it took forever for me to get head over heels for him, either; I was sprung after our second date. Though you *were* trying to clown me for that, if I recall correctly..."

"Yeah, I did. But I let it go after a couple of days. You've been keeping up your shock for some months now."

"Well, hell, can you blame me?" Cassidy asked, her head jutting forward slightly as she held up her glass of rum. "You've gotta admit, Jackie, even *you* didn't see this coming."

"I've admitted that. But not expecting it doesn't mean it can't turn out to be one of the best things to ever happen to me."

"So you're more into him than you were into Ringo?"

"Definitely. My relationship with Ringo was unhealthy; I looked at him like a possession. I loved him and believe he loved me, but I'm not sure how we would've worked long-term. To be honest, I'm not even sure I ever thought about that; I was too busy being proud of having one of the sexiest, most-desired men in Brodence in my bed. We're better off as buddies, if that. But it goes deeper than that with Myles."

"Can you see yourself marrying him?"

"Actually yes, one day," Jackie admitted, unable to resist a smile. "It's not something we've talked about yet but I wouldn't be mad at having that conversation at all. Myles really has the potential of taking over my whole heart, Cassidy. I need to make sure I don't do anything to mess this up."

"How do you think you would do that?"

Jackie thoughtfully hunched a shoulder, contemplating as she raked her short nails across her forearm. "Overall, things are good with us. I'd even say great. But our differences can still bring some tension. He tends to think that I'm trying to change or control him, simply because I ask him to ease up on the suits or not talk to me like I'm a business associate."

"Those things bother you that much?"

"I wouldn't say they *bother* me...it's just something he can tweak, you know? I mean, what's wrong with that?"

"What's wrong with him staying the way he is? You became attracted to him for a reason. He was stuffy when you met him and you're still falling for him. Why try to change who he is now?"

"Hey, it's not like he never makes any of the same suggestions to me," Jackie defended. "He's asked me to change from jeans to a dress when we went out to dinner a couple of times. If we're in the car and I'm listening to some rap, he always manages to find an excuse to turn the music down. And don't even get me *started* on how often he straightens up behind me when I throw my clothes on the floor or don't put something back in the right place right away. It's like it makes him itch if everything isn't just so."

"Oh my god," Cassidy laughed, downing the rest of her rum before returning the glass to the coffee table on one of the coasters Myles had insisted on getting for Jackie. She tucked the long red hair of her wig behind her ear. "I'm wondering if you hear yourself right now."

"What?"

"Are you trying to change him?"

"Not *change*. Just tweak. Like I feel he might be doing to me, purposely or not."

"Then you two need to have a talk, then, because that can't work long-term. One supposedly-harmless suggestion too many could send your relationship off the rails before it gets to wherever you're trying to go."

"Look, I sincerely like Myles the way he is. But I don't see what's so wrong with making suggestions for improvement. Shouldn't we *all* be open to that?"

"Tell yourself that the next time you get pissed off when he turns down your Jay-Z."

Sighing, Jackie ran a hand through her short black hair. "You know what the hell I mean, Cassidy."

"Who's benefit is the improvement for; his or yours? And who determines that it's an 'improvement' at all? Just you? It's not like you're asking him to stop smoking or eating fried food for every meal or driving with his knees. There's nothing wrong with what he's doing except for the fact that *you* don't like it. And the same can be said for the shit he bugs you about."

"Ugh," Jackie groaned, sinking against the back of the couch. "I guess you have a point."

"Jackie, girl, all I'm saying is those things are pretty meaningless, in the grand scheme of things. If he wears a suit twenty-four-seven or never listens to hip-hop or continues to be a neat freak, is that going to make you stop wanting him?"

Jackie pondered her answer, though she knew what it was. "No."

"And do you think the same could be said for him if you never again wore a dress or kept being a slob? I know you can't read the man's mind, but, still. Do you?"

"I am not a damn slob. But no; I don't think those things are ultimate deal breakers for Myles. He wouldn't be with me now if they were."

"My point exactly. So just enjoy your nerd-boo and quit worrying about insignificant shit."

"Well, I guess you told me, huh?"

The friends shared a laugh. Jackie managed to put her relationship concerns out of her mind for the rest of the evening and just enjoy her girl's night, feeling more encouraged than when it began.

The next night, Jackie couldn't help but be a little nervous about her date with Myles. Not only because of what she had to tell him regarding the land development situation, but also because she sensed he wouldn't be thrilled with the plans she'd made for the evening. Cassidy's advice rang through her head and part of her felt she should change course, but she managed to convince herself it would be fine. Plus, she'd already bought the tickets and wasn't trying to waste her money.

Myles arrived to pick her up, right on time, as usual, and they shared a lengthy kiss that had Jackie momentarily considering cancelling their plans altogether and just spending the evening fooling around in her bed, but she made herself pull away and grab her purse and keys, insisting on driving.

"What are you up to, Jackie?" Myles asked with a suspicious smile.

"You'll see."

"Where are you taking me?" He slid into the passenger seat of Jackie's Mustang, pulling the seatbelt across his chest.

"It's a surprise. So stop digging and just ride."

"Am I going to enjoy this surprise?"

Jackie's smile faltered slightly. "I hope you'll be open to *trying* to enjoy it."

Myles's eyes narrowed slightly as his smile flattened. "Jackie..."

"Will you relax? It's not like we're going bungee jumping."

"I'd like to think you know better than that."

"What happened to my man that enjoyed trying new things?" Jackie asked playfully, trying to ease the budding tension. "Where's your sense of adventure? Your carefree attitude?"

"Are you confusing me with someone else?"

Jackie laughed, unable to resist. Myles couldn't help but chuckle, himself.

"Just saying, baby, keep an open mind," she requested, glancing at him when they stopped at a red light. "That's all I'm asking. Okay?"

Myles eyed her warily but eventually gave a reluctant nod. "All right. Am I at least dressed appropriately?"

Jackie eyed his tailored charcoal gray suit. "Ehh, you might stand out a little bit. But you're used to that. And if you'll notice, I didn't comment on your clothes or suggest you wear something else so you should be glad about that."

"I suppose."

That reluctant agreement immediately went out the window when they pulled up to an amphitheater and Myles saw the marquee displaying the event for the evening.

"Is this a joke?" Myles asked incredulously, turning to her with fire in his hazel eyes. "Did you seriously try to trick me into attending a *rap concert*??"

Sighing, Jackie rubbed her forehead with her fingertips. She should've expected this reaction but had been hoping to be pleasantly surprised. "Can we not turn this into a major deal? And nobody *tricked* you."

"What do you call purposely omitting where we were going and refusing to give me any details after you insisted on driving so I'd have no means to leave?"

"You have means to leave. There are several rideshare options you can use if you just absolutely want to. But I hope you won't. I thought you agreed to keep an open mind."

"That's before I knew you were bringing me to an event you knew full well I wouldn't agree to attend otherwise. I do not like rap music, Jackie; that's not a secret."

"Okay, well I didn't love racquetball but I went with you to play that, didn't I?"

"You never even played racquetball and had to do it to determine you didn't care for it. And I accept that. But my distaste for rap is *not* new information. So I'm not sure what you were trying to accomplish with this."

"I just..." Jackie looked at him, seeing how upset he was, and realized she messed up. Cassidy's advice to her from the night before blared through her mind yet again. "I'm sorry. Okay? I guess I was just hoping you'd be open to trying something new. This rap artist isn't one that talks about violence or degrades women or uses tons of profanity. They rap about conscious issues that you actually care about. I sincerely thought you might like it."

"You should've just told me that up front, then, instead of using trickery."

"It's not...all right. I'll concede that I should've been straight up. But is it such a terrible thing to step out of your comfort zone every now and then?"

"I'm out of my comfort zone by even being with you, Jackie. And I'm not so inflexible that I *never* want to try anything new, as evidenced when I was eating potato chips and hot sauce with you the other night or when I sit through seemingly countless episodes of that *Custom Salvage* show you love so much. But when you do things like this," he waved a hand towards the amphitheater, "It makes me think again that you're trying to mold me into something you want me to be. Am I not good enough for you as I am?"

She looked over at him, the admonishment clear even in the dim light. "Come on, baby, don't trip. You know better than that."

"Do I? Because I'm starting to wonder if you sincerely want me for me or if I'm nothing more than a project for you. And if that's the case-"

"Oh my god, are you serious?? Do I take it there when you try to tell *me* what to wear to one of your fancy restaurants or get onto me for using too much slang you don't understand? I could ask if you're trying to change me with all that shit. *Are you*??"

"My making a few suggestions or observations here and there isn't the same as *deceiving* you into doing something I know you wouldn't want to do simply because I think you should. And you know it, Jackie, so don't try to turn this back around on me."

"Why do you feel the need to make *suggestions or observations* at all if you truly like me for who *I* am?"

"You tell me. Why do *you*?"

"Myles..." Jackie covered her face with her hands with a deep sigh. "I don't want to argue with you."

"Then you shouldn't have lured me here under false pretenses."

"Didn't I already apologize for that? How long are you going to keep harping on it?"

"Until we're out of this parking lot."

"Wow. So you won't even go in, considering I spent money on the tickets and we're already here? All that stuff about having an open mind was meaningless, huh? Even after I told you that this isn't the kind of rap you hate so much? I took you into account when I chose this, hoping you'd be willing to compromise, but I guess I should've damn known better."

"Like I said, it's how you went about it. You could've told me all of this before we left the house when I asked you where we were going if your intentions were sincere. But the fact that you felt you had to execute it the way you did shows otherwise." Myles turned away from her, looking at the people milling around the parking lot towards the building through the window. "And to answer your question, no I am not going in."

"Fine. Be a big-ass baby about it. I don't even care. But I should've known you saying you'd keep an open mind was cap!"

"As usual, I don't know what that means. My goodness. Can you please talk regularly, for *once*?"

"What's *regular*?? You know what..." Jackie sucked her teeth and put the car in reverse, having never even turned the engine off as they sat there arguing. She zoomed out of the parking lot, annoyed with both Myles and herself. She knew she had handled the situation poorly, but she still couldn't understand why Myles was so incredibly unyielding. Even if it was just because he didn't want her to waste the money she'd spent on the tickets, Jackie would have appreciated that, even if his sour attitude stayed put. But now they were mad at each other *and* she was out two hundred bucks.

They ended up going to get something to eat, since Jackie announced she was hungry and Myles grumbled his agreement. They didn't say anything else to each other, each still carrying major chips on their shoulders from their date night being ruined, and each too stubborn to be the one to try to mend fences. For the time being, they were perfectly fine eating together in silence.

Jackie's mood certainly didn't get any better when they were approached by a familiar face who, as far as Jackie was concerned, had the worst possible timing.

"Jackie, I've been meaning to call you."

Casting a tentative glance across the table at Myles, Jackie sighed and looked up at Chanel.

"Chanel," she greeted dryly, resisting the strong urge to tell her to get lost.

"I don't mean to interrupt your..." Chanel looked back and forth between Jackie and Myles with a growing intrigued smirk, "Is this a date?"

"Yes. And you *are* interrupting, so-"

"Wait...Chanel?" Myles spoke up, looking up at their visitor with a slight frown. "The Chanel that's going around trying to oust our landmark businesses?"

"Oh joy, another fan," Chanel sighed, her smirk disappearing. "That's not exactly what I'm doing-"

"That's not how it looks to me. Ms. Lula over at Lula's Cup has told me that you've pestered her to exhaustion. I can only imagine she's not the only one."

"Look, I'm just doing my job. Everything can't stay the same forever. And it's not like I'm the only one who believes some change is necessary around here. Right, Jackie?"

Jackie's face flamed as Myles's glare turned to her, his eyes widening slightly.

"*Is* that right, Jackie?" he snipped, his hazel eyes now shooting accusatory daggers.

"Of course it is," Chanel forged ahead before Jackie could. "She and I are on the same page when it comes to all the necessary land development. And it's a relief because outside of her, I have next to no allies in all this."

Jackie's hand actually itched with the urge to give Chanel one good slap across the face. She'd totally thrown her under the bus, and Jackie chose to believe it was purposeful. Maybe Chanel was getting tired of being the sole receiver of vitriol and wanted to share some of the score.

"Oh, so you're an *ally*?" Myles sneered, folding his arms across his chest. His gaze was still locked on Jackie's, agitation growing with every second she sat there dumbfounded. He figured Chanel's words were true because Jackie would have already vehemently denied them if they weren't.

"Chanel...go away," Jackie ordered through gritted teeth, throwing a murderous look to the stunned land developer.

Realizing she must have said something she shouldn't have, Chanel held up her hands. "Sorry if I spoke out of turn. I'm not trying to cause any trouble, in this city and especially not with your man, here. My whole point was-"

"Bitch, you are *two seconds* from getting the beatdown of the fucking century and I swear I won't feel one ounce of remorse about it. I *said* get the hell away from here!"

"Ugh, fine. I'm gone." Chanel turned on her heel and quickly strutted off.

Jackie made herself turn her eyes back to Myles, who was sitting there fuming so hard she could almost see it radiating from him. As if their evening wasn't already going bad enough.

"Myles...look. I know you're upset-"

"I was upset about the nonsense with the rap concert. This? *This* pisses me off."

Chapter 15

As soon as they were back at Jackie's, all hell broke loose.

"So you're in on this bullshit, too, huh?" Myles roared, making Jackie rear at both his volume and his language. She'd never heard him speak that way before and didn't think she ever would. "You're in cahoots with that woman??"

"I am not in *cahoots* with anybody! It's not like I told them to come around here trying to change anything!"

"But you apparently have no problem with them doing, it, from what the woman said. Or was she lying?"

"She..." Jackie knew she couldn't do anything but be honest. "No, she wasn't lying."

Myles straightened, his chest heaving with anger. "Wow. So all those times I vented to you about what was going on with Ms. Lula and the other businesses around here, I was apparently trusting the wrong person with that."

"Myles, come on...don't take it there."

"Why shouldn't I?"

"I get that this means a lot to you but please understand...it's not like I'm going around co-signing and campaigning with Chanel on all this. And I told her that shit in confidence; it wasn't supposed to be broadcasted."

"I'm glad she told me because *you* certainly didn't. And likely wouldn't have."

"Myles, I was going to tell you. This was what I was starting to say a couple days ago when you got called away for that meeting. I had every intention of telling you tonight."

"How convenient," he scoffed, shaking his head as he looked away. "Was this going to be before or after your ill-advised rap concert?"

"Oh my *gosh*!" Jackie exclaimed, running her hands down her face before clawing them in the air in front of her. "How long are you going to fuss about something I've already apologized for?? I said I was sorry about that, dammit! Can we focus on this *latest* thing you're pissed at me about, please??"

"Fine, let's! Tell me how you've waited this long to inform me of your opposing stance on something that you *know* means a lot to me! I've confided in you about how I felt about all of this more than once, Jackie; the other day wasn't the first time!"

"Honestly, I didn't expect you to get this incensed about it! Baby, I really need you to calm down enough to where you can think rationally and at least *try* to see my side on this."

"What??"

"Myles, I had no malicious intent. But you've gotta remember, baby, I didn't grow up here like you did...I don't have the same affiliation and affection for these places that you do. I respect them; hell, I love Ms. Lula, too. I don't want to see anything bad happen to her, or any of the other businesses Chanel is targeting."

"So why don't you see a problem with what she's trying to do, then?"

"I just don't think it'll be the end of the world. It's not like Chanel is trying to burn everything down. When she approached me about my land, I figured I could just build a better garage somewhere else. I don't have the same attachment as everybody else but it doesn't mean I don't care. I specifically told Chanel that I was fine with going with the majority on all this, *not* that I love what she's doing."

Myles just looked at her for a moment before shaking his head and blowing out a long breath. He removed his glasses and rubbed his eyes wearily, then gazed at the floor for several beats before looking back up at her with tired eyes.

"I get what you're saying," he finally informed.

Some of the twisted tension in Jackie's belly unfurled at his comment and she blew out a quiet breath of relief.

"But I still don't think you really understand the enormity of what it would mean to this city if Lula's Cup closed," Myles continued, a tiny bit of the bite returning to his voice. "It's not just a coffee shop; it's a landmark around here. My parents would take me there when I was a child. Ms. Lula would babysit me and Mollie while they went off to one of their many obligations and weren't able to take us with them. She loved us as if we were her own children."

Jackie stilled.

"Not to mention what she does for so many other people around here. Someone's house burns down or gets broken into, she's the first one to organize a help drive. A new business opens, she's welcoming them and sending over business. She'll employ the homeless without even batting an eye if they're willing to work. She holds dinners for anyone that has no family or anywhere else to go, on Thanksgiving or Christmas or just a random night of the week. We had a shady mayor for years and she was one of the few who had the guts to stand up to him, organizing boycotts and rallies when he tried to cut school funding and was suspected of taking bribes. All kinds of people have been to her shop, and they love Ms. Lula as much as I do. I could keep going about the things she's done for the people of this city and the impact she's made. After all that, Ms. Lula deserves to go out on her *own* terms, and not be bullied out by someone whose pursuit of dollar signs makes them blind to history."

Hearing all of that made Jackie feel like a heel. She had no idea about everything Ms. Lula had done, and she was sure that probably wasn't even the half of it. Even though she hadn't been the one putting pressure on Ms. Lula or anyone else, now the fact that she even marginally agreed with who was made her feel awful.

"I'm so sorry," she finally muttered, moving closer to Myles. She placed her hands on his chest but he kept his head turned away from her. She stared up at him pleadingly, willing him to give her those eyes of his that she loved so much. "Really. You're right; I didn't realize how deep it was."

Myles turned his head in her direction but kept his face lowered. He started to turn away again but Jackie caught his face between her hands, bringing it even with hers.

"You *have* to know that I would never intentionally do anything that would bring you stress or that I knew would hurt you," she insisted. "Tell me you know that, baby."

"Jackie, I just..." His jaw clenched under her hands. "Maybe we're not-"

"No" Her voice was strong and defiant. "I'm not gonna let you use this as an excuse to push me away. I own my part in this but it doesn't have to affect our relationship,

Myles. What we have is too real to let it go just because of a difference of opinion."

He eyed her. "I wouldn't really call this a 'difference of opinion', Jackie."

"Whatever you want to call it. This doesn't have to come between us. Do you really want to walk away from me? From us, just over this?"

Several beats passed before he finally took light hold of her wrists. "No. I don't *want* to, Jackie. I have real feelings for you. I'm just..."

Jackie's head jerked expectantly. "You just *what*?"

"I'm just starting to wonder if we're *too* different," he finally replied. His hands slid down her arms, then down her sides before falling away. "If we were to stay together...would we just end up resenting each other because of our differences?"

"No," Jackie automatically replied, her voice emphatic. "At least, I don't think so."

"You seriously think that? You can see yourself enduring the things that annoy you so much about me long-term?"

"I'd like to think we're both mature enough to recognize minor things for what they are. Things might get on my nerves in the moment but that doesn't affect my feelings for you. When I said I was falling for you, those weren't just words. I meant it."

"I believe you." He stepped back, releasing himself from her hold and looking at her with a thoughtful expression. "Everything I've said about my feelings for you has been sincere, as well. Believe me, I want this to work. I'm just starting to wonder about the feasibility that it actually can."

"Just because we've had a couple of disagreements?"

"Jackie. You're more intelligent than that. It goes deeper than what happened tonight. This is no longer just a matter of a difference of personality or habits; this is a difference of values. That's not as easily ignored."

Folding her arms, Jackie looked away. "Are you ending this, Myles?"

He hesitated, his shoulders sagging. "I honestly don't know what I'm doing. And I probably shouldn't make any declarations until I do."

"So what does that mean?"

"It means I need time to figure it out. I need to step back from this."

"Wow." Jackie scoffed, feeling her skin burn. "Just like that. I do something you don't like and now you're questioning our whole relationship."

"Please don't make it sound so menial."

"It's not?"

"I'm not enjoying this, Jackie. When I came here earlier, it was with the intention of spending a beautiful evening with my lady, not any of this. My desire for you isn't in question. I want you, Jackie. But-"

"What we want isn't always what's good for us," Jackie concluded for him. She stared at him with stinging eyes, wondering how the hell they ended up at this point. She, too, had been looking forward to their evening together and couldn't believe this was how it was going to end. "I get it."

"So you agree?"

"No. I personally don't think this isn't something we can get past if we both want to. I'm ten toes down and I *thought* you were, too. But I can't force you to stay, and I'm damn sure not gonna beg. So if you feel 'taking a step back' or whatever is what you need to do, then have at it."

She expected him to go right for the door, but Myles didn't move. He just stared at her with a remorseful expression, as if he was already questioning his decision.

"Please don't resent me for this," he asked of her. "Can you promise me that?"

"I can't promise anything, Myles."

"Jackie-"

"I'm hurt. I'm pissed. And I can't keep standing this close to you knowing you're not as sure about us as I am. So...just go."

Briefly hanging his head, Myles turned for the door, his eyes still on Jackie, who was looking everywhere but at him. "I know what I said a moment ago, but I'm *not* ending this. I just want to make that clear."

"Sure. But *I* want to make it clear that I won't sit on my hands forever while you're figuring your shit out. So take that into account while you're doing all this soul searching."

Jackie finally let her eyes meet his and they shared a long look, saying nothing. Their gazes were just starting to melt towards longing before she snapped out of it, catching herself, and stormed off towards her room. Myles just looked after her, opening his mouth to call her back but nothing came out. He hesitated several more moments before finally making himself trudge towards the door, hoping he hadn't just made the final blunder between him and Jackie.

Cassidy knew something was going on with Jackie, but her friend was being uncharacteristically tight-lipped about whatever it was. Though her snappiness and biting everyone's head off said plenty.

But when Cassidy returned from running a couple of errands to find Jackie straight going *off* on a customer, she knew it had to be something major.

"I don't give a fuck what you think you know or what they do at some other janky-ass garage!" Jackie practically yelled, her neck rolling in glaring 'pissed off' fashion. "I done told you before not to come in here trying to tell me how to do my fucking job! If you think you know so damn much, take your raggedy-ass car back and fix it your fucking *self*!"

"Jackie! What in the world is going on here?!?"Cassidy demanded, looking back and forth between her fire-breathing boss and the customer who was stunned mute. He looked frozen in place.

"I have *told* this man ten times what needs to happen for me to properly finish fixing his car," Jackie immediately responded, her voice accusatory as she jabbed a finger in the customer's direction. "But he keeps coming in my face challenging every damn thing I say, telling me what they do at other places and spouting shit he read on the internet. And I'm telling him if he wants to YouTube how to fix his little wind-up car, then good luck. And when you fuck it up even more than it already is, don't even bring it back here. 'Cause I am *over it!!*"

"Go to the office," Cassidy ordered to Jackie, pointing the way with one hand and pushing her towards it with the other. "Get yourself together. I will deal with this."

Jackie looked like she had more she wanted to say to the red-faced customer but at Cassidy's pointed glare, she turned and stomped off to her office, slamming the door behind her and making Cassidy jump. Momentarily closing her eyes, Cassidy forced a tight smile to the customer and began the butt-kissing mission to ensure he didn't not only take his business elsewhere, but also bad-mouth them to anyone who would listen.

It was another twenty minutes before Cassidy finally joined Jackie in the office. Thankfully, it was the end of the day, so all the doors were locked and there would be no more customers for Jackie to take her clear frustration out on for the day. Jackie had already sent her other employees home, not wanting to be bothered.

"What the hell was that, Jackie??"

Jackie banged her fingers on the keys of her laptop, eyes on the gibberish she'd been filling her screen with to try to calm herself down. It hadn't worked. "I *told* you I didn't wanna talk about it!"

"Well, that's out the window now, isn't it? Because you just acted a complete ass to a customer out there, something you'd surely fire one of us for if we did, so 'I don't wanna talk about it' just isn't gonna fly anymore."

"Who's the fucking boss around here??"

"What I saw out there wasn't boss behavior, with you getting in your damn feelings so much that you're cussing out paying customers. *I* just had to clean up *your* fucking mess, so the fact that you sign my paychecks is irrelevant right now. Answer me; w*hat* is going on with you?"

Jackie just kept banging on the keys, staying stubbornly silent.

Cassidy went and stood right in front of her, frowning at her defiant friend. "This is your best friend from tenth grade talking right now, Jackie, not your employee. Now dammit, what is it?"

Jackie's fingers steadily slowed until she finally plopped against the back of her chair. Squeezing her eyes shut, she rubbed her fingertips across them, a headache sprouting like mental weeds. "I'm just in a bad mood."

"No shit. Why?"

Sighing, Jackie squeezed her eyes even harder to keep the sudden tears at bay. "Because I realized I'm completely in love with Myles after he told me he needed a break from me."

"Oh..." Cassidy's frustrated frown melted into a compassionate one as she perched herself on the edge of the desk, eyes aimed on her anguished friend. "Girl...why didn't you say anything?"

"For what? What's the point? Breakups happen. It's not supposed to be the end of the world."

"Do you think you're not supposed to be hurt about this? And I thought you said he just needed a break."

"It doesn't feel like just a break. It's been three days and we haven't communicated at all. He said he wasn't ending it but I've been preparing myself for the kiss-off text or email to come any day now. I even ripped my affirmation board off the wall because I'm too pissed and in too much pain for some fucking mantras."

"Did you two have a fight or something?"

"You could say that." Jackie recalled what happened on her date with Myles, from her trying to trick him into going to a rap concert, to the run-in with Chanel, to the blow-up afterwards.

"And the thing that frustrates me the most is that I see his damn point," Jackie concluded, adjusting the scarf covering her hair. "The more I thought about it, the more I started to wonder if he didn't do what I would've eventually done my damn self. Myles and I *are* widely different and probably all wrong for each other. He gets on my last nerve and I *know* I get on his."

"But you're still in love with him."

"A lot of good that is."

"Jackie, girl, you and Myles being different doesn't have to mean you're wrong for each other. You might each be just what the other needs. I know you've been happier since you got with him."

"Yeah, well." Jackie sighed, leaning her head back and closing her eyes again. "Looks like I'm gonna have to find a way to be happy *without* him, too."

"Will you stop? The man didn't break up with you. Do you know how many times Orion and I took breaks from each other? More than I can count. And we always went right back to each other because that's where we both wanted to be. Stepping back from something you love for a minute doesn't mean you don't want it anymore."

"I think this whole thing with Ms. Lula might be his breaking point."

"I doubt it. You explained yourself and he said he understood. He seems intelligent enough not to let something like that be the deciding factor about your relationship. Speaking of that, though, why the hell didn't you tell *me* that you would be okay with selling the garage if it came to that?"

Jackie's eyes opened. She'd momentarily forgotten that she hadn't in fact shared that with Cassidy when she started spilling her guts about Myles.

"I'm sorry," she sighed. "I guess I didn't want you to get upset at me, too."

"Either way, we're supposed to be in this together. I didn't leave my rising career to come work for you only for you to be keeping secrets."

"Rising career? You worked in a call center. And you hated it."

"That's not the point. I was still good at it. But as soon as you offered me this job, I jumped, didn't I?"

"You were looking for another job anyway, Cassidy."

"Quit trying to make yourself less wrong."

"You're right." Jackie held up her hands in concession. "I definitely should have been up front with you about all that. Part of me didn't think it was that big of a deal but I can admit that I didn't want anyone giving me the side-eye like they've been giving Chanel. Regardless, though; like you said, we're in this together and I should have told you."

"I accept your apology. Have you calmed down now? Do you feel any better?"

"Marginally. Thank you for stepping in out there; now that I think about how I was acting, I'm thoroughly embarrassed. Was he pissed?"

"He was pretty freaked out. I think I smoothed things over enough, but he won't be bringing his car back here. Hopefully he won't go bashing us online. I'm just grateful that no one else was in there and that he wasn't savvy enough to record the whole thing."

"Ugh." Jackie rubbed her temples, her headache beating like a punishment for letting her emotions cause her to lose a paying – if however difficult – customer. "I really need to get it together. I cannot believe I let my relationship issues jack me up so much that it messes with my money."

"Another indication that your boo Myles is something special." Cassidy stood from the desk, going around to grab Jackie's arm and pull her from the chair. "Enough of this self-defeatist stuff. We're going to get everything closed out and then go to dinner. Maybe even find a karaoke night somewhere."

Not having the energy to protest, Jackie just let her friend push her out of the office so they could get closed up. She wasn't really in the mood to go out but it beat sitting at home drinking rum and overanalyzing her relationship with Myles like she'd been doing.

And trying to ignore the sexual frustration and withdrawal she was already experiencing from not getting to be up under Myles for three days.

Once they got the garage shut down and locked up for the night, Cassidy ushered Jackie across town to a small bar that she found on Brodence's social media that claimed to be having karaoke that night. Jackie, having cleaned up at the garage and now donning jeans and a fitted tee, told herself to try to have fun. She missed Myles but she couldn't keep stressing over him.

After a couple of beers and several comical performances, Jackie had managed to laugh and forget about her issues for a while. She even got onstage with Cassidy for an off-key rendition of "The Boy is Mine." The song choice was Cassidy's.

"*Please* tell me we can blame your tone-deafness on the alcohol."

Jackie whipped around to see Mollie looking down at her with good-natured amusement, her boho locs hanging over her shoulder and a hand on her hip. Jackie giggled.

"I'm blaming everything on the alcohol tonight."

"Girl, you're talking my language. It's how I'm gonna justify going home with that couple over there and banging both of them 'til the sun comes up."

Almost spitting out the beer she just sipped, Jackie gawked at her before her eyes darted around the room for the couple in question, wiping at her chin with the side of her hand. "What? Who??"

"Them over there," Mollie confirmed, pointing discreetly to a man and woman sitting at the end of the bar, talking amongst themselves. They looked like the last people that would be having a threesome, with their nondescript clothing and poised mannerisms. They looked out of place just sitting there.

"*Them?*" Jackie confirmed, not being nearly as discreet as she pointed for confirmation. "Are you serious??"

"Don't let the muted looks fool you. They're some freaks. It's always the most conservative ones, you know."

Mollie flipped her hair from her shoulder. "I've had a rough past few days and they're about to be my stress relief."

"I get it, at least about the rough past few days part. Well, hey, if you're all down, then get it, girl."

"Consider it gotten. I'm glad I ran into you, though. You're coming to our folks' anniversary party, right? I'm supposed to finalize all the invitations and you just saved me a stamp."

"You could've just called and asked if I was still going."

"Calling is so passé."

"Girl..." Jackie couldn't help but chuckle. "I'd like to go but honestly, I'm not sure. That might be something you need to ask your brother."

Mollie's narrow eyes turned curious. "What does that mean?"

"It means Myles and I are kinda up in the air right now. He's wondering if he really wants to be with me and I'm giving him his space. For the time being, anyway." She glanced back towards the stage where Cassidy was trying her best with an Anita Baker song.

"Oh, hell, I thought it was something major," Mollie scoffed, waving a dismissive hand. "Myles isn't going anywhere."

Cassidy's performance forgotten, Jackie whirled back around. "And how do you know that?"

"Because I know my brother. Because I believe in love. Because I might've overheard him telling Daddy the other day that he's head over heels for you and wants to figure out how to make it work."

Jackie gasped, her heart instantly pounding faster. "Mollie, don't play with me. Are you being for real right now?"

"I like to mess with people but I wouldn't joke about matters of the heart and shit. I heard him loud and clear when I was pretending not to be eavesdropping. He's just confused and befuddled right now 'cause he's new to this kind of relationship; you know, the kind with a woman who isn't some kind of cardboard cutout of supposed idealism. There might be part of him that's looking for an excuse to run but that's not what he really wants to do. I'd bet my cats on it."

Jackie's eyes fell to the floor, giddiness tingling her skin at this information. "I'll be damned..."

"But you didn't hear that from me," Mollie added, pointing a brief finger. "And since I'm running my mouth about stuff, I'll go ahead and tell you that I don't think you should leave how long y'all stay on ice up to him. If you give him unlimited time, he'll take it, overanalyzing everything to death and dissecting it like some business deal. Go and *demand* that he tell you this shit himself. Get your man. 'Cause he absolutely still wants you, girl."

Jackie just sat there processing all this as Mollie flounced off towards her freak-in-the-sheets entertainment for the evening, her smile growing by the second.

"Thank God for nosy little sisters."

Chapter 16

"Is that a Polo shirt you're wearing?"

Myles looked down at his outfit before glancing back at his stunned mother. "Yes..."

"Since when do you wear those?"

"I'm not understanding what the big deal is. And may I come in, please?"

"Oh, oh, of course," Agatha stammered, shaking her head as she stepped aside to let her son into the house. "I apologize. The lack of your customary suit threw me off. I don't even remember the last time I've seen your arms."

"It's a casual visit; I figured there was no need to dress so formally. And why are you answering the door? Where is Lloyd?" Myles asked, referring to his parents' live-in help that had been there for years but tended to be seen and not heard, he was so quiet. Agatha had protested even needing anyone in such a capacity but her compounding health issues caused her protests to be basically ignored. She now loved Lloyd, even though she constantly had to be reminded to let him do what he was there to do.

"He's fixing dinner. I'm capable of answering the door myself. I wish you all would stop treating me like I'm made of candy glass."

"No one thinks you're made of candy glass. Whatever that is. But I don't know why you're so resistant of getting proper rest. You're in a position where you don't have to strain yourself doing anything unnecessary."

"I came and opened the front door; I didn't swan dive off the roof. Chill out. You want something to drink? You hungry?"

"I could eat. And I'll get my own drink, thank you. Where's Dad?"

"At a meeting. He should be back in a little bit. Come on in here."

Myles followed his mother into the den, which was one of her favorite places in the house. French rap music flowed through the wall speakers, and Myles almost chuckled to himself. He'd temporarily forgotten that his mother loved listening to that. It was only because it was in French that Myles found it tolerable. He wondered if Jackie would like it.

"What's been going on with you, sweetheart?" Agatha asked him once they were both settled. She curled up in the corner of her huge couch that she fell in love with as soon as she saw it on the furniture showroom floor; it was a little big for the room but she didn't care. Patting the cushion next to her after Myles poured himself some Malbec at the bar, she pressed a button on the remote on the end table next to her, lowering the volume of the music. "You look like you've got something on your mind."

"A couple of things." Myles took a sip of his drink, eyes on the wall-to-wall built-in bookcase in front of him.

"Talk to me. Is work going okay? A hitch in your foundation plans? A problem with you and Jackie?"

Myles's jaw twitched at the mention of his woman's name. They still hadn't spoken since he told her he needed some time days earlier, and trying to distract himself with work and crime shows and endless games of racquetball wasn't helping. He missed her something terrible, but he was still flummoxed about their situation. Of if they even had a situation and he was making an issue out of nothing. That's what his dad Hamilton surmised when he came over to talk to him about it a couple of days before; Hamilton thought Myles was just freaking out because he was experiencing a level of feelings he hadn't before, and with a woman he'd never expect to fall for in a thousand years. They'd had a long father-son talk, with Hamilton giving Myles some much-needed advice on love and relationships. Myles had felt encouraged, though he still hadn't reached out to Jackie. Everything in him wanted to, but he kept making excuses to himself to put it off.

"It's not about Jackie," he finally grunted, grateful that it seemed his father had kept their talk to himself. "I'm worried about Ms. Lula. I went by to see her this morning and that Chanel woman was there. I admittedly lost my temper when I saw her; we had some words before Ms. Lula had to pull me aside and calm me down. I just wish I could make that woman and all of her unwanted development plans go back to where they came from."

"Lula is a tough old bird; she can handle whatever they try to throw at her," Agatha insisted. "This certainly isn't the first time someone's tried to come for her business. With everything she's been through already, this is kid's stuff."

"I don't know, Mom. Maybe it's *because* she's already been through so much that she won't have the energy to contend with this, too. I'd hate to see her give in just to get some peace."

"I assure you, Lula will be just fine, baby. Her coffee shop will be fine, too. It's too important to this community. But I love that you're so concerned about her." She smiled at him, her head resting on one of the large couch cushions and her thin arms folded loosely over her stomach. "I'm so proud of the man you've become."

Myles couldn't help but smile at that. He loved hearing that he made his parents proud. "Thank you, Mom. I credit my amazing parents." His smile grew when Agatha blew a kiss at him.

"Thank you, sweetheart. And don't you stress over Lula; everything will turn out like it's supposed to. Now," Agatha slightly adjusted her position, her smile widening with eager excitement. "Tell me how things are going with Jackie. I really like her. And I like her for *you*, son."

Myles's eyebrows lifted. "You do? Why is that?"

"Because I can see she makes you happy. I saw the way you two were gazing at each other at Mollie's showcase; I've *never* seen you look at anyone like that. You've certainly seemed less uptight since you've been seeing her. I mean, you're wearing that short-sleeved shirt and everything."

"Mom..." Myles couldn't help but chuckle. "I...I admit that Jackie has had an effect on me, almost without me realizing it. Though I..."

Agatha nodded encouragingly. "You...?"

Myles briefly wavered on how much he should say. Or if he should say anything at all. "Jackie means a lot to me. I'll admit I have feelings for her that I haven't felt for anyone else. Frankly, I'm in love with her, Mom. But there's still this lingering concern that she's trying to change me."

Frowning slightly, Agatha sat up straight. "Why would you think such a thing? Change you how?"

"How I dress. How I speak. My tendencies and preferences...she's made several comments about them over the course of our relationship. I can't tell you how many times we've butted heads over my wearing suits all the time. I've wondered if she could fully accept me the way I am."

"You don't think she can?"

"She says she can. She's insisted that she's not trying to control or change me. And to be fair, she's had the same concerns about me doing that to her. It's one of the reasons I've wondered if maybe we're too different, despite how we feel about each other...and if those differences would eventually be detrimental."

"Do you think, at her core, Jackie would be a different woman if she didn't have whatever issues you apparently quibble with her about?"

Myles's eyes turned thoughtfully to his clasped hands. "I think the way she is is what endears me to her. Even the parts that agitate me."

"Exactly. And she might be able to say the same about you. Come here, sweetheart."

Myles slid closer to his mother and she immediately slid her hand down his arm until it clasped his. She looked at her son like the adoring mother she was. "I've never asked you this but since we're talking about it...why *do* you stay so buttoned-up all the time? And please don't say there's no reason. Ever since you could dress yourself, you've chosen shirts and ties over t-shirts. You've even worn suits to family picnics."

Wincing slightly in recollection, Myles considered his mother's words. It hadn't occurred to him how long he'd been dressing the way he had. "I could say it's just what I like to wear; and it is. But I can admit that it started because I felt like...well, I felt I had to live up to the image of being the son of Agatha and Hampton Cornwall."

"Really?"

"Yes. I've always been proud to be your son, though I can admit my reasons for that have matured as I have. Over the years, it's become more habit than anything else. Though I *can* concede that there have been times when I felt out of place or even ridiculous donning a suit when everyone else was dressed so casually."

"So why did you keep doing it? You know you never have to put on airs for us. Hell, I was the one walking around here wearing Mickey Mouse ears."

"Oh, I recall," Myles chuckled. "And I can also admit that there's some stubbornness involved. Whenever someone – usually Mollie – makes some kind of comment on my clothing it just makes me that much more determined to continue wearing it. It's as if I'd be admitting I was doing something wrong if I were to change based off their comments. The same can be said for Jackie; now that I think about it, I didn't want her believing she could make me change what I felt was a part of me simply because she thought I should."

"Sweetheart, I obviously don't know Jackie as well as you, but call it women's intuition when I say that I think her requests were more about wanting you to let your guard down around her more than about changing *you*. It's like your suits are an armor you're hiding behind or something."

Myles chewed his bottom lip as he considered his mother's assessment. "I've never considered that."

"I've literally *never* seen you in jeans. It's still blowing my mind that you're not wearing a jacket and tie right now, or at least a button-down. Just curious, why aren't you?"

"As simplistic as it sounds...it's hot."

Agatha burst out laughing, causing Myles to chuckle. "I'll take it."

"And..." Myles made himself continue, "Jackie bought me this shirt and I've never worn it. So..."

Grinning, Agatha squeezed her son's hand. "I love to see you sprung. Don't let this woman get away."

"Mom..." Myles ducked his head, actually blushing.

"Myles, baby, stay true to yourself, but don't be afraid of or resistant to change. It's not conceding. We grow, we evolve; it's the fun of life. Some changes are for the better. And it doesn't take anything away from you to take what your woman likes into account, as long as you're not compromising your values to do it. And hopefully she's willing to do the same for you. I couldn't *begin* to tell you all the ways I've changed since I met your father, and I'm sure he can say the same; we've only been better together for it. It can be the same for you and Jackie, if that's what you both want."

Myles did want that. Any recent thoughts of his future always included Jackie. Despite whatever concerns he had about their differences, he couldn't help but imagine her right by his side. The few days they'd been apart only cemented that he didn't want to lose her. He could only hope his foot-dragging hadn't made her realize she was better off without him.

Finally getting his nerve a few hours later, Myles grabbed his phone to call Jackie so they could talk but she beat him to it; the phone rang in his hand with a call from her asking if she could come over. He readily agreed, though he was nervous as to what the outcome of their conversation would be. Would she finally decide she was tired of him and his crap and end it? Would she agree that they were just too different and were better off apart?

Since it would be a good hour or so before Jackie would arrive, Myles turned on some smooth jazz to calm his nerves and concentrated on assembling more care kits for the homeless to keep his mind from spiraling. It was something that always centered him, and that's what he needed right then. His troubles momentarily disappeared as he lovingly placed the various toiletries and snacks and bottles of water into the totes, smiling to himself. It truly did his heart good to give those out to the homeless and see the genuine appreciation in return, and know that he was easing their burdens even in a small and somewhat temporary way.

His mind drifted to the progress he was making with Veronica on the homeless foundation. They'd filed all the necessary paperwork, finished assembling the board, secured several donors, and were getting the website and social media campaigns up and running as they brainstormed their introductory event. Myles looked forward to every Zoom call or meeting they had, as eager as anyone to get things up and running. He was also putting in time on his own passion project for the homeless, making sure his proposal was as fine-tuned as he could possibly get it. He planned on having Ethan look it over to get another perspective and make sure he wasn't missing anything.

He was so deep in his thoughts about all of this that he was almost startled when the doorbell rang. He absently glanced at his watch, frowning curiously at the intrusion, then he remembered Jackie was coming over and hurried to the door, his frown melting into one of eagerness and anxiety.

"Hey," Jackie greeted him once they were face-to-face.

Myles's eyes roamed over her, taking in her chest-hugging powder blue v-neck sweater, fitted dark jeans, and blue and white wedge sneakers. Silver hoops hung from her ears and a silver chain was nestled in her ample cleavage, and the urge to bury his face there was strong enough to knock Myles over.

"Are you gonna invite me in or..." she asked after a few moments of Myles staring at her, an amused smile on her glossed lips.

"Oh, um, of course..." Myles stepped aside, his face heating at his behavior. "Please, come in."

She smelled like bubblegum as she walked past him, something Myles never cared for but on her it was the most delectable and enticing fragrance. His urge to wrap himself around her and not let go intensified.

Jackie was having a similar reaction to seeing Myles again. She'd missed him so much it ached and couldn't take another night in limbo, so she called and asked to come over. And seeing him in the shirt she'd bought him, actually showing off those smooth toned arms of his and looking absolutely delicious, made her want to jump him first and talk later.

But she told herself to get it together; they had things to handle first.

Placing a hand to her chest, she glanced around his living room, taking note of the boxes of supplies and canvas totes, as well as the notepad on the glass coffee table where it appeared he was checking items off a list.

"Are you putting together your care kits?"

"I am." Myles moved further into the room, sliding his hands into his pockets. He seemed to be purposely keeping distance between them, though she could feel his nervousness from where she stood. She wondered if he could feel hers, too.

"I've always loved that you have such a passion for this," she commented softly, looking around her and feeling herself fall for him even deeper. "It really says something about what kind of person you are."

"It's important to me. Though I admit I got engrossed in this tonight to help take my mind off of what might come of this conversation." He rubbed the back of his neck. "I can't help but think that..."

When he didn't finish, Jackie stepped closer to him. "You can't help but think what?"

He eyed her for a moment before dropping his hand to his side with a steeling breath. "Did you come here to end it? Have I blown it again with you, Jackie?"

"No." She quickly closed the rest of the distance between them, blindly tossing her purse on the couch before taking his face in her hands. Her chest thumped as she assured, "I came here to tell you I'm *not* losing you. That I'm in this and I don't care how different we are. I don't care if you wear suits everyday and never listen to rap and clean up behind me 'til the cows come home. You mean more to me than any of that insignificant shit. We've both fumbled in this relationship but that doesn't mean we shouldn't be together. Unless..." She swallowed, "That's not what you want-"

"No, it is!" Myles insisted, grabbing hold of her waist and pulling her closer. "It is absolutely what I want. *You're* what I want, Jackie. This, us...it's all I want."

Her fingers flexed slightly. "Are you sure?"

"I've never been more certain of anything. I've missed you more than I can express."

"I've missed *you*. Myles..."

"And for the record, I in turn don't care if you never dress formally or leave your clothes on the floor or pop that god-forsaken gum you like to chew when you work in my ear. I've never felt for a woman what I feel for you and I'm not letting you go."

Jackie had never felt such relief as she felt in that moment. Even with Mollie's assurances (and her eavesdropping report) Jackie had still been worried that Myles might have talked himself into believing they were better off apart. Knowing that he wanted her as much as she wanted him made her want to dance on the roof.

"I love you, Myles," she stated with every ounce of feeling in her body, looking right into his eyes. "I'm *so* fucking in love with you. And I need to know you won't run from this again."

"I'm not running anywhere." His hand grabbed her face, brushing his thumb along her bottom lip. "I'm in love with you, too. I'm yours, Jackie." He licked his lips. "Indefinitely."

The drop in his voice and the look in his eyes instantly had parts of Jackie's body clenching and tightening. She felt her nipples harden against his chest. Unable to help it, she eased her tongue out and tasted Myles's thumb before dipping her head and taking it into her mouth, giving it a few soft suckles before slowly sliding her mouth from base to tip. His hazel eyes darkened behind his glasses as his breathing deepened, and he quickly leaned down and took her lips in a kiss that went from zero to sixty in seconds. Jackie threw her arms around his neck, unable to get close enough to him, as they wildly made out in the middle of his cluttered living room.

"Before I take you to my bed and ravage you," Myles grunted, briefly tearing his mouth from hers, "I just want to make one more thing clear, for the record."

"What's that?"Jackie panted, her hand fisting his shirt.

"In regards to what we said a moment ago; I want it to be said and agreed..." His hands slid into the back pockets of her jeans and pulled her against his throbbing erection, "That you're mine."

Jackie had never wanted a man as much as she wanted Myles in that moment. Literally jumping into his arms, she wound herself around him as she savored those lips of his she'd grown to love so much, holding the side of his neck in a possessive grip.

"A thousand percent agreed. I am absolutely all yours, Mr. Cornwall," she concurred against his lips. "And you're damn sure mine. *All* mine. Now I believe you said something about ravaging me?"

Grinning, Myles hurriedly carried Jackie to his bedroom.

"If how you just put it on me is how it's going to be from here on out now that we've re-committed to each other, I'm here for it," Jackie teased some time later, her naked body on top of Myles's. "You must've really missed all this, huh?"

Myles chuckled, running his fingertips through her super-short hair. "You have no idea."

"Believe me, you're not by yourself. Who would've thought we'd go from me wanting to throw you out of my garage to us being in your bed all tangled and naked and in love and shit?"

"You have such a way with words."

"You like it."

"I like *you*. I don't always love the language. But I realize that's just part of your package and I accept that."

"Yes, I know you don't always love my potty mouth. I can be eloquent when I need to be, though. I'll be totally ladylike at your parents' anniversary party."

Myles's smile dimmed slightly. "About that..."

"What?" Her own smile fading, Jackie eased up slightly, her hand braced against his chest. "Should I not have assumed I'd be going with you? You *do* want me there, right?"

"Of course," he quickly assured, rubbing her arm. "I had every intention of taking you, Jackie; that's not it."

"Then what's wrong?"

"I did something that in hindsight might have been rather presumptuous and I wouldn't blame you if you took offense to it."

Her eyes narrowed slightly. "What did you do, Myles?"

"I..." He sighed. "I bought you a dress to wear to the party."

"You what?"

"I got it a few weeks ago, thinking I was helping you out because I know you got rid of most of your formal wear and you don't love shopping that much. But now I realize that was a liberty I probably shouldn't have taken. You're more than capable of buying your own dress and I shouldn't have done that without talking to you first."

Jackie peered at him, seeing the regret in his eyes. Only a teeny tiny part of her was annoyed at what he did; it was true that she didn't love shopping, much less for something she'd likely only wear once, and hadn't been looking forward to it. She'd been planning on dragging Cassidy with her to find something and hope she didn't run out of patience for the whole activity before she did.

"Where is it?" she finally asked, sliding off of him. "Show it to me."

Myles wordlessly sat up and swung his legs off the side of the bed, grabbing his glasses off the nightstand and sliding them onto his face as he stood. Jackie had to will her body to calm down at the sight of his strong back and ass as he walked into his closet. She eased into a cross-legged sitting position as he emerged with a long garment bag, the nervousness on his face evident.

"I can take it back if you don't like it. Or if you just want to get your own dress," he assured. "I won't be offended."

"Noted."

Myles unzipped the garment bag and laid it on the bed next to Jackie, who immediately reached inside and removed the dress, standing on the bed to get a full-length look at it. Part of her expected Myles to say something about her doing that, but he just eyed her silently, waiting for her reaction.

It was a satin chiffon corset floor-length dress in a beautiful deep wine color, and Jackie had to admit that Myles had damn good taste. She could only imagine how much it cost and her pride started to compel her to ask so she could repay him, but the larger part felt relief that he had spared her from doing something she hadn't really been looking forward to, anyway.

"Are you upset?" Myles finally asked, unable to take the silence anymore. Jackie was just standing there on his bed looking the dress over with an unreadable expression on her face and he couldn't tell if she was pleased or if she was getting ready to go off.

Jackie looked down at him, finally breaking into a smile. "No, baby, I'm not upset."

Myles breathed a small sigh of relief. "Seriously?"

"Yes, seriously." She lowered back to her knees, carefully laying the dress down beside her, giving it a lingering look before turning her eyes to him. "It's beautiful. And if I'm honest, better than anything I probably would have picked out. Thank you, baby, for real."

Finally breaking out into a smile, Myles stepped forward and wrapped his arms around her. "My pleasure. And despite you being okay with it this time, going forward I won't make such a move without consulting you first."

"I'm not gonna front; you did me a favor. I didn't want to spend hours looking for a dress. Your eye for formal stuff is better than mine, so I'm more than good. How'd you know what size to get, though?"

"I might have peeked into your closet a while back to get an idea of that. If it needs to be altered, there's time to have that done. You want to try it on?"

"Yeah, I will. After I properly thank you. Why don't you get your sexy ass back on this bed?"

Myles smirked before grabbing her chin and tilting her head back, laying a deep kiss on her that had them both moaning with rejuvenated passion. He pushed her onto her back with his body, his other hand lifting her smooth thick thigh around his waist.

"Thank me later," he whispered as he kissed his way down her neck. Her bubblegum body oil mixed with the lingering sex scent in the air had him feeling extra heady; he'd never felt high off a woman before but he surely did now. His hand squeezed her ample breast before lightly running his palm across the nipple, his mouth closing around the other. Jackie arched into him, groaning and cursing at how good it felt as she held his head in both hands. "There are some things I want to do to my woman first."

Jackie gasped as Myles slid down her body, removing his glasses again before spreading her legs and sliding his tongue between them, followed by his fingers, driving her as crazy as she drove him.

Chapter 17

Myles wanted to be annoyed by Ethan's incessant teasing, but he could only make himself get marginally affronted. He actually found himself blushing and chuckling at his friend's ribbing.

"Myles and Jackie, sittin' in a tree..."

"How old are you, again?"

"K-I-S-S-I-N-G..."

"Ethan, we're at work."

"First comes love-"

"Did I do this kind of foolishness when you were gushing about Eniah?"

"Good-natured teasing really isn't in your blood, man. That's *my* job. And when you come in to work, *late*, all flush-faced and distracted with your shirt on inside out, you leave me no choice."

"My shirt was not on inside out."

"It was partially untucked. *And* your tie was askew. Which for you might as well be the same thing."

Myles tried to fight his smile as he pretended to read something on his computer screen. True enough, he'd been almost thirty minutes late to work because it had been hard to peel himself off of Jackie's warm luscious body that morning. And he might not have taken the same care as he usually did when he got dressed, when he finally made haste to get out of the house. Ethan had taken one look at him and grinned, surmising the exact reason for his tardiness and slightly unkempt appearance.

Myles was never one to be late for anything but he couldn't even make himself care. Ever since he and Jackie reconciled three weeks earlier, they'd hardly spent a night apart. And while he absolutely couldn't get enough of her physically, they didn't spend all of their time together in bed. They talked as Jackie helped him assemble care kits. She even looked over his proposal for the homeless shelters, dusting off her corporate eagle eye to give him some tips to sharpen it even more. They cooked together, engaging in more of their friendly competitions. Myles massaged her tired body after long days at the garage bent over and under cars, and listened to her vent about difficult customers. They took turns choosing activities for their date nights, each promising to be open to trying new things, and respectful if it turned out to be something they didn't care for.

And the pride Myles experienced when he was out with Jackie and noticed other men checking her out was another first. The fact that it was his hand she was holding or his arm she was snuggled underneath or his ear she was whispering dirty things into made him feel like the king of the world.

He was riding such a high that he'd only been marginally disappointed when his first submission of his homeless shelter proposal was politely rejected. It was a minor setback, but he wasn't discouraged. He was savvy enough to know that the first cast of the line hardly ever got a bite. He'd hook what he was aiming for soon enough; he just had to find the right fish.

"Are you and Eniah still coming to my parents' anniversary party this weekend?" Myles asked Ethan, changing the subject.

"Of course. She's almost narrowed down which dress she's going to wear. Do you know she actually bought three different ones?"

"Why?"

"My lady is kind of a clotheshorse. You should see her closet. I'll probably have to have one specially built once we're married because there's no way all of my things and hers can fit into a regular one."

Myles looked at his friend thoughtfully. "You've been alluding to marriage with her for a while now. Is that something you're saying because of infatuation or are you actually planning to propose?"

"It's not infatuation, first of all; I'm in love with her," Ethan corrected, crossing one long leg over the other. "And yes, I have every intention of proposing."

"Does she know? I mean, do you think she's on the same page as you, as far as that?"

"I do. We've talked about it several times and she's been very clear about wanting to be my wife one day. We both want to take our time so it's not like I'll be popping the question tomorrow, but Eniah is everything I've wanted in a partner and I know in my gut she's the one for me. I want her to be the mother of my children, for us to grow old together; all that."

Nodding slowly, Myles rubbed his chin. "Wow."

Ethan peered at him as Myles turned his attention back to his computer. "Do you have similar thoughts about Jackie?"

An automatic smile tugged at Myles's lips. "It would be dishonest to say I haven't."

"But?"

"There's no 'but.' It's nothing I'm rushing into but I can absolutely see my future with Jackie. The more time we spend together...well, I probably shouldn't say it."

"Yes, you should. Say what?"

"This will probably just invoke more teasing but I feel Jackie becoming ingrained in me. I can hear her voice in my head when I get agitated and it calms me down. I sleep better when she's next to me, either with us cuddled together or on opposite ends. I've never had fun with a woman like I have with her; she makes me laugh, which is something I didn't even think I'd appreciate in a partner. And even when we butt heads, I'm assured that we'll work through whatever the issue is because we've made that commitment to do so. I actually bought a pair of jeans."

Ethan's jaw dropped and Myles couldn't help but chuckle. "*You* bought jeans?? I haven't seen you wear any of those the entire time I've known you."

"Yes, I know. But I had a talk with Mom a while back that got me to thinking about the reasoning behind why I do some of the things I do...it made me realize some things. The same way I crafted this image when I was younger and stubbornly adhered to it all of these years, I can alter it now that I've matured and evolved. And not just with how I dress but in other areas, as well."

"Well, I'll be damned. I am pleasantly surprised, man. I had a feeling when we met Jackie that day that she was going to be impactful. And I know this isn't just about her but there's something to be said about the influence of the right woman."

"I can't disagree."

"Now let me hear some slang."

Myles looked at him in mild alarm. "I beg your pardon?"

"Just seeing how far this evolution of yours goes, that's all. I can count on my hand the times I've heard you say anything remotely indelicate and I'm just curious if your speech is one of the ways you'll be loosening up or if you'll forever talk like someone's pen-pushing professor."

Myles laughed, surprising them both. "I'd like to think so but that's not as easy for me as putting on a pair of jeans or tennis shoes."

"Oh, come on. And they're sneakers."

"What is it you would like for me to say, Ethan?"

"Don't tell me you don't know *any* slang, Myles. You might not say it but you hear it. Channel your inner Jackie or Mollie and give me something. *Anything*."

Already feeling silly, Myles sat back in his chair and rubbed his forehead. The way he spoke was so innate that it was difficult for him to step outside of it, but he was up to the momentary challenge.

"Ugh...'I'm gon' make it do what it do.'"

Ethan broke out into a huge grin, actually clapping, causing Myles to chuckle and shake his head.

"My man!" Ethan exclaimed. "You're like a brother and I love you the way you are but *man*, I loved hearing that! The way you went off on Morton and Dennis that time, I *knew* you had it in you somewhere!"

Myles had forgotten about that incident when he essentially threatened his immature coworkers for talking disrespectfully about Jackie the day she surprised him at his office in her dirty work clothes. The memory actually made him grin right along with his cheering friend.

It was the night of Agatha and Hampton's anniversary party and Jackie was blasting Wale as she got ready. Cassidy was sprawled out on Jackie's bed, eating from a pack of Oreos as she regaled her bestie with the latest happenings between her and her husband.

"You will not *believe* how loud that man snores!" Cassidy exclaimed before sliding the crème-covered half of the cookie she just broke apart along her tongue, taking a moment to savor the sweetness. "I actually went to sleep on the couch last night and I might as well have stayed in the room, it was still so damn loud. Even turning on music didn't totally drown it out."

Jackie just chuckled as she smeared lipstick over her lips, silently debating the color. She was a little nervous about the evening and had invited Cassidy over to help her take her mind off of it. "This can't be a new issue, Cassidy. Did he just start snoring last night?"

"That is not the point. It's like it's gotten louder. I told him he might need to start using one of those machines when he sleeps but he told me I was just being dramatic. As *if!*"

"The man knows his wife, all right."

"Um, excuse you? I am *not* dramatic."

"And I don't curse, eat meat, or work on cars for a living. There, now we're both liars."

"Whatever." Cassidy flopped onto her back, the dark blonde hair of her wig fanning out around her. She blindly reached for another cookie before turning her head to her friend. "Why do you look nervous?"

Jackie stilled momentarily as she dug for her other tube of lipstick, opting to change. "What are you talking about?"

"Are we really gonna waste time with that?"

"Honestly, girl, I don't even know," Jackie finally acquiesced, not having the energy to pretend otherwise. "I've been around Myles's people before and it's not like I don't feel I can hold my own around them. I'm not sure what the hell it is that has my hands shaking and me second-guessing every decision about what I put on."

"At least you don't have to worry about that with your dress. That shit is fire. Your man needs to do *all* your shopping for you."

"Shut up." Jackie couldn't disagree with her friend, though, about the gown Myles had bought for her. Not only was it beautiful, it fit pretty much perfectly. The more she looked at it, the more enamored she got. And once she tried it on, that was it; she loved it. As corny as it sounded, she actually felt like a princess. Especially when she found out he'd gotten her shoes that were equally as perfect, too.

"Do you think Myles is gonna propose tonight or something?" Cassidy asked her.

"Oh no, I don't think we're there yet."

"Do you want that, though? One day?"

Jackie hunched a shoulder, though she couldn't hide her automatic smile. "I might've fantasized about being Mrs. Myles Cornwall a time or two...or fifty. I know for sure that he has me and my heart on lock and I haven't even thought about anyone else but him since we got together. It's wild how much I love that man."

"Considering how you all started, I can agree. But I love seeing you together. And I love how happy you are with him. Seems like he's just as sprung, too; when he came by the garage the other day, the man couldn't keep his eyes off you. I half expected him to come pull you out from under that hood you were working under and take your dirty self right there in the bay."

"Good." Jackie grinned, abandoning her search for the other lipstick. She told herself to chill out; there was no need to psych herself out about this evening. She smoothed her hands down the back of her freshly-tapered short haircut and adjusted her chandelier earrings. She turned to her friend, striking a pose and sticking her leg out through the high slit in the dress. "How do I look?"

"Amazing, girl. That appliqué on the bodice is hot and not to mention, it makes your boobs look heavenly. You're gonna blow Myles away when he sees you in that."

"That's the plan."

"You're going bare-legged, though? No pantyhose?"

"No, I hate those things. Why?"

"Just wondering. Those scars on your legs are front and center."

"Oh yeah." Jackie glanced down. Years of working in a garage and getting on her knees to change tires or do other things had left some marks on her legs, even though they were usually covered when she worked. The scars didn't bother Jackie and she never made special effort to hide them.

"They're not *that* bad. Mostly healed and faded. I doubt anyone will even notice 'em. I consider them badges of honor."

Cassidy chuckled. "You don't think Myles will care?"

"Maybe if this were a few months ago, he might've. But he knew what my legs looked like when he bought me this dress with this big-ass slit in it so clearly they're not a factor for him, either."

"Hey, I love it. What time is he getting here?"

Jackie checked the time on her phone. "Any minute now."

Cassidy snapped a few pictures of Jackie, joking that there was no telling when or if she'd see her all dolled up like that again. When the doorbell rang, Jackie shook her head.

"I gave the man a key and he still insists on ringing the doorbell," she muttered, starting to head for the door. Cassidy was right on her heels.

"What?? *You* actually gave a man a key to your place? You didn't even do that with-"

"That name isn't allowed in this house anymore, you know that," Jackie cut her off, turning and pointing a momentary finger at her friend before continuing to the front door. "He's such a non-factor he's not even worth talking about."

But when she checked the peephole, Jackie realized how wrong she was. Ringo was standing on her doorstep.

"What the hell..." Cassidy muttered from behind Jackie after she yanked the door open.

Ringo's eyes were on Jackie. "Hey, Jacks."

Blinking out of her momentary shock, Jackie's anger immediately flared as she placed a hand on her hip. "Why in the fuck are you here??"

"What's up with all the animosity? I *know* you're not still pissed about our last conversation."

"I'm not pissed about the conversation. I'm pissed at your lack of respect. I told you about popping up at my house. *And* how to address me."

"You're still on that shit?" Ringo tried to step inside, but Jackie's hand to his chest kept him where he was. He actually looked floored at her blocking him. "Seriously?"

"You know as well as anyone that I don't play. What do you want? I'm busy."

"Yeah, I see. You and Cassidy playing dress-up or something? Because you don't even get down like this." Ringo's eyes traveled down Jackie's frame, taking note of everything from her professionally-styled hair to her made-up face to her fancy jewelry to her classy but sexy gown to her jeweled stilettos. Everything looked so expensive, which also wasn't usual for Jackie. She didn't have fancy tastes. He figured this had to be for someone else's benefit, and the realization made him frown in displeasure. "Who are you seeing that has to make you over like this? And since when do you let anybody do that to you?"

"You don't know what you're talking about. Nobody is trying to 'make me over' and I'm damn sure not allowing anything I don't want. Now again, what are you doing here?"

"Can I come in?"

"No," Cassidy spoke up before Jackie could.

Ringo sucked his teeth. "Nobody was talking to you, Cassidy."

"Don't be getting an attitude with her!" Jackie snapped. "Since you want to hear it from me, *no*, you cannot come in. I'm getting ready to go out and don't have time for whatever nonsense you're coming with this time."

"It's not nonsense. I'm coming at you on the serious tip this time. Look," Ringo sighed, figuring he might as well go ahead and say what he came to say on the doorstep since he knew Jackie wasn't going to acquiesce and let him in, "I thought about everything you said the last time I was here. And you had a point. I *don't* like being alone, and that was a big part of why I showed up that morning after Sharonda ended it with me. But I think you were wrong about us not being any good for each other. We are. Or at least, we can be."

"I disagree."

"Because you're still pissed at me and you're in your feelings. But if you take a minute to-"

"That ain't it, Ringo. You remember the part that day about me no longer being available? That's still true. I'm in a relationship that I'm certainly not stopping or ruining for your ass. And he's on his way, so-"

"Wait...not that corny-looking dude that I ran out your house that morning?"

Jackie rolled her eyes. "Quit trying to jack your own dick, Ringo. You didn't do a damn thing to him. And that was months ago, anyway; we're way more solid now. That is the man I'm gonna marry at some point. So you might as well-"

"Marry? You? You and *him*??"

"You heard me," Jackie stated emphatically, straightening her spine. "I'm in a healthy *grown* relationship now and don't have the time or desire to go backwards."

"Especially with a man who is so willing to jump from one woman to the next like it's nothing," Cassidy couldn't help chiming in. "Jackie deserves somebody who's all in, who has her back, who puts it down, and who isn't ready to throw in the towel every time she messes up."

Ringo's nostrils flared as he glared at Cassidy, then Jackie. Then just like that, his angry expression faded. "Jackie...all right, look. I hear you. I know I put all our shit on you but I know I made some mistakes, too. I'm asking you to please give me a minute. If your stance doesn't change after that, then I'll leave and won't bother you no more. Can you at least give me that?"

Jackie knew there wasn't anything he could possibly say that would make any difference and started to tell him so when Cassidy suddenly grabbed her arm and pulled her back a few paces into the living room. Jackie, stumbling slightly, looked at her in confused annoyance.

"What the hell??"

"Let him say what he needs to say so he can go on about his business," Cassidy whispered. "Then he can leave."

"*Or* he can leave now, because nothing he says will change anything."

"You know that and I know that but it wouldn't be the end of the world to give the brother some peace of mind. He's like a kid who won't go to bed without a bedtime story. Give him what he wants but make it quick."

"You were the main one telling him he couldn't come in here."

"Yeah, well..." Cassidy sighed, her eyes drifting over Jackie's shoulder. "That's shot to hell now."

Jackie whirled around to see that Ringo had stepped inside and was closing the door behind him. When he began to remove his shirt, Cassidy gasped and Jackie's jaw hit the floor.

"Why the fuck are you taking your shirt off??"

"I'm just reminding you of some of the fun we used to have," Ringo commented, his voice casual as he started unbuckling his belt. "For old time's sake. Your girl can stay, too."

Cassidy released a surprised squeak. Jackie wondered if she had somehow hit her head and was hallucinating, because this could not seriously be happening.

"Have you lost your fucking mind??" she exclaimed, snatching his shirt off the ground and shoving it into his hard chest. "We're not doing a threesome with you!"

Actually chuckling, Ringo took hold of Jackie's wrist, trying to pull her closer before she snatched it away. "I was talking about putting on a private show for you, Jackie. But I like that your mind went there."

"No thank you. We are *not* interested. This is why you wanted to come in here? Did you seriously think a damn striptease was going to get me to give up the man I love to get back with you?"

"It's worked before."

"That was then and this is now. I'm a different woman now, Ringo. I've matured and grown. It takes more to move me than some abs and hip thrusts like it did back in the day. I've moved on, Ringo." She looked into his eyes, hoping she was getting through to him finally. "You need to accept that."

Ringo noted the seriousness in Jackie's eyes and the sincerity in her voice, and his shoulders slumped slightly in realization. She meant every word she was saying and he knew it; she wasn't just blowing smoke or trying to punish him. He swallowed hard and his hand fell to his side as it hit him that his roller coaster ride with Jackie was actually over.

They stood there staring at each other for so long that they momentarily forgot that they weren't in the room alone. But another squeak from Cassidy snapped them out of their trance, and a new voice in the room had them both whirling around.

"What do we have here?"

Jackie gasped upon seeing Myles standing there, looking especially dapper in his custom black wool tuxedo, his hazel eyes taking in the scene in front of him. He looked at Ringo, and Jackie could see the recognition flash in his eyes.

"Baby..." Jackie hedged, unable to read Myles's eerily-calm expression, "I'm not sure what you're thinking, but-"

"What I'm thinking about your ex in your house shirtless and standing in your personal space while you're wearing the dress I bought for you?"

Jackie's face flushed, and Cassidy hurriedly spoke up in her friend's defense. "It's not like that, Myles. Ringo showed up here *unannounced* to try to get her back and thought taking his clothes off was going to be a way to do it, and she checked him. Nothing out of pocket happened."

Myles's hand fiddled with a button on his suit jacket, his other hand encased in his pants pocket. His gaze slid around the three of them, taking everything in. Jackie could almost see his mind processing everything, assessing the situation, and checking for signs of dishonesty.

"Any time you're ready to run again so I can handle my business, feel free," Ringo couldn't resist taunting, the smugness in his expression ticking off the ladies in the room. But to everyone's surprise, Myles actually appeared amused.

"Not this time," he replied, unfazed. His fingers stopped fiddling with the button and his hand rested on his stomach, eying this man who had the gall to stand in his woman's house with no shirt on and look at Myles as if *he* was the interloper. And Myles knew he couldn't much blame him for that, with the way he bolted the first time Ringo showed up unannounced while he was there. The way Myles handled that situation always bugged him, and he was almost glad that Ringo had dared to show up again so he'd have a chance to redeem himself. "Circumstances are not the same now as they were then. Jackie wasn't officially my woman at that point. Now she is. So that means, sir, that you don't have any 'business' left to handle here."

"Oh is that right?" Ringo challenged, stepping away from Jackie to square up to Myles.

"Wait a minute, now..." Jackie warned, moving to step between them before Cassidy grabbed her arm. She shot her friend a look, silently instructing her to let Myles handle it.

"That it is," Myles responded to Ringo, looking down at him. "Now how would you like to do this?"

Ringo cocked his head slightly. "Do what?"

"I'm asking how you would like to make your exit. Willingly, or with my assistance. I'd greatly suggest the former."

"Why? Is that your siddity way of trying to warn me you'd beat my ass?"

"No. It's my way of reminding you that this is not how you endear yourself to a lady that you claim to care about. And I believe you probably care about Jackie. So you should respect it when she rebuffs your advances." He stepped closer, his eyes hardening. "Or are you the kind of man that needs to resort to cheap tactics to break down a woman's defenses because your ego can't handle being denied?"

Jackie saw the twitch in Ringo's jaw, and she anxiously eyed the scene in front of her, almost not believing it was happening. Her man and her ex facing off in her living room; one of them clean-cut with glasses and suited up in a tuxedo and the other half-dressed with locs and tats, their differences as vast as the Pacific ocean. It was a physical embodiment of how much Jackie had changed in the past several months, because there was a time when the offer of a private strip show from Ringo would have gotten him just about anything he wanted. And a man like Myles wouldn't have even been on her radar.

But now, Ringo didn't even appeal to her anymore. Myles Cornwall was all the man she wanted and needed.

At Ringo's convicted silence, Myles smoothly leaned down and retrieved Ringo's shirt from the arm of the couch where he'd dropped it. "I'll take your silence as you seeing my point. You're smarter than I thought. Now, take your shirt," he jammed it into Ringo's chest with enough force to send him back a couple of steps, "And enjoy your evening *somewhere else*. And do not bother Jackie again."

Ringo actually looked stunned as he began to inch towards the door under Myles's watchful eye. When he started to turn and say something else, Myles held up a hand.

"Ringo, is it? You should be aware that this is the only tactful warning you will receive. My patience evaporated when I handed you your shirt. I am a completely different man when I get incensed. You should consider *very* carefully if whatever you're about to say is worth risking it."

His head rearing slightly, Ringo sized Myles up for a moment, and Jackie and Cassidy stood by with baited breath waiting to see what he'd come back with. Jackie's eyes flitted to Myles, her man, standing there in his tux and glasses as suave and authoritative as any iteration of James Bond. This was a new side of him that she hadn't seen yet, and it did something to her. Her hand slid up the back of her neck and down to her chest, every inch of her skin now tingling so much she almost couldn't keep still. Her other hand gripped the skirt of her gown, needing to occupy itself.

She half expected Ringo to try to save face and step to Myles again, but to her surprise, he finally sucked his teeth and stalked to the door, yanking it open and slamming it behind him.

"Well I'll be damned..." Cassidy muttered.

Jackie's eyes were on Myles as he moved over to the front window to make sure Ringo actually left, then locked the door. He slid his hands back into his pockets as he turned towards the women.

"We don't want to be late," he said to Jackie, smooth as ever, as if that whole scene hadn't happened.

Jackie felt like she was going to explode. Her eyes never left him as her breaths started to deepen. She knew she needed to get her hands on this man before she lost it.

"Cassidy...get home safe, girl."

Cassidy glanced at her friend and grinned, recognizing that look. It was pure heat. She was surprised Jackie wasn't already kicking off her shoes and unzipping her gown, the way she was openly lusting over Myles right in front of her.

"Don't hurt him, girl," she chuckled under her breath, sliding her sandals back on before grabbing her purse and moving swiftly for the door. "Good night, Myles. And please tell your parents happy anniversary for me...if y'all end up even making it to the party, that is."

She left, leaving them alone. As soon as the door was closed, Jackie did in fact kick off her shoes.

"Get naked, Myles."

A knowing smirk spreading across his lips, Myles eyed her up and down before glancing at his watch. "As tempting as that is, we don't have time, Jackie. We can and will get into all of that when we return home later, believe me."

"Then drop those pants. I can't wait until later. If you hurry up and bend me over the back of the couch, we can get a quickie in before they have time to get wrinkled. And if they do, I have an iron."

Myles bit his lip as Jackie hiked up her gown and turned around, treating him to the sight of her sheer lace panties, looking over her shoulder with that lustful expression that always went straight to his groin. Just like that, he no longer cared about what time it was.

"My parents will understand," he muttered, unbuckling his belt.

By the time Myles and Jackie arrived to the anniversary party, it was in full swing. They strode into the banquet room hand-in-hand, both still tingling from their impromptu and intense lovemaking on Jackie's couch. What was intended to be a quickie to hold them over blossomed into more as soon as Myles put his hands on her.

"You think they'll be able to tell I just got off your lap?" Jackie muttered through her smile as her eyes flitted around the crowded room. She knew her face was probably still flushed and she could only hope nothing was out of place, but she knew her man's meticulous eye would've caught it if there was and he wouldn't have let her leave the house until it was fixed.

"Mollie probably will," Myles admitted good-naturedly. "You know she seems to have a nose for that kind of thing. She's like a bloodhound for anything resembling debauchery."

Jackie laughed. "Oh well."

It was a full house, with seemingly most of Brodence there to celebrate Agatha and Hampton's anniversary. There were several photographers as well as people filming things on their phones, no doubt broadcasting that they were in the presence of such influence. Myles wondered if Mollie and Ethan had arrived yet as he snaked through the crowd to find his parents. When Jackie gently tugged on his hand, he turned, looking at her curiously before leaning down to where he could hear her over the music and chatter.

"Where have I seen that woman before?" she asked him, her eyes aimed somewhere to the left.

"Who?" Myles looked in that direction, trying to determine who she meant.

"That woman there in the pink ball gown that looks like it's straight out of a Disney movie. She looks familiar."

When Myles realized who she was referencing, his frown morphed from curious to aggravated. What was *she* doing there?

"Yes, you've met," he confirmed with a sigh. "The day of your impromptu visit to my office."

"Oh, *right*..." Jackie actually smirked, clearly not as put off by the woman being there as Myles. "She still has eyes for you, apparently. She's staring you down hard."

Myles only grunted.

"Hello, Myles."

Reminding himself to remain cordial, Myles righted his expression. "Cynthia, good evening. I can't say I was expecting to see you here."

"My father was actually supposed to attend but he got called out of town unexpectedly so he asked me to come in his stead and help celebrate your parents," Cynthia explained. Her eyes had the unmistakable lustful slant as they slid up and down Myles's frame. "You're looking as handsome as always."

"Thank you. But I pale in comparison to my love, here." Myles slid his arm around Jackie's shoulders, pulling her closer. "You remember Jackie Malone?"

Cynthia's eyes finally tore away from Myles to look at Jackie, silently giving her a critiquing head-to-toe sweep much like she did when they first met in Myles's office. Only this time, the flash of intimidation was clear instead of the disdain that had been there when she met Jackie in her dirty work clothes.

"Yes..." Cynthia replied, drawing the word out slightly. "Vaguely. You were the homeless woman that showed up at Myles's place of business, correct?"

Myles's nostrils flared but Jackie only chuckled. She knew Cynthia knew better than that. She threw a low blow because she clearly still wanted to be on Myles's arm and Jackie was there instead. But Jackie wasn't about to take the bait and go off like she would've done a few months ago.

"You're partially right," Jackie confirmed. "I *was* at Myles's place of business but I own the same house now that I had then." She linked her fingers through Myles's over her shoulder. "Myles has spent a good amount of time there, haven't you, baby?"

"Absolutely. We've christened just about most of it by now, too."

Cynthia's face turned almost as pink as her dress and Jackie had to stop herself from laughing out loud. She was pleasantly surprised at the level of petty Myles exhibited with that comment.

"Oh..." Cynthia croaked, placing a hand to her throat, then her flushed cheek. "I, um..."

"Jackie is an accomplished and successful entrepreneur, Cynthia," Myles continued, looking down at Jackie with a proud smile. He pressed a kiss to her forehead. "She owns The Auto Loft and is the best mechanic in Brodence, and that's not even the half of it. I can only imagine what she's going to do next. You could learn a thing or two from her, actually. Now, if you'll excuse us..."

Jackie felt like she was floating as Myles took her hand and led her away. It did something to her to hear him say such things on her behalf, and she knew it wasn't just to show Cynthia up; he actually meant it. Her eyes softened as she looked up at him, and her heart beat faster when he smiled and blew her a kiss.

They finally spotted Myles's parents and made their way over to them. Mollie was standing near them, her arm resting on the shoulder of a man who was several inches shorter than her whose powder blue tie matched perfectly with Mollie's satin slip dress.

"There you two are!" Agatha exclaimed happily as soon as she saw them approaching. She excused herself from the woman she'd been talking to and turned to them with her arms wide open. "I'm so glad you made it!"

"Yeah, we were wondering if something happened," Hampton added, waiting for his wife to finish her enthusiastic hugs before stepping forward for some of his own. "Our son is perpetually punctual so we were starting to get a little worried."

"Are you two all right?" Agatha asked, looking over Myles and Jackie with concern.

"We're fine, Mom," Myles assured, placing a comforting hand on her shoulder. "We were just running a little behind, that's all."

"That was my fault, Mama Cornwall," Jackie spoke up, addressing her as Agatha insisted she should a while back. "Myles was ready to leave on time as usual but he got caught up...helping me with something."

"*Mmm-hmm*," Mollie hummed, eying them both with a knowing smirk that grew into a grin when Jackie flashed her a look that clearly said to shut up. "I just bet he did. Good job on that, big bro!"

Myles had to fight to keep his smile at bay as he glared playfully at his sister. "Right," he cleared his throat. "Thanks. Well, it's good to see you all."

"Uh-huh. I bet *everything* is good with you right now," Mollie teased, loving the caught expressions on Jackie and Myles's faces. "Just how many rounds of 'help' did you manage to get in before you-"

"Mollie!" Jackie cut her off, unable to resist a giggle. She wasn't embarrassed about her and Myles being on fire for each other but she didn't necessarily want to get ribbed about it in front of his parents.

"Okay, okay," Mollie conceded, still grinning, briefly holding up a hand. "I'll just make up my own number."

"What is happening?" Agatha asked, looking back and forth between the three of them.

"Nothing, Mom, don't worry about it," Myles quickly spoke up, the smile still on his lips. He wasn't upset at his sister's teasing but like Jackie, he wasn't eager for his parents to hear about his pre-event romp. "Who is this gentleman you have with you, Mollie?"

"Oh, this is my date, Kevin O'Neal," Mollie introduced, standing to full height and turning to her date with a smile and a flourishing sweep of her hands as if she was a game show hostess presenting a prize before grabbing onto this arm and leaning into him. "We met at the bakery a couple weeks ago and we got into a debate about whether peach or apple cobbler was better. We decided to get together for a taste test and since then it's been *onnnn* like donkey kong."

"What?"

"I'll explain it to you later, baby," Jackie told her man with a chuckle. To Kevin she said, "It's nice to meet you. I'm Jackie Malone."

"You too," Kevin smiled, showing off a gold tooth. Jackie noted his smooth dark skin and stocky build, and also how Mollie couldn't seem to keep her eyes or hands off him. Her smile widened at the realization that Myles's sister was sprung. "Though I feel like I know you already with how much Mollie has mentioned you. She probably wouldn't have gone out with me if I hadn't agreed to bring my car to your garage the next time I need something serviced."

"You won't regret it if you do," Myles spoke up. "Jackie is a wizard with cars."

"And her garage is just lovely," Agatha added. "I almost didn't want to leave when I stopped by recently. It's so good to have a woman-owned business like that here in Brodence."

"I love to see our people doing big things," Kevin stated. "You know, my sister has a podcast and also mentors teenage girls; she's always looking for successful, empowering women to highlight. I know she'd love to talk to you, if you're interested."

"Absolutely," Jackie nodded. "I love sharing how I got to this point and – not gonna front – it could only be good for business."

"Most definitely. I'll get your information before we leave."

"This is quite a turnout," Myles commented to his parents, glancing around the room. "I'm not sure why but I didn't expect it to be quite this many people here."

"You know your mother; she can't hardly turn people down when they ask for an invitation," Hampton replied with a wink at his wife. He looked like the older version of Myles in his tuxedo. "*I* wanted to cap the guest list at a hundred, max."

"Why not do it big? We never know how many of these we're going to have," Agatha retorted, sliding her arm through her husband's. She looked radiant in her strapless purple gown and matching silk shawl. "I'm the last one to take any day or celebration for granted."

They all stood around talking for a while longer before the three couples dispersed and enjoyed the party. There were an abundance of drinks, hors d'oeuvres, and music that ranged from The Temptations and Al Green to the Count Basie Orchestra to Jill Scott. Myles had never been one for big parties but he found himself having a great time with Jackie. She looked amazing both on his arm and by herself, and whenever she stepped away, he found he could hardly tear his eyes from her. Pride surged through him having her by his side, especially when she more than held her own with the wealthiest or most influential people in Brodence. Her confidence radiated, presenting herself as every bit worthy as a garage owner as those who owned multimillion dollar corporations, not cowering to anyone or feeling intimidated in the least. Myles watched her almost in awe.

Jackie was equally as impressed and enamored with Myles. He made sure to introduce her whenever someone stopped him to talk, making sure Jackie wasn't excluded in any way. And any opportunity he had to say her name or promote her business, he took it. She could see the pride in those hazel eyes of his behind his glasses, and it warmed her all over. It meant a lot to her that he was integrating her into his circle like he was, not just to appease her, but because he genuinely believed she belonged there. He *wanted* her there. Her love for him surged, and she felt a huge sense of gratitude that they had worked through their issues to get to this point together.

Myles also floored her when he didn't scoff at or refuse her request to stay on the dance floor when the music changed from a slow to an up-tempo one. She could see the flash of self-consciousness cross his face, but she just reached up and caressed his cheek before sliding her hand behind his neck, gently pulling his ear closer.

"Don't worry about anyone else in here; you're the sexiest man in the room, my hot nerd," she muttered, unable to resist a brief pull of his earlobe between her teeth. "Just focus on you and me."

Her words put him at ease, and he cupped her chin and took a lingering kiss before they resumed their dancing, enjoying each other. They danced through three songs and almost didn't see Chanel when she cautiously approached.

"Oh hell," Jackie muttered under her breath.

Myles looked at Chanel and pursed his lips, determined to not make a scene at his parents' party. The displeasure at seeing her there, however, was glaringly evident.

"I come in peace," Chanel quickly stated with her hands up, noting the glares they were both giving her. "Not causing any more trouble."

"Why are you even here?" Jackie demanded, asking the very question that Myles had refrained from asking, himself.

"My date is cool with Mr. Cornwall and I'm his plus one," Chanel replied. "Though I admit I'm not much in the partying mood. All of my development plans in Brodence are now officially defunct."

His eyebrows shooting up in surprise, Myles asked, "Since when?"

"As of this morning. I got a call from my superiors and was told that everything has been shut down effective immediately and we're taking our focus to surrounding cities. Apparently the mayor decided to put the kibosh on the whole thing. All of my time and work here has turned out to be for nothing. Though I'm sure that's good news for the two of you."

"Wow, just like that, huh?" Jackie marveled. "And yes, that *is* good news, but I can't help but be curious as to what happened."

Just then, Myles caught Agatha's eye across the room. Her eyes flitted to Chanel before giving him a knowing wink. Myles grinned.

His parents didn't throw their weight around often, but he was certainly glad they had this time. One phone call from Agatha or Hampton Cornwall was enough to stop or start just about anything in Brodence. No wonder Agatha had been so confident that Ms. Lula and her café would be just fine.

"Beats me," Chanel shrugged. "But, oh well. It's just on to the next one."

When she sulked away, Myles and Jackie turned to each other and broke out in celebratory laughter. They wrapped their arms around each other, holding tightly as they swayed side to side. They slipped into their own little world despite all the activity going on around them.

"You happy, baby?" Jackie whispered in his ear.

He eased back to look at her. "As I've ever been."

They stayed at the party another couple of hours, mingling and laughing with Ethan and Eniah for a while, before the urge to be alone with one another overtook them both. They found Mollie's date Kevin so he and Jackie could exchange contact information before saying goodbye to Myles's parents, wishing them happy anniversary again before scurrying out with their hands linked.

They were almost to Myles's car when they heard a frantic voice nearby. Cynthia was parked a little ways away, practically shrieking to someone on her cell phone as she anxiously paced back and forth in front of her car, whose trunk was wide open. Myles was going to mind his business and continue on to his car but Jackie immediately released his hand and headed over to Cynthia.

"What's going on?" she asked with concern, her eyes going to Cynthia's BMW.

Cynthia whirled around, looking surprised to find Jackie there. Her eyes were wet with frustrated tears. "My car won't start. And I can't seem to get anyone to come and tell me why or fix it. I asked a couple of people inside but none of them apparently know the first thing about car repair. It'll be at least two hours before Triple A can get here and my mechanic actually hung up on me when I called him at home."

Myles couldn't help but stifle a laugh, knowing her mechanic was Chet. He now realized how inconsiderate and unreasonable it was to expect his mechanic to be at his beck and call twenty-four-seven and that was clearly a realization Cynthia still had yet to come to.

"Babe, hold this for me," Jackie requested, handing her clutch to Myles. To Cynthia she ordered, "Pop the hood."

Cynthia blinked, clearly thrown. "What?"

"Pop the hood so I can see what's going on with it. Did you accidentally leave your lights on or something like that?"

"No. At least, I don't think so..."

"In any case, calm down; there's no need to panic," Jackie assured her, actually giving Cynthia's arm a comforting rub. "Pretty much anything is fixable; it's just about determining how simple or difficult it'll be to fix. I'm gonna help you, all right?"

Her words seemed to put Cynthia at ease. Nodding and expelling a relieved breath, Cynthia quickly ended her call and flashed a grateful smile to Jackie. "Thank you."

"Don't mention it. Why is the trunk open?"

"I thought it was the thing for the hood."

Jackie chuckled as she rounded the car to the driver's side, opening the door and easily finding the latch to open the hood. Myles watched in awe as she lifted the hood, then proceeded to gather the long skirt of her gown and tie it in a knot on the side to keep it from dragging on the ground as she assessed what was in front of her. There she stood, in her custom formal gown and heels, chandelier earrings dangling and sparkling, leaning underneath the hood of his ex-girlfriend's car, and Myles had never in his life been more turned on. She looked unbelievably sexy with her soft shapely legs on display as they were, her cleavage jutting from the strapless bodice of the dress, not caring about her nails or potentially getting dirty. And the fact that she was doing it, voluntarily, for a woman who wasn't very nice to her made it all the more attractive to Myles.

It turned out the battery was just dead so Jackie had Myles pull his car around, retrieving his jumper cables so she could jump off Cynthia's battery. It was almost amusing that Myles hadn't even owned any jumper cables until Jackie got some for him.

Jackie had Cynthia's car purring back to life in no time, and after instructing her to get her battery replaced and informing her that some of her fluids were low, Jackie turned to leave when Cynthia stopped her with a hand on her arm.

"Thank you so much, for helping me," she said humbly. Her eyes flitted to Myles before adding, "I know you didn't have to."

Getting the silent message, Jackie just smiled and shrugged. "No big deal. Glad to do it."

"What do I owe you?"

"Girl please, you don't owe me anything for that. Jumping off a battery is light work."

"In any case, I wouldn't feel right if I didn't repay you in some way. I was freaking out with no clue what to do, and you were kind enough to assist me despite how I've spoken to you. And if I'm completely honest, I think I left my lighted visor down when I was doing last-minute primping to try to entice Myles, and it's been on for hours since I got here embarrassingly early. I had every intention of using tonight as an opportunity to get Myles back, only to see that he's clearly moved on. I feel ridiculous enough. Please, let me do *something*."

Jackie gave an acquiescing sigh. "All right, then. You can bring your car to The Auto Loft to get your battery replaced and for any future services. I'll gladly take your money then."

Cynthia laughed, to Myles's utter surprise. He didn't think he'd ever heard her laugh so boisterously.

"That decision was made as soon as you opened my hood," Cynthia revealed. "What else?"

"You can give a sizeable donation to Myles's foundation for the homeless. There are big plans in the works and we need all the funds possible to help alleviate this issue and get as many people back on their feet as we can. Every little bit helps."

"Consider it done," Cynthia agreed without hesitation. "And it'll be far from a little bit."

"Good," Jackie said, accepting the wet wipe Myles handed her and cleaning her hands. "Then we're square."

They wished each other good night, with Cynthia promising Myles she'd be reaching out to him regarding her donation the following Monday and Jackie making sure Cynthia pulled out of the parking lot without issue. Myles gazed at Jackie as he held his passenger door open for Jackie and she proceeded to get into his car, her dress still tied and showing off her sexy legs, whistling to herself as if what she'd just done was no big deal at all. But it certainly was to him.

They went back to Myles's house, and they were barely through the door before Myles suddenly yanked Jackie to him by the arm and laid a deep, urgent kiss on her, his hands wasting no time going underneath her dress.

"Myles," Jackie breathed in both surprise and arousal as he lifted her off her feet, pulling her legs around his waist before backing her against the nearest wall, grunting as he sucked her neck. She held onto him, leaning her head to the side to give him better access as her eyes slid closed. "Baby..."

"I've got to have you," he grunted against her neck, grinding his erection against her. "I need you *now*, Jackie."

"Yes...yes, baby, I'm all yours." Jackie didn't know what brought on all this aggression but she didn't care. She loved this side of him and could only hope this wouldn't be the last time he displayed it. "Take me, Myles."

And Myles did. He yanked down the top of her dress to help himself to her full breasts, sucking and savoring her pebbled nipples as if they were coated in crème fraîche. Her gasps and whimpers of pleasure only egged him on as he continued down her body, lowering her feet to the floor before he got onto his knees, lifted her leg over his shoulder, and dove for her wet lower lips, his arousal and eagerness doubling when he realized she never put her panties back on after their earlier tryst.

Jackie clutched his head as she grinded against his face, the pleasure so intense that her standing leg felt as if it might give out at any second. Myles had not only been inexperienced with receiving head before Jackie, but with giving it as well...he'd revealed to her that he'd only done it one other time before. But not too long after Jackie began going down on him did he start returning the favor, and Jackie was blown away with how quick of a study he was. After a couple of times of her telling him how she liked it, he took over the reins and proceeded to have her losing her mind every time he put his head between her legs. And he enjoyed pleasing her as much as she enjoyed pleasing him.

He wanted to take her to his bedroom, but his overwhelming urge had him frantically unbuttoning his pants right there and kicking them and his underwear aside carelessly, causing Jackie's jaw to drop in shock. But she didn't have time to marvel over his lack of concern for his expensive clothing being on the floor because when he slid inside of her, all other thoughts evaporated.

"Ooh *fuck*, Myles," she breathed, clutching his shirt as he stroked her with overflowing need.

"You like it, Jackie?"

"Baby, I *love* it..."

"You love *me*?"

"I absolutely fucking love you. And I love how you're giving me this dick...*fuck*!"

At that, he gave her several more hard strokes, Jackie's pants getting more intense and loud with each one. When he rammed into her and held it there, Jackie's mouth went slack and her eyes popped open, feeling bursts of pleasure explode all over her body. Her nails dug into his shoulders as she clenched several times on him, earning a tortured grunt from him and a sexy bite of his bottom lip.

"You're driving me crazy, Jackie," he growled, his hips slowly resuming their rhythm. "I couldn't wait to get my hands on you again."

"You? I've been craving this since we left earlier."

"Do something for me..."

"What, baby?"

He leaned in, his lips right against her ear when he whispered, "Tell me this pussy is mine. And *all* mine."

Jackie wondered if she was dreaming. Myles had *never* used such language with her before, even when they were deep in the throes of passion. Really, while he'd been far from mute during their lovemaking before, he'd never been *this* expressive. Jackie didn't care what prompted it; hearing him talk dirty to her was like pressing the accelerator on her arousal and she was going to ride it out until neither of them could move.

"This pussy is *all* yours, Mr. Cornwall," she readily confirmed. "Just like this delicious dick better be mine."

"No question about it. And I plan on giving you a lot of it tonight."

And that he did. He sexed Jackie against the wall, on the arm of the couch, and even the dining room table before they finally made their way to his bed. He couldn't get enough of her any more than she could of him, their hands or mouths never leaving each other's bodies for more than a couple of seconds. Myles had never felt more wired, more physically addicted to anyone as he did to Jackie.

And not just her body or what she could do to him under the sheets. He thought he knew her pretty well already but that evening put her in a whole new light for him, and he was even surer that she was it. There would be no one else for him. His desire to spend his life with her had been cemented, and if he had a ring, he'd have been sliding it onto her finger right then. He'd never been more certain about anything in his life.

"I don't know what got into you tonight but I'm here for it," Jackie breathed when they finally calmed down a long while later. She looked over at him with a lovesick smile. "I love ending my nights with you, baby...you have no idea."

"It's definitely mutual." Myles rolled on top of her, his eyes roaming her face before taking it in his hand and giving her a long, impassioned kiss, his feelings for her overwhelming him again. "You mean everything to me, Jackie. Tonight only proved how much I want you by my side, for good. I want you in my heart, my house, and my bed, and I never want you to leave. I want *us* to be celebrating a milestone anniversary with all of our loved ones one day. I never would have imagined it when we met the way we did and because of how different we are but...you are who I want and need forever. I love you so much, sweetheart."

"Oh, Myles..." Tears welled in Jackie's eyes at his words. It was the first time he'd called her anything other than Jackie and the term of endearment made her heart want to burst out of her chest.

Aside from that, it thrilled her to hear that he wanted to spend his life with her, because that was absolutely what she wanted, too. Her love for Myles had only deepened since they reconciled a couple of months earlier and there wasn't a doubt in her mind that he was the man she'd been manifesting on her affirmation board all this time.

"Baby, I love you too," she replied, sliding her hands up his bare chest and grasping the sides of his neck. She grinned at him through her ecstatic tears. "And I want everything you just said. I want your last name. I want to come home to you. I want to have your babies. You have my whole heart, Myles. And I'm ten toes down on that."

"As am I," Myles concurred, pressing himself closer to her. "So that's twenty toes down, it seems."

They shared a look for a moment before they both burst out laughing, Jackie throwing her head back. Myles buried his face in her neck and she immediately threw her arms around him as their laughs continued, eventually petering into moans when Myles started kissing and licking her damp skin. Before too long Myles had Jackie's arms stretched above her head, their fingers and eyes locked as he slid back inside of her, her begging him not to stop and him promising he never would.

Epilogue

2 years later

Myles glanced at his watch as he headed from the homeless shelter. He'd lost track of time checking up on things and speaking with the facility director, Dirk, who had made worlds of progress since Myles met him on the street that random night. He was one of the first people that took advantage of the job and housing placement services that A Loving Chance, the foundation Myles helped to start, offered. It turned out Dirk had a degree and was a former teacher who was left with nothing after his wife and his best friend that she was sleeping with behind his back swiped all the money from their joint accounts and skipped town while he was at work one day. Then it was just a steady decline from there, but Myles was glad to see that things were looking up for him now.

As far as Myles's pet project, he smiled when he thought about the progress that was being made at that very moment. It took a while, but he had finally gotten the funding he needed to procure a huge plot of land on the outskirts of Brodence to build his community of small homes that would be rented or sold in conjunction with the foundation's housing placement program. Construction had already begun, and it thrilled him every time he visited to see the progress. In addition to housing, there was going to be a childcare facility, a small café, an activity center, and a shuttle to the main parts of town for those without transportation. He couldn't wait until everything was completed and he was able to hand over the keys to a new home to someone for the first time.

Part of him couldn't believe that Cynthia, of all people, had such a big hand in helping to make his dream project finally become a reality. Or more specifically, her father. Cynthia did make a large donation to the foundation as promised after Jackie helped her with her car the night of Myles's parents' anniversary party, but she also got her father involved. He reached out to Myles directly, and upon hearing his plans and seeing his proposal, offered to put up the bulk of the funds himself. Myles almost thought he was the subject of a practical joke.

When he stopped at a red light, he quickly made a call to Jackie, hoping she wasn't tied up.

"Hey baby."

Myles grinned, thrilled to hear her voice. "Hey, sweetheart. I just wanted to check on you. Are you all right?"

"I'm fine, Myles," Jackie chuckled. "And you *just* called to check on me before you went to the homeless shelter barely two hours ago. Is this how you're gonna be throughout my whole pregnancy?"

"Probably. And I make no apologies for it. My wife that I'm crazy about and who refuses to slow down at work is carrying our first child so I'm going to be overprotective. Get used to it."

"I already know." Jackie laughed again. "And I love you for all the concern but you know I wouldn't do anything to put our baby or myself in jeopardy. I'm just in my first trimester. The doctor said I'm still good to work; I just have to be extra careful and not overdo it. Please try not to worry so much."

"I'll try," Myles conceded, though they both knew better. He'd been a hovering husband ever since they got the positive pregnancy result almost two months earlier, especially since Jackie was considered high-risk because of her age.

"You heading back to the office?"

"I was actually going to come by there to see you; the meeting I had this afternoon was postponed. Have you eaten?"

"We both know you're gonna bring something regardless," Jackie replied, the smile in her voice evident. "I'll be here. I'm mostly staying in the office today because, thanks to you, now my employees hardly let me do much of anything, either. Thanks for that."

"Again, I hope you're not expecting me to apologize."

Myles stopped and picked up some Chinese food for Jackie before heading over to The Auto Loft. Jackie's business was in a new location , having expanded in the previous six months thanks to business going through the roof after Cynthia sung her praises for Jackie helping her after the anniversary party. And Jackie's guest spot on the podcast Mollie's man Kevin (who she was still dating and now living with) recommended her for got her a lot of attention, also. Not only was Jackie able to get a larger facility with more bays, she could hire more employees and offer more services. Myles was extremely proud of her; he knew this was what she always wanted.

He entered the lobby and was immediately greeted with the usual 90s R&B music, and smells of fresh coffee and muffins from Lula's Cup. Cassidy smiled when she looked up and saw him enter.

"Hey Myles," she greeted. "I figured we'd see you in here at some point today."

"Just came to bring my wife some lunch," Myles stated with a smile, holding up the bag of takeout.

"Sure. As if you need an excuse."

"True."

"I guess it's a good thing that you knocked Jackie up *after* we got back from our girls trip to Jamaica that you sent us on. You know Orion is *still* trippin' that he couldn't go?"

Myles chuckled. He knew Jackie and Cassidy kept that Disrespect Jar to put money in towards a girls trip, so he sent them on an all-inclusive weeklong vacation to Jamaica. They certainly deserved it, but it was also because it never sat right with him that he'd been the cause of anything having to be added to it. His behavior during his first visit to Jackie's garage still embarrassed him when he thought about it.

But look where they were now. Who would've thought?

Myles chatted with Cassidy for a couple more minutes until a customer came in, then Myles headed back to Jackie's office. He could see through the narrow window in the short hallway that every bay was occupied in the service area, and he couldn't help but smile.

He knocked on the door a couple of times before poking his head in. "Hey, sweetheart."

Jackie looked up from what she was writing, her lips spreading into a wide smile. "There's my hot nerd. Come bring me those lips."

Myles just shook his head, smiling himself as he entered the office and closed the door. He crossed over to the desk, placing the bag of food on the end of it before bracing his hands on either side of Jackie's notebook and leaning over. She met him halfway, grunting with satisfaction as they shared a deep, tongue-filled kiss.

"See, that's how I got into this condition in the first place," she joked, wiping her lip gloss from his lips when they finally parted before easing back into her chair. "If you hadn't practically tackled me when I got back from Jamaica..."

"I was powerless. You modeled all those new bikinis for me. Pair that with how much I'd been missing you and I had no choice but to 'get it in', as Mollie would say."

"You're getting better with the slang, I see. And trust, I'm not complaining. You know I love it when you get aggressive. I'll just be glad when I can do the fun stuff and get up under a car again. I miss it already."

"I'll concede that I've been somewhat overly cautious, so if you want to get back out to the garage doing some of the more tame jobs – and I do mean *tame* - I'll understand. I don't want you to be unhappy."

She grinned at him, sliding her hand over his. "Oh, baby...I'm not *unhappy*. I just miss doing what I love. But I know it's only temporary. And I know you just want me to be safe and careful. It's not like I don't have plenty of other stuff to do, anyway."

"What are you working on?" Myles asked, peering at her notebook.

"Concepts for the next round of videos for the YouTube channel. Irv and I are going to film everything later on this week."

"You're up to almost thirty thousand subscribers now, right?"

"Which is still blowing my damn mind. I love that you came up with that idea. I'm almost embarrassed I didn't think of it myself."

"You came up with the auto maintenance and repair class for women and that's been hugely successful. So that deserves plenty of credit."

After helping Cynthia the night of the anniversary party and seeing how clueless she was when her car battery died, Jackie wanted to teach women how to be more self-sufficient when it came to cars. She started a weekly class where she taught things like how to change a tire, jump off batteries, change oil, and other basic things. It floored her to see how many women couldn't even do something as simple as change their windshield wipers. Cynthia hadn't even known how to pop the hood of her car let alone anything else. Jackie didn't want any more women in Brodence or surrounding cities helpless on the side of the road and frantic, having to rely on someone else to come rescue them because they had no clue what to do when their car malfunctioned.

"I guess," Jackie conceded. "And I've got that online entrepreneurial panel tomorrow; I almost forgot about that. I just want to get all of this stuff done and out of the way so we can enjoy Ethan and Eniah's wedding weekend that's coming up."

"And you will. No working, Mrs. Cornwall."

"I could say the same for you, Mr. Cornwall, what with how you're always over at the homeless shelter or doing something for your pet project. And it's not like your main job is some kind of cakewalk, especially since you got that promotion last year."

"We're *both* going to be fully invested in celebrating with Ethan and Eniah and not worrying about any of this." Myles rounded the desk, grabbing the arm of Jackie's chair and turning her to face him. He lowered to his knees, gently easing her legs apart.

She smirked at the mischievous look in his sexy hazel eyes, which only got more prominent when he removed his glasses and laid them on the desk. "On your knees on the floor in your suit?"

"I'm not concerned about my suit." He unzipped her coveralls, yanking them open and down far enough over her shoulders to where he had access to her full, luscious breasts. Her nipples were already hardened through the thin tank top she wore underneath, and he eagerly licked his lips.

"Myles," Jackie breathed as he nipped at her buds through the fabric before pulling it down and out of his way. "You didn't lock the door..."

"Do you want me to stop?"

He was now licking her, and her head fell against the back of the chair. She couldn't help the loud moan that escaped as he began sucking her extra-sensitive nipples. "*Fuck*...you stop and I'll kill you."

"As I thought."

Myles proceeded to deliciously torture his wife at her desk, actually having to clamp his hand over her mouth when she started to scream as he brought her to orgasm. He loved pleasing her so much it was almost addictive, and especially now that she was carrying his child, she was even more desirable to him.

Seeing her slouched in her chair with her coveralls bunched around her waist and her tank top and bra pulled under her breasts that were heaving in satisfaction had Myles biting his lip and already ready for more. He stood, hastily removing his suit jacket.

Jackie's eyes opened and widened when she saw Myles unbuttoning his shirt. "Baby..."

"Take all that off," he ordered, motioning to her clothes before unbuckling his belt. "I'm not done."

"You...*you* actually want to get *naked* in my office?" Jackie confirmed, whispering the word 'naked.' Though her arousal was already rejuvenating at the sight of her usually decorum-conscious husband getting undressed in her office right in front of her. "I've never been able to get you to do that before."

He paused in removing his shirt, one shoulder exposed. "Do you want to question me or do you want to fuck?"

That did it. She bolted from the chair, pushing her coveralls down to her ankles. "Oh you already know. Put me on the desk and fuck me, then."

In no time, they were both naked except for their socks, and Myles had Jackie laid out on her desk, pumping furiously as he held her thighs at his waist. Jackie sat up and wrapped her arms around his neck, mashing her lips to his in a sloppy kiss as they continued to go at it, panting dirty talk against each other's lips. Myles's hands gripped Jackie's fleshy behind, one of her legs draped over the crook of his arm, pulling her to him at a steadily increasing pace that had Jackie begging him not to stop. They barely even noticed when the bag of food he brought for her fell to the floor, along with a couple of car catalogues. They just kept going.

Jackie was on her back again with Myles hovering over her, squeezing both of her breasts as he stroked her. He was getting close but was trying to hold off, wanting Jackie to come again first. Jackie was gripping the edge of the desk over her head, rolling her hips against her husband's, releasing all kinds of indecipherable phrases and noises as she felt the orgasm coming. They were both so focused that they were oblivious to everything else and almost forgot where they were.

So it was a mild shock when the door burst open.

"I just wanted to make sure – OH MY GOD!" Cassidy shrieked, immediately squeezing her eyes shut before slapping a hand over them, turning away. Their heads jerked up, seeing Cassidy's reddened face as she blindly bumped into the doorjamb.

Myles covered Jackie's body with his, not as mortified as he might've been a couple of years earlier in such a situation. Now, he was unfazed, even amused at the way Cassidy was fumbling for the doorknob with her eyes still squeezed shut. His hips had slowed, but hadn't stopped.

"What is it, Cassidy?" Jackie grunted. She shot Myles an admonishing look for still stroking her while someone else was in the room, but she wasn't any more able to stop than he was and was still moving right along with him. Another tiny moan escaped before she could stop it.

"I heard stuff falling and just wanted to make sure nothing was wrong! Can't you two lock the damn door?? I didn't need to see this shit!" Cassidy exclaimed before finally managing to yank the door closed, leaving them alone again and muttering about being traumatized.

Jackie looked up at Myles, whose eyes were already on her. They couldn't help but burst out laughing.

THE END

Thanks so much for reading *Don't Make Me Over*! I loved writing Jackie and Myles's story and I hope you dug it as much as I did.

Whatever you thought of this story, please consider leaving a review or rating. And if you want to show *extra* love, share that you read it on social media! ☺

You can find me on Instagram, Threads, FB, and TikTok at @authorjessicaterry. And don't forget to subscribe to my email list at jessicaterry.com.

Also by Jessica Terry

Some Like 'em Thick
It's All Right...Now
Not By a Long Shot
Get Right
Decisions and Consequences
Take One For the Team
When You Share Too Much
Backtalk
Emasculated
Restless
The Beginning of Again
Always and Nevers
She is Me
Split By the Bell
The Karma Call
Forehead Kiss
All Because of Ava
Love Intolerant
Mr. Time Waster
The Stubborn Kind
From Meltdown to Mistletoe
Mrs. Soul Crusher
I Want Us
Trade Rumors
Sugar Daddy Sweet Tooth
More Than What It Is
Hooked on Valentine's

Forced
Holliday Drama
Couple's Night
Liz and Luther
Chillin' on Thanksgiving
The Hired Gift

The Introvert Series

An Introvert's Christmas
Wooing the Introvert
The Introvert Roast
I, Take Thee Introvert
The Introvert Series Compilation (paperback only)

Discussion Questions

1. After reading the first chapter, what did you think of Myles?
2. Were you down on Jackie after she propositioned Ringo, knowing he was in a relationship?
3. Could you sense who Myles was really setting Jackie up with before it was revealed?
4. Did Ringo overreact to what Jackie did during his video call?
5. When Jackie went off on Myles at her place for complimenting her corporate accomplishments, did you see her point or did she blow it out of proportion?
6. What did you think of Jackie telling Myles he wasn't ready for sex?
7. Do you think Ethan would have been a better fit for Jackie?
8. Was Jackie wrong for her stance on the development efforts going on around town?
9. What did you think of Mollie? Would you want to see this character again in a future story? What about Chanel?
10. What did you think about Jackie's constant fussing about Myles showing support for her business? Did she come across as insecure or did you agree with her?
11. Cassidy and Ethan serve as both best friends and voices of reason for Jackie and Myles, respectively.

Was there ever a point where you disagreed with their advice?

12. Did you ever feel Myles or Jackie was trying to change each other? What changes did *you* feel they each needed to make for their relationship?

Did you love *Don't Make Me Over*? Then you should read *The Introvert Series Compilation* by Jessica Terry!

In this compilation of shorts from The Introvert Series:

An Introverts Christmas:

When Lola gets dumped right before Christmas, her friends make it their mission to cheer her up, to her chagrin.

Wooing the Introvert:

Cupid's bow strikes Lola at a Valentine's Day party, though not all of her friends are thrilled about it.

The Introvert Roast:

Lola meets her man's family for the first time on Thanksgiving, and the drama only increases when an unexpected guest shows up.

I, Take Thee Introvert:

Lola is over the moon when her man pops the question...but then she remembers they have to tell people about it.

Read more at https://www.jessicaterry.com/.

About the Author

Jessica Terry caught the writing bug at a young age and loves little more than holing up at home in Douglasville, GA, cranking out contemporary novels. And eating. www.jessicaterry.com

Read more at https://www.jessicaterry.com/.

www.ingramcontent.com/pod-product-compliance
Lightning Source LLC
LaVergne TN
LVHW090549110826
845146LV00001B/78

9798999506986